'A roller coaster ride of gun-blazing action, fascinating historical references, and a nail-biting battle of wits ... Move over Dan Brown, and give Boyd Morrison a try.' *Lisa Gardner*

'A rip-roaring thriller which has the reader entranced from first page to last ... Hold on tight as the pace is akin to that of a white water raft ride – furious bouts of life threatening action then a spell of calm before the next onslaught on your senses!' *CrimeSquad.com*

'Heart-stopping action, biblical history, mysticism, a stunning archeological find and mind-boggling evil results in a breath-catching adventure ... a pitch-perfect combination of plot, action and dialogue.' **RT Book Reviews**

'Full of action, villainy, and close calls. Fans of James Rollins, Matthew Reilly, and Douglas Preston take note.' **Booklist**

'The perfect blend of historical mysticism and clever, classical thriller plotting. Imagine the famed Ark rediscovered and reinvented to form the seeds of a modern day conspiracy. Boyd Morrison manages that flawlessly in this blisteringly-paced tale.' *Jon Land*

'*The Noah's Ark Quest* by Boyd Morrison skillfully entwines Biblical history, archaeology and religious fanaticism with high technology to create a riveting adventure of high-stakes terror and international intrigue. Wow. This is one fine heart-stopping thriller.' **Douglas Preston**

'A perfect thriller.' **Crimespree Magazine**

THE
ROSWELL
CONSPIRACY

BOYD MORRISON

sphere

SPHERE

First published in Great Britain in 2012 by Sphere
This paperback edition published in 2012 by Sphere

A CIP catalogue record for this book
is available from the British Library.

ISBN 978-0-7515-4800-6

Typeset in Sabon by M Rules
Printed and bound in Great Britain by
Clays Ltd, St Ives Plc

Papers used by Sphere are from well-managed forests
and other responsible sources.

MIX
Paper from
responsible sources
FSC® C104740

Sphere
An imprint of
Little, Brown Book Group
100 Victoria Embankment
London EC4Y 0DY

An Hachette UK Company
www.hachette.co.uk

www.littlebrown.co.uk

*Have you read the other thrillers
in the Tyler Locke series?*

The Noah's Ark Quest
The Midas Code

For Randi, my idol

PROLOGUE

July 23, 1918

I van Dombrovski sloshed through the muddy bog, stopping only to catch his breath. Tracking dogs howled in the distance, their task slowed by the stench of rot suffusing the air. He checked his holstered Nagant revolver to verify that it hadn't come loose. When the time came, he would need it to ensure the future for his beloved Tsar Nicholas.

The rain clouds parted briefly, and he ducked to avoid the glow of the full moon that would make him visible among the shattered trees that surrounded him. The showers gave way to hordes of mosquitoes and horseflies, but Dombrovski's head-to-toe wool clothing and the netting over his face protected him from the bloodsucking insects. The heat from the outfit was bearable only when compared to the unrelenting swarms that had driven half of his team mad during their trek to this forsaken stretch of Siberian wilderness.

His heart pounding loudly in the sudden silence, Dombrovski poked his head up and searched for any sign of his adversary, who would also be keeping well ahead of the baying hounds. Vasily Suzdalev must be close. The footprints in the mud meant they'd been circling each other, but the rain had drowned out any noise of Suzdalev splashing through the swamp.

Dombrovski could see nothing but death, an entire forest of eighty million trees denuded and scythed flat. Although he had been in the Tunguska region for more than a week, he was still agog at the expanse of devastation caused a decade ago. According to the reports of the Evenki natives, the Tunguska cataclysm had happened in mere seconds, a blinding flash in the sky followed by a sound like a million cannons firing at once.

By Dombrovski's estimation the razed area measured twenty kilometers in every direction from the center of the blast, larger than Moscow. He knew of no power capable of such an event. Yet despite the unprecedented scale of the destruction, the area was so sparsely populated that no one had been killed by the explosion.

Suzdalev, a Bolshevik agent for Lenin, had come to this desolate region two years ago and discovered a metallic substance never before found on this earth. During the subsequent lab tests, an accident destroyed the specimen, and now Suzdalev was back on another expedition to find more. Dombrovski had been sent to retrieve the secret material from him before Suzdalev could return to Moscow with it and seal the fate of Mother Russia.

Dombrovski would sacrifice himself rather than let the

communists claim it for their own. They had already killed his wife and daughter. He would not let them destroy his country as well.

The clouds shielded the moon again, and raindrops pelted him anew. With one last look around, he hoisted himself up onto the log he'd been crouching behind and ran along it to avoid the quagmire. Where the tree ended at a splintered stump, he leaped over to the log next to it. A hand shot up and snagged his boot while he was in mid-air, causing Dombrovski's foot to miss the log. His chest slammed into the trunk and he fell backward into the mud.

Suzdalev, who must have been lying in wait for Dombrovski to make exactly that move, jumped onto him and kneed him in the stomach, driving the air from his lungs. Suzdalev scrabbled at the pistol holster, trying to draw the Nagant.

Dombrovski grabbed a handful of muck and threw it in Suzdalev's face. The Bolshevik wiped at his netting in an attempt to clear it. Dombrovski launched a fist at Suzdalev's neck. Suzdalev grasped at his throat and collapsed from the blow. Dombrovski rolled over and pulled the pistol free. He staggered to his feet, keeping the gun aimed at Suzdalev, who was on his hands and knees wheezing. The man was no longer a threat. If he'd had a weapon, Dombrovski would already be dead.

More baying. The dogs were closer, and Dombrovski could now hear the shouts of the fifteen armed men with them.

"Where is it?" Dombrovski demanded.

Suzdalev sat back on his haunches and spit mud from his lips. "It won't do you any good."

"You're wrong. It will be a powerful weapon for the tsar—"

"By now the tsar has been executed, along with the entire royal family."

Dombrovski narrowed his eyes. "What do you mean?"

The clouds parted again, and he could see Suzdalev's smile just below the shadow from his hood. "I mean the Romanovs are no more. It is only a matter of time before the glorious revolution transforms our country into a workers' paradise."

"How do you know the tsar is dead?"

"As one of Comrade Lenin's most trusted agents, I am privy to much. Nicholas was scheduled to be shot on the night of July eighteenth."

Almost a week ago. As isolated as they were, it would take news even of such momentous proportions quite a while to reach them. Suzdalev might be telling the truth. But it made Dombrovski's task that much more important. If the Reds took over and gained possession of Suzdalev's secret, the communist revolution might not stop at Russia's borders.

Two dogs barked as they latched onto a stronger scent.

"I know you found another sample of xenobium," Dombrovski said. "Tell me where it is, and I'll kill you quickly."

"I hid it an hour ago. You'll never find it."

Dombrovski shot him in the left knee, drawing a scream from Suzdalev and shouts from the dogs' handlers.

"You're lying." If Suzdalev had hidden the specimen during his midnight escape, there would have been no way for him to find it again among the countless identical logs. He had to have it with him.

Dombrovski spied a knapsack inside a cavity beneath the log. With the pistol trained on Suzdalev, he snatched the pack and rifled through it until it was empty. The material was not inside. He checked Suzdalev's pockets with the same results.

"Where!" Dombrovski shouted and fired into Suzdalev's right knee.

Another scream. More shouts. The trackers were almost upon him.

Then Dombrovski spotted a glint reflecting the moonlight next to Suzdalev. The Bolshevik followed his eye and grabbed for it, intending to fling it away, but Dombrovski stepped on his hand. Suzdalev must have tried to bury it beside him after he'd been defeated in the melee.

Dombrovski plucked it from the mire and wiped it on his sleeve. No bigger than a piece of hard candy, the multicolored surface of the xenobium shimmered in the light. Whoever could puzzle out the secrets of this object would have a tool to dominate the world.

Dombrovski bent down and ripped the net and hood from Suzdalev's head. The ravenous mosquitoes descended. Dombrovski could see the pure hatred in Suzdalev's eyes.

"I warned you, *tovarisch*," Dombrovski said, spitting the despised word for *comrade*. "You should have told me. Now you will suffer the way my family did."

Suzdalev launched himself forward but cried out in agony when his legs wouldn't support him. "Your kind will be extinct soon!" he shouted as he swatted at his face. Even the thick mud was no match for his insect tormentors. "You cannot stem the tide of history!"

Dombrovski said nothing. He pocketed the object, took the pack's rations, and left Suzdalev cursing and writhing in pain, at the mercy of Siberia's natural horrors. With no food and dozens of kilometers to the nearest settlement, his last days on shattered knees would be excruciating.

It took less than five minutes for the tracker team to catch up with Dombrovski. The team's leader, his rifle at the ready, eyed him warily. "Did your idea work?"

Dombrovski nodded. "The dogs drove Suzdalev straight to me. Our mission is accomplished." He would secure the specimen in a lead-lined case when they returned to camp.

"So now we return to Yekaterinburg and rescue the tsar, sir?" the man said.

Dombrovski would have to confirm Suzdalev's claim about the death of Nicholas. If he was correct, it was only a matter of time until the civil war was lost to the Reds.

"Perhaps not, my friend. When we return to civilization, we may need to find a different path."

As he led his team away from Suzdalev's final resting place, Dombrovski was already formulating a new route and a new plan. He had to get Suzdalev's find as far from the communists as possible. Instead of taking the Trans-Siberian railway west toward Moscow, they would head east—to Vladivostok and eventually, to America.

QUEENSTOWN

ONE

They called it the Snow Farm, and Tyler Locke had to admit this winter brought a bumper crop. White stretched across the rolling hills unbroken until it reached the rocky peaks in the distance. As he strolled out the lodge entrance, Tyler zipped up his leather jacket and put on gloves. Although there were no clouds to block the morning sun, it was still a nippy negative ten Celsius outside, not the temperature he was used to in mid-July.

With a wave to the bellman, Tyler walked out into the frigid air. He squinted against the blinding white before donning his sunglasses. In the distance, clusters of Nordic skiers whisked across groomed courses. Behind him he could hear the whine of car engines being pushed to their limits as they raced around a track.

A silver Audi S4 rounded a bend piled high by the Snow Farm's massive snow blowers. The Audi drifted one direction, then the other, throwing up a rooster tail of snow behind it. The turbo howled as the car accelerated toward the hotel entrance. Just when it looked like the driver was going to blow past him, the antilock brakes chattered, and the car skidded to a stop in front of Tyler.

The driver's door flew open, and a black man bounded out with a quickness that must have amazed the bellman watching from inside. Though Grant Westfield's six-foot frame was two inches shorter than Tyler's, he was built like a tank and moved like a Ferrari. If Tyler shaved off his short brown hair and quadrupled his time in the weight room, he might look half as formidable.

Not that Grant was looking particularly intimidating at the moment. Tyler barked a laugh when he saw that his friend had squeezed all 250 pounds of muscle into an enormous orange parka. To Tyler, Grant looked like the unholy offspring of the Michelin Man and a pumpkin.

"Where did you get that?" Tyler said.

Grant patted the car and smiled. "Isn't it cool? I talked the guys at the Proving Grounds into letting us borrow it for the day."

New Zealand's Southern Hemisphere Proving Grounds, located halfway between Wanaka and Queenstown in the South Island's Southern Alps, is the leading facility for auto companies that want to torture-test their upcoming cars in winter conditions while the US, Japan, and Europe bask in summer. Tyler and Grant were there to put a top-secret hybrid prototype through its cold-weather paces for an unnamed manufacturer. Now that they were done with their main work, they had one more job to do before they took a few days off to explore some of the adventures for which the Queenstown area was famous.

Skiing, however, would not be one of the activities. Unlike Tyler, Grant hated the cold.

"The car is great," Tyler said, "but I was talking about your nuclear-powered parka."

Grant stretched out his arms and then adjusted the black ski hat that covered his shorn head. "It's awesome. Even Antarctica is afraid of this parka. You don't like it?"

"*I'm* afraid that if I sit next to it for more than an hour, the radiation will make me as bald as you are." He rounded the front of the Audi, but Grant blocked the opening.

"What are you doing?" Grant said.

"I'm driving."

"The hell you are. I procured the vehicle, so I get to drive."

"When was the last time you drove in snow?"

"Two years ago. When we were in Whistler for that job at the Olympics."

"Exactly," Tyler said. "You tore the bumper off my Cayenne."

"An accident. Could have happened to anyone."

"In the condo parking lot?"

Grant shrugged. "Then this is just the practice I need. Four-wheel drive, top-of-the-line snow tires, electronic stability control."

"Ten airbags."

"Right! You'll be plenty safe. What more could you want?"

Seeing that Grant wouldn't relent, Tyler trudged back to the other side and got in. Before he even had his belt on, Grant punched the accelerator and they were fishtailing down the road.

"Where to?" Grant asked.

"Left when we get to the highway. The sheep station is north of Queenstown. My phone's map says no more than an hour to get there, even with your driving."

"Man, I cannot believe we are doing this."

"Aren't you a little curious to see what she's got?"

"Come on. This lady must be senile. A seventy-five-year-old woman claims to have witnessed the crash of an alien spacecraft at Roswell and has a piece of the wreckage, and you think she'll hand us anything other than some unidentifiable hunk of twisted metal? If she's creative, it'll at least be from a 1947 Buick. Who is she anyway?"

"Fay Turia. Born Fay Allen. Raised on a ranch near Roswell, New Mexico, until the age of ten when her father's cousin got him a job as a foreman at a sheep station in New Zealand. The whole family moved down here, and she hasn't lived in the US since."

"You checked her out?"

"As much as I could," Tyler said. "She emailed me a copy of her birth certificate to prove she was born in Roswell. It was legit."

"So she lived there. Why does she want to hire us?"

"She called Gordian the foremost airplane accident investigation firm in the world."

"Well, that's true. At least she's perceptive in that respect."

Gordian Engineering was the company Tyler had founded. With a bachelor's degree in mechanical engineering from MIT and a PhD from Stanford, he'd since happily stepped down from his role as president of the firm and now served as its chief of special operations, which meant he could pick and choose the projects he wanted to pursue. Grant was his best friend and the company's top electrical engineer. Their complementary skills let them oversee a wide range of projects, including forensic accident analysis, demolition, loss prevention, and automotive testing.

But this request was not in the normal line of inquiry. Most of their jobs were for large multinationals that could afford the rates they charged. An individual asking for their assistance was highly unusual.

"Did she ever say why she waited sixty-five years to come out to the world?" Grant asked.

"She said she's been doing her own investigation on the down low because she heard too many stories about what the government did to the other people who came forward about the crash. But now she's stuck and wants to see if we can help her out."

"And you agreed to this out of the goodness of your heart?"

"She sweet-talked me into it. Of course, I wasn't going to take on the job officially."

"Probably not something we want to add to our website."

Tyler laughed. "Right. I told her if she could wait three months, we'd be in her neck of the woods for another job and would stop by to see what she had. So here we are."

"She's a kook."

"Likely, although she sounded remarkably with-it on the phone. I'm sure whatever the object is, we'll turn it over, frown at it with concern, take a sample and some photos, and then tell her that its origin is indeterminate. We won't give her a conclusive answer, but we won't dash her hopes for an alien artifact, either. After that we can head into Queenstown."

"I hear they've got a good pizza place there called The Cow," Grant said. "Then we can figure out what to do for fun. You know, I do have the parachutes in the trunk."

Tyler smirked at him. "You don't give up, do you? I told you. Bungee jumping, yes. Skydiving, no. At least with the bungee you're already tied to the bridge."

For the next thirty minutes, Grant steered them down a twisty cliff-hugging road called the Crown Range, where the drop-offs were so steep and Grant's driving was so suspect that Tyler started to wonder just how much more adventure he could stand during the trip.

Once they got below three thousand feet, the snow cleared and Grant upped the speed. They made up so much time that Tyler texted Fay that they'd be twenty minutes early.

Tyler guided Grant through green pastures and farmland dotted by quaint bed-and-breakfasts. When they turned onto Fay's road along a deep ravine carved by the

Shotover River, Grant sighed as it climbed back above the snow line. In another few minutes they saw a sign for the Turia Remarkables Sheep Station, named for the jagged Remarkables mountain range looming over Queenstown's Lake Wakatipu. Fresh tire tracks split the driveway's snow.

"Maybe this means she left," Grant said hopefully. "I'm starving."

Tyler looked at his watch: 9.40 a.m. Twenty minutes early for their appointment. "That would explain why she hasn't texted back."

They followed the tracks for half a mile until they reached a stately white clapboard home with an attached garage. Behind it was a large red barn. Except for a few evergreens surrounding the house, the countryside was bare of trees. A fence disappeared into the hills on either side.

The snow tracks separated into a pair that led to the garage and a second set leading to a Toyota sedan parked in the circular driveway in front of the house. Grant pulled up next to it.

Tyler got out and laid his hand on the Toyota's hood. Still warm, just like he expected. No rancher would drive a sedan. Two pairs of footprints wound to the door. Fay must have visitors.

No sheep or ranch hands were visible, probably out working somewhere on the station's two thousand acres.

"Nice place," Grant said.

"Looks like ranching has been good to her. Shall we say howdy?"

Grant nodded, and they crunched through the snow. When they were within ten feet of the front door, two shotgun blasts erupted from inside the house.

Their Army training kicking in, Tyler and Grant both dived to their bellies without hesitation. Grant gave him a look and silently mouthed, "What the hell?"

Tyler was about to suggest they make a hasty retreat to the Audi when he was stopped by a woman's shout, followed by a third shotgun blast closer to the right side of the home. Tyler turned his head and saw a man skid around the corner of the house.

He raised a pistol, but before Tyler could yell, "Don't shoot," the stranger fired wildly in their direction, bullet impacts kicking up snow all around them.

That was all the prodding they needed to find cover. Grant scrambled toward the house and rammed the front door open like a charging rhino. Tyler was hot on his heels and slammed it closed once he crossed the threshold.

The hallway seemed shrouded in darkness until Tyler realized he was still wearing his sunglasses. When he doffed them, he saw that shards of a broken lamp littered the floor and buckshot holes peppered the wall.

From his right came the unmistakable sound of a pump-action shotgun chambering a new round. Tyler looked up to see a striking woman who had to be seventy-five-year-old Fay Turia, though she didn't look a day over sixty. In her white hair cropped just below the ears, slim sporty figure, and bright green eyes, Tyler perceived the echo of the stunning beauty she must have been fifty years ago. Only the wrinkles around her eyes and neck and several liver spots on her hands betrayed her true age. She held the shotgun firm to her shoulder, as if she were not merely comfortable with the weapon but adept at handling it.

"Who are you?" she growled. The yawning barrel was the size of a manhole at this distance. Smoke wafted from it.

Tyler put up his hands. "I'm Tyler Locke. You must be Fay. I believe you invited me and my friend, Grant Westfield, for a friendly visit."

Recognition dawned on her face, and the scowl melted away, replaced by a toothsome smile.

"Welcome to my home, Dr. Locke," she said cheerfully, as if she were about to serve tea and crumpets instead of hot lead. "Would you mind terribly calling the police?"

TWO

Nadia Bedova stared at the water glass, hoping that Vladimir Colchev would not show up. Nestled next to her feet was the package that he'd requested.

Her seat at the outdoor café afforded a spectacular view of the Sydney Harbour Bridge, clusters of tourists visible along its spine partaking in the BridgeClimb. A cruise ship docked across Circular Quay provided the backdrop for ferries, catamarans, and jet boats motoring past the ivory shells of the famed opera house.

Despite her calm expression, Bedova's stomach churned as she waited. Four of her fellow operatives from Russia's foreign intelligence service—the Sluzhba Vneshney Razvedki or SVR for short—were stationed at key locations nearby: two in the crowded walkway between the café and water, one at another table outside, and a fourth inside the restaurant housed under a five-story apartment tower. In addition to the mass of tourists strolling along, bikers and skateboarders occasionally rolled through. None of them would escape the operatives' notice. They were here to apprehend Colchev or, if necessary, to kill him.

His actions had driven her reluctantly to this point. If he had just disappeared, he might have been left alone. But his last contact with her made it obvious that the SVR would have to bring him in or get rid of him once and for all.

A voice issued from the tiny microphone in her ear. One of the men in the walkway.

"I see him. One hundred meters behind you and coming this way."

Bedova didn't turn. "Is he alone?"

"Yes."

The agents had already checked everyone else in the vicinity, and nobody seemed suspicious or put in place to help Colchev. He really was on his own, just as he'd said on the phone this morning.

She felt him touch her shoulder and didn't flinch. She looked up and saw him smiling back at her. He was as fit as she'd ever seen him—broad shoulders, slim hips, steely gray hair—and she suddenly experienced a rush of memories of when they'd been together.

He bent down and lightly kissed her cheek. Then he came around the café's front railing and took a seat opposite her. Now that he was in the shade, he removed his sunglasses and the intense eyes she remembered drilled into her.

"You look lovely, Nadia," he said in a silky bass, using his native Russian.

She responded in kind. "I miss you, Vladimir. Why don't you come home?"

"You know I can't do that. At least not yet."

"When then?"

"I have something to do first."

"Is that why you needed this?" Bedova handed the bag over to him. He unzipped it, confirmed that the contents were complete and intact, and then closed it back up.

"Thank you, Nadia. I know procuring this must have been difficult." He withdrew an envelope from his jacket and slid it across the table to her.

"I can't take that," she said.

"You deserve it. For everything you've done."

She ignored the bulging envelope and leaned forward, taking his hands. "You must tell me what you're doing. I want to help you." She knew all four operatives, as well as her superiors back in Moscow, were hanging on every word.

Up to this point, the only intel they'd had to go on was courtesy of a single encrypted communication intercepted from one of Colchev's known associates that referred to "Wisconsin Ave" and an event taking place on July twenty-fifth, less than a week away. The belief within the organization was that he was planning a rogue op using former SVR operatives turned mercenaries and that the target was somewhere in America.

"I wish you could come with me," Colchev said, "but the risk is too great."

"When I volunteered for the SVR, I knew the risks."

"I meant the risk to my mission."

"You don't trust me?"

Colchev turned to watch a passing ferry. "What I'm planning takes a special conviction. Honestly, I don't think you would have the stomach to follow through."

"Why?"

"It's better that you don't know."

She let go of his hands and sat back. "Did you know I have spoken to the head of the SVR?"

Colchev's head snapped around. "Why?"

"I didn't tell him about our meeting. I wanted to know what he had planned for you if you returned."

"A sham trial followed by a swift execution, I expect."

"No, he said that he understands that the situation wasn't your fault. And he knows that you have another operation in motion. He wants to know if there is any way he can help you."

Colchev was silent as he examined her for deceit. Like him, she was an expert at lying, which she was doing now. Her objective was to find out about Colchev's current plan. The director was hoping that Colchev would bring her onto his team or at least give her some hint of his mission. Barring that, the four operatives were instructed to move in and take him as soon as he walked out of the café with the bag. Bedova couldn't have asked for a more wrenching assignment: to bring in the man she had once loved to be executed just as he'd theorized.

Colchev had created the spy ring that included Anna Chapman and nine other spies who were exposed by the US counterintelligence agencies in 2010. To prevent divulgence of their intelligence-gathering methods, the Russians retrieved them by swapping four imprisoned Russian intel officers who had been moles for the Americans. Nobody had been happy about the deal, but the SVR couldn't allow the spies in America to reveal any more than they already had.

Someone had to be blamed for the debacle, and the obvious choice had been Colonel Alexander Poteyev, the SVR agent convicted of selling the spies' identities to the Americans for thirty thousand dollars. But internally, the fault rested with Colchev, the man responsible for setting up the entire operation in the first place. If he wasn't incompetent for letting the Americans discover the spies, then he was complicit. Either way, he had to be dealt with. Permanently.

"Nadia," Colchev finally said, "they have already tried Poteyev in absentia and found him guilty of treason. He's now a non-person in Russia. If it weren't for the CIA's protection, he'd be dead by now."

"Why didn't you go into protective custody like Poteyev?"

Colchev's jaw worked back and forth, and then he spoke in a hush. "Because I'm not a traitor. I didn't sell out my country. I hate America for everything they've done to Russia. I'm a patriot."

"Then prove it. Come back with me and tell them the truth."

"They aren't interested in the truth. They want a show trial to save face. It will accomplish nothing."

"Then what are you going to do?"

"I have assets in the US that I never revealed because I feared Poteyev's treachery myself. Because they weren't compromised, I saw my opportunity to act independently, and I'm taking it. I'm going to prove my allegiance to Russia and the SVR. And when I do, my men and I will be welcomed back to our homeland as heroes."

"But what can you possibly do that we can't?" Bedova asked.

"Something that takes will. Now that I'm a non-person, whatever I do can be blamed on a rogue spy. I didn't ask for this status, but since I have it, I will take advantage of it and do what Russia never could without fearing retaliation. Once they see the results, they will do everything they can to reward me."

"I don't understand." Her gaze lingered on the bag holding the equipment Colchev had requested. "How will Icarus make this operation possible?"

Colchev tilted his head as if considering a decision. "Are you sure you want to be a part of this?"

She had reached him. Now she had to delve into his mission. "Are you planning an attack?"

He smiled. "I am planning to strike a blow that will change the course of history and Russia's place in it. I have—"

Colchev's phone buzzed. He stood and picked up the bag. This was it, as soon as he left the café, the operatives would move in and grab him.

But instead of leaving, he put the bag on his seat and held

up a finger. "Excuse me while I take this call. Then I'll share my plans with you."

He stepped away to a pillar by the side of the restaurant, just out of earshot.

"Can you hear anything?" she said without moving her lips.

"Nothing," one operative said.

"Keep an eye on him," said another.

"He won't leave without the bag," Bedova said. "He needs it for some reason, and he's about to tell us why."

Bedova felt a rush of air blow by her, and the swift hand of a bicyclist snatched the bag from Colchev's seat. He threw the satchel over his shoulder and pedaled away furiously, scattering yelling pedestrians in every direction.

The thief, who was wearing shorts and a T-shirt, must have thought it was Bedova's luggage carelessly placed across from her, but he would get a rude surprise when he saw that it held no money, jewelry, or electronics.

Before she could call for help, the other operatives were shouting in her ear.

"Get him!"

"He's too fast!"

"Cut him off!"

The operative seated at the café tried to jump across the railing to stop the cyclist, but he was too late, as were the agents in the walkway and the one bursting out of the restaurant's interior.

Bedova knew that Colchev would be just as concerned

with retrieving the sack, but when she turned, she couldn't see him. The wail of an alarm coming from that direction cut through the other noises.

"What happened to Colchev?" she said.

"He was right there a moment ago!" came the harried reply. "I looked away for a second, and then he was gone."

Bedova grabbed the envelope and leaped out of her chair. She ran through the café to see a fire exit from the adjoining apartment tower click shut. The alarm it had tripped continued to shriek. Because it was a metal door with no exterior handle, someone inside must have opened it for Colchev.

Only then did she realize that the whole scenario had been a setup. Colchev had chosen the restaurant, no doubt paying off the waiter to steer Bedova toward the seat she'd taken. He had used the cyclist as a distraction, giving him enough time to duck into the building.

She took off after the other men chasing the rider, who disappeared around the corner of the building.

Pumping her arms, she sprinted after him, rounding the building not far behind the other agents. As the cyclist came into view, she saw him dump the bike at Macquarie Street. A van screeched to a halt next to him. He hopped in and the van sped away.

She heard it stop again only a few seconds later. She kept running, and when she got to the street, she could see Colchev climbing into the van. He caught sight of her and gave her a wave. He mouthed "*Spasebo*" and the door shut. The van accelerated and whipped around the corner.

"Did you see the plate?" one agent said.

"Don't bother," Bedova replied. "It'll be a stolen number."

Their own van arrived a minute later, but by now the trail was too cold. Colchev could be heading in any one of six directions.

Bedova patted the envelope in her pocket and withdrew it. She opened it to find a stack of hundred-dollar Australian bills. They were wrapped in a white sheet of notepaper.

She unfolded it and saw Colchev's handwriting.

I don't blame you for trying, Nadia, because you are a patriot, too. But don't get in my way again.

THREE

Tyler was surprised when the men who'd attacked Fay didn't jump into their car and drive away, instead taking up positions covering both sides of the house with their pistols. Tyler, Grant, and Fay had retreated to the top floor to wait there until the cavalry arrived. The only time she had left them was to duck into the living room and retrieve a canvas satchel that now sat by her side.

"Have you ever fired a Remington twelve-gauge, dear?" Fay said to Grant. The weapon that had loomed like a howitzer in Fay's hands looked like a pea shooter in Grant's.

"I've handled a few in my day," Grant replied.

"He was in the Army Ranger battalion," Tyler said. "He could shoot an RPG if you had one."

"No, the New Zealand government won't let us own those, I'm afraid," Fay said. Tyler didn't know whether or not she was seriously chastising her adopted country for not allowing her to own a rocket-propelled grenade until she winked at him.

"You don't have any more ammo, do you?" Grant asked. "We're down to four shells."

"No. It was my husband's gun, God rest his soul, and I hadn't fired it in years until today."

Fay's initial calm demeanor hadn't been an act. Once they'd heard that the police were on their way, Tyler had expected her to collapse from the strain. Instead, she'd methodically related the events preceding their stumble through the front door, although she did give Grant the shotgun, which he kept trained on the stairwell.

Fay had been traveling in the US for the past two weeks, and she had returned to Queenstown that morning, in time for her meeting with Tyler. Five minutes after she got home, two men knocked at the door. New Zealand normally being a safe place, Fay didn't think twice about letting them in, especially when they said they were there representing Tyler Locke, who unfortunately wasn't going to be able to come himself.

The men, both of whom spoke with American accents, seemed to know everything about the meeting, including the ten o'clock appointment they'd set, so she showed them her artifacts from Roswell. The lean blond man who'd shot at Tyler and Grant called himself Foreman, and the other one, a hulking giant sporting a black goatee, went by the name of Blaine. They wanted to know whether she'd ever come in contact with an opalescent metallic material, and she told them she honestly didn't know what they were talking about.

Fay was already beginning to suspect their motives when she went into the kitchen to fetch a pot of tea and saw Tyler's text message that he would be early.

Calling from the kitchen, she asked Foreman and Blaine where Tyler was, and they claimed he hadn't been able to make the trip from America. Instead of coming back with a tray of Earl Grey and scones, she entered the living room holding the shotgun.

The men put up their hands and moved as if to leave, but one of them drew a pistol, and that's when the shooting started.

"I guess those two will think twice before underestimating an old lady again," she said.

Fay certainly didn't fit the image of an elderly pensioner. Tyler guessed she kept herself fit working the sheep station. Her hands were callused and she had lines on her face from being outdoors in the sun, but the sweater she wore left no doubt that she had some muscle on her bones, holding the shotgun with ease. She was the antithesis of a doddering grandmother.

"I wouldn't mess with you," Tyler said. "Plus you seem pretty fresh for someone who slept on a plane last night."

"Try Ambien. It does wonders for a person. Fourteen hours from LA through Auckland, and not a bit of jet lag. You should try it the next time you travel."

"As long as Tyler isn't the one doing the flying," Grant said.

"Oh, are you a pilot?" When Tyler nodded, she patted his arm and then gave it a squeeze, feeling his bicep. "You are a catch, aren't you? Smart, good-looking, *and* talented. If I were forty years younger, I'd save you for myself."

Tyler didn't know what that meant, but he felt himself blushing. Grant chuckled and shook his head.

"Maybe we should get back to focusing on the two men with guns outside," Tyler said. The car hadn't started, so he guessed they hadn't gone far. "How long before the police get here?"

"About ten more minutes, give or take."

"They'll leave as soon as they hear the sirens. It would be suicide for them to make a frontal assault."

"Their whole plan seems risky," Grant said. "Why aren't they leaving already?"

"Fay, do you know why they wanted your artifacts?" Tyler asked.

Fay shook her head and clutched her satchel tightly. "I don't know. Only my granddaughter has seen what's in here."

"Would she have told someone about it?"

"Absolutely not."

"I know why they aren't leaving," Grant said with a sniff. "Do you smell that?"

Tyler saw the first wisps of smoke curling up the stairwell, followed by the crackle of flames from the back of the house.

"I'll call 111 back and tell them to send a fire engine," Grant said as he handed the shotgun to Tyler and pulled out his phone. "And I'll get something to cover our faces." He went into the hallway bathroom.

For the first time, Fay lost her composure. Her face

seethed with rage. "Those bastards set my house on fire! I should have killed them when I had the chance."

Tyler crabbed to the rear window and poked his head up. The back door was engulfed in fire. "Did you have any accelerants outside?"

Fay thought for a moment, then nodded. "Lighter fluid for the barbecue."

"That must be what they used. The cedar siding will go up fast."

"If they came for my Roswell artifacts, why do they want to burn them now?"

Tyler shrugged. He was just as confused by the situation as Fay.

Smoke billowed through the hallway. He and Fay crouched to get under the thickest of it.

Tyler edged over to the front window and took a peek. He saw Blaine run around from the back of the house and take up a spot behind the Toyota. At this distance the shotgun would be at a severe disadvantage. Instead of solid slugs, the gun was loaded with birdshot, which had a minimal effective range. There was no way to get all three of them to the Audi safely.

Blaine reared back and threw a glass container with a lit rag protruding from it.

The front of the house burst into flames. Now they were trapped from both sides. They'd all succumb to smoke inhalation long before the police arrived if they stayed inside, but jumping through one of the windows would make them easy targets.

Grant came back from a bathroom with wet hand towels to put over their noses and mouths.

"The firefighters are on the way," Grant said, "but it'll be a while. I suggest we get out of here."

Tyler remembered the tire tracks leading to the garage. "Do you have a car, Fay?"

"A Land Rover. We can get to it from the kitchen."

That's what Tyler had been hoping to hear. Since the garage was attached to the house, they wouldn't have to go outside to get in the vehicle.

"We'll have to risk a getaway," Tyler said. "Let's go before we can't breathe."

They all scooted down the stairs. Fay grabbed Tyler's hand. "This way."

The three of them scuttled to a door in the kitchen. They had to shield themselves from the flying shards of glass as the back windows shattered from the heat. When they entered the dark garage, Fay slapped a set of keys into Tyler's hand.

"Your reflexes are probably quicker than mine."

Tyler gave the shotgun to Grant. "See if you can take one of them out when we pass."

They scrambled into the SUV, Tyler in the driver's seat, Fay in the passenger seat, and Grant in the back.

"Ready?" Tyler said, the key already in the ignition.

Grant thumbed the window switch. "Ready."

Fay clicked her seat belt and nodded.

"Okay," Tyler said, "everyone keep your heads down."

Tyler started the engine and flicked the transmission into drive. He didn't bother with the garage door opener. He slammed his foot to the floorboard, and the Land Rover's nose tore into the aluminum door, wrenching it from its tracks. Flames licked at the truck as they sped out, the garage door still clinging to the hood until a flick of the steering wheel sent it flying.

The gunmen were crouching behind the Toyota, ready for their quarry to pile out in a panic away from the fire at the back of the house. It only took a moment for them to refocus their aim, but it was enough time for Grant to lay down some covering fire. Two quick blasts disintegrated the Toyota's rear window and pockmarked the quarter panel.

Tyler checked the rearview mirror and saw that one of the men had been hit by a couple of pellets. The slight injury did no more than cause him to curse loudly and return fire, his pistol cracking as bullets plunked into the back of the Land Rover.

In this snow there was no way the two-wheel-drive Toyota sedan would be able to keep up with the four-wheel-drive SUV, so Tyler intended to gain a lead and rendezvous with the police, who should be on their way up the mountain.

It sounded like a great plan until a pistol shot behind them was followed by a loud thump from under the vehicle. A bullet had punctured the right rear tire. The Land Rover's back end swerved sideways as Tyler struggled to maintain control. Now he not only had to outrun their trigger-happy pursuers, but he would have to fight the SUV's insistent urge to plunge off the snowy cliff-side road into the river far below.

FOUR

Morgan Bell wasn't getting much cooperation from Charles Kessler, Lightfall's project lead. That pissed her off.

"Dr. Kessler, we have full authorization to be here," she said, pointing at her credentials. It stated that she was a special agent with the Air Force's Office of Special Investigations.

Kessler peered at her ID in mock studiousness. "Never heard of OSI."

"That doesn't matter. I know you've been contacted by our superiors about our investigation and that you were instructed to give your full cooperation. We need to talk. Now."

By "we" she meant herself and her partner, Vince Cameron, who stood next to her watching a dozen laboratory technicians carefully packing equipment into shipping crates. Their voices echoed from the Wright-Patterson lab's high ceiling. Morgan had visited the sprawling Dayton, Ohio Air Force base many times, but she'd never been inside this building.

"Agent Bell, I'm very busy here," Kessler said, his eyes sweeping the room before locking on a skinny man in glasses and a lab coat who was wrestling a box onto a hand cart. "Collins! Make sure the OC-5 analyzer gets packed in there."

Collins looked up and nodded vigorously. "Yes, sir."

Kessler pointed at a guy with long greasy curls and more forearm hair than she'd ever seen before. "Josephson. Help Collins."

Josephson looked less eager than Collins. "Dr. Kessler, I'm supposed to be packing the calibration equipment."

"And if you had that done yesterday, maybe I would have sent Collins on the transport flight to accompany the equipment instead of you. Now move."

Josephson shrugged and moseyed over to Collins.

Kessler turned back to Morgan. "The transport flight is scheduled to take off in three hours, and as you can see we are behind schedule."

"Sounds like poor planning on your part," she said.

"Who *are* you?"

"Dr. Kessler," Vince said, "we're sorry to bother you at a critical time. We just need a word with you in private. I promise it won't take more than a few minutes."

Kessler smoldered and then said, "Fine. My office is over here." He stalked away, leaving them in the dust.

Vince grinned at Morgan as they followed him. "Have you heard of the phrase, 'You'll catch more flies with honey than vinegar'?"

Morgan didn't return the smile. "Yes."

"Don't you think that tactic might come in handy once in a while?"

"I use it if I need to."

"Do you ever need to?"

"No."

"See?" Vince said. "That's your problem."

"It's not a problem. That's what I have you for."

"I knew I had a purpose."

They entered Kessler's office and closed the door. Kessler sat down at his desk in a huff. "So what is the OSI anyway?"

"You ever watch the show *NCIS*?" Vince said. "You know, Naval Criminal Investigative Service? We're like them, only for the Air Force instead of the Navy."

"I don't watch TV."

"We are the primary law enforcement agency for the Air Force," Morgan said. "Our mission is to identify and neutralize criminal, terrorist, and intelligence threats to the Air Force, Department of Defense, and US government."

"Well, I'm pleased to tell you, Agent Bell, that we're on your side."

"Are you sure about that? Because we have evidence that there is a leak in Project Lightfall."

Kessler sat up in his chair. "What do you mean?"

"Does anyone in the program ever use the term, 'Killswitch'?"

Kessler was aghast. "How do you know that word?"

"That's the nickname some people on your staff have used to refer to the Lightfall weapon, isn't it?"

Kessler furiously tapped on his desk with his index finger to punctuate his points as he spoke. "Agent, this is an unacknowledged Special Access Program. Information is strictly on a need-to-know basis. Most members of Congress don't even know about Lightfall."

"Well, there are no senators here, so we should be fine."

"Dr. Kessler," Vince said, "both Agent Bell and I have top clearances, as I'm sure you were told. And we are on a need-to-know basis in this case. If someone is trying to steal information about Lightfall, our mission is to identify that person or persons and bring them to justice before we have a further national security breach."

Kessler didn't look happy, but he nodded. "All right. Yes. The staff started referring to the weapon as the Killswitch, and the name stuck, much to my chagrin."

"The National Security Agency intercepted a message hidden in a public Internet discussion forum dedicated to videogames." Vince referred to his notebook. "It said, 'Kill Switch hints? Stuck on level seven. Died twenty-one times the first day, then twenty-five times the next. Need help.' The username was PG0915. Only one person responded. A man named George Hickson. His answer was, 'Did you try the black box cheat code?'"

Kessler frowned. "Hints and cheat codes? Is Kill Switch a game?"

"Yes. It was released nine years ago."

"So? It's just some kid who can't play very well. What's the problem?"

"Because elements of the message seem to have connections to the Lightfall program, we think it may be a code. When is the Killswitch supposed to arrive in Australia?"

"Two days from now. The weapons test is scheduled for ten days after that." Kessler's eyebrows knitted together. "What are you getting at?"

"The arrival date is July twenty-first," Morgan said. "Seven twenty-one."

"Are you serious?" Kessler said with a laugh. "That has to be a coincidence."

"What happens on July twenty-fifth?"

Kessler shrugged. "We'll be prepping for the test firing."

"And what about the username?" Morgan asked. "PG0915. You're using the Pine Gap facility for the test prep. PG may mean Pine Gap."

"More coincidence."

"And what if 0915 is a time?"

"Oh, come on. Did you track this person down? It's probably some pimply-faced teenager in his mother's basement."

"We did try to find this person," Vince said, "but whoever it was used an anonymizer to register the username. George Hickson didn't pan out either."

"Then what do you want me to do?"

"It's possible that hostile forces are targeting one of those dates for some reason," Morgan said. "Perhaps someone is planning to take photos or smuggle information about the weapon out of Pine Gap. They may even try to sabotage the weapon somehow. It's our recommendation that you postpone the test until a later date."

Kessler's face darkened. "Agent Bell, do you know how much has been spent getting ready for this test?"

"That's irrelevant."

"Over one billion dollars and seventy thousand manhours of work."

"And all of that time and money will be wasted if someone steals information about the weapon or disables it somehow."

"I don't believe this."

A knock at the door.

"Yes?" Kessler said.

The door opened and Collins poked his head in. "Sir, we're having a problem with the magnetic flux density analyzer."

"What's wrong with ... Never mind. I'll be there in a few minutes."

"Yes, sir." Collins closed the door.

"Why is this test being conducted in Australia?" Morgan asked.

Kessler sighed. "We have to use the Woomera Test Range in South Australia."

"We have test ranges here in the US."

"Woomera is the biggest land-based weapons testing area in the world. It's larger than England and allows the evaluation of rockets and explosives far from prying eyes. No facility in the US is that isolated."

"Who chose Australia as the test site?"

"The Australians. This is a joint project with them."

"I know. Do you think someone on the Australian side could be the leak?"

"It's only a handful of people on their end, but go ahead and waste your time delving into that side of it."

"We will investigate every possibility thoroughly," Morgan said. "In the meantime I'm going to recommend that you postpone the test until we can verify who sent that message."

"Agent Cameron," Kessler said, turning dramatically toward Vince, "you seem to be the more reasonable person here, so I'll address this to you. Unless I get a call from the Secretary of the Air Force himself telling me to call off the test, we are going forward with it. Now, you are the investigators, so investigate. You may interview whomever you want. Look into their backgrounds. Put extra security on the transport. I don't care. Just stay out of my way."

Before Morgan could respond to the disdainful comments, Vince stopped her. "Putting extra security measures on the transport will only draw attention that what they're transporting is valuable. We might as well put a sign on the plane saying, 'Top-secret weapon inside. Please don't steal it.'"

Kessler waved a hand. "Security is your job, not mine."

"Dr. Kessler," Vince said, "are any of your employees gamblers?"

"I have no idea. I don't get involved with their private lives."

"Any of them been acting strangely at work?"

He spoke without hesitation. "Not at all."

"You're absolutely sure you don't remember anything out of the ordinary?"

"Not that I recall."

"You seem to be very blasé about the possibility that your project has been compromised by potential spies," Morgan said.

"I handpicked all of the scientists and engineers on this project myself. I work with them daily. I can state for a fact that none of them is a spy."

"What about you?"

Kessler's eyes burned into Morgan's. "Are you insane? I've spent the last ten years of my life on this program. I've staked my entire reputation on it. Why would I do anything to sabotage it?"

"You tell me."

"I can't, because this is ridiculous. You're fishing for something to justify your jobs. Unless you can come up with a more credible threat than a stupid message on a discussion forum, we will continue as planned. Now, if you'll excuse me, I have to make sure Collins will be finished in the next thirty minutes."

He stood and walked to the door, waving Morgan and Vince out of his office. He shot Morgan a withering stare as he locked it, and he was gone.

"What do you think?" Vince asked her.

"I don't like coincidences," Morgan said.

"Neither do I."

While Vince took a bathroom break, she called her section head. The conversation didn't go well. She hung up and waited.

When Vince returned, he said, "By the fact that we aren't hustling after Kessler, I'm guessing the boss said he wasn't going to the director with this."

Morgan shook her head. "He doesn't think there's enough to warrant canceling the test."

"It *is* pretty flimsy evidence."

"Not too flimsy to merit two tickets to Australia, though. We're on United out of LA this evening. I convinced him to send us to Pine Gap just to keep an eye on things."

Vince groaned. "Are you kidding? Fifteen hours on a flight to Sydney? At least tell me we're flying business class."

Morgan shook her head. "Coach."

Another groan.

"It gets worse. Did you look at Pine Gap on the map?"

"No. Why?"

"Sydney isn't our final destination. We've got a connecting three-hour flight. Pine Gap is in the middle of the Australian outback, near Alice Springs."

This time Vince didn't groan. "You just love trying to make me miserable."

"No," Morgan said. "You do just fine on your own."

FIVE

I f the bullet had gone through one of the front tires, the Land Rover would have skidded off the road and plummeted into the Shotover River long ago. And although the right rear tire was punctured, it hadn't shredded, so Tyler was able to open up some distance between him and the rear-wheel-drive Toyota on the snowy road. With the curves throwing off their aim, the pursuers' shots went wild. So far luck had favored the pursued.

But two new problems faced them. Grant was now out of shells, and they had come down to an elevation where snow no longer covered the road. At the speed Tyler was going, the pavement would rip the punctured tire to tatters in minutes.

"Where are the cops?" Tyler said to Grant in the back seat.

"The dispatcher says they're about two miles away."

Tyler saw in the mirror that the Toyota was closing fast. "If we stop, we'll never be able to hold out until the police get here."

"There's a small town up ahead," Fay said. "Arthurs Point. We could run into a shop and get help."

"Do the shop owners carry guns?"

"Shop owners in gun shops do."

"I don't suppose there are any gun shops in this little town."

"I don't think so."

Hiding in a store might work, or it might get innocent bystanders killed. Given that the gunmen were still in hot pursuit, it didn't seem like they cared much about witnesses.

Tyler saw a red sign flash by for Shotover Jet, the jet boats that take passengers on a high-speed ride down the Shotover River canyon. Grant had shown him a brief video of the boats when they were planning their trip to Queenstown, but Tyler hadn't thought about it further because of the cold weather.

"Fay," he said, "do the jet boats run in the winter?"

"Oh, yes. Year round."

He glanced in the mirror and saw Grant nodding. "It'd be hard for them to follow us."

Bullets hammered the tailgate.

"Down!" Tyler shouted, but nobody had to be told to duck.

The Toyota was less than a hundred yards behind them.

The rear wheel was now grinding along the asphalt, throwing up a shower of sparks. At any moment the wheel itself might fly off, and then they would be easy prey.

"Since they're after *me*," Fay said, "the noble thing for me to do would be to offer to have you drop me off to distract them while you get away, but I have to admit I'm too scared to make the gesture."

"Don't worry, Fay," Tyler said. "That's not an option."

"Good, because if you're thinking of using the jet boats to get away from these men, the turnoff is coming up on the right."

Tyler was impressed. Even though she was frightened, Fay still kept her wits. Sure enough, a new sign for the jet boats pointed to the right. Tyler cranked the wheel and grimaced as the rear hub squealed against the road in protest.

Tyler approached a fork in the road. "Which way?"

Fay indicated a gravel lane straight ahead. The Land Rover passed a parking lot where startled tourists watched the SUV flash by. Tyler slammed on the brakes as they turned down a tree-covered decline.

He accelerated again when they reached a rocky beach along a bend in the river. On the right were several of the bright red jet boats still stowed on their trailers. Two boats were in the water, and Tyler could make out the twin-jets poking from the back of the sleek craft just above the waterline. Each of the identical boats was big enough to hold twenty passengers, and an aerodynamic roll-bar stretched across the rear, giving them the appearance of sports cars.

Not that Tyler knew much about boats. Cars and planes were the vehicles he spent his time on. But Grant was a fanatic for boats. He had several of them back in Seattle and hosted a party on his thirty-foot Bayliner every August on Lake Washington to watch the Navy's Blue Angels perform their air show. In addition to the cabin cruiser, he also owned a jet boat for water skiing.

If they made it onto one of the Shotover boats, Grant would be the one driving.

To their left, a group of passengers were waiting for their ride, already decked out in weather gear and life jackets. Several of them yelled as Tyler skidded across the stones.

One of the docked jet boats was unloading tourists, and the other was empty. Tyler had been hoping there would be only one boat, but with the Toyota rushing down the road toward them, blocking their sole way out, they were committed. Standing and fighting wasn't an option.

He stopped and the three of them jumped out. Fay sprinted for the empty boat. Seeing that he didn't have to help her, Grant waved the shotgun around in the air, sending the tourists and jet-boat operators scattering back toward the guest center in terror.

With the Land Rover covering their escape, they pounded across the dock and climbed into the boat. Passengers were rapidly evacuating the other one.

The Toyota smashed into the SUV, and more shots split the air. Tyler felt a round zing past him as he helped Fay into the boat. Grant tossed the shotgun on the deck and leaped in, quickly examining the dashboard. He found the ignition and hit the button. The engines turned over, burbling with barely restrained power.

While Fay belted herself into her seat in the front row, Tyler threw the lines off. "Clear!" The massive Blaine sprang out of the car and ran along the dock, snapping off shots from his pistol. Tyler dropped to the deck.

"Hold on!" Grant yelled.

He threw the throttle forward. With a deafening roar, the jet boat surged into the river. As the boat pulled away, Blaine jumped from the dock and landed in the back row.

"Watch out!" Tyler shouted to Grant, who turned around and saw that they had a hitchhiker. Blaine raised his pistol to fire. Tyler, in the front row of seats next to Fay, was too far away to do anything. He pulled her down to get her out of the line of fire and told her to stay as low as she could.

In the middle of the river, Grant turned the steering wheel all the way right, and the boat whirled around in a 360-degree spin. As he struggled to keep from being tossed out of the boat, Blaine was thrown into the handlebar in front of his seat and dropped the pistol into the third row.

"He lost it!" Tyler yelled as he saw Foreman draw a bead with his own pistol from the dock. "Go! Go!"

Grant goosed the throttle, and the boat darted ahead just as rounds slammed into it. Tyler couldn't hear over the cacophonous engines, but Foreman rushed through the fleeing passengers from the other boat and screamed at the operator, who dived over the side into the freezing water. Foreman climbed in, obviously intent on continuing the pursuit.

Having regained his footing, Tyler vaulted into the second row of seats and leaned down, searching frantically for the dropped pistol. Blaine had the same idea and spotted it before Tyler did. He bent over to snatch it, but Tyler grabbed his arm to prevent him reaching it. Neither would let go of the other, and both of them fell into the third row as they entered the narrow canyon downriver.

Because of the precise control the engine nozzles afforded them, the Shotover Jet boats could come within a foot of the canyon walls, nearly brushing the rocky outcroppings as they rocketed down the river at sixty knots. Though it seemed dangerous, the highly trained operators made it a safe thrill.

Tyler just hoped that Grant had as much skill as the normal operators, because they were coming awfully close to hitting the cliffs.

However, that wasn't his biggest problem at the moment, which was that Blaine was mercilessly pummeling his midsection with fists the size of canned hams. Tyler threw his own punches, but because he was on his back and constricted on either side by the seatbacks and railing, he couldn't get much power behind them.

Blaine's face was so close that Tyler got a noseful of his fetid breath and saw that his attacker had the scarred remains of a disfigured left earlobe, no doubt the result of a previous fight. The man was a professional, not giving Tyler the opportunity to move his arms. There was no way for him to reach into his pocket and get to the knife on his Leatherman multi-tool.

A punch to the temple set stars whirling in front of Tyler's eyes. Blaine bent over to retrieve the pistol so he could finish the job. At the same time, Grant juked the boat left, causing Blaine to reel backward. Seeing his slim opening, Tyler kicked out with both feet.

He caught Blaine in the stomach, which combined with the momentum of the boat, launched him over the side just as the boat passed another outcropping of rock.

Blaine crunched into the sandstone as if he'd fallen from a ten-story building. His inert crushed body flipped backward into the roiling water and disappeared beneath the wake of the jet boat.

Tyler, the adrenaline masking the effects of the pummeling, bent over and picked up the pistol, a .45 caliber Heckler and Koch. He checked the magazine. Six rounds left, including the one in the chamber.

The jet boat behind them had made up the distance while Grant had been maneuvering to help Tyler get rid of Blaine. Barely a boat length separated them.

Rounds thudded into the back of the boat. Tyler popped up and fired off three quick rounds from the HK, but the motion of the boats made it impossible to get a clean shot. His bullets missed, but the other boat swerved away, giving Tyler a chance to climb to the front.

Fay was belted in and leaning down in the seat as far as she could. Tyler squeezed her shoulder, and she replied with a thumbs-up.

"Where does this river go?" he asked her.

"It ends up in Lake Wakatipu. We can get all the way to Queenstown."

That might have worked but for an ominous sputter coming from the rear of the boat. Black smoke trailed behind them.

"He hit one of the engines," Grant yelled. "I'm shutting it down. Any rounds left in your hand cannon?"

"Three."

They were coming to the end of the canyon. The river widened ahead, looping around low stretches of stone beach like the one at the dock, which would leave them fully exposed to gunfire from their flank.

"I say we turn around. Those tourists at the dock would have called the police. They should arrive by the time we get back."

"Let's do it," Tyler said. "I'll distract him with a couple of shots."

"Got it."

Tyler belted himself in, leaned out and squeezed off two rounds, causing Foreman to duck again. At the same moment, Grant twisted the steering wheel and Tyler's stomach along with it. The boat did a 180, dug in, and then launched forward. Foreman didn't have time to shoot, but Tyler saw him do his own turn. They left him far behind, but with two working engines on the pursuing boat, Foreman would likely catch them before they reached the dock.

They roared back up the canyon, the sound of the single engine echoing off the steep walls. Tyler peeked above the gunwales and saw the other boat gaining quickly, but he didn't fire. With only one round left, he'd have to make it count.

More bullets raked the stern.

"We're not going to make it," Grant shouted. "Any ideas?"

"Keep sweeping back and forth. Make sure he can't pull even with us until we reach the other side of the canyon. Then let him come up on the right. Remember the rock beach back at the dock? Maybe we can strand him on it."

Grant nodded. "Better than nothing."

Even at their slowed speed, it took no time for them to race back to the northern entrance of the canyon.

"Ready?" Grant yelled.

Tyler held up the pistol in response. Grant steered left and ducked down, and Tyler could hear the trailing boat pull alongside. Foreman was waiting until he was next to them before he dealt the *coup de grâce*.

Tyler sat up and took aim. If he was lucky, his shot would kill the gunman.

He wasn't. The shot went wide, but it was close enough to make Foreman flinch.

Grant rammed their boat into the other one. Because Foreman was holding the pistol, he had only one hand on the wheel and wasn't able to react quickly.

Tyler saw the surprised expression on the gunman's face when he realized he was headed directly for the rocky beach at full speed. Foreman tried to bump his way to the left, but Grant wouldn't let him budge. At the last second, Grant spun the wheel, putting their boat into a slide and missing the beach by inches.

Foreman wasn't as nimble. He went into a slide as well, but it was the worst possible decision.

Had he simply gone straight forward, Foreman's boat would have slid up onto the beach and come to a stop. Instead, the skidding motion meant that the side of the boat's hull hit the rocky shore at fifty knots.

The boat rolled spectacularly, the engines whining as they sucked air. The roll-bar would have protected Foreman if he'd been belted in. Instead, he was ejected into the path of the somersaulting boat and crushed by the hull.

Grant eased back on the throttle and guided the boat toward the dock. Four policemen who'd been watching the chase covered them with rifles as they approached, shouting at them to put their hands in the air. Grant put his hands up and let the boat drift close enough for one of the policemen to tie them off. Tyler dropped the pistol onto the deck and raised his arms.

"It's okay, Fay," Tyler said. "You can get up now. Just do it slowly. Your local constables look like they have itchy trigger fingers."

Fay sat up and peered at the men. Her eyes lit up when she recognized one of the officers. "For goodness sakes, Michael Brown! Stop pointing that thing at us. These aren't the bad guys."

The tension drained from Brown, and he lowered his rifle, signaling the others to do the same.

"Mrs. Turia?" Brown said. "We had a report that you'd been taken hostage."

"Don't believe everything you hear." She unbelted herself and stood. Tyler held her hand as she stepped out.

Tyler, his eyes still fixed on the policemen as he climbed onto the dock, heard a woman yell, "Nana!" She rushed past the policemen and threw herself into Fay's arms. Tyler thought she could be the granddaughter Fay had mentioned, except that this woman had much darker skin than Fay. The two of them hugged tightly until the woman pushed back to hold Fay at arm's length. "I was horrified when I heard about the fire at the house. Are you okay? Tell me you're okay."

"I'm fine, Jessica, thanks to these young men." She gestured at Tyler and Grant.

The woman turned, and Tyler got his first good look at her. Everything about her screamed athlete, from her drawstring pants and black hoodie stretched over her lithe build to the stylish shag of shoulder-length chestnut hair. She wore no makeup and none was needed. With creamy brown skin, rounded cheekbones, and full lips, she had no trouble drawing furtive glances from the young police officers.

Despite all that had already happened this morning, it was this moment that really shocked Tyler. He blinked a few times, not believing that he was seeing her for the first time in over fifteen years, half a world away from where they'd last seen each other.

Eyes like melted chocolate stared at him in surprise, and memories came flooding back like a cresting wave.

"Tyler?" she said. "What the hell is going on?"

Tyler opened his mouth, but the words wouldn't come. He turned to Fay. "Your granddaughter is Jess McBride?"

Fay's sheepish look told him that she had known from the beginning that Jess had been Tyler's college girlfriend.

SIX

I t had been four hours since Popovich and Golgov, traveling under the names Foreman and Blaine, were supposed to report in that they had disposed of Fay Turia. But when Vladimir Colchev checked his messages upon landing in Alice Springs, there were none waiting.

Before his three-hour Qantas flight from Sydney, Colchev had meticulously rechecked the Icarus prototype he'd procured from Nadia Bedova. As he'd expected, it was complete and ready for use. She wouldn't have risked sabotaging it because he might have noticed during the handover.

As Colchev had been finishing the examination in Sydney, Popovich texted him a brief message.

We are in her house. She has engraving but no X. Orders?

To Colchev the information was both interesting and unfortunate. Interesting because he didn't know the engraving still existed. However, he had a high-resolution photo of it, so it was worthless to him. The unfortunate part was that she had no xenobium. If she had, it would have made his mission much more simple.

Colchev had texted back immediately.

Destroy engraving. Term woman.

He didn't need any loose ends at this late juncture. Termination of the Turia woman was the best option, and he'd had every confidence that his men would carry out his orders. That was why the lack of communication with Popovich since then was so troubling.

Colchev exited the plane and emerged from the covered staircase to a cloudless azure sky. The midday sun beat down, but its rays could heat the mild winter breeze to only a few degrees above room temperature.

Waiting for Colchev at the gate was Dmitri Zotkin, a whippet-lean operative whose trim mustache and beard matched his short dark hair. Dressed in khakis and a denim shirt, he could have passed for a guide coming to take Colchev on a tour of the outback.

They exited the airport without a word, and Colchev tossed his duffel into the rear of Zotkin's SUV. They both got in, and Zotkin drove out of the airport.

"Why haven't we heard from Golgov or Popovich?" Colchev said.

Zotkin cleared his throat. "They failed in their mission."

"How do you know?"

"We've been monitoring news reports from Queenstown. Police say that two men were killed in an apparent kidnapping attempt."

"Damn it! Is the woman alive?"

Zotkin nodded. "Her house was burned to the ground, but she survived. No word on her condition."

"What about our men? Have they been identified?"

"No names have been released."

Like all of the men who were in Colchev's operation, Golgov and Popovich spoke fluent English in a neutral midwestern accent, and their passports were stellar fakes. Still, their deaths added to the mission's risk.

"Is there anything leading back to us?" Colchev said.

Zotkin shook his head. "I've already sent the scramble signal to their phones. Any data or phone numbers on them have been destroyed."

Colchev pounded the dashboard with his fist, shaking it until the glove box popped open. He closed it, sat back, and sighed. "They were good men."

"At least they died for their country."

They had been a loyal part of his foreign intelligence service team before Colchev's failure, and now the former SVR operatives wouldn't even get the honor of a Russian state funeral. He unrolled his window and breathed in the cool desert air. When his team had achieved its mission, he would make sure Golgov and Popovich's part in the operation was recognized, that they would receive the honor they deserved as heroes of the Motherland.

Colchev snapped back to focus on his goal now. Because Fay Turia had no xenobium, their path was clear.

"How are the preparations going?" he asked.

"We're almost ready. The last shipment arrived this morning, and they should be finished loading it by the time we get back."

Zotkin turned onto a road going north into Alice Springs.

"What about the CAPEK vehicle?" Colchev asked.

"It is in working order, and we have a meeting set up with the project lead tomorrow morning."

"Excellent."

"And your informant still says the Killswitch will arrive on time?"

Colchev thought back to the message on the discussion forum. The username they'd agreed on had been compromised, so the pre-arranged replacement had been used. The only thing it said was "Confirmed", meaning the operation was a Go according to plan.

"The Killswitch will be here in the morning," Colchev said. "Do you have all the documentation in order?"

"The uniforms, vehicles, and papers are all ready." Zotkin cleared his throat. "What about Nadia? Did you get Icarus from her?"

"Everything went as expected."

"I knew she'd never join us."

"I didn't think she would."

"But you let her live."

"We are patriots, Dmitri. So is Nadia. You would have me kill one of our own?"

"If necessary."

"It wasn't necessary."

Zotkin grunted but didn't say more. How to deal with Bedova was the one disagreement he and Colchev had. Zotkin had advocated wiping out her whole team as soon as she delivered Icarus, but Colchev knew that killing a fellow member of the SVR would make their reintegration into Russia much more difficult once the mission was over.

"If we see her again, we'll do what we have to," Colchev said.

Zotkin gave another grunt, but he seemed satisfied.

As they continued driving, they went over details of the operation. Although they had planned it down to the last detail, there were always contingencies to consider. A mission this complex required precise timing and complete understanding of the situation by all involved. The biggest question mark was his man on the inside of Lightfall. If he came through, the rest of the operation would go smoothly.

By the time Zotkin turned into the warehouse parking lot, Colchev was confident they were as ready as they could be.

The depot had once been used as a transfer station for trucks bound for Darwin and Adelaide, but it had been shut down years ago. Through a shell company, Colchev had rented it out as a staging point for their own operation, and the owners had asked no questions about their business.

Four semi trailers and a shorter truck were backed up to the warehouse loading platforms, and two SUVs occupied the lot. He and Zotkin got out and went into the warehouse, where a forklift was busy moving a pallet from the small truck to one of the trailers. Half a dozen men were assisting in the work.

Colchev stopped the forklift driver. "How long until you're done?"

The driver pointed at the trailer closest to them. "This is the last load. We should be done setting the rest of it up in two hours."

"What about the detonators?"

"Ready for rigging."

"We'll do it today. From now on, I want two men on watch, rotating every four hours."

"Yes, sir." The forklift driver carefully set down the pallet and went back to the small truck for another one.

His men formed a chain to move the pallet's load, twenty-five-pound clear plastic bags full of tiny pink pellets. Golgov and Popovich had been instrumental in obtaining them.

Colchev smiled as he read the bag's large block letters. ANFO. It had taken his team months to acquire the quantity they needed. And just as he'd planned, the last payload had arrived in time for the operation to be set in motion.

Short for ammonium nitrate/fuel oil, ANFO was one of the most common explosives in the world. Colchev walked over to the trailer to get a good look inside. His smile widened when he saw the fruition of so much hard work.

For the entire length of the interior, bags of ANFO were stacked from floor to ceiling.

SEVEN

After four hours in the police station, Tyler was famished. Before he'd had a chance to talk to Jess, they'd all been hauled away from the jet boat dock to be questioned at the Queenstown police department. An incident like this was extremely unusual for peaceful New Zealand, so he was sure they'd already made the worldwide news reports.

Tyler lost count of how many times he went over the story for the interrogating officers, all without stopping for lunch. No doubt they were comparing his tale to Grant's and Fay's. They were eventually convinced that Tyler was telling the truth, that unknown assailants attacked Fay and that Tyler and Grant had come to her rescue, although Tyler wasn't so sure that she had really needed rescuing.

What the police wanted to know now was why she'd been targeted. So did Tyler. As he told the investigators, it must have something to do with her Roswell artifacts, but he had no idea why anyone would want them.

By mid-afternoon Tyler had told the detectives all he could, and he was released. The police seemed content to chalk this up to a strange robbery gone awry, and with both assailants dead, they considered the danger over.

The policeman who escorted Tyler out told him that someone would be coming by shortly to return the Audi using the keys Grant had given them. Tyler met Grant at the front of the station. When they saw the mass of news media outside, they took a seat in the waiting area.

"Well, this has been fun," Tyler said. "Where's Fay?"

"The cops interviewed her before they got to us," Grant said. "They told me she left two hours ago to check out what's left of her house."

"I hope she's able to salvage something."

"At least she's alive."

Tyler couldn't disagree, but the attitude that *it could have been worse* was small consolation for someone who just lost everything they owned.

Grant patted his stomach. "I'm as hungry as a vegan at a pig roast. As soon as we get the car back, we're heading to that pizza place and I'm ordering an extra-large pepperoni. Then you're going to tell me all about Jess."

Tyler rolled his eyes. He should have known that would be Grant's first topic of conversation.

"I'll tell you now, because there's nothing to it. She and I went out for a year at MIT. It didn't work out and we broke up. End of story."

"Uh huh. And how come I never heard about her before?"

"Do I know about all your old girlfriends?"

Grant smiled. "Good point. But now that she got us into a shootout in the middle of a foreign nation, maybe it's time you spilled it."

Tyler sighed. "All right. I was a junior and she was a freshman in a history elective I was taking. She sat next to me one day, and we started talking. I thought she was cute, and after about a week, I asked her to go to a party with me. One thing led to another, and we were a couple."

"You thought she was *cute*? When she was a college freshman, did she look anything like she does now? 'Cause I got a look at her down at the dock. She's not cute. She's smokin'."

"I noticed her. *Everyone* noticed her. A girl at MIT who looks like that had her choice of guys."

"And she sat next to *you*? What was wrong with her?"

"Maybe she liked a man in uniform," Tyler said with a shrug. "I was wearing my ROTC class A's that day."

Grant nodded knowingly. "That's why I wear mine whenever I go to a wedding. Never fails. So why'd you break up?"

"Pretty simple. I wanted a long-term relationship. She was new to college and didn't want to settle down just yet. So that was it. Three months later I met Karen."

But in fact their relationship had been far more serious than he was letting on to Grant. The eight months he'd dated her had been intense, but that was a lifetime ago. Jess was the first girl he'd ever fallen in love with, and she'd broken his heart. But he harbored no ill will toward her because if he hadn't broken up with Jess, he would never have gone out with Karen, his wife and the love of his life. In a way, he owed Jess for giving him the best years he'd ever had.

Grant had been great friends with Karen, though she had teased him mercilessly about his serial love life. Grant had been the only reason Tyler had lived through the terrible year after she was senselessly taken from him in a car accident.

A policeman came in through the front door, and the sounds of shouting reporters briefly invaded the station. He spotted Tyler and Grant.

"Dr. Locke and Mr. Westfield, your car is waiting."

"They brought the car here?" Grant said. "That's service for you."

They walked outside and were immediately surrounded by the growing crowd of news people and cameras. Tyler saw the Audi and silently pushed his way through the cacophony of shouted questions.

He stopped when he saw Jess driving and Fay in the passenger seat.

Fay waved from her open window. "Get in!"

Not wanting to get into a discussion in front of the media, he and Grant crammed into the back seat. Jess hit the accelerator and zoomed down Camp Street.

"What are you doing here?" Tyler said.

"Didn't you want your car back?" Jess said.

"Yes, but where are we going?"

"Back to my house."

"Your house?"

"Well, we can't go back to *my* house," Fay said with a mixture of anger and sadness. "It burned to the ground before the fire brigade could get there." A sob caught in her throat.

"I'm sorry, Fay," Tyler said.

"I wish we could have done more," Grant added.

"You boys did all you could. I would have gone up in smoke, too, if you hadn't shown up when you did."

"They couldn't save anything?" Tyler said.

"All that's left is what I have with me."

There was silence for a moment until Grant opened his mouth.

"So, Jess, how do you know Tyler?"

Tyler had to stifle a groan.

"Tyler didn't tell you about our hot love affair?"

"I heard it was quite passionate," Fay said.

"Good God," Tyler said. He didn't think the day could have gotten worse.

"Why *did* you break up with my granddaughter?"

"Do you think this is really the best time to talk about our dating history?" Tyler said.

"It's okay, Nana," Jess said. "He's always been a little touchy about sharing his feelings."

"College was a long time ago," Tyler said.

"Yeah," Grant said. "Tyler now regularly gets choked up by greeting card commercials."

"You are not helping."

"What? This is fun."

"Can we please get back to the issue at hand?" Tyler said. "Which is that two men burned your house down and tried to kill you this morning for something you supposedly found after the Roswell incident. Do you know why?"

"That's why I wanted to consult with you," Fay said. "Jess said you were the best forensic airplane crash analyst in the world."

"Jess told you to hire me?"

"Not in so many words," Jess said. "That's why I was surprised to see you earlier. When Nana said she was looking for someone to look at her piece of wreckage, I must have off-handedly mentioned you worked for Gordian."

"It wasn't off-handed," Fay said.

"Nana!"

"She was reluctant to call you. She had no idea I asked you to consult with me."

Jess glanced in the mirror at Tyler, then looked at Fay. "Wait a minute. Is this why you asked me over to lunch today and wouldn't tell me why?"

"I thought it might be nice for you two to get reacquainted."

"Why are you even here?" Tyler asked Jess.

"In the car or in New Zealand?"

"In Queenstown."

"I live here now. Moved here three years ago after a stint doing encryption analysis for a global private security firm in Auckland."

"I thought you were going to be an economist."

"Oh, right, I was still an economics major then. No, I switched to mathematics. I thought I was going to work for Wall Street, but the thought of spending every day dressed in a suit made me want to throw up, so I went into code-breaking. It paid almost as well, and I could come to work in sweats if I wanted to."

"What are you doing here?"

"After my parents died, they left me some money, and I wanted to be closer to Nana. Since I have dual citizenship with the US and New Zealand, it was easy to buy a part ownership in a business here."

"In encryption?" Grant asked.

Fay shook her head. "Jessica has a stake in one of the biggest extreme sports tourism companies in Queenstown."

"I'm not much more than an investor, but I come up with some of the ideas for new activities. The best perk is that I get to beta test all of the new experiences. Other than that, I spend most of my time on the slopes or the hiking trails around Queenstown."

Tyler was surprised by none of this. One of the things that had attracted him to Jess in the first place was her out-going nature, willing to try anything and everything, convincing him to take risks that he might not have without her. She was an excellent skier, rock climber, and swimmer, and she loved spending time outdoors. Jess had always been more interested in play than work, so it sounded like the new gig was a perfect fit for her.

Jess turned into the drive of a small bungalow with an expansive view of the lake and the Remarkables range behind it.

They got out and Fay took Grant's arm. "I bet you're as hungry as I am. Come help me make lunch."

"Happy to," Grant said, and they went into the house, leaving Jess and Tyler alone outside.

"Nice place," Tyler said.

"It does the job. I'm not here much so I don't need a lot of space." She turned to him and gave him a serious look. "I was sorry to hear about your wife's passing."

Tyler did the head bob he always used to acknowledge that kind of sentiment. He'd gotten accustomed to it over the years, and everyone seemed to understand what the gesture meant.

"And I'm sorry about your parents." After an awkward silence, he said, "Jess, what's going on here?"

"With my grandmother?"

He nodded.

"She's told me her story so many times, I'd come to think of it as a myth. Now I don't know what to think."

"What story?"

"She'll have to tell you. She's much better at it."

"I'll be interested to hear it. Then Grant and I will have to be on our way. Given what happened today, we thought it would be prudent to head back to Seattle tomorrow."

"That's why I asked Nana to take Grant inside. I want to hire you."

Tyler was taken aback. "I wasn't going to charge Fay for the consult."

"No, I want to hire you to find out why someone tried to kill her. She's the only family I have left in the world, and I owe it to her. Especially now that she has nowhere else to go."

Tyler hesitated, so Jess went on. "If you're worried about the price, I can afford whatever you charge."

"It's not that. It's just . . . I mean, Roswell?"

"I know it sounds crazy, but you have to admit there must be something to these artifacts she has if someone wanted it badly enough to chase you down the Shotover River for it."

Tyler looked out over the water, then back at Jess. "I can't make any promises. I need to hear what Fay has to say."

Jess smiled. "Oh, and by the way . . ." With both hands she pulled Tyler's head down and planted a kiss on him. For a second he was a college junior again, and his stomach did a flip as he lost himself in the moment.

Jess stepped back and said, "That's for saving Nana's life this morning." She walked into the house, leaving Tyler to wonder what just happened.

EIGHT

Jess was pleased with herself. Not because she had kissed Tyler. Ever since she'd seen him this morning, she'd had the overwhelming urge to do that. What she was proud of was that she had the willpower to go no further.

Tyler had aged well. He used to be as lanky as dried linguini, but obviously he'd filled out during his Army years. Though the sun had weathered him a bit, the lines on his face and long jagged scar on his neck added a rugged dimension to his tousled hair, strong jaw limned with a two-day stubble, and alert blue eyes. Now she recalled why he was the one she'd approached in history class. At first he hadn't gotten the hint, so she'd maneuvered herself into getting invited to a party he was attending.

She smiled at the memories and opened the front door of her house. Jess turned to Tyler and said, "Well, aren't you coming?"

Tyler recovered from his flabbergasted reaction and nodded, walking in her direction.

She found Fay and Grant making ham-and-cheese sandwiches in the kitchen.

"I think we all need a drink," she said, and grabbed four bottles of Newcastle from the fridge. She popped the top on hers and took a long draft.

Tyler came in, spotted the beers, and drained half a bottle without a word.

"We haven't been properly introduced," Jess said to Grant. "My name is Jess McBride. Only Nana calls me Jessica."

"Grant Westfield," he said, wiping some mustard on a paper towel before shaking her hand.

"You work for Gordian Engineering, too?"

"Electrical engineer. Tyler recruited me into the firm. We did stints together in both Iraq and Afghanistan when I served in his combat engineering battalion as his first sergeant."

"Then he abandoned us to join the Rangers," Tyler said.

"*His* battalion?" Jess asked.

"Tyler was captain of the unit. And I didn't abandon him. He left to start Gordian."

"Why do you look familiar?" Fay said to Grant.

"You might remember Grant as the guy who gave up his pro wrestling career to join up," Tyler said.

Jess didn't follow sports much except during the Olympics. She looked at Fay, who shook her head.

"No, I think it's because you remind me of that man on the reality show. The handsome bald one. I can't remember which one now. It'll come to me. But you do look a little like my husband. He had your type of muscular build."

Tyler knew Jess's background, but Grant gave her a new once-over at this tidbit of info.

"My grandfather was full-blooded Maori," Jess explained. "That's why you'd think I was Nana's adopted grandchild."

"Nonsense," Fay said. "She looks exactly like her mother, who looked just like me."

"And it seems like she got her sense of adventure from you," Tyler said.

"That's why she's so good at coming up with the company's tour packages."

"Like what?"

Jess ticked them off using her fingers. "We've got six bungee-jumping locations, skydiving tours, kayaking trips, heli-skiing, white-water rafting. Just about anything you can name. Except jet boats. And we're working on that."

"Sounds like you've got a budding empire," Tyler said.

"It's in full bloom," Fay said. "Jess's company made twenty million dollars last year."

"Okay, Nana. They don't need all of the details."

"I'm just so proud of you, honey."

"I know."

Now it was Tyler giving her a new appraisal. "Well, we've gone through a lot to get to this point, Fay. What exactly is it that you wanted me to take a look at?"

Fay went to her satchel and removed a hunk of silver metal the size and shape of a Frisbee cut in half. One edge was a smooth curve while the other was jagged, as if it had been hacked apart with a rusty can opener. Jess had seen it a hundred times, but now the attack gave it greater significance.

Fay gave it to Tyler, who held it carefully so that he didn't cut himself, weighing it with his hands. "Too strong to be aluminum. Feels like a titanium alloy. Or possibly magnesium. I'd have to take it back to a lab to make sure."

"Can you tell me if it's from a spaceship?" Fay asked him.

Jess noticed Tyler's lip curl at the ridiculous question, but he inspected the object carefully before answering. "It definitely looks like it's been involved in a crash of some kind." He pointed at the tears in the metal. "You can see evidence of explosive impact here, along with some melting of the material. But this could be from an aircraft. I've seen thousands of pieces like it."

"From sixty-five years ago?"

"Well, no. My expertise is on recent accidents. But I have seen wreckage from old World War II bombers. Maybe that's what you found."

"Oh, no. This is definitely from the Roswell crash."

"How do you know?"

"Because I found it there."

"Perhaps a plane crashed in the area."

"No."

"I'm sorry, Fay," Tyler said. "I'm having a hard time believing this came from a spaceship, but it's not because of you. I'm just an inveterate skeptic. If this is from Roswell, why are you just investigating it now?"

"She's been investigating it for the past five years," Jess said. "Ever since my grandfather died."

"I didn't tell Henare—that was my husband—about my experience at Roswell until very late in life. I thought he would send me to a loony bin, so I told him about it only when he was dying. I was shocked when he said I should go on that quest, that he'd be with me every step of the way. Since then I've been trying to track down the origin of what I learned at Roswell. I was hoping you could point me in the right direction. All I want is an answer. I don't care what it is, but I'd like to know before I end my days on this planet."

Grant stopped cutting the sandwiches, and Tyler guzzled the rest of his beer. Though they hid it well, Jess saw the dubious look they exchanged.

"Fay," Tyler said, tossing the bottle in the recycling bin, "I'm happy to take this piece of metal back to Gordian and test it every way we can. But I can tell you now that unless we find it's made of some material that we've never seen before, the results will be inconclusive."

"Did you show that to anyone else?" Grant asked. "The guys at your house today must have heard about it somehow."

Fay gave them an embarrassed look. "Oh my goodness, I did talk about it, didn't I? When you told me it would be three months before you could see me, I didn't think it would hurt to go to Roswell for the annual UFO festival and see if I could get some information from the people there, although plenty of them are kooks."

"Who did you talk to?" Tyler said.

"Lots of people. You could tell that ninety percent of them were just what I thought Henare would think of me: crackpots, all of them with wild tales that I knew were absolute hogwash, but there were also lecturers and authors there who've spent years researching the incident."

"Did any of them seem to take a particular interest in your story?"

"Sure. I don't know if they believed me, but a lot of people were interested."

"Did you show anyone your artifacts?"

"No, but I did mention the piece of wreckage in an interview."

"There's even a video," Jess said.

"What video?"

"I can show it to you after lunch," Fay said.

"Do you know anything about the multicolored metal Foreman and Blaine were after?" Tyler asked.

Fay shrugged. "I've never seen anything like that."

"You mentioned in the house that you had 'artifacts' plural. Is the second one another piece of wreckage?"

"Not wreckage really. But it's from the crash."

Fay pulled out her real treasure from the satchel, a battered piece of wood in a plastic sheath.

She handed it to Tyler, who peered at the engraving. His

eyes lit up when he recognized the drawings etched into the smooth wood. Jess wasn't surprised that he knew what they were.

"Where did you get this?" he said.

"At Roswell. The same day I picked up that piece of metal from the wreckage of the spaceship."

"You found it in the wreckage?"

Fay looked at Jess, who nodded for her to continue.

"It was given to me," Fay said. "By an alien who survived the crash for a short while."

Grant, who had been taking a swig of beer, coughed as some of the liquid went down the wrong way.

"Excuse me," he said. "Did you say alien?"

Tyler furrowed his brow at Jess, but she was glad to see that he didn't immediately dismiss the statement. He was obviously willing to listen to more.

Jess picked up two of the plates and nodded for Grant to get the others.

"Let's take our lunch into the dining room," she said. "Nana has a tale to tell you."

NINE

Fay galloped across the grassy plain atop her Appaloosa, Bandit, trying to outrun the approaching storm. With darkness falling, her father would soon come looking for her, and he'd tan her hide if he found out she'd gone riding without finishing her after-school chores. As she felt the hot wind in her face and watched Bandit's silky mane toss from side to side, Fay thought it would be worth the risk.

In just a few days, he'd be yanking her from everything she'd ever known in her ten short years. She'd never even been out of New Mexico and now her father wanted to uproot the entire family so he could go run his cousin's sheep ranch near someplace called Lake Wakatipu on the other side of the world. And the worst part was that they'd have to leave Bandit behind. She'd argued that it wasn't fair, but nothing she could say would change his mind. The best she could do was spend as much time as she could with her beloved horse, so she'd taken him for long rides every evening whether her dad liked it or not.

But he'd be extra mad if she got stuck out in a thunderstorm. Flash floods could happen in the blink of an eye, and to get home she'd have to cross many arroyos on the Foster sheep ranch where the foreman, Mac Brazel, let her ride undisturbed.

The clouds rolled in, lightning piercing the sky every few minutes. She was still seven miles from the barn and safety. At this rate she'd be soaked by the time she got there, and there'd be no way she could hide what she'd been doing if she walked into the house drenched and covered with the smell of horse. Then her behind would get the belt for sure. She pressed her heels down and urged Bandit to go faster.

A new sound intruded over the pounding hooves. Faint at first, the hum grew steadily, coming from the west behind her. Too constant to be thunder, it sounded like an engine, but no one would be idiot enough to try to drive a truck through the uneven terrain.

Fay looked over her shoulder to see where it was coming from, but the plain was empty to the horizon. The sound grew louder still, and she realized that it wasn't coming from behind her. It was overhead.

With White Sands Proving Grounds only thirty miles away, she'd heard some of her friends talk about planes that sometimes flew high above the Army base. Two years ago, she'd even heard the faraway boom of something her father later called an atom bomb. That had gotten the kids talking when the news had been made public. To them, nothing was better than a government secret, unless it was a secret weapon that could destroy an entire city.

But the noise she heard now wasn't a bomb, and it wasn't the drone of aircraft propellers. This was more like the whine of a thousand trumpets blowing in unison. And it was heading straight toward her.

She pulled up sharply on the reins, and Bandit whinnied as he came to a stop. Fay looked up into the low-hanging clouds hoping to catch a glimpse of the noise's source. Then, just like heavy seas parted by a ship's prow, the clouds slid aside, and a flying object like nothing she'd ever seen screamed out of the sky.

Her mouth agape, Fay struggled to keep Bandit from bolting as a giant, silvery disk descended directly at them. Not knowing which way to go, she kept the horse still. The flying disk had no propellers, just two gaping black openings on either side. The craft had to be wider than the local high school's football field.

Before she could decide on a direction to go, it roared overhead, deafening her and spooking Bandit. He reared up, bucking Fay, and while she sailed through the air, she realized that the object that she'd thought was a disk was actually the shape of an oblong wing with no body. Then she hit the ground, smacking her rear harder than her dad would have and rolling away from Bandit's panicked stomping.

Fay raised her head in time to see the silver wing plow into the ground a quarter-mile in front of her, spraying dirt into the sky as it skidded to a stop.

The whine from the craft didn't end, but she could see no further movement.

Wincing from her bruised backside, but otherwise in one piece, she cooed at Bandit until he calmed and came to her. She climbed back on and tentatively rode toward the motionless air vehicle.

She knew she should just ride straight on and tell her father what had happened, but she also felt intense curiosity about the craft. Her father had taken her to an airfield one time to see the Army planes, and they'd all had white stars and numbers painted on the sides. This object had no markings whatsoever.

When she reached the front of the craft, Fay dismounted the horse and tied him to a scrub brush to keep him from bolting. She could see now just how huge the thing was, the wing standing more than five times higher than her thin frame.

As she walked along the wing's length, she ran her hand over its smooth skin, the metal cold to the touch. She didn't notice the cracked square of glass lying on the ground until she was right next to it.

No, not glass, because it wasn't shattered, but it was transparent like a window pane. She looked up and saw the space where the pane would go. The frame around it had been ripped apart from the force of the crash. Although the front of the craft was partially buried in the earth, it was too far above her to see inside without hoisting herself up. Now she wished she hadn't dismounted Bandit.

Her heart raced as she tried to decide what to do. If someone was hurt, Fay had to help them, but she was terrified about what she might find. Living on a ranch, she'd seen death and injuries: broken bones, impalements, rotting sheep that hadn't been discovered for a week. But this was different. There might be injured men inside.

Her dad had raised her to be tough. She'd become the son in the family after her brother died when she was two. Her father took her shooting and roping, taught her how to shear and hunt and fish. Fay convinced herself she could handle whatever she discovered in there and then report back. It would take only a moment to investigate.

Wrapping her leather gloves around the frame, she prepared to pull herself up when a silver hand shot out of the opening and grabbed at her wrist.

Fay fell backward and screamed. She shrieked even louder when she saw the face that peered out the window.

Although it was the size of a human and had two arms, its bulbous silver head was two sizes larger than a man's, framing two circular black eyes and a wide slit where the mouth should have been. The grotesque face lacked any nose. She screamed again when the creature climbed over the window's sill and landed next to her, breathing heavily before collapsing to its knees. Blue fluid bled from its stomach. It put its three-fingered hands to its head, shaking it back and forth as if it were trying to decapitate itself. After a moment, it gave up and sank to all fours.

With a guttural tone, the thing babbled at Fay in a

language she'd never heard. She shook her head in disbelief, and before she could scramble away, the creature
lunged at her and grabbed her leg. She tried to twist free,
but its grip was too strong. He crawled toward her and
took her hand.

Fay was scared beyond reason, sure that the thing was
preparing to eat her, but instead it stood and pulled her to
her feet. Without letting go of her hand, it loped toward
Bandit, babbling nonstop the entire way, as if it were terrified about something inside the downed craft.

She struggled but couldn't break free. When they reached
Bandit, the creature patted the horse on the neck, then
threw Fay onto the saddle. To her dismay and surprise, the
thing climbed awkwardly up behind her and lashed the
reins, launching Bandit into a canter with surprising skill.

It was only then that Fay realized that the whine from
the craft was getting louder by the second. They fled
across the plain in the direction of a slope leading down to
an arroyo a half-mile ahead. For some reason, the creature
was desperately trying to put distance between them and
the craft.

Lightning flashed, followed seconds later by the crack of
thunder. The storm would arrive in minutes.

When they reached the slope, the creature dismounted
and pulled Fay off, leading them down into the dry
streambed, soon to be swollen with water from the coming
storm. With one hand on Bandit's rein, it pushed her against
the twenty-foot-high vertical wall of the arroyo and covered

her body with its own. As it did so, a tremendous blast like a thousand thunderclaps split the air.

The thing hadn't been trying to kidnap her. It had been trying to protect her.

Bits of debris rained down around them, but none of them were large enough to injure them or the horse.

After a minute, the thing rolled over and lay on its back, wheezing with great effort. Its shaking hand snaked behind its back and withdrew something from a hidden pouch. It pressed the object into Fay's hands.

No longer terrified by her savior, she looked down and saw with astonishment a weathered piece of wood no bigger than a schoolbook. On it was an engraving of a rough triangle with a large dot on the left side next to a squiggly line coming from the triangle's center. Carved on the reverse side were four simple images recognizable as a spider, a bird, a monkey, and a person.

She stared back at the creature. "You want me to give this to someone?"

The creature pointed at her. The gift was meant for her.

"The Army, maybe?"

At the word "Army" it violently shook its head and shoulders and pointed at her again. The piece of wood was for her alone. Then the creature spoke with a voice so warped that Fay could barely understand the syllables.

"*Rah pahnoy pree vodat kahzay nobee um.*"

Fay shook her head. It sounded like gibberish. "I don't understand."

It repeated the phrase again slowly. "*Rah pahnoy pree vodat kahzay nobee um.*" It gestured for her to repeat it, and she did so three times until she got it verbatim.

With its hand shaking even more forcefully, the thing drew a figure in the dirt. It was an upright rectangle. Inside the rectangle the creature wrote a K, a backwards E, and a T before it was too weak to go on.

It raised one hand to Fay's face, and she didn't recoil. The hand stroked her cheek once, then fell away.

The shaking stopped and the labored breathing abruptly ended. The creature that had saved her life was dead.

Fay bawled at the thing's sudden end. She stayed crouched over its motionless body until the rain began to gush from the sky, washing away her tears.

She couldn't stay, and she couldn't move the heavy corpse. She'd have to leave it where it was.

The thing obviously didn't want her to report what had happened, but she couldn't just leave the creature there for no one to find for days or even weeks, its body at the mercy of scavenging coyotes.

Fay knew that Mac Brazel and little Dee Proctor rode the fence line every Thursday, so they'd be coming in this direction the next morning. She could leave clues that would lead them here.

She climbed onto Bandit and took one last look at the creature, who now seemed so vulnerable and unthreatening lying against the streambed wall. She kicked and Bandit trotted up out of the arroyo through the water coursing down in a torrent.

As she topped the slope, Fay was amazed to see that virtually nothing was left of the craft but small chunks littering the ground around her.

She picked up a dozen of the silvery metallic scraps and rode Bandit toward the fence line, scattering pieces behind her every few hundred yards. The shiny metal would lead the way back. When she reached the fence, she dropped the last few bits where she knew Mr. Brazel and Dee would see them.

But two remnants of the crash she kept with her, safely tucked into her vest. One was a curved piece of the silver craft itself, its jagged edges wrapped in her bandana. The other was the strange wooden carving.

She wouldn't tell anyone what she'd seen. Something about the way the creature pointed at her gave her the sense that she would get into all kinds of trouble if she volunteered the story.

If the creature wasn't washed away by a flood, Mr. Brazel would find it. He would come across the wreckage, too, and then tell the government authorities about it. After it made the news, she imagined that the discovery of such an alien craft would be the talk of the town in nearby Roswell.

TEN

After Fay finished her story, no one moved. Tyler stared at his empty plate and mulled over what he'd just heard. Grant had a look like he was trying not to show he thought she was nuts. Jess twirled her knife back and forth in her fingers and kept her eyes on the table.

"Why didn't you tell anyone about this back in 1947?" Grant asked.

"I was afraid. When Mac Brazel reported the spaceship wreckage, the Army came in, covered the whole thing up, and convinced everyone Brazel was crazy. If people wouldn't believe the ranch foreman, why would they believe a ten-year-old girl? I don't even know what they did with the alien body. Took it back to Area 51, I suppose."

"But you went to the UFO festival a couple of weeks ago. Why?"

"I had tried on my own for five years to find the truth, and I never got any closer to answering my questions. I was at a dead end. I had nothing to lose. Or so I thought." Tyler felt Fay's eyes fix on him. "I can tell you don't believe me."

He ran his hand through his hair, trying to think of a way to put his next words delicately.

"I like you, Fay," Tyler said.

"Oh, this isn't going to be good."

"You really think you met an alien?"

"He certainly fits the description of other encounters that have been reported: the gray body and huge head, the bulging black eyes, the slit for a mouth."

"And you believe those stories?"

"I can tell you don't believe in UFOs and aliens."

"I believe in UFOs. They're unidentified flying objects. Any time someone can't figure out what something is flying through the sky, it's a UFO by definition. That doesn't mean they're spaceships from another world."

"How can you be so sure?" Fay asked. "'There are more things in heaven and earth, Horatio, than are dreamt of in your philosophy.'"

"Sounds familiar," Grant said to Tyler, who squinted as he tried to recall which Shakespeare play the line was from.

"*Hamlet*, Act One," Jess said to Grant, then looked at Tyler. "Did you take *any* English courses at MIT?"

"Just one," he said. "Science Fiction and Fantasy. I can give you a great analysis of the human compulsion for self-destruction symbolized in *A Canticle for Leibowitz*."

"So you're a science fiction fan who doesn't believe in aliens," Fay said.

"It's the fiction part that's important. I do believe it's

probable that alien life exists in other parts of the universe. It's even likely that some of that life is sentient and intelligent. Astronomers are finding new planets all the time. Eventually, we'll confirm that some of them are capable of supporting life."

"Then why is it so impossible to believe that some of those civilizations have visited Earth?"

"I didn't say it was impossible. I'm not an absolutist. Shakespeare was right. I don't know everything. But I'm also a scientist, so I go by evidence. No one has yet produced incontrovertible video, photographic, or physical evidence that spacecraft have visited us."

"Don't we have stealth aircraft that you can't see on radar?"

"Yes."

"Then why couldn't the aliens have something similar but more advanced?"

"They could," Tyler said, "but then you run into another issue. Current scientific knowledge states that faster-than-light travel is literally impossible. An alien civilization would have to send ships that take thousands of years to get here."

"Maybe they did," Fay said.

"But why do the ships always land in Podunk little towns in the middle of nowhere? No offense."

"None taken. Maybe it's because they know humans have itchy trigger fingers, so they're trying to feel us out. Maybe they've been in our solar system for hundreds or thousands of years just observing us."

"Why?"

"They could be waiting us out. Seeing if we kill ourselves. Then they can just move in."

"They've been waiting for thousands of years and have never made their presence known?"

"They *have* made their presence known," Fay said. "I may not have a college degree, but I've been studying this for years now. There are eerie similarities among cultures around the planet. Simultaneous development of key technologies. Common structures like pyramids built by the Egyptians, the Inca, the Mayans, the Cambodians, the Indians. I've been all over the world and seen them with my own eyes. You can't just dismiss the strange coincidences. What I find hard to believe is that humans could build such advanced structures and technology with the primitive tools they had."

"I don't think that gives much credit to human ingenuity and creativity. We're a pretty smart bunch of people. I've been around the world, too, and I've seen things you would have a hard time believing if you hadn't been there." Tyler exchanged a knowing look with Grant, who'd been with him to witness those incredible sights.

"And what about my own experience?" Fay said, exasperated. "Are you saying I'm making it up?"

"Fay, I don't want to sound patronizing, but this was sixty-five years ago. You were ten and probably had never left your county at that point in your life, so anything outside of your experience would have seemed exotic. I'm sure you saw something you didn't understand, but that doesn't make it a flying saucer from another world."

"Then what was it? A weather balloon?"

"It sounds like some kind of aircraft."

"And the alien?"

"It could have been a man in a flight suit."

"Then why couldn't I understand what he said?"

"Maybe he was injured in the crash and that messed with his language skills," Grant said. "I've had a couple of concussions, and I could barely pronounce my own name for a while after each one."

"And the blue blood?" Fay said.

"Are you sure it wasn't just water?" Tyler said. "You said yourself there was a storm coming."

"It wasn't water. It was bright blue, like glass cleaner."

Tyler turned to Jess. He knew she would have an equally hard time with the belief in aliens. Time to put her on the spot.

"What do you think about all this?" he said to her.

Jess cleared her throat before speaking. "To be honest, it's a pretty fantastic story, and I didn't believe it for a long time." She looked at Fay with chagrin. "Sorry, Nana."

"But you believe it now?"

"I don't know what to believe. But those men thought she had something worth killing for."

"Fay, you said you were in a video. Can you show it to us?"

"I'll bring it up on my computer," Jess said. She left and came back a minute later with a laptop. They all crowded around while Jess brought up the video on YouTube. The username said UFOseeker0747. According to the stats, it had been viewed over fifteen thousand times.

"Who was this video for?" Tyler asked.

"A young man named Billy Raymond was filming it for his UFO blog," Fay said. "When I was in Roswell a few weeks ago for the festival, he was interviewing attendees. I only appeared on screen for a minute."

Jess started the video and skipped forward to the five-minute mark.

The interviewer was off-camera inside some kind of conference center. Crowds milled in the background, and it looked like he was wrapping up an interview with a woman dressed in a flowing kaftan covered with a field of stars. Then the video cut to Fay in the same location.

"*This is Fay Turia,*" Raymond said. "*Have you ever had an encounter with UFOs or aliens, Fay?*"

"*As a matter of fact, I have,*" Fay said. "*I saw the crash at Roswell and met an injured alien who gave me an artifact. I'm writing a book about the encounter now.*"

"*You were actually there? Amazing! Can you tell me anything about the incident or the artifact itself?*"

"*I'm not ready to just yet. I also have a piece of the wreckage. I have an expert coming to look at it soon, and I'll be including his findings in my book.*"

Suddenly Tyler felt guilty for not acting earlier on her

request. Maybe her house would still be standing if he had.

"*Come on, Fay! You're killing me! Can't you give us just a hint about what happened to you to convince my viewers that you were really there?*"

"*Well, I can tell you what the alien told me,*" Fay said reluctantly.

"*The alien spoke to you? What did it say?*"

"Rah pahnoy pree vodat kahzay nobee um."

"*Huh. Any idea what it means?*"

"*I was hoping someone here could tell me.*"

"*Any luck?*"

Fay shook her head.

"*Well, Fay, I hope you find out. That'll make a hell of a book. Can't wait to read it. When your book comes out, I'd love to do a follow-up interview.*"

"*Happy to.*"

The video cut to another attendee, and Jess paused the playback.

"After we were done," Fay said, "I gave him my name, email, and address, but I haven't heard from him since. I only found the blog and the video because he had transcribed the dialogue and mentioned my name."

"Did you ever find anyone who had an idea what the phrase means?" Grant asked.

Fay shook her head.

"Anyone could have seen this video or read his blog and

heard you talk about the artifact," Tyler said. "What you said got someone's attention."

"But it makes no sense," Jess said. "The piece of wreckage, the wood engraving, the opalescent metal those men asked Nana about. Why is any of it valuable?"

"The whole scenario does seem extreme for UFO hunters," Grant said.

Tyler picked up Fay's weathered piece of wood to examine the engraving again. It was clear that the drawing on one side was a map, detailed enough to pinpoint a location depending on the scale. It could be a city or an island, but without a starting point, it was useless.

Tyler flipped the wood over and ran his fingers across the grooves etched in the surface.

"If I didn't meet an alien," Fay said, "how do you explain that?"

The four primitive etchings were of a monkey with a spiral tail, a tarantula, a condor with its wings spread wide, and a human-like figure with one arm raised.

Tyler had recognized the images immediately, remembering the *Chariots of the Gods* TV special from his youth that speculated about gigantic messages drawn in the desert. The 1,500-year-old drawings—many of them hundreds of feet in length—could only be seen in their entirety from the air, so the theory was that the multitude of animal symbols, straight lines, and wide pathways were actually created to signal ancient aliens about potential landing sites.

The four images on her piece of wood were identical to

ones that were part of an ancient archaeological enigma: the mysterious Peruvian geoglyphs known as the Nazca lines. Fay believed that Tyler was holding in his hands proof that aliens had visited Earth.

ELEVEN

Morgan could tell that Vince was not happy with the flight arrangements, mostly by the way he'd been bitching about it ever since they were changed. Even though the United flight from LA would have been more comfortable, the military would have had to shell out big bucks for the full-fare coach seats. Not only was the Air Force saving money by having them travel on the C-17 carrying the Killswitch to Pine Gap, but the two of them could do it without being noticed as extra security. The flight would make one stop at Hickam Field in Honolulu and then it was straight on to the Alice Springs airport, with in-flight refueling from a tanker on the way.

They were sitting in two of the permanent side seats in the cavernous main cargo hold. Crates of equipment bound for Pine Gap were chained to pallets running down the center of the plane. Some of it was Dr. Kessler's, but most of it was routine machinery and supplies used to run the facility. The only passengers were Morgan, Vince, and Kessler's technician Josephson, who slept on a seat at the far end of the hold.

"Why couldn't we go with Kessler and the rest of his team?" Vince said.

"Their charter flight was full," Morgan said without looking up from her e-book reader. It was loaded with every book by Charles Dickens and Jane Austen, so she had plenty to keep her occupied. She found that losing herself in nineteenth-century English literature was a strong inoculant against stress.

"This sucks," Vince said. "At least in coach you get dinner and a movie."

"I told you to bring some books."

"I was going to watch a few DVDs, but I forgot to charge my computer, and they don't have any outlets down here."

"That's too bad."

"Then we get a flight attendant who thinks he's a comedian." Vince aped the loadmaster's Alabama drawl: "'You have a life jacket under your seat, but if we crash into the ocean, we're all going to die anyway, so don't worry about it.'"

"You sound worried about it. He said don't."

"If I liked the water, I would have joined NCIS."

"Get some sleep."

"Sleep? On these seats? Sure. And then once I get my eight hours in, what do I do with the other twelve?"

"You could keep whining. That seems to be working for you."

Vince crossed his arms in a huff. He stayed quiet for a whole five minutes. Elizabeth Bennet had just received an all-important letter from Mr. Darcy when Vince interrupted Morgan's reading.

"I'd feel better about the transport from the airport to Pine Gap if we went with the weapon."

"The truck will have four armed agents in it. What would you add to the equation?"

"We could follow in our own car."

"It's a nondescript truck. A chase car would draw attention."

"Do you think the leak is an Aussie?"

"We shouldn't talk about it outside of a secured facility."

Vince exaggeratedly looked around at the hold. "Where do you think they hid the bugs?" he said in a stage whisper.

He had a point. On board an Air Force cargo jet was about as secure as they could get. The noise from the engines would make it impossible for Josephson to hear them, even if he were awake. And they wouldn't have much time to plan once they arrived in Australia. She closed the cover on her e-reader with a sigh.

"Since the person who posted it used an anonymizer," Morgan said, "we can't pinpoint where it came from. So it could be anyone on the team from the US or the Australian side."

Since they'd discovered the posting three days ago, Morgan and Vince had been working nonstop trying to trace where the message had come from. Backgrounds, relationships, and possible motives for everyone involved in the project had all been checked. On the US side, the trail was cold.

"Maybe we should look at it from a question of motive."

Morgan nodded. "All right. There's greed."

"Could be. There are a dozen countries that would be willing to buy the Killswitch technology. But nobody on the team seems to have sufficient money troubles to sell out their country."

"And none of them has any suspicious bank deposits. But we can't rule it out because a lot of these people are smart enough to hide overseas accounts."

"Unfortunately, we don't know if they want to steal the Killswitch itself, steal the technology, or sabotage the test."

"It's doubtful they'd attempt to steal it before we get to Pine Gap," Morgan said.

"Why?"

"Because of the xenobium stored there. It's the only known sample in the world, and the Killswitch is useless without it."

"Xenobium. Ever since I heard the name, I keep thinking it's a heartburn medication. 'Xenobium—Relief is on the way.' What do you think it is?"

"I don't have enough information to speculate."

"We don't need info to speculate."

Morgan eyed the six-foot-long crate and shrugged. "Kessler will give us the rundown on it in Australia."

She and Vince had received only a minimal briefing on the Killswitch, so they didn't yet know how it worked, only that it was an unprecedented new weapon that fried electronics with an electromagnetic pulse, or EMP, and that xenobium was the material used as the explosive trigger.

"The forum didn't say anything about the xenobium," Morgan said. "It's possible that someone is trying to sell the plans for the Killswitch and didn't mention the xenobium because he's trying to have his cake and eat it too."

Vince clucked in disapproval. "You mean, sell somebody a worthless weapon? That's a recipe for getting yourself killed."

"It may be enough for someone to know how it works. If they had the plans, they could build it themselves."

"Then where do they get more of the xenobium?"

Morgan shook her head, but said nothing.

"Of course, this could all be coincidence," Vince said, "and we're just getting a free trip to Australia on the dime of the American taxpayer."

"You don't think that."

Vince smiled. "No, I don't. Neither do you. So what's the plan?"

"We should get our interviews of the team underway as soon as we arrive. Maybe we'll get one of them to crack."

"And I'll double check the security plan for moving the Killswitch to the test range. If someone's planning to steal it, the likeliest scenario would be during transport, because that will be the first time the xenobium will be with the weapon outside of a secure facility."

Vince went silent and sighed. After two more sighs,

Morgan took pity on him and lent him her laptop so he could watch his DVD.

With Vince plugged in and tuned out, she went back to reading her novel. Though she tried to immerse herself again in the machinations of nineteenth-century British landed gentry, Morgan couldn't keep her eyes from flicking to the crate holding the Killswitch.

TWELVE

Colchev sat at a metal desk in the Alice Springs warehouse office and watched the news report from Queenstown for a second time. The laptop's streaming video cut from a view of Fay Turia's smoldering house to the overturned jet boat lying behind a body covered in a sheet. Colchev's lip curled in anger at the thought of his men being killed on what should have been a routine operation.

As the anchor continued her narration of the events, the video showed two men exiting the police station. The first was a huge black man dressed in the brightest orange parka Colchev had ever seen. Bald, with a neck as thick as a telephone pole, the man was identified as Grant Westfield, an electrical engineer and former professional wrestler who was known as "The Burn" before he left the sport to join the Army.

The slightly taller white man who followed Westfield was identified as Dr. Tyler Locke, another engineer with a company called Gordian Engineering. Though not as bulked-up as Westfield, Locke in his leather coat didn't conform to the doughy awkward lab denizen that Colchev had worked with in the past. They both looked like men who could take care of themselves in a fight. Colchev had been surprised his men could be defeated by civilians until he saw Locke and Westfield.

The two men ducked into a silver Audi and left without responding to questions shouted by the journalists. Colchev found Gordian's website and read the short bios for each of them. As he suspected, both were decorated combat veterans. Locke was a mechanical engineer skilled in forensic investigation and explosives while Westfield specialized in system failure analysis and demolition.

It wasn't mentioned on the Gordian site, but Colchev found several news reports connecting Locke and Westfield to the discoveries of Noah's Ark and King Midas's tomb. Apparently, these men were gaining a reputation for finding ancient artifacts. Perhaps they were working with Fay Turia to interpret the map on the wood engraving.

That thought gave him renewed confidence that he'd been right to seek her out. She'd come to his attention through a blog from a Roswell conspiracy theorist. Colchev had standing Web searches in place for any spelling variation of xenobium connected to Roswell, and her video had come back as a match. When he saw Fay talking about her experience at Roswell, he was sure she had a link to the xenobium that he needed.

His mole within the Lightfall program thought the xenobium that Australia possessed was the last remaining specimen in existence, but Colchev knew otherwise. Colchev's research indicated that another sample of it had been hidden by the ancient Nazca civilization of Peru somewhere amongst their colossal desert drawings, but until he'd discovered Fay's Roswell UFO convention video three days ago, he had no idea how to find it.

Zotkin knocked on the office's open door. "We're ready for you."

Colchev closed the laptop and followed Zotkin to the closest trailer backed up to the warehouse's loading platform.

Four barrels had been anchored to the trailer's floor and filled with loose ANFO pellets. Two blocks of C-4 plastic explosive lay next to each barrel. In addition to Zotkin, four other men watched as his electrical expert, Gurevich, crimped wires together.

Colchev inspected the work. Everything seemed to be connected properly, but he had to be sure this setup would function as intended.

"Let's test it," he said.

While he waited for Gurevich to hook up a temporary extension to his wiring, Colchev thought it apt that yet another explosion would complete a mission that had begun at the site of the Tunguska blast in Siberia over a hundred years ago.

According to reports Colchev dredged up long ago from dusty archives, explorer Vasily Suzdalev had been the first to the disaster area in 1916, eight years after the explosion.

When he came back two months later, he carried with him an unusual metal he'd dubbed xenobium for his speculation that it had come from space. During the return journey to Moscow with his prize, Suzdalev became extremely ill, not realizing then that he'd been suffering from radiation poisoning while carrying the postage-stamp-sized specimen in his pocket. The elemental structure of xenobium would remain a mystery because scientists who were testing its electrical properties applied a power surge that detonated it, resulting in the complete destruction of a five-story-tall brick building.

When the fledgling Soviet government realized the potential of such a compact explosive, the Reds sent a now-recovered Suzdalev back to Tunguska in 1918 to find more of it, this time with a leaded case to carry any samples he might find. But a spy told the White forces of his mission, and they dispatched their own representative, a scientist and former soldier named Ivan Dombrovski, to track down Suzdalev and retrieve the weapon that might be used to defeat the communists.

It was only much later, after the tsar had been executed and Dombrovski fled to America, that Suzdalev's corpse was found in the swampy tracts of Siberia by some native tribesmen. The Soviets assumed Dombrovski had given whatever he found to the United States in return for asylum. A new search of the Tunguska area revealed no more samples of the xenobium. The secret of its source location died with Suzdalev.

The Soviet Union sent spies to the US to discover if Dombrovski had gleaned any info about where to find more of the precious metal. Unfortunately, an attempt to steal back the Tunguska sample from the US went horribly wrong, leading to Dombrovski's death and the destruction of the xenobium he'd spirited out of Russia. Instead of a victory for the Soviets, the operation had been a catastrophe.

The one piece of useful intelligence had been that Dombrovski explored the world for years trying to track down another source and apparently found two strong leads: a map and proof that more of the xenobium existed. Somehow, Dombrovski had used the map to find a huge sample in the Nazca region of Peru, even taking a photo to document that it was real. But for unknown reasons, Dombrovski did not take the specimen, leaving it in South America. With Dombrovski dead and most of his records burned in a lab fire, the failed Soviet operation had destroyed any possibility of following his trail, and it was thought that the xenobium was lost forever.

Then Colchev had had a stroke of luck. For many years he had cultivated a source within the American military weapons development community, and during their communications the mole claimed that the Australians had some xenobium of their own. It matched all the properties of the Tunguska material, and the Americans were designing a weapon to take advantage of its unique nature, paying the Australians a hefty sum to use xenobium as its explosive trigger.

Tomorrow the Killswitch weapon system would land in Australia, and with the detonation of the truck bomb it would be Colchev's. Four days after that, July twenty-fifth would become a day to remember for Russia.

Gurevich unspooled the temporary cable to the center of the warehouse and connected it to a tiny detonator. He stood and said, "It's set."

All of them stepped back from it as far as they could. Colchev removed a small state-of-the-art signaling device that operated on a coded spread-spectrum frequency. It had a wireless range of twenty miles, far greater than required for his purposes.

Zotkin and the rest of the men looked at Colchev expectantly, the validation of their hard work over the last nine months held in the palm of his hand. He knew how they felt. This moment represented years of Colchev's life.

His specialty in the SVR had been recruiting and handling foreign intelligence resources. He'd received four commendations for the information he'd gathered. Obtaining the Killswitch prototype would have been his greatest achievement, but the capture of Anna Chapman and her comrades had caused his fall into disgrace before he could accomplish his goal. His superiors were so shortsighted and timid that they abandoned the mission to obtain the Killswitch technology to avoid any chance of further embarrassment.

Since they lacked the conviction to follow through, Colchev would show them what could be accomplished with the proper will and expertise. They would see how

Russia could be a great country again, no longer under the heel of America's mighty capitalist domination.

Colchev went to university during the Glasnost years, watching his country's steep decline in global stature. He had never known insecurity until the Cold War ended with the fall of the Berlin Wall. Certainly there were indignities to be suffered during the communist regime—long lines for bread and toilet paper, tight restrictions on travel, the omnipresent gaze of the internal intelligence apparatus. But the people knew what it was to be safe back then. Colchev's father, Yuri, had a steady job at a factory and there was always food on the table.

Perestroika ripped all that away. When the Soviet Union crumbled, it was the collapse of an empire that had ruled a quarter of the Earth's land area. He hated America for claiming victory in the Cold War and laughing at his nation's woes.

The economy fell off a cliff when Boris Yeltsin became president, and Colchev's father lost his job. Crime in Moscow grew rampant. Yuri tried to open a little store with the paltry savings he had, but the fledgling Russian mafia exacted revenge when he refused to pay the protection money they demanded. On the way home from work late one night, Yuri was shot dead in the street.

His mother never recovered. Vodka became her medicine, and she took ample doses. Colchev could have turned to the mafia himself, but he vowed never to join those pigs, who he felt were destroying his country and turning it into a kleptocracy. He wanted to help restore Russia to its former greatness, and he had an aptitude for languages, so when the foreign intelligence community recruited him, he knew it was his calling.

He rose quickly through the ranks, focusing on his career so tenaciously that he stumbled through two failed marriages. As a fellow agent, Nadia Bedova had understood him. She knew, more than either of Colchev's ex-wives, that the job was everything. The Chapman debacle was grievous but not insurmountable. In the end he would prevail.

Colchev smiled and pressed the button on the handheld device. The isolated detonator went off with a bang, and his men cheered in unison. Neither of the sounds were loud enough to draw undue attention in this industrial district of town.

He congratulated each man with a traditional Russian bear hug, finishing on a hearty backslapping embrace with Zotkin. Gurevich unclipped the temporary wires inside the trailer and began inserting detonators into the bricks of C-4, which would be buried in the ANFO barrels.

Colchev stood quietly and admired the work of his team. In less than a week, his sacrifice would be rewarded and his reputation restored. After July twenty-fifth, he would return to his country a hero for devastating their greatest enemy, the United States of America.

THIRTEEN

Nadia Bedova stood patiently as the bodyguard frisked her. With a touch that was quick and efficient, he showed he was a pro by not lingering on her breasts or rear. She had come unarmed to the Sydney office tower knowing that she'd never be allowed to enter with her weapon.

Satisfied that she was clean, the guard led her down the hall to the penthouse suite of Mulvey Gardner Trading. Andrew Hull, the company's owner, had established the innocent-sounding firm to provide a front for his arms deals; it was one of the biggest such organizations on the Pacific Rim. Bedova had used his services herself many times. If Colchev were conducting some kind of operation in Australia, Hull would have information about it.

Inside the corner office was a portly man in his forties who strode over to her with an outstretched hand. As he got closer, she could see evidence of the Australian's recently implanted hair plugs.

"Ms. Bedova," he said with a smile. "It's always a pleasure to see you."

"Mr. Hull." She shook his hand and sat.

"May I offer you a drink?"

"No, I don't have time."

"Ah, business only. Unfortunate. To what do I owe the pleasure of your company?"

"You've spoken to Vladimir Colchev recently."

Hull didn't look away, but his smile faltered ever so slightly.

"I'm afraid I can't discuss my business with other customers."

"Even if that business was conducted with money stolen from Russian coffers?"

"It's no matter to me where the money comes from," Hull said. "Surely you can see that having to worry about the source of the funds would be bad for business."

"I need to know what you got for Colchev."

Hull laughed. "There's nothing to tell. Besides, even if there were, I wouldn't stay in business very long if my clients felt that their trust in me could be violated so easily."

"Your business will be even more short-lived if my superiors feel that you are dealing with our rogue agents behind our backs."

The smile vanished. "My understanding was that Mr. Colchev resigned and is now operating independently."

"Oh, he's operating independently. With funds he stole from the SVR. How much business do you conduct with Russian arms suppliers?"

Hull remained silent at the rhetorical question. She already knew that more than half his income came from supplying Russian arms to rebel groups across Asia. If her country were to turn off the spigot, he would be hammered by other dealers vying to take his place.

"What are you offering?" Hull said.

"Besides your continued good standing with the Russian state? If the lead you give me results in the capture or death of Colchev, you will be paid five hundred thousand Australian dollars."

Hull shook his head. "If you fail and Colchev finds out I led you to him, he'll come after me. That would also be bad for business."

In addition to the phalanx of guards she'd come through, Bedova could see that the penthouse was clad in glass thick enough to withstand an RPG blast.

"All right. I'm authorized to make an *upfront* payment of a half million."

"Plus a bonus? Double, say?"

Bedova paused, then nodded. "That should pay for your security for quite a while."

"Hmmm. One million dollars. You must want him badly. Why?"

"His departure didn't go well, and he had a high-level clearance. If one of your key employees suddenly left and took your greatest secrets to a competitor, what would you be willing to pay to stop him?"

"I see your point." He pursed his lips in thought, then

said, "All right. I agree to your terms. But I require the deposit before I tell you what I know."

Bedova nodded confidently. She made a call and had the $500,000 wired to Hull's account. In reality she was authorized to pay only half a million dollars. She'd figure out what to do about the bonus payment later. When he was satisfied with its completion, he turned from his computer.

"Now tell me what you know," Bedova said.

"Three weeks ago, Colchev came to me with an urgent request. He'd had difficulty securing some materials he needed."

"What materials?"

"ANFO. Detonators. Primer cord."

"How much of the ANFO did he buy?"

"Forty tons of it."

Bedova eyes widened. "Did he say what he planned to do with it?"

Hull laughed again. "No, and I didn't ask."

"If he's plotting a terrorist attack, weren't you afraid of it being traced back to you?"

"That's a risk we always take in this line of work, but my involvement was merely as a facilitator. I simply paired him with a seller, a treasurer at a mining company in the Northern Territory who had a surplus that he was trying to get rid of."

"Where is the attack taking place?"

"That I don't know."

"Where did he tell you to have the ANFO shipped?"

"To a warehouse in Alice Springs." He gave her the address. "The last shipment arrived yesterday morning."

"So the attack could happen at any time?"

"I suppose so." He paused. Bedova could see he was trying to decide whether to tell her something else. "It's obviously in my best interests for you to succeed."

"You know more?" she asked.

"Colchev may be gone when you arrive."

"If we miss him in Alice Springs, we may lose him for good, so you better share what you know."

"I don't think his ultimate objective is in Alice Springs."

"Why?"

"Because he asked me to put him in touch with someone in the Baja cartel."

Now Bedova was even more confused about Colchev's intentions. "The Mexican drug gang?"

Hull nodded. "And before you ask why, I don't know."

Bedova had her suspicions why. If Colchev needed something smuggled into the US, no one had a better system than drug runners.

She leaned forward in her chair. "Did he mention Wisconsin Ave?"

"No."

This wasn't making sense. Why would Colchev need Icarus for any of this?

"If you're lying to me," she said, "I will find out. Your suppliers will dry up, and your customers will know you are *persona non grata*."

Hull put up his hands in acquiescence. "I assure you that's all I know. If you can't find him, I think that says more about the Russian intelligence forces than it does about me."

Bedova looked at him for several seconds. Hull was a skilled liar. If he was holding back, she would never know. But she didn't think he would give her a false lead.

She stood. "One more thing."

"Yes?" he said, coming around his desk.

"If you attempt to warn Colchev that we are coming, you won't live to the end of next week."

"No need to threaten me, Ms. Bedova. I'm fully invested in your success. Literally."

She nodded and walked out. While she rode the elevator down, she texted her team.

Find out how quickly we can charter a flight to Alice Springs.

FOURTEEN

" I don't care what it costs," Jess said to Tyler and Grant, putting her phone away and taking a seat on the sofa next to Fay. "We need your help."

While Jess had taken a call, the rest of them had moved to the living room for coffee and gone over Fay's story twice more. The tale was the same all three times, so Tyler was confident Fay wasn't lying. Whether she had all the facts right was another matter. Memories could grow hazy over that stretch of time.

Jess seemed surprised that Tyler hadn't jumped at the chance to join them on their quest. "Come on? What do you say? Want to have an adventure?"

Tyler glanced uncomfortably at Grant, who shrugged as if to say, "Why not?"

"Don't you think a private detective would be a better choice?" Tyler said. "We're engineers."

"But you're also investigators. Who else would I hire? Some local PI who tracks down ex-husbands late on their child support?"

"You need some kind of international investigation firm."

"How much more international can a firm be than Gordian? Your website says you have offices in thirty-five countries."

"But you also want to find out how the Roswell incident is connected to the Nazca lines. Don't you want an archaeologist?"

"I've already talked to a dozen archeologist," Fay said. "They all thought I was crazy."

"Besides," Jess said, "Nana has been working on this for five years nonstop. She could have a PhD in the subject by now if she had gone to school for it. I bet she knows as much about the Nazca culture as anyone."

"What do you want us to do?" Grant said.

"We want you to help us track down whoever it was that attacked me," Fay said. "They have to have some answers about the engraving."

"At the very least we have to know why they want the artifact," Jess said.

Tyler's eyes went to the engraving. "Did you show it to the police?"

"Yes," Fay said. "They didn't believe me. They think this is about something else."

"Like what?"

"They said they think it was a pair of robbers who showed up under false pretenses to get the cash in my house."

"How much cash?"

"I have a safe with a hundred thousand dollars inside.

Part of Henare's life insurance payout. I use the money to pay for travel to Peru twice a year to study the Nazca lines and their ancient city of Cahuachi. The safe's fireproof, so it survived. The police think I must have told someone about it, but I didn't. I have no idea how thieves could have known about the money."

"Why would they burn down your house and chase us if they were looking for cash?" Tyler said. "Burglars would have bugged out when things got hairy."

Fay shrugged. "I'm just telling you the police's current theory. I'm sure it'll change, but they said the investigation might take a while."

"And we don't have that much time," Jess said. "More men could come back at any time."

"Or never," Grant said.

"Maybe. But until we find out what was so important about this piece of wood, Nana and I will be looking over our shoulders constantly. Even if she gives it to someone else, she may not be safe."

Tyler sighed and looked at Grant. "What do you think?"

"I'm up for it if you are. We were going to take a few days off anyway."

Jess and Fay looked at him expectantly. Finally, Tyler said, "All right. We'll do what we can."

Jess pumped her fists in the air. "Yes! I knew you wouldn't let us down."

"Thank you so much," Fay said.

"The only problem is that we don't have many leads,"

Tyler said. "We'll contact Billy Raymond and see if anyone has asked him about Fay, since the video seems the likely place where these guys heard about you."

"I'll get on that," Grant said, and took out his phone as he left the room.

"We can take the piece of wreckage and the engraving back with us to Seattle for analysis in our lab. We might get some new info about the materials used."

"We might want to put that off for a while and go another direction," Jess said. "The phone call I took was from a contact I have with the police."

"You have an in with the cops?" Tyler said.

"I still do occasional decoding work for them."

"Do the police have a lead?" Tyler said.

Jess nodded. "Yes, they do, but they think it's pretty thin. One of the tourists at Shotover Jet posted a video online of you three commandeering the jet boat. He also caught the men chasing you on camera. Apparently it's plastered all over the Web."

"Someone recognized Foreman and Blaine?" Tyler asked.

"So he claims. An Australian student at a Charles Darwin University extension campus. He emailed the police telling them that he thinks he saw one of the men last week."

"Where was this?"

"At a research facility just outside Alice Springs in central Australia. The student's name is Jeremy Hyland."

"Are the police following up on it?"

Jess shook her head. "Foreman and Blaine's passports had no stamps for Australia, so the New Zealand police thought it was just the ramblings of an overexcited kid, even though he provided a pretty detailed description of Blaine. They're swamped with the rest of the investigation right now, so his lead is a low priority."

"Why do you think he's right?" Tyler asked.

"Because I called Hyland. He said he's pretty sure he saw Blaine at his university facility. He was driving the car of a man who came to see their research."

"Pretty sure doesn't sound very sure."

"He also mentioned that Blaine was missing part of his left ear."

That got Tyler's attention. He thought back to his fight on the jet boat and remembered Blaine's torn left earlobe up close, just before Blaine was crushed against the rock outcropping, most likely mangling the evidence of the disfigurement.

But Fay had noticed it, too.

"That's him!" she blurted out. "It looked like the lower part of Blaine's ear had been ripped off. He *must* be the man the student saw."

"And even better," Jess said, "the student claims to have seen Blaine's passenger just yesterday driving down the main highway through Alice Springs."

"What is Hyland's research about?" Tyler said. "Anything to do with Roswell?"

Jess shook her head. "He works on a project called

CAPEK. It stands for Computer-Automated Payload Extension Kit. It's autonomous vehicle research funded by the trucking industry."

Tyler chuckled. "They named their robotic truck after Karel Capek."

"Who's that?" Fay said.

"He's a Czech writer who coined the word 'robot' in a play called *R.U.R.*, which stands for Rossum's Universal Robots." When Tyler saw Fay and Jess's surprise at his knowledge of this bit of trivia, he added, "Another work featured in my sci-fi course."

Jess took the wood engraving. "Why are the men who are willing to kill for Nana's artifact interested in a robotic truck in the middle of Australia?"

"I guess we'll have to ask the researchers," Tyler said. "And I think we should do it in person. We might be able to track down the man who was with Blaine."

"I was hoping you'd say that. Because we're going with you. There's a flight to Sydney that leaves Queenstown in two hours. Then we can catch a connection to Alice Springs."

Before Tyler could protest, Grant returned with a grim expression.

"What's the matter?" Tyler asked.

"It's Billy Raymond, the guy who shot Fay's Roswell video," Grant said.

"What about him?"

"Three days ago he was killed."

PINE GAP

Starbucks hadn't yet opened a franchise in Alice Springs, so as he steered the rented Jeep out of the city, Tyler drank a cup of truck-stop coffee strong enough to be used as an industrial solvent. He supposed that made sense, given the vast stretches of outback drivers would have to cross to get anywhere else.

Alice Springs was the largest town for eight hundred miles, and in the short time he'd been there, Tyler had sensed an independent nature that was likely characteristic of the 27,000 inhabitants. Despite its geographic isolation, the town was no stranger to strangers. Visiting ranchers, miners, explorers, and truckers making the long haul between Adelaide to the south and Darwin to the north were the lifeblood of the city.

Still, the group he was with surely stood out. Grant was next to him, with Jess and Fay in the back. The four of them together wouldn't go unnoticed for long, which was why they'd kept a low profile coming into town.

Tyler involuntarily glanced in the mirror at Jess and she caught him looking. They'd had no time alone to talk during the trip, and maybe that was for the best. He was still attracted to her, still felt the pull between them, but trying to start something up again after all this time, under these circumstances, was a ridiculous thought. In any case he didn't get the sense that she wanted anything from him except help in solving their mystery. He would approach this job as a professional, nothing more.

Right. If that were true, why couldn't he stop looking in the mirror?

To distract himself, Tyler focused on the upcoming meeting with Jeremy Hyland at the CAPEK facility. With no inkling to how CAPEK might be connected, they thought it safer to use Tyler's status as chief engineer at Gordian to arrange a nine a.m. meeting with the student, without mentioning his tip to the New Zealand police.

Because the flight from the US to New Zealand was so long, Tyler hadn't used one of Gordian's Gulfstream private jets for the trip, which meant they'd had to fly commercial to Alice Springs. With the connection, the flight from Queenstown had taken seven hours, and during that time they'd rehashed the events of the previous day and the possible meaning of Fay's artifact with no further insight.

The only new information they'd gleaned during the stopover in Sydney was that Billy Raymond had been struck by a pickup in a Phoenix shopping mall parking lot. There were no witnesses to the hit-and-run. The pickup, stolen earlier that day, was eventually found, but the police had no further leads. They believed the culprit was a car thief or joyriding teenager who got scared and fled the scene.

Nobody in Tyler's group, however, thought Raymond's death was coincidental. For some reason, Blaine, who'd traveled all the way to New Zealand to steal a seemingly worthless artifact, kill Fay Turia, and burn down her house to cover the evidence, had been at a high-tech experimental research facility in the middle of Australia less than a week before. And his likeliest connection to Fay was Billy Raymond, now lying in an Arizona grave.

Though Tyler didn't believe in alien visitors to Earth, he did think Fay's relic had some significance that they hadn't yet divined. They were obviously missing crucial information that would shed light on why the wood engraving was so important, and they were all hoping Jeremy Hyland could point them in the right direction.

"I'm coming in with you to see Hyland," Fay said.

A night's sleep in the local motel obviously hadn't changed her mind.

"Fay," Tyler said, "we don't know how CAPEK figures into this."

"Blaine's partners could be watching the place," Grant said.

"I'd feel better if you stayed in the car until we check them out. In fact, I'd rather you stayed back at the hotel."

"I didn't come three thousand miles to wait in the car like a little girl. If this Hyland kid knows something, I want to be there."

Tyler looked in the rearview mirror at Jess. "Your call. Blaine's friends might still be around."

"If that's the case, then they probably saw *you* on that tourist's video of the jet boat dock," she said. "We'll all go in."

Tyler shook his head. "All right."

The trip from Alice Springs to the project headquarters north of the city took fifteen minutes. They turned onto a dusty road labeled with a small sign saying, "Charles Darwin University—Transportation Research Center".

Though CDU had an extension in Alice Springs, the newly created research facility was located outside of town so that its vehicles could access the Northern Territory highways more easily during road testing. A half-mile down the road, Tyler saw the low-slung building rising from the scrubby desert. Because it was a Sunday, only a few cars were parked in the lot.

Tyler was about to park in front of the entrance when he noticed that a garage door was open on the side of the building. He wheeled the Jeep around and stopped next to it. He could see a man hunched over the hood of a car.

The four of them got out. The clear blue sky was cloudless all the way to the low mountain ridges to the south. The winter air was cool but pleasant, requiring nothing heavier than a windbreaker. Grant would have been sweltering in the parka, which meant Tyler was spared another day with Sergeant Traffic Cone.

The man inside the garage heard the doors slam and looked up. He couldn't have been older than twenty and had grease stains on his sunburned cheeks. Tyler recognized him as Jeremy Hyland from the bios and photos posted on the CAPEK project's website.

"You Dr. Locke?" Hyland said with a heavy Australian accent.

"I am," he said and introduced the others, eliciting a round of *g'days*. "You must be Jeremy."

"That's right. I'd shake your hand, but I'm not very presentable at the moment."

"Thanks for taking the time to meet with us."

"No worries. Any chance to meet the chief engineer from Gordian."

"You've heard of his company?" Jess asked.

"Heard of them? Any engineer would give their right arm to work there. Say, would you put in a good word for me at the Sydney office?"

"I'll see what I can do," Tyler said.

"So what can I help you ... " All of a sudden, Hyland's eyes went wide with recognition. "Hold on! You three were in the video!"

Tyler nodded. "That's actually why we're here."

Hyland grinned. "Wait'll I tell my mates. I couldn't believe it when the jet boat rolled over onto the beach. That was bloody bonzer!"

"We understand you recognized one of the men chasing us."

"I emailed the Kiwi police about it, but I suppose they thought I was some kind of nutter."

"You sure it was the same guy?"

"He was sitting in the driver's seat of a car right where yours is. I was walking by and only saw him from the side. That's why I wasn't sure it was him in the video. But that mess of an ear was hard to forget."

"What about the man he was chauffeuring around?"

"I never spoke to his boss. I went back to work while my professor gave him a tour of the place. Said he was some kind of corporate sponsor."

"Do you remember the boss's name?"

Hyland shook his head. "Some gray-haired bloke. Wasn't old, though. Looked like he could wrestle a croc and win."

"How about his company?"

"Sorry. You'd have to ask Professor Stevens."

"Where can we find him?"

"Don't know. CAPEK and the van were gone when I got here this morning. He left a message that he was taking it out for a run."

"You mean the robotic truck?"

Hyland nodded. "Beautiful piece of work, if I do say so myself. Gonna revolutionize shipping in Australia, although the truckies won't care for it."

"The truck drivers?" Fay said. "Why?"

"Well, it's a robotic truck, you see. We've got thousands of miles of desolate roads running through the outback. CAPEK is the first step in making them autonomous vehicles. Operating in remote regions to start with, of course. Private mines. Sheep stations. Like that. But eventually they could travel all the way from Darwin to Adelaide using GPS and on-board cameras."

"How close are you to becoming operational?" Grant asked.

"We're there now if the government would certify us. We've put forty thousand miles on CAPEK so far, though we've had someone in the driver's seat the whole time in case there's a problem. Haven't had a single incident."

"Did you have a test today?" Tyler said.

"It wasn't on the schedule. I imagine Professor Stevens wanted to do some fine-tuning."

"How does it work?"

"The truck can be driven normally, but once the robotic system is activated, the driving functions are totally autonomous. We have a chase van used for control and monitoring. The truck uses sensors, GPS navigation, and computer-controlled servomechanisms to stay on the road, and the person monitoring in the van gives it commands to start, stop, and turn. Eventually you'll be able to plug in a destination with no further input. While we're testing, you usually need three people to operate it: one in CAPEK, one to drive the van, and one in the back of the van monitoring."

Hyland frowned.

"What's the matter?" Tyler asked.

"Oh, nothing. It's just that I was surprised they took it out without me. It being winter break, the only other student around is Milo Beech."

"So it's just the three of you? Isn't it odd for you not to go with them?"

"I suppose it's not that unusual. The professor must have had his reasons. And it's easy enough for two people to do. They find a stretch of road, park the van, and drive the truck up and down to collect data."

"Can you call the professor?" Tyler asked. "We'd like to talk to him."

Hyland shook his head again. "When he left me the message that they'd be taking it out this morning, he told me he'd be turning off his phone so he wouldn't be distracted during the testing. But he should be back after lunch."

"What time?"

"Two o'clock should do it."

"You sure we can't contact him sooner?"

Hyland looked to each of them in turn as if he were making up his mind about something, then nodded.

"I suppose it'd be all right to tell you where you can find him."

"You just said he's not answering his phone," Fay said. "How can you find out where he is?"

"I'll show you." He beckoned for them to follow him into the garage.

Hyland sat at a computer terminal and everyone gathered around him. He talked while he clicked through the screens. "Of course, when there's a fleet of robotic trucks in operation, we'll need to know where they are at all times, so we have a system to track their GPS signals."

The map on screen was scaled to one inch per hundred miles, so the blinking dot representing the truck didn't tell them much. Hyland blew up the map by a factor of ten.

"That's weird," he said.

"What's weird?" Tyler asked.

"Well, I expected them to be out the back of beyond, but they're in Alice Springs. The truck's not moving. Wonder what he's doing there."

"Can you overlay a satellite map on that?"

"No worries."

A few clicks later, an overhead view of Alice Springs appeared.

If the satellite map was up to date, the truck was currently parked next to a warehouse, right in the middle of town.

SIXTEEN

While the C-17 taxied to a remote area of the Alice Springs airport's tarmac, Morgan called Dr. Kessler. Vince was already standing; Josephson was busy checking the moorings to make sure none of the equipment had come loose during the flight.

"Yes?" Kessler answered.

"Are you ready?" she said.

"I saw you land as we were driving in. We'll be there in a minute."

She hung up.

"I hate flying on planes with no windows," Vince said. "I wanted to see Ayers Rock."

"That's over a hundred miles west of here," Morgan said. "You wouldn't have seen it anyway."

"Still. Where's Kessler?"

"On his way."

The cargo plane lurched to a halt. The loadmaster scrambled down the stairs from the upper deck and opened the side door. Per procedure, he wouldn't open the rear doors until the cargo was ready to be unloaded.

Morgan followed him out to see two local police cars guarding the street entrance. They'd stop anyone who tried to get within a hundred yards of the plane.

Vince stretched his arms and put on sunglasses as he peered at the sparse trees dotting the red landscape.

"That is a whole lot of nothing," he said.

"You're from West Texas."

"So I know what I'm talking about."

So did Morgan. She grew up in Ohio, but her pilot training had been at Laughlin Air Force Base in Nevada. The terrain here looked familiar to her, except there were no tall mountain ranges surrounding the airport like they did in Vegas—just a few ridges in the distance.

The sound of a truck's engine made her turn. A nondescript white two-axle truck was stopped by the police, and the driver flashed his identification. The policeman waved him through. Morgan walked toward the back of the plane to meet the truck at the cargo door.

Kessler got out of the passenger side, and three men emerged from the rear of the truck.

"Welcome to Australia, Agent Bell," Kessler said. "Agent Cameron. Have a good flight?"

"Peachy," Vince said.

"Have there been any new developments while we were in the air?" Morgan asked.

Kessler shook his head. "We're all settled in and ready to get prepped for the weapon test."

"I'll need to see your IDs," she said to the men with

Kessler. All of them were carrying pistols. She peered in the back of the truck and spotted three automatic rifles.

They looked at the scientist as if to ask if she were for real. Kessler nodded that she was, and they showed her their IDs. All of them were NSA agents on the Pine Gap security team.

"All right," she said to the loadmaster. "Let's go."

He lowered the ramp and released the clamps on the crate carrying the Killswitch. The four security men kept watch as Josephson and the loadmaster used a hand truck to move the crate off the plane. It took only a few minutes to lash it securely to the truck's floor.

Once Kessler was satisfied that it was in place, two of the security men and Josephson climbed inside with it.

"Are you staying here or going with it?" Morgan asked Kessler.

"Josephson can take care of it. I'll stay here to supervise unloading the most delicate equipment. You may ride back with me."

"How long will you be?"

"No more than ten minutes."

Morgan nodded as she watched a semi pull into the airport entrance, where the police allowed it to enter. It stopped next to the C-17. At the same time a forklift motored over to the plane.

"Are we cleared to go, Dr. Kessler?" one of the security men said.

"Yes," Kessler said. "Close it up. Collins will meet you at

the base to unload. Make sure you stay with the crate until it reaches the lab."

"Yes, sir."

The rear door of the smaller truck was shut, and the two other security team members climbed into the front seats. Morgan watched them drive off.

While she waited for Kessler's men to load the semi rig with the rest of the equipment, she called back to the office to see if they'd made any progress tracking down the origin of the Internet videogame forum message.

Tyler parked the Jeep down the street from the unmarked warehouse where the CAPEK truck was located. He'd driven slowly past it and they had seen the robotic semi and chase van next to a dozen white trailers, four of which were backed up to the warehouse loading bays. Cars and trucks passed them periodically, so the Jeep's presence wouldn't be noticeable.

"Hyland thought this was an odd place to bring the truck," Tyler said. "I agree."

"What do you think it's doing here?" Grant asked.

"Only one way to find out."

"If you're going inside," Jess said, "we're going with you."

"That would be no," Tyler said. "Something about this doesn't feel right. Until we know it's safe, you're staying in the car."

"Should we call the police?" Fay said.

"We don't have any reason to just yet."

Grant pointed at the warehouse. "We've got movement."

Two men walked quickly from the warehouse. One of them, a powerfully built man in his forties, had steel-gray hair. They climbed inside the van.

"Neither of those guys looked like students to me," Grant said.

"Looks more like our mysterious sponsor."

"And the other one wasn't Stevens. He must be in the warehouse."

"We're going to see if we can get a better view of the place from the other side," Tyler said. "We'll also try to snap a photo of our mystery man's face. Jess, you take the wheel. Drive us down past the next warehouse. We'll hop out and you continue on."

"Where?"

"Drive around the block and come back here to keep an eye on the place. We'll turn off our cell phone ringers but leave them on vibrate. If you see anything suspicious, text me, then call the police. We'll call when we're ready to be picked up."

"I don't like this."

"Neither do I," Tyler said as he backed the Jeep up the street until they were out of view of the warehouse. "But we need to get some answers, and I'm not ready to put Fay in harm's way again."

Getting shot at and having her house burned down was bad enough. If it was the same guys, they might want to finish the job. Tyler was already queasy about putting her in this much jeopardy.

"You don't even have guns," Jess said.

"This is just a recon mission. If we see any weapons, I'll text you to call the cavalry."

Jess reluctantly nodded. "All right. But be careful."

"What do you think?" Tyler said to Grant. "Should we be careful?"

Before Grant could answer, Jess punched Tyler in the arm. "Okay, wiseass. Out of the car."

As he passed her outside, he said with a smile, "That's *Doctor* Wiseass to you."

"Tell me when it's on your business card."

Tyler and Grant got in the back and put their phones on vibrate. Jess drove to the empty warehouse next door as if she were delivering something in back. When they were on the opposite side, Tyler and Grant jumped out. Jess made a U-turn and headed back to the street.

Grant peeked around the corner at the warehouse and switched his cell phone to camera mode. "There's a Dumpster thirty feet away. We'll be able to see him if we hide behind it. I think that's about as close as we can get."

Tyler smiled. "We could always bust into the warehouse unannounced."

"Going into a warehouse potentially full of gunmen with no intel and armed with whatever large rocks we can pick up from the dirt? Even a rookie lieutenant would think we'd be nuts going with that plan."

"And so instead we take pictures."

"Then we'll text the photo to Hyland," Grant said.

"Right. If he positively identifies the guy as Blaine's cohort, we'll ask the police to come on down and knock on the front door."

"Sounds easy enough."

A woman spoke from behind them. "No, it's not."

Tyler turned expecting to see that Jess had ignored his instructions. Instead, a blonde woman walked toward them flanked by two serious-looking men.

All three of them were aiming pistols at him and Grant, who raised their hands to show they were unarmed.

"What?" Grant said. "They have cameras that can see all the way over here?"

"If you mean the men inside that warehouse," the woman said, "I'm not with them."

"Who are you?" Tyler said.

"Nadia Bedova. Russian intelligence."

Tyler looked at Grant, who stared back at him with the same astonished look he must have had on his own face.

"What the hell is going on here?" he said.

"Dr. Locke, you and Mr. Westfield are going to help me disarm a bomb."

SEVENTEEN

"**S**earch them," Bedova said.

While she and one of the men kept their guns trained on Tyler and Grant, the second man frisked them. He found their phones and Tyler's Leatherman multi-tool. She held on to the phones but tossed the tool back to Tyler.

"I can't have you attempting to make a call, but you may need that for your task," Bedova said, nodding at the Leatherman. "You can lower your hands."

Tyler narrowed his eyes at Bedova. "How do you know our names?"

"When I saw you driving down the street casing the warehouse," she said with the slightest accent, "I used our facial recognition software to identify you."

"You have us on file?"

"Do you really think you could stay off our radar after finding Noah's Ark and the tomb of King Midas?"

Grant raised a hand. "My first question, and, I think, the most relevant: uh, bomb?"

"The silver-haired man you saw going to the van is

Vladimir Colchev," Bedova said. "According to our intelligence, he's been trying to acquire explosives from mining companies around the country for months, apparently unsuccessfully. But we know that this week he procured forty tons of ammonium nitrate/fuel oil explosive and had it shipped here. We think he's planning to use it. Today."

Grant whistled. "That would put a nice dent in Ayers Rock."

"Who is Colchev?" Tyler asked her.

"A Russian national wanted by my government. He has a highly trained team ready to follow his orders. Now a question from me. Why are you here?"

"Concerned citizens."

"You're not even Australian. I already have a potential international incident on my hands, so either you cooperate or I'll shoot you both now and take my chances without you."

Tyler cleared his throat. "Well, that seems like a fair trade. Two of his men attacked a woman in Queenstown, New Zealand yesterday. Burned her house to the ground and tried to kill her."

"Did they succeed?"

Grant shook his head. "They're both currently resting comfortably in the morgue."

"Do you know why they attacked her?"

"Haven't a clue," Tyler lied without hesitation.

"Then why are you here?" Bedova asked.

"We got a tip that one of the assailants had been seen in

Alice Springs," Grant said, "so we came to do a little private detective work and ran into you lovely people in the process."

"Did you talk to the man before he died?"

"Fay did," Tyler said. He saw no reason to hide her name since it was all over the news.

"Did he say anything about Icarus or the date July twenty-fifth?"

"Not that we know of. What's Icarus?"

"How about the Baja drug cartel or Wisconsin Ave?"

Tyler was confounded. A rogue Russian spy is willing to kill for a relic from Roswell, then buys enough explosive to depopulate central Australia, and now the agent after him is asking about Mexican narcotics gangs and Greek mythology? If Tyler lived through this, he was going to love to hear the explanation behind it.

He shook his head in answer to her question. "Never heard of them. Maybe a little context would be useful."

Bedova stared at him. "I need you to look at the bomb he's built and tell me if it can be disarmed."

"Why do you want our help? Why not just call the police?"

"We obtained a layout of the warehouse, so we have our assault planned out, but we're waiting on our bomb expert. When you showed up, I saw an opportunity to keep this quiet. He's coming from Singapore and won't be here for another five hours. From our observations, Colchev is getting ready to make his move sooner than that. Are you going to help us or will you let him detonate a truck bomb in the middle of the city?"

"What you're really saying is that you want us to save you the trouble of an international incident started by your rogue agent."

"Will you do it?"

Tyler looked from the pistol to Grant. "What do you say?"

He could see that Grant was thinking the same thing. The odds were that she was sharing so much information with them because she was planning to get rid of them right after she did away with Colchev. Still, they had little choice, and if a bomb that size exploded, it could kill everyone within a quarter-mile, including Jess and Fay where they were parked.

Grant nodded and regarded Bedova with a dead-eyed gaze. "I couldn't be more enthusiastic about assisting you."

"Good," she said, ignoring his sarcasm. "If you try to get away, I will shoot you both and then kill your friends waiting for you in the Jeep."

Tyler mirrored her unflinching stare. "We're not going anywhere." *Yet*.

"The plan is that we wait for Colchev to come out of the van. As he's entering the building, my two men on the other side of the warehouse will move in. We won't kill him until we're sure that there's no danger of someone detonating the bomb. We think it's in one of the four trucks backed up to the warehouse."

"What if he's divided the explosives among the four trucks?"

"Then you'll have to assess all four and tell me if you can disable them."

"And if we can't?"

"Then we'll call the police," is what Bedova said, but Tyler didn't think for a second that she actually would.

"All right," Tyler said, furiously trying to think of a way out of their predicament. For now, going along with her was the only choice. "Lead the way. It's your party."

Bedova looked at him, perplexed. She obviously didn't understand the idiom, but let it go. She tilted her head. Tyler guessed that she was listening to an earpiece hidden by her hair.

"He's on the move," she said. "It's time. Stay behind me."

With no one in sight, Bedova sprinted toward the warehouse. Tyler ran crouched next to Grant, with Bedova's two men bringing up the rear. In the Army when he'd done this kind of thing, Tyler usually had a helmet, flak jacket, and M4 assault rifle, so now he felt practically naked. By the way Grant clenched his fists, Tyler could tell that his friend also missed the heft of a weapon.

They reached the door of the warehouse. Tyler could hear the shouts of men working inside. Bedova picked the lock and pulled the door ajar. She paused as she scanned the interior, then nodded. They all kept low as they crept inside.

Now Tyler saw why Bedova had chosen this entry. This

door must have served as the entrance to the warehouse office. Its interior wasn't visible from the main warehouse floor.

She kept below the level of the windows and went to the open door on the other side of the room. Tyler and Grant followed. Without speaking she pointed toward the front of the warehouse.

Tyler could see into the cargo area of the closest trailer. The shadows hid most of the contents, but five feet inside he could barely make out four oil drums with wires leading from them.

They'd found their bomb.

With a series of hand gestures, Bedova indicated for one of her men to take Tyler and Grant over to the trailer and keep an eye on them while they examined the device. At the same time, she'd make her assault.

She and the first man dashed out of the office. Tyler and Grant crabbed over to the trailer with the operative assigned to watch them. The two of them entered the trailer while the Russian stayed nearby and kept a lookout.

Tyler's eyes were still adjusting to the dark as he moved past the barrels. He stopped when his foot bumped into something pliant.

Grant pointed behind one of the drums. A body. Tyler recognized the face from a photo at the research center. It was Professor Stevens. Another limp figure lay next to him. He didn't recognize the man, but it had to be the student, Milo Beech.

Tyler knelt and felt for a pulse. They were both alive. He lightly slapped Stevens' face, but the professor didn't move. Same for Beech. Tyler put two hands together at the side of his head to indicate to Grant that they were out cold, probably drugged.

Now that his eyes had adjusted, Tyler could see the truck's interior past the drums. Stacked floor to ceiling were twenty-five-pound bags full of pink ANFO pellets. Enough space to hold all forty tons of it.

Grant examined the wires from behind one of the barrels so he wouldn't block the dim light coming from the warehouse.

"Doesn't look like it's booby-trapped," he whispered. "But I don't see a timer or receiver for a radio-controlled detonation."

"When Bedova's got the place secured, we can—"

Shouts inside the warehouse interrupted Tyler. The man who'd been guarding them took cover behind a forklift. Tyler and Grant edged out the rear of the trailer where Tyler spied Bedova and the rest of her men surrounded by Colchev's operatives.

She spoke to Colchev in soothing Russian that suggested a history between them. Colchev shook his head and answered in English.

"Remember what my note said, Nadia?"

Bedova nodded, but she didn't lower her gun. "I can't let you do this, Vladimir."

"And I can't let you leave."

"You can't go back to Russia. Not ever."

Colchev slowly shook his head. "In four days they will welcome me with open arms after they see what I've achieved."

The operative behind the forklift, the last of Bedova's men still hidden, stood to shoot, but one of Colchev's operatives spotted him and hit him with a three-round burst to the chest. The man fell backward, his finger on the trigger of his weapon. Automatic fire spewed toward the ceiling, the suppressor muting the shots so that they weren't much louder than the pings of the bullet impacts.

In response silenced gunfire erupted from every direction. Bedova's team scrambled for cover, blasting away as they ran, but they were caught in a crossfire. Two of Colchev's men had perfect sightlines on her team and cut down their targets with lethal precision. Within seconds, Bedova's three other men were dead.

Bedova showed no fear as she returned fire, dropping to one knee and taking aim at Colchev in a textbook stance. She got off three rounds, but Colchev was too quick. He rolled to the side as bullets pinged off the metal walls behind him. He came to rest in a prone position and pulled his trigger just once. Bedova's head snapped backward, and she crumpled to the floor.

"Cease fire!" Colchev shouted. He got to his feet and walked over to Bedova's corpse, where he knelt beside her, softly caressing her hair. Tyler saw no satisfaction, only remorse.

Tyler was about to suggest they make a break for it when Colchev stood and started to turn toward the open trailer. Tyler and Grant scrambled behind the barrels before they were spotted.

"Close everything up and take the bodies into the office," Colchev said. "We are leaving now."

Footsteps pounded toward the trailer, and Tyler and Grant tried to make themselves as small as possible. Any attempt at escape would be suicidal.

Still, the alternative wasn't much better. The trailer door was slammed shut and latched from the outside, leaving Tyler and Grant in total blackness with an eighty-thousand-pound bomb.

EIGHTEEN

Jess checked her phone again to make sure it was getting a signal. Tyler still hadn't called. She wasn't worried just yet, but she thought it shouldn't have taken this long to do his reconnaissance.

"What do you think they're doing in there?" Fay said. Since the gray-haired man walked back from the van to the warehouse, they'd seen no movement at all.

"I don't know. Maybe Tyler and Grant will be able to tell us."

They went silent, waiting for the cell phone to buzz.

Fay turned to Jess. "You haven't spoken to Tyler much since we left New Zealand."

Jess sighed. "Not much to say."

"Did you talk to him about Andy?"

Jess shook her head. "Not yet."

"I'll leave that to you." Fay took a deep breath. "Are you ready to tell me why you broke up with Tyler?"

"We didn't have the same priorities at the time."

"Were you in love with him?"

Jess hesitated. "I suppose I was."

"And now?"

"Of course not."

"Liar."

"I haven't seen him in over fifteen years."

"I can see it when you look at him. The chemistry is still there."

"Well, I can tell you this is just a job for him. He's a professional and it'll stay that way. I wish you'd told me you were going to call him."

"You are a pill, Jessica," Fay said.

"I know."

"I just want to see you happy before I die."

Jess's heart sank. She squeezed Fay's hand.

"I know, Nana. But you're a tough lady. You'll be around for a long time."

Fay smiled with a tinge of sadness. "I only wish your parents could see what a lovely woman you've become."

Jess was about to reply when she saw movement in the parking lot of the warehouse. Two men went to the CAPEK truck. One of them got in while the other stood behind it.

They watched as the truck backed up to one of the trailers and was hooked up by the man behind.

"Is this what Tyler wanted to see?" Fay asked.

"I don't know."

When the tractor and trailer were attached, the rig moved around until it was directly in front of a second trailer. Then the rig backed up, and the second trailer was hooked up.

They continued this choreographed hookup process for ten minutes until all four trailers were attached in a line.

"What did Tyler say that was called?" Fay said.

"A road train."

They'd seen a dozen of them on their way out to the CDU facility and back. Tyler had told them they were the longest street-legal trucks in the world. With minimal rail service in the Australian interior and huge distances to cover, road trains were the most economical means to transport goods between remote outposts.

The two men who'd been attaching the truck got into a white Ford sedan and sped off. Jess and Fay ducked so they wouldn't be seen. When they sat up, Jess saw the gray-haired man and a companion getting into the van.

Jess was surprised to see the CAPEK truck start and rumble forward. She gawked at the sight of the massive vehicle roaring off with no one in the driver's seat.

The truck turned at the end of the road. A few minutes later, the van drove off, leaving the warehouse lot empty. All the loading bays were open.

"What in the world is going on?" Fay said. "Where are Tyler and Grant?"

Jess called Tyler's phone but got no answer. She started the engine. "We're going to find out."

She sped over to the warehouse. It was unlikely anyone was still inside with all the vehicles gone and the warehouse interior exposed.

She got out but left the Jeep running. Fay joined her.

Jess pushed herself up onto the raised loading platform and stood. Fay, who was an experienced rock climber, clambered onto the ledge without assistance.

The cavernous space was still. Surely Tyler and Grant would have called by now if they were watching the warehouse from outside.

"Hello?" she called. No one answered.

As she tiptoed into the open space, her heart thudded. She hoped the worst she'd discover would be that Tyler and Grant couldn't respond because they were tied up and gagged. But then something Jess saw in a side room made her freeze.

Two boots. A woman's. Jess could only see the lower part of her legs. They were motionless.

"Wait here," she said to Fay.

"Why?" Fay spotted the legs. "Oh, my God!"

"Stay here!"

Jess moved forward until she was standing in the doorway. Now the whole body was visible.

The woman was dead, her eyes staring unfocused at the ceiling, a dime-sized hole in her forehead.

The sight was made all the more horrifying by the bullet-riddled bodies of four other men piled behind her, the smell of blood thick in the air. They couldn't have been dead for more than fifteen minutes.

Jess only got close enough to see that none of the corpses was Tyler or Grant. She ducked out and caught her breath, trying not to hyperventilate or vomit.

"Call the police," she gasped to Fay.

"Is she dead?"

"Yes. Tell them there's been a murder."

As Fay made the call with her cell, Jess took out her own phone and dialed Tyler.

He didn't pick up. She was about to hang up and try again when she heard the buzz of a vibrating cell phone coming from the office.

Jess steeled herself to walk back into that charnel house, phone in hand.

At the door Jess listened for the sound and her stomach lurched when she realized why Tyler hadn't picked up her call.

The buzz was coming from the pocket of the dead woman.

NINETEEN

Rummaging around in the pitch-black through an unconscious man's pockets was not Tyler's idea of fun, but it was the only reason he was now holding a cell phone, courtesy of Professor Stevens. Colchev must have been expecting it to be incinerated in the blast. Unfortunately, the phone was more useful as a meager light than as a communications device.

While Tyler focused the light on the C-4 explosive in Grant's hands, he checked the phone for a signal. No bars. The few times he'd gotten a signal, it dropped before he could complete a call to the police. Tyler didn't know Jess's email address or phone number, so he'd sent a short email to Fay: *This is Tyler. We're in the truck that just passed you. Call the police. Bomb inside the truck.* He could only hope that it would be sent in the miniscule gaps in the blockage.

Grant, cursing under his breath, pressed the plastic explosive into the door panel where the external latch would be.

"How's it coming?" Tyler said.

Grant glanced up at him. The whites of his eyes were like beacons next to his brown skin. "You know, when I said I was looking for some thrills during our trip, this wasn't what I had in mind. More light, please."

Tyler angled the phone so that Grant could see while he inserted the detonator.

"Just be thankful it's not summer. It'd be a hundred and twenty degrees in here by now."

"It'll be two thousand degrees if you don't give me some more light."

Tyler shifted the phone closer. "Better?"

Grant nodded and unspooled the wire to attach it to Milo Beech's identical phone. "If we die, just remember that this contraption was your idea." He deftly crimped two wires together using Tyler's Leatherman. "Any signal yet?"

Tyler looked at his phone's display. "Still nothing. And we could be only a few minutes from the target."

"Yeah, but what's the target?"

That was the million-dollar question. They had no idea where the truck was headed, so there was no way to know how much time they had left.

When it had been clear they weren't going to get a signal, Tyler decided that they'd have to take matters into their own hands to stop the truck. And the first order of business was making an exit for themselves.

With the rear door locked from the outside, the C-4 they'd scavenged from one of the barrels had been the only option for escape. The truck-bomb design consisted of detonators inserted into four blocks of C-4 buried in the barrels full of ANFO. The blast from the plastic explosive would set off the barrels of ANFO, causing a chain reaction that would blow up the whole truck. Cutting the wires had disabled the bomb, but they'd found no timer or receiver to set off the weapon. It had to be somewhere on the truck, but tracing the wire to its source proved impossible.

Although they had dealt with the bomb, they still needed to find a way out of the truck. When the explosive didn't detonate, Colchev would open the trailer to find out why.

"That should do it," Grant said. He gave the C-4 putty one last pat and stood. "You sure you can't think of something better than this?"

Tyler forced a smile. "Would you rather wait in here until the truck comes to a full and complete stop?"

"Not really. But it feels like we're going about sixty. Gonna be a bumpy landing if we jump."

"Then we'll have to stop the truck."

Grant raised a finger. "One teensy problem with that plan—"

"It's more of a goal than a plan."

"The guys operating this thing have guns and we have persuasive verbal skills. Oh, and they have enough ANFO to divide Australia in two."

They both turned toward the stacks of explosive. Tyler estimated that the truck carried a destructive power equal to the payload of a B-2 bomber. The Oklahoma City bomber, Timothy McVeigh, used seven thousand pounds of ANFO to take out half of the Alfred P. Murrah building. A truck filled with eighty thousand pounds of the same material would level a city block.

To make an exit out of the trailer, Tyler and Grant would have to blow up four small wads of C-4 within five feet of the truck's deadly load. Grant had taken the C-4 and detonators from the ignition barrels to form the crude breach charges. Because Stevens' and Beech's phones could also function as walkie-talkies, Grant rigged one unit to send the detonation signal when it was contacted by the other. He'd attached two arm's-lengths of wire from the phone's speaker to the detonator so that the cell wouldn't be destroyed by the explosion.

"We'll be okay," Tyler said as much for himself as for Grant. "As long as we don't get any fires started in here, the ANFO should be stable."

"That's comforting."

"Look on the bright side. We should be out of the city by now. If it does blow, we'll only take out a few kangaroos at most."

"And us."

"And some terrorists."

"You are just a positive guy, aren't you?"

Tyler grinned. "I try. Now let's do this before I decide it's moronic."

He followed Grant behind one of the barrels and crouched down. Even if the load didn't detonate, the shrapnel from the blast could be deadly.

Grant nodded that his phone was ready to receive. Tyler closed his eyes, covered his ears, and hit TALK.

The explosion sucked Tyler's breath away and assaulted his nose with the signature smell of burnt tar he always associated with C-4. He held his breath to wait for the smoke to dissipate through the new hole in the truck door.

He opened his eyes to see sunlight blazing into the trailer. He peeked over the barrel to look at Grant's handiwork. The charge had blasted a perfect hole in the bottom of the door, taking the external latch with it.

"Nicely done," Tyler said.

Grant stood. "Well, we're still here." He went to the rear of the trailer and pushed the roll top door up on its tracks until it was wide open. Wind swirled into the truck, but the turbulence did little more than muss Tyler's hair.

Except for the occasional scrub brush, the rusty outback consisted of nothing but dirt and rocks, with low mountain ranges in the distance. The rapidly receding asphalt pavement disappeared to a point at the horizon. Tyler didn't like the idea of leaping out onto it. Unless they could clad themselves in bubble wrap, the impact wouldn't be fun. Without helmets, they'd be lucky not to bash their heads in.

"They're not slowing down," Grant said. "They had to have seen the explosion from the chase van."

"They might be guiding the truck by GPS. I know I wouldn't want to be this close to a truck full of ANFO."

"I'll see if I can find any landmarks." Grant poked his head around the corner on the passenger side. When he pulled back, his expression was even grimmer than before.

"It's worse than we thought."

"Why?"

"Take a look."

Tyler exchanged places with him and peered around the edge, squinting as the wind lashed his face. At first all he noticed was the white side of the trailer pasted with the name "Western Lines". Then he blanched when he saw the source of all the bumping and clashing metal they'd heard before heading out on the highway.

They weren't on a conventional tractor trailer. They were on a road train. Instead of just a single trailer, there were three more identical ones hitched in front of it. That explained why the detonator's receiver was nowhere to be found. It must have been in one of the other trailers.

Bedova was wrong about the amount of explosive Colchev had acquired. If the other trailers were as chock full of ANFO as this one, the road train was hauling 320,000 pounds of the stuff, enough to destroy not just a city block, but an entire downtown.

TWENTY

After the car carrying Kessler, Morgan, and Vince was cleared through the front gate of Pine Gap, it was just a short drive to the main part of the facility. Although Morgan had been expecting the dazzling white buildings she'd seen in the photos, the six spherical radomes housing the satellite uplink equipment were far larger than she thought they'd be.

They came to a stop in front of a two-story building that would have looked right at home in an American office park. The semi following them continued around the building.

"Welcome to Pine Gap," Kessler said as he got out.

Joint Defence Facility Pine Gap, run by both the US and Australian governments, sprawls across a dusty plain eleven miles southwest of Alice Springs. The National Security Agency station, shielded by mountains on all sides, is so secret that it's the only facility in Australia designated as a "prohibited" flight area, meaning no aircraft flying lower than 18,000 feet are allowed within 2.5 miles of the base.

Speculation about the facility's true purpose has been rampant. Morgan knew that its widely believed function as an ECHELON listening post was correct. The NSA ECHELON program samples cell phone, email, and text messages from around the world for any specific keywords deemed critical to protecting US interests, and Pine Gap is important for communicating with satellites orbiting over the southern hemisphere. But few knew of the facility's other role in preparing weapons to be evaluated at the Woomera Test Range.

"When can we start the briefing?" Morgan said.

"Follow me and I'll show you to an office you can use while you're here. Then I'll need to instruct my people where the equipment from the truck should go. It ought to take about ten minutes. When I'm done, we'll begin the briefing."

He took them inside the structure and guided them to a small room with two desks and chairs. After giving them the security password to the internal WiFi system, Kessler walked out.

Vince leaned over to Morgan. "What's your secret?"

"What do you mean?"

"We've been in the air for twenty-four hours, and you look like you're ready to run a marathon. I'm about to keel over."

Morgan shrugged. "I don't need much sleep."

"That's it? You don't need much sleep?"

"Right."

They both sat and started setting up their laptops to securely access the OSI network when the door opened and Collins poked his head in.

The technician scanned the room. "I thought Dr. Kessler might be here."

"He just left. Is there a problem?"

"No, I just need to let him know that we're ready to receive the Killswitch."

Morgan looked at Vince in confusion, then back to Collins.

"What do you mean?" she said.

"Wasn't the Killswitch coming separately from the semi?"

"Yes," Vince said. "Kessler said you were expecting it."

"I am," Collins said with a puzzled look. "That's what I'm trying to say."

"Isn't it here already?" Morgan said. She and Vince stood. Something was very wrong here.

Collins looked as if he were being asked a trick question. "If the Killswitch was here, I wouldn't be telling you we're ready to receive it."

"The truck left ten minutes before we did," Vince said. "Josephson was with it. He should have been here by now."

"Are you sure the Killswitch truck isn't somewhere in the facility?" Morgan said.

Collins nodded slowly, his face dawning with horrified comprehension. "I'm absolutely positive. The truck with the Killswitch on board never arrived."

While Zotkin drove the van, Colchev sat at the control station in back. Although they were six miles behind the road train, the video feed from the cab allowed Colchev to monitor the truck's progress on its suicide mission. He had a driver's eye view of the road, only eleven miles of which were left before it reached its destination. More cameras on either side gave him panoramic views to the left and right. When the truck blasted through the Pine Gap gate, which would prove no match for the massive protective steel bull-bar frame over the engine bay, he'd be able to see it wend its way into the center of the complex before the contents of the four trailers blew the facility off the map. Then his plan to bring victory to Russia over America would be inexorably underway.

Colchev's training kept him from shaking with anticipation, but his muscles ached from the tension he forced himself to contain. There was no going back now. Either he would succeed spectacularly or he would compound the failure that had brought him to this desperate position in the first place.

But that desperate position gave him strength. Nothing would stop him because he had nothing to live for if the mission was a failure. He had warned Nadia not to pursue him, but she had always been stubborn. He once thought he'd loved her, but he realized long ago that a man like him had no use for such feelings. Then she had shown up at the warehouse, just as he'd suspected she would but hoped she wouldn't. It had been disappointingly easy for his men to catch her team in an ambush.

That had always been Bedova's weakness, thinking she was better than Colchev was.

Now that he'd been forced to wipe out her team, he

would become enemy number one to his former masters. But a successful mission would convince them that the deaths had been necessary, that they had resulted in a greater good. He would be able to return to his Mother Russia with honor. Any other outcome was unacceptable. Then he would remain an embarrassment to his country, a pariah consigned to a fate worse than death.

Colchev pushed those thoughts aside and focused on the present. The only thing that mattered was making sure the road train reached its destination. Once it did, the rest of the mission would be relatively easy, and he would have free rein to carry out the ultimate attack with impunity.

Through the windshield of the truck cab, he could see the white Ford sedan a half-mile ahead of the road train, providing escort until the truck exited from the public highway. Two men inside the car were on the lookout for any potential interference, primarily from the police. Once the truck made its turn, there would be no reason for the car to accompany it onto the private road. Colchev would then guide it the rest of the way.

He noticed on the GPS map that the gap between the truck and van was growing.

"Speed up," Colchev said to Zotkin. "You're falling behind."

"Yes, sir," Zotkin replied.

Colchev felt the van accelerate and turned back to the monitor. He was annoyed to see that his men's pace car was decelerating.

He leaned forward. "Escort One," he said into the mic to the car's driver, Gurevich, "why are you slowing? Keep the interval at five hundred meters."

"Sir, I don't know how it happened," Gurevich said, the concern in his voice evident. "We've been watching the entire time, and no vehicles have approached."

"What are you babbling about? Is there a police car there?"

"No, sir. There's a man on top of the truck."

Colchev adjusted his earpiece. "What are you saying?"

"I can see someone walking along the top of the trailers. He just jumped from the second trailer to the first."

Colchev shook his head in shock. This was not happening. If he was hearing Gurevich right, someone had stowed away on the truck. But when? All the trailer doors were locked, and the professor and his student had been injected with enough sedative at the CAPEK facility to knock them out for hours. The two men hadn't been shot during the abduction because telltale blood splatters might have raised alarms at CAPEK. But Nadia Bedova and her men had come along and forced him to leave a mess behind.

Colchev suddenly realized the stowaway must be one of Bedova's men. She'd been smarter than he'd given her credit for.

"Send the order to stop the truck," Gurevich said, "and we will kill him."

"No. That truck stops for nothing. You will have to take

the intruder out while it's in motion." The road train was only nine miles from the target, and with the bodies they'd left behind in the warehouse, they were committed. Any delay would make it easier for the authorities to intercept the truck if the stowaway had called for help.

"Will we set off the explosives with a stray shot?"

Colchev thought that scenario was extremely unlikely. ANFO was a stable explosive, and a bullet impact would have no effect. Colchev was more worried about an errant round disabling the robotic truck's control system.

"Do not shoot unless fired upon," Colchev said. "Escort Two will have to get on the truck and eliminate him. You will not deviate until the task is accomplished. Understood?"

There was a pause on the other end. The Ford was now close enough to the road train that Colchev could see the men on his monitor, conferring in the car. The passenger, Lvov, didn't gesticulate or get upset. He knew his job. Gurevich was just outlining the plan to him.

"Understood," Gurevich replied to Colchev. "We'll pull alongside the cab and Escort Two will climb on."

Colchev saw the sign for the coming intersection a half-mile in the distance.

"You're approaching the turnoff. The truck will slow to turn. Your best chance will be right before it speeds up again."

"Acknowledged."

The road train began to slow, and the nose of the cab dipped as the brakes were applied more abruptly than

Colchev expected. It must also have been more sudden than the man on the truck expected because he fell onto the hood of the vehicle, filling the windshield and blocking Colchev's monitor view with the back of his leather jacket.

The man flipped over and clutched at the lip of the hood to keep himself from sliding off, bracing himself with his feet against the tubular bullbar, the Australian version of a cow catcher. At first all Colchev could see was the top of the man's head, his brown hair whipped by the wind. To stretch the length of the hood, the man had to be at least six feet tall—big enough to pose a problem for Lvov.

The stowaway looked up, and Colchev saw blue eyes peering back at him through the video camera. Colchev stared in stunned disbelief when he recognized the man as Tyler Locke.

How had Locke ended up here? Colchev wanted to reach through the screen and throttle him, but he was six miles away, helpless to do anything himself.

He leaned forward, his own eyes never leaving Locke's. He spoke slowly and distinctly into the microphone so that Gurevich would have no doubt that dying would be preferable to failure.

"I don't care how you do it," Colchev said, "but get that bastard off my truck."

ven as he was trying to keep himself from sliding off the hood and getting crushed by the road train's eighty tires, Tyler couldn't help but be mesmerized by the truck's empty cab. Invisible hands made minute adjustments to the steering wheel.

I guess it's getting harder to find suicide bombers these days, he thought.

Tyler marveled at the engineering involved in creating a two-hundred-ton remote-control truck. Then the howling wind reminded him he was in danger of becoming outback roadkill, and he looked for a way off the hood.

The situation hadn't turned out exactly as he'd planned. It had been Tyler's bright idea to jam the pliers of his Leatherman multi-tool into the trailer's rear door track to hold it open while he gripped the door's handle to pull himself onto the roof. Although Grant steadied him as he scrambled up, the abrupt encounter with the airstream nearly blew him onto the asphalt. Once Tyler was safely up and found his footing, he'd run along the trailer roofs, leaving Grant to implement their backup plan.

Tyler intended to climb down next to the cab's door, but while he was still on its roof, the road train had unexpectedly slowed, tossing him onto the hood instead.

Tyler swiveled his head to see why the truck was slowing. He squinted at a white car that turned off the highway just in front of him. It looked like the truck would follow.

As the road train made its turn, Tyler used the momentum to swing his legs over to the side and down onto the running board. With one hand on the mirror, he maneuvered over to the door handle. He pulled on it and realized he shouldn't have been surprised to find it unlocked. Colchev wasn't expecting stowaways on board.

He got into the cab and searched the interior for a simple DISENGAGE button, but he couldn't see one. In the middle of the dashboard was an LCD screen the size of a laptop's. He touched the dark screen, and a window lit up with the CAPEK logo.

Having successfully negotiated the turn, the road train accelerated again. A sign flashed by.

NO THROUGH ROAD

JOINT DEFENCE FACILITY PINE GAP

PROHIBITED AREA

TURN AROUND NOW

Tyler had never heard of Pine Gap, but it sounded like the kind of place a terrorist would want to target. He had no doubt security cameras along the road had already spotted the truck, but they might think it was just a shipment to the base that hadn't been properly recorded on the schedule. Guards would try to wave him down at the front gate and only realize their mistake when it barreled through. Stopping the truck before it got there was Tyler's best option.

Tyler scanned the screen hoping for an obvious solution to his predicament. A button at the bottom said MENU. Tyler tapped on it, and an inscrutable list of acronyms and commands filled the screen. It would take some study to figure out what series of commands led to the STOP command, so Tyler did what he thought would shut down most any cruise control.

He jammed his foot on the brake pedal.

The truck began to slow, but he could feel the accelerator fighting him. Either the auto-shutoff had been disabled or Colchev was in the van countermanding his efforts.

Tyler tried turning the wheel to jackknife the truck, but it spun freely in his hand. Normally a truck's steering was controlled by a rack-and-pinion mechanism, but the CAPEK vehicle's steering was drive-by-wire, controlled by a computer that sent commands from the steering wheel to a motor adjusting the position of the front wheels. The drive-by-wire system had been disengaged.

Tyler looked for an ignition key but found only a red START button. Pressing it had no effect. He pushed the brake pedal as hard as he could, and the road train slowed to ten miles per hour.

The walkie-talkie on Tyler's cell phone squawked.

"Tyler," Grant said. "You there?"

"I'm here and inside the cab."

"So you're stopping us?"

"Not exactly. We'll have to go with plan B. Get Stevens and Beech out of there."

"Will do," Grant said. He'd have to drop them off the back of the truck and hope the speed would be low enough to prevent serious injury.

"Is the device ready?" Tyler said.

"Almost. I just wanted to let you know I'd be incommunicado momentarily. I'll be out of here in thirty seconds. Can you keep us crawling for that long?"

"Will do. Should give us plenty of open space."

"And remember. Do *not* call me."

"Got it," Tyler said and hung up.

A face popped up in the driver's side window. Tyler had been so distracted that he'd lost track of the white car. The man outside with the thin nose and hideous underbite had climbed aboard to expel Tyler.

Colchev's man ripped the door open, and Tyler gave him some assistance. Tyler pushed the door wider, slamming it out of the man's hand and throwing him off balance. But he recovered easily and lunged inside, grasping Tyler in a chokehold.

Tyler kept his foot on the brake pedal as long as he could, but with his neck lodged in the crook of his assailant's arm, his vision tunneled at a rapid pace. He threw an elbow backward with little effect, and he couldn't use his other hand or he'd lose his grip on the cell phone. With only seconds before he blacked out, Tyler twisted in the man's grip and launched himself through the driver's side door, landing on the hood of the white sedan.

The surprised driver swerved and slowed as he brought a pistol to bear. Tyler rolled so that he would land in the dirt and not on the blacktop where he'd be drawn under the truck's wheels. Bullets blasting through the windshield missed him as he tumbled off the car and onto the hardpan, shielding his head from the impact, but subjecting his arms and legs to a multitude of bumps and bruises. He winced as he sat up and opened his palm to see that the phone was still intact.

The car accelerated away to catch up with the cab. Tyler turned and saw Grant fifty yards behind him, waving. Two limp forms lay next to him.

Tyler sprinted toward Grant and pointed at a boulder the size of a Volkswagen beside the road.

"Get to cover!" he shouted.

Grant gave the thumbs-up and picked up one of the men as if he were no heavier than a feather pillow. Tyler ran to the other man and saw that he was the smaller of the two, Professor Stevens. Tyler threw the dead weight onto his shoulder in a fireman's carry and hustled behind the boulder.

When he reached the relative safety of the rock, Tyler lay Stevens down and gasped for air.

"Glad you could join us," Grant said, and looked at the

car driving alongside the cab of the accelerating truck. "They with the Auto Club?"

Tyler nodded. "And they're very upset about what we've done to their truck."

"So we're not too excited about seeing them again?"

"I think they'd let their guns do the talking."

The man who'd jumped Tyler was now perched on the running board, looking for a graceful way back into the car. Colchev obviously wasn't planning on stopping to let him off.

"How much distance you figure we need?" Grant said.

"I'd like two miles, but I don't think we're going to get it."

The man leaped onto the top of the car, which immediately began to slow down. The truck, which was now more than a mile from Tyler and Grant, sped away from the sedan.

"It's now or never," Tyler said. They both crouched behind the boulder, covering Stevens and Beech. If this didn't work, they'd only have seconds to warn Pine Gap before those men returned to finish them off.

Tyler waited for Grant to cover his ears, then pressed the TALK button on the phone and covered his own.

Grant's phone was now hooked up in an electrical circuit with one of the detonators sitting in an ANFO barrel in the back of the truck. It received Tyler's signal and sent a current through the detonator.

The world ripped apart as if a volcano had erupted in the

middle of the desert. The deafening blast, louder than a thousand sonic booms, shattered the air and transformed the earth into an undulating ocean of dirt and sand.

Even with the boulder protecting them, Tyler could see the reflected glow of the gigantic fireball through his closed eyelids. His bones rattled from the overpressure wave, and the heat from the explosion singed his hair.

Shards of metal rained down around them. Tyler covered his head with his arms, but it would do little good if any large engine parts were flung this far. He just had to hope the boulder would do its job.

After what seemed like an eternity, the reverberations of the blast subsided. Tyler opened his eyes.

Tyler checked Stevens and Beech. Both were breathing and uninjured.

Grant blinked like he was coming out of a coma.

"You all right?" Tyler said.

"Definitely two miles next time," Grant replied.

They stood and staggered from behind the rock to survey the damage.

As the dust settled downwind, they could see that the road train had been wiped from the earth. In its place was a crater a hundred feet wide. The car had vanished, reduced to mere fragments by the explosion. Any remains of Colchev's men would be microscopic.

Grant handed Tyler his Leatherman without taking his eyes off the wreckage.

"Thought you might want this back," he said.

"Thanks," Tyler said as he mechanically replaced it in his belt holster.

"So," Grant said, "shall we call the police now?"

"I doubt that'll be necessary," Tyler said as he gazed in awe at the smoking hole in the ground. "I imagine we'll have plenty of company in a few minutes."

TWENTY-TWO

Thirty seconds after he lost the video and data signals from the road train, Colchev felt the shock wave from the immense explosion shake the van like a paint mixer. He tried reaching the men in the Ford, but all he got was static in return. He tore his headset off and smashed it against the console, swearing a stream of Russian curse words in violation of his own directive.

Locke had somehow caused a premature detonation, literally vaporizing his carefully designed plan. At least the man was likely dead, but his operatives were also gone.

Colchev sat back in numbed silence to consider his next move. If someone at the base had discovered the Killswitch didn't arrive from the airport, the explosion of the truck bomb was intended to bring any investigation to a dead stop. But with Pine Gap still intact, the Americans would act quickly to track down the weapon. That meant he had to act decisively. Quitting just as they were starting was not an option. He'd never get a chance like this again, so he could not waste time hesitating.

The van slowed.

"Keep driving," Colchev said, moving to the van's passenger seat. "Head to the rendezvous." A mushroom cloud rose in the distance.

"What the hell happened?" Zotkin said. "Wasn't that early?"

"We lost the truck," Colchev said.

Zotkin's grip on the steering wheel tightened until his knuckles were white. "How?"

"An intruder got on board and blew it up. It was Tyler Locke, the engineer who killed Golgov and Popovich in New Zealand."

Zotkin gaped at him. "Locke is here?"

"He must have been with Bedova."

"Did he survive?"

Now that Colchev thought about it, there was a chance Locke was still alive. He had to operate under that assumption.

"He may have made it," Colchev said, "but there's nothing we can do about that now. The site will be crawling with police before long. Gurevich and Lvov are dead, too."

Given how soon the explosion happened after Lvov got out of the CAPEK cab, they had to have been caught in the blast.

Zotkin's jaw clenched. "The US government will put every resource they have into finding the weapon."

"We have a solid plan for getting the Killswitch back to America. Our larger concern is retrieving the xenobium to power it."

"Can we still accomplish our mission?"

"Absolutely," Colchev said, betraying not a flicker of doubt in his voice. He did, however, have grave doubts. Without the xenobium, the Killswitch was just a regular bomb, and not a very powerful one at that. With the xenobium, the Killswitch could change the world.

Colchev's phone rang, and he answered the blocked call warily. Other than his operatives, only his mole at Pine Gap had this number.

"Yes?" Colchev said.

"It's me," a man's voice replied. They didn't risk using names. The call was forwarded by a VOiP service, so there would be no way to trace it to Colchev from the source. Still it was a risk they'd avoided until now. His mole was desperate.

"What do you want?"

"I want to know what the hell happened!"

"The package wasn't delivered as planned."

"I know that! Don't you think I heard? What am I supposed to do now?"

"Can you get out?"

"No. They put us on immediate lockdown."

"What about the trigger?"

"I can't smuggle it out now, for God's sake! You'll have to wait."

"We can't. I'll have someone check the drop in Sydney tomorrow. If the—" In his anger at the ruined scenario, Colchev almost said "xenobium", but mentioning the word would raise alarms. "If the trigger isn't in the planter box by midnight, our business is concluded."

"You can't leave me hanging out to dry! It's only a matter of time before they realize I helped steal the weapon."

"You knew the risks, and you were paid a lot of money to take them."

A long pause. "I'll tell them everything."

"What will you tell them? You have no idea where we're taking the package. *I* will be fine. *You*, on the other hand, will be executed for treason. So keep your wits about you and figure out another way to get me the trigger. And don't bother trying to call me again."

Colchev hung up and opened his window. He erased the phone's contents, removed the battery, wiped both parts clean of fingerprints, and tossed them into the desert.

"Do you really think he can do it?" Zotkin asked.

Colchev shook his head. "Doubtful, but there's nothing we can do to help him at this point." Without the truck bomb to divert attention from the theft, it would be almost impossible for his mole to get the xenobium out of Pine Gap undetected. Colchev massaged his forehead to ward off the headache he could feel coming on.

"If he gets caught, he'll reveal the location of the dead drop."

"Which is how we'll know if he was caught." His capture wasn't a concern because he couldn't tell the authorities anything useful. Colchev had led him to believe he was stealing the Killswitch weapon for some American mercenaries planning to sell it on the black market.

"What about the xenobium?" Zotkin said. "We can't use the Killswitch without the trigger."

"We have proof that there's more xenobium in Peru. And now we know how to find it, thanks to Fay Turia."

Zotkin opened his mouth to voice further concerns, then thought better of it when he saw Colchev's icy stare.

Five minutes later, Zotkin turned onto a dirt path and drove for a half-mile until he parked the van behind a rocky tor. He opened his phone.

"We're ready." After a moment, he hung up. "They'll be here in four minutes."

Colchev nodded. They wiped down the van and jogged back to the highway. The van would eventually be found, but their trail would go cold here.

They reached the road just as two cars arrived. Both were beige sedans, the first with only two men inside, the other with four. The contents of the stolen Killswitch crate had been divided between the trunks.

Colchev and Zotkin got in the back of the lead car, and they sped away.

"Buran," Colchev said to the driver, "you and Vinski will wait at the dead drop tomorrow. Be aware that the location may be compromised. If the delivery is made, pick up the trigger and rendezvous with the package in Mexico."

"What about us?" Zotkin said.

"We'll follow the trail that Fay Turia led us to in case we need a backup source of xenobium."

The cars stayed at the speed limit as they headed south. In ninety minutes they'd be at the remote airfield where they'd parked a chartered PC-12 Pilatus prop plane. Four hours after that, they'd be at Bankstown airport on the west side of Sydney.

Using Zotkin's phone, Colchev called the pilot of their private jet and told him to be ready to leave Sydney's main airport by eight a.m. the next morning. Because of today's setback, they had an enormous amount of work to accomplish. There were only four days left until zero hour.

TWENTY-THREE

Sitting in the back of the unmarked black van, Grant worked his jaw trying to get his hearing back. The buzz in his ears was now down to a dull roar, and since they weren't bleeding, he assumed he hadn't ruptured the eardrums. His clothes were caked with dirt from his tumble out of the truck. His shoulder got the worst of it when he hit the ground, but he seemed to be intact, the benefit of learning how to take a fall during his wrestling days.

Tyler sat across from him, rubbing his elbow. Dust cascaded from his jacket.

"You okay?" Grant asked.

"Just a little impact with a car hood. Nothing that a beer won't take care of."

He nodded at the stoic security officers in the front seat and smiled at Tyler. "At least they didn't handcuff us."

Tyler shot him a grin. "Considering what we did to their nice road, I wouldn't have been surprised if they had."

Within minutes of the explosion, police, firefighters, and ambulances descended on the site like locusts and cordoned it off from the local press. When Tyler mentioned Jess and Fay during questioning, they got even more attention from the police. They were told that Jess had discovered the five bodies of Bedova and her men at the warehouse.

The police had been about to bring them in for further interrogation when a Pine Gap security team took custody of them and swept them into the security van.

"Do you have any idea why they're taking us to Pine Gap?" Grant said.

Tyler shrugged. "You got me."

"They probably want to give us a medal. Thank us for stopping a major terrorist attack."

"I doubt they were terrorists. If they're rogue Russian operatives like Bedova said, it's more likely that they're mercenaries. Besides, they weren't the sacrificial types."

"Because of the robotic truck?"

Tyler nodded. "They went to a lot of trouble to steal the CAPEK prototype and put together a hundred and sixty tons of ANFO. Do you know anything about Pine Gap?"

"One of the cops said it's some kind of NSA listening post. The people stationed there mix with the locals, but no one ever talks about what goes on inside."

"Whatever it is, the people who put this road train together knew what they were doing. They had a definite plan, and it wasn't to make a political statement. Otherwise they wouldn't have been after Fay's artifacts."

"But all this having something to do with Roswell? I

know we've seen some funky stuff in our time, but that's just crazy."

"I don't believe in little green men any more than you do. But there's something big going on here."

"Must be, for them to bring a couple of civilians into a spook palace."

Not that they were typical civilians. Because Gordian did so much work with the Pentagon, Tyler and Grant had secured top-secret clearances. But that didn't mean they could just stroll into the most secretive US base in the southern hemisphere. Someone with juice had to make that happen.

They reached the front gate of Pine Gap. Though the security was formidable, the road train had been so massive that halting its momentum would have been impossible, especially with no driver to shoot.

The guard checked the passengers' credentials, including Grant's and Tyler's, while a second one used a mirror on the end of a stick to check the underside of the van for contraband or bombs. After a lap around the van, the guard waved them through.

A minute later the van screeched to a halt, and one of the security men got out and yanked the side door open.

"Let's go," he said.

Tyler climbed out and Grant followed, putting on his shades to shield his eyes from the harsh midday sunlight. He breathed in the clean air, unsullied by the smoke that was downwind and just visible over the ridgeline.

He rotated to get a lay of the land. Low white buildings

were spread out over a ten-acre area. To the north were ivory-colored domes that protected sensitive communications equipment from the outback sand that billowed through the site. Nothing else distinguished the facility from an office complex you'd see on the outskirts of any US city.

Grant imagined the road train making it to the spot where he was now standing. If it had detonated here, every building would have been reduced to rubble.

A slender woman strode toward them, her thick auburn hair swaying with each step. Dressed in stylish gray pants, matching suit jacket, and tailored green blouse, she didn't cut the figure of a scientist, but the sensible rubber-soled shoes didn't peg her as an administrator, either. She would have been a knockout if she weren't scowling.

She stopped in front of them. "Dr. Locke and Mr. Westfield, may I see your IDs?" She inspected their passports dispassionately and handed them back. "I'm Special Agent Morgan Bell, Air Force Office of Special Investigations."

"Nice to meet you, Agent Bell," Grant said. "Call me Grant. And you're welcome, by the way."

She didn't take the bait. "Anything you see, hear, or read on this base is classified at the highest levels. You shouldn't even be standing here."

"*You* wouldn't be standing here if it weren't for us," Grant said.

"That doesn't change the fact that you are a security risk that we don't need right now."

Grant looked back pointedly at the plume of smoke still

rising to the east. "Seems like the security risk has already occurred."

"Are we suspects?" Tyler asked.

Morgan shook her head. "We checked you out after the police identified you. Because of your security clearances, we felt it was prudent to debrief you here since you may have information vital to US national security. You should feel lucky that our position here kept you from being investigated for the murder of seven people."

"Hey!" Grant protested. "*We* only killed two of them. And that was so we could save your butts. Not to mention those of Professor Stevens and Milo Beech, who I understand are doing just fine."

Morgan took one step closer, so that Grant could feel her breath on his lips. "Mr. Westfield, I will let others bestow whatever honor you think you deserve for this morning's actions. But I have bigger problems right now. You are here at my discretion, and you will do as I say when you are on this base. Follow me," she said, and turned on her heel.

Grant leaned over to Tyler and whispered, "Oh, I like her."

"You would," Tyler replied. "Because she definitely doesn't like you."

"What's life without a challenge?" Grant caught up with Morgan and matched step with her.

"What?" she said.

"I just thought maybe you'd feel better about us being here if you knew more about us."

"I wouldn't have agreed to this if I hadn't read your file."

Morgan opened a door and led them inside the building. "I know everything I need to know."

"Oh yeah? What do you know about me?"

"Electrical engineer from the University of Washington. Performed for professional wrestling's meathead fans who think it's a real sport before gaining a conscience and becoming a combat engineer. Thinks he's some kind of badass for subsequently joining the Rangers. Now works for Gordian and is currently annoying me."

"I also love hot cocoa, Shetland ponies, and moonlit walks on the beach. So tell me about yourself."

She wasn't buying. No smile. "No," she said, and sped up.

"Well, I tried," Grant said to Tyler.

Morgan stopped at a door and nodded at a series of small cubbyholes.

"You'll need to put any communications or recording devices you have in there. Although the room is completely shielded, no cell phones or PDAs are allowed inside."

Tyler took Stevens' phone from his pocket and put it in one of the empty slots. Morgan looked at Grant, who raised his arms.

"The one I had was turned into dust particles by the truck bomb. Oh, and I'd appreciate your getting mine back from the warehouse when you have a chance."

Morgan rolled her eyes and went through the door. Grant smiled, thinking this was the most fun he'd had all day.

Tyler followed her, then Grant. He entered an immense laboratory filled with testing equipment, some of which he was familiar with, some that was new to him. Two men in lab coats were having an animated conversation with a guy in a dark blue suit. They stopped talking when they saw the newcomers enter.

Morgan introduced them quickly. The suit was her partner, Vince Cameron. Dr. Charles Kessler, the older lab coat, seemed to be in charge of the place. The intensely uncomfortable-looking younger lab coat was technician Ron Collins.

"I must reiterate my protest," Kessler said as he sneered at Grant and Tyler. "These men are a security threat to the entire project."

"The Secretary of the Air Force himself vouched for them," Morgan said.

Grant wasn't surprised about that. Tyler's father had been a two-star general in the Air Force and was a friend of the secretary. A quick call would have verified Tyler's credentials.

"Besides," Morgan said, "they may be our only hope for finding the crate quickly."

"Protecting the weapon is your job. If you were doing it correctly, we wouldn't need them."

Morgan stepped forward until she was nose to nose with Kessler. "Dr. Kessler, I don't give a damn what you think of me. I care about my country's national security. If you endanger it further, I will arrest you for obstructing my investigation. Am I clear?"

Grant chuckled. Even if Kessler couldn't see it yet, there was no way he was going to win.

"What was in the crate?" Grant asked.

Kessler glared at Morgan for a moment, then said, "Fine, you win." He turned to Grant. "She's talking about the Killswitch weapon systems. They were stolen from right under Agent Bell's nose."

For the first time, Morgan's stoic demeanor dissolved. "What do you mean 'they'?"

"I didn't tell you before because it wasn't relevant. As we do with all our testing programs, we built in redundancy in case we had a malfunction. When the terrorists took the crate, they didn't steal just one Killswitch. They stole two."

TWENTY-FOUR

While Fay rested in the SUV after talking with the police for over an hour, Jess stood outside with the Alice Springs detectives and finished detailing the events leading up to the discovery of the bodies in the warehouse. When she'd presented her credentials as a New Zealand police consultant, they'd been forthcoming in what they'd learned so far about the case and the contents of the road train.

It wasn't until after the police arrived that Fay had received the email from Tyler saying he and Grant were inside the road train. As they were conveying the message to the officers, a massive explosion from the truck bomb detonated south of town. Jess and Fay were in shock at losing them until the police received word that Tyler and Grant had gotten out safely, saving the lives of the professor and his student as well.

As to the bodies inside the warehouse, those five had been traveling under Russian passports and had arrived only this morning. It would take a while to verify the identities, and federal authorities were on their way to take over investigating the biggest terrorist attack in the country's history.

Jess had tried to convince them that this wasn't just an act of terrorism, but once they learned that Pine Gap had been the target, she'd gotten nowhere. The secret base had been the site of numerous demonstrations in the past, so the police felt it had been only a matter of time until some wacko took a more drastic step like this.

When Jess was finally released, she returned to the Jeep to find Fay lying in the front seat with it tilted as far back as it would go. She opened the door as quietly as she could, but Fay sat up immediately, then fell back with a moan.

"How are you feeling, Nana?" Jess said as she shut the door.

"Oh, just a little tired. I shouldn't sit up that quickly."

"You shouldn't be out here at all. I'll run you back to the hotel so you can take a nap."

"No, I'm more hungry than anything. Any news about Tyler and Grant?"

"They're fine. Apparently they're still being detained for questioning."

Fay looked worried. "The police don't think they had anything to do with this, do they?"

"I doubt it."

"Where are they?"

"I don't know. I gave the police my phone number so Tyler could call us when he and Grant are ready."

"Did they tell you anything about those poor dead people?"

Jess put the Jeep into gear. "Just that they were Russian nationals."

"Russians? I am so confused by all of this."

"So am I," Jess said. "As far as we know, the men who attacked you in Queenstown were Americans. They were part of a group who hijacked an experimental robotic truck that they used to pull four trailers filled with explosives to blow up a secret American base in the middle of Australia."

Jess kept an eye on her rearview mirror. Although she thought the hijackers would be miles away by now, she was still worried they would make another attempt to get the relic from Fay.

"Maybe they thought my piece of the wreckage or the wood engraving might be valuable," Fay said. "Maybe they needed the money to fund this attack."

Jess shook her head. "An attack this complex had to have taken a long time to plan. And there are a lot of easier ways to finance the operation."

"What if they were planning to sell it for some other reason? What if the Russians thought it was some kind of alien technology?"

They entered the central business district. There were several restaurants to choose from.

"Nana, I don't think they came all the way to New Zealand for an artifact that they'd never even seen, just because they thought it might have some alien—"

A sudden realization popped into Jess's head. Her skill with codes included recognizing patterns where there didn't seem to be any. Now that she had more info about the men who'd attacked Fay, the link became clear.

Those Russians were killed by associates of men who had come all the way to New Zealand based on what Fay had revealed in the video. Because of something she said.

Jess slammed on the brakes and pulled to the side of the road.

"What's the matter?" Fay asked.

Jess turned to her. "What exactly did the creature on the spacecraft say to you?"

"You mean the alien language? Why?"

"I don't think it was an alien language."

"Jessica, I know you don't believe that it happened to me, but it did. I'm not going to lie just because it makes me sound crazy."

Jess smiled. "I don't think you're crazy, Nana. I think everything happened to you just the way you said it did, and someone else knows it did. That's why they came for your artifacts. Specifically the wooden engraving."

Fay embraced her granddaughter with delight. "I'm so glad you finally believe me. The US government has always been so successful at covering up the incident, I didn't think anyone ever would."

"I don't think that the US government is behind the attack."

"Well, I wouldn't be surprised. Any time someone has

gotten close to revealing the truth about the Roswell incident, the US has hidden the evidence and labeled the person a nut or worse. Mac Brazel—remember the foreman of the ranch in Roswell?—he got the worst of it."

Until the events in Queenstown, Jess had never given much thought to Roswell except when Fay would retell the story about the alien or her trips to Peru to decipher the engraving's clues. Jess would listen politely because she knew it was important to her grandmother, but it wasn't something she took seriously. As long as the travel kept Fay busy and happy after her grandfather's death, that's all Jess cared about. Now she wished she'd paid more attention.

"I didn't tell you this morning," she said, "but I stayed up last night researching the Roswell incident. Did you know there was a book out recently about Area 51? The author claimed a source told her that Stalin created child-sized people with grotesque features. They were sent over to the US in a top-secret Soviet airplane to crash and cause hysteria in the populace."

"That sounds more ridiculous than an alien spacecraft landing."

"I know. It sounds insane, but we just heard that the men who attacked you killed five Russians. Could there be some link between Roswell and the Soviets?"

"But I saw the alien with my own eyes!"

"Maybe you were supposed to think it was an alien."

"Well, it wasn't child-sized, I can tell you that for sure.

It picked me up and put me on Bandit like I weighed nothing."

"Even outlandish stories have a kernel of truth to them. What if the Russians are involved? We won't know until we figure out what that piece of wood from Roswell means and why it depicts the same figures found in the Nazca lines. And I think the key is what the creature told you. Can you repeat it?"

"*Rah pahnoy pree vodat kahzay nobee um.*"

Jess opened her cell phone and dialed a number in her contact list.

"Who are you calling?" Fay said.

"Michael Silverman. He's a professor of Russian at the University of Auckland, and a well-known authority on its different dialects. I confer with him from time to time when I need something translated."

He answered on the third ring. "Hello?"

"Mike, it's Jess McBride."

"Hey! How's my favorite codebreaker?"

"I'm fine. Listen, I don't have much time and I need to ask you a favor."

"Find another Russian virus on your system?"

"No, but I do need something translated." Jess put the phone on speaker. "Mike, I've got you on the line with my grandmother, Fay Turia."

"The one who does all the adventures around the world?"

"The same."

"Hi, Fay. Jess talks about you every time she calls."

Fay smiled. She leaned over and talked loudly into the phone. "Nice to talk to you, Michael."

"So what do you need translated?"

Jess nodded for Fay to speak. "*Rah pahnoy pree vodat kahzay nobee um.*"

"Say that again?"

Fay repeated it, and they heard typing. The phone went silent for a minute.

"Mike, you still there?" Jess said.

"I'm here. You sure that's Russian?"

"That's what we were hoping you could tell us."

"Well, the pronunciation is way off if it is. I parsed the sentence into its syllabic components. The only part of it that could be remotely Russian is *pree vodat kah*. If I'm hearing it right, it means 'leads to'."

"So if it's Russian, it means '*rah pahnoy* leads to *zay nobee um*'?"

"The last part might be a single word. Zaynobium. Don't ask me what it means. I just tried plugging several different spellings of it into Google and got nothing except a link to a video of your grandmother."

The word was meaningless to Jess. She looked at Fay, who shrugged back at her.

"What about the first part?" Jess asked.

"That's interesting. The first thing that popped into my head was a slightly different pronunciation. Rapa Nui."

"As in Easter Island?" Fay said, her eyes shining with revelation.

"It's just a guess," Silverman said. "Sorry I couldn't be more helpful."

"No, Mike," Jess said. "You've been very helpful. Thanks." They said goodbye and hung up.

Jess was mesmerized by the chain of events. A supposed alien crash lands at Roswell, hands Fay a wooden engraving showing figures from the Nazca lines, and utters a phrase implying that the map on the other side depicts Easter Island.

"What do you think Zaynobium is?" Fay said, but Jess couldn't even hazard a guess.

Fay thought about it for a moment and then bounced in her seat with excitement. "Maybe that's the alien home planet!" She took the wooden tablet out of her bag and looked at it again with new eyes.

"Let's talk about it over lunch." Jess moved to get out of the car, but Fay put her hand out to stop her.

"Where are you going?"

"To that restaurant."

"But we have to find Tyler and tell him what we found out."

"Nana, you need to eat."

"I can eat later. Do you realize this is what I've been searching for the past five years? Rapa Nui could be the missing piece of the puzzle!"

"But how could Easter Island be linked to both Roswell and the Nazca lines?"

"Some anthropologists think the Nazca people could

have migrated from South America to Polynesia." Fay removed the ancient engraving from her bag and reverently ran her fingers over the grooves etched into the wood. "The person who made this map might be a descendant of those voyagers. If he left clues to the lines' true purpose, it would mean that somewhere on Easter Island lies the answer to one of the world's greatest mysteries."

TWENTY-FIVE

T
yler and Grant had spent the last hour seated at a conference table, reciting to Morgan, Vince, and Kessler the sequence of events over the past two days that led them here. They included everything, including the cryptic items that Nadia Bedova asked about outside the warehouse.

"Do you know what Bedova meant by Icarus?" Morgan asked.

Tyler knew the myth to which it referred: the boy who escaped Crete only to fly too close to the sun, which melted his waxen wings and caused him to fall to his death. "Sounded like a code name to me," he said. "Maybe it's a Russian spy."

"Or a secret project," Grant said.

"And you don't know what's happening on July twenty-fifth?" Vince said. His eyes had flinched noticeably when Tyler had told them that part. It obviously struck a nerve.

"No idea," Tyler said.

"What about Wisconsin Avenue or the Baja cartel?"

Tyler shook his head. "Perhaps if you shared some information about the Killswitch, we could be of help."

Kessler straightened in his seat. "That is my project. And its real name is Lightfall. 'The Killswitch' is Collins's nickname for the device, and everyone on the team started calling it that." He was obviously unhappy about sharing this information.

"I'll bet it's not a new kind of blender," Grant said.

"You are an idiot," Morgan said. "This is a DARPA black project. Lightfall is a weapons program."

"What does it do?" Tyler asked.

"I don't have time for this," Kessler said, jumping out of his seat. Tyler could imagine how shaken the scientist must be, knowing his life's work had been stolen.

"Dr. Kessler," Morgan said, "this is more important than anything else you could be doing right now. Please sit down."

Kessler looked at the door and grumbled, but he took his seat, massaging his temples as if he were soothing a headache. After a few moments, he said with a tired voice, "You, of course, know what an EMP is."

Tyler nodded. "When an H-bomb explodes at high altitude, it blasts out an electromagnetic pulse that fries anything with a computer chip."

"So the Killswitch is a nuke?" Grant said.

"No, it is much more sophisticated than that," replied Kessler. "Under Project Lightfall, we designed the bomb to emit the pulse without a thermonuclear explosion. The weapon has the capability to penetrate hardened bunkers and vehicles, even at low altitudes, and it leaves no residual radioactive fallout."

"So it could be used in conventional wars," Tyler said.

"It's not my place to say where or how it's used. That's for military commanders and politicians to decide."

Grant grunted.

"I suppose you have a problem with me being a weapons developer," Kessler said.

"Not at all. When I was in the Rangers, I wouldn't have minded setting one of those babies off over a tank division that I was about to engage. Would have made my job easier."

That seemed to calm Kessler. "We were planning to do our first test next week at the Woomera range south of here."

"Why Australia?"

"The Australians have material critical to operation of the weapon. It was a joint development."

"What material?"

"You don't need to know that."

Tyler was confused. "If the weapon was stolen, then why the truck bomb?"

"A cover-up attempt," Morgan said. "If that truck had made it through the gates and blown up Pine Gap, everyone here would have been killed. The ensuing investigation would have come to the conclusion that the weapon was destroyed in the explosion."

"How powerful is the bomb?"

Kessler rubbed his mouth. "It depends on the yield of the trigger. That's what we were hoping to find out with the tests. But my estimate says that an airburst at an altitude of thirty-five thousand feet would disable everything within a thirty-mile radius."

Grant leaned forward, slack-jawed at the weapon's destructive potential. "That's the size of Washington."

"Or Paris. Or Beijing. If the Killswitch is used to take out a major city, the effects would be catastrophic."

"Now you see why we need your help," Vince said. "You can identify the thieves."

"How did they steal it?"

"We're still tracking that down. But it looks like it was done in transit, on the way here from the Alice Springs airport. The truck never showed up. With the police investigating the warehouse deaths and the explosion, we're stretched thin looking for it."

"What about the airport?" Tyler said. "Roadblocks?"

"The Alice Springs airport is tiny, so we're checking every plane flying out. Roadblocks are more difficult. We can't have the police stop every car and truck leaving the area to do a thorough search without telling them what they're looking for."

"You can't exactly put out an all-points bulletin advertising that the US military lost something that could send Sydney or Melbourne back to the Stone Age," Grant said.

Vince nodded. "The press would get hold of it in no time, and then we'd have a panic on our hands."

"But it can't be set off," Kessler protested. "Not without the trigger."

Morgan sat with a mixture of sigh and growl. "Dr. Kessler, it's about time you tell us exactly how the Killswitch works. And I mean everything."

Kessler stood and glared at Morgan. "I reiterate my protest. These men are not properly vetted—"

"Your protest is noted," she said. "Continue."

He seethed for a long minute before finally throwing up his hands in defeat. "All right," he said, pacing as he spoke. "Do you know what hafnium is?"

Tyler didn't hesitate. "It's a metallic element. It doesn't have many uses, but it's important in the cladding of nuclear fuel rods to control the reaction."

Grant tapped the table. "Wasn't there something about a bomb that used a hafnium isomer? I read about it a few years ago. DARPA was developing it, but there was some controversy over whether it actually worked."

"How do you know that?" Kessler said in amazement.

"Well, we *are* experts in explosives. Reading the literature on the subject is kind of a job necessity."

"After those articles came out, all future press communication on the process was halted," Kessler said.

"Let me guess," Tyler said. "Because it works."

Kessler nodded. "It's called induced gamma emission. And yes, it works. Hafnium-3, the isomer you mentioned, is the most powerful non-nuclear explosive in existence. One gram of it has the explosive power of three hundred kilograms of TNT."

Grant whistled in appreciation. "Good things come in small packages."

"The Killswitch uses an isomer trigger. Without it, the weapon is nothing more than a very expensive bomb. All other EMP weapons with an effective range of more than half a mile are either nuclear or the size of a house, making them impractical in battle situations. Using a hafnium isomer to generate the gamma radiation necessary, we were able to shrink the weapon to only fifty kilograms, and half of that weight is for the plastic explosive to set off the isomeric reaction in the trigger. Most of the design expense went into compacting the weapon into such a small size."

"So the Killswitch is triggered by hafnium-3?" Tyler asked.

"No. Production of hafnium-3 is prohibitively expensive. It would cost a billion dollars for just a few grams. We have something even more powerful. A hafnium isomer called xenobium. It's more stable than hafnium-3 and twice as powerful."

Tyler chewed his lip. "You glossed over the fact that both hafnium-3 and induced gamma emission weapons emit gamma rays. How deadly is this xenobium?"

"It can be carried safely in a shielded lead container."

"And the gamma rays from the explosion of the Killswitch?" Morgan said.

Kessler looked around the table and cleared his throat. "At low altitudes the explosion would produce a lethal dose of radiation for anyone within a mile or more, depending on the size of the xenobium trigger."

"Sounds like a nuclear weapon to me," Grant chuffed.

"It is non-nuclear in the sense that it is not a fission or fusion device, and as I mentioned there is no lingering radioactive fallout. Beyond the immediate region around the explosion, the effects are not fatal."

"Supposedly. Didn't you just say that you haven't tested it yet?"

"Of course. All our calculations are purely theoretical at this point."

Everyone went silent at the potential catastrophe if the weapon was set off in a populated area, possibly on July twenty-fifth.

"Do the hijackers have this new isomer?" Tyler finally asked.

"They don't. All one hundred grams are stored ten stories under Pine Gap, locked in a hardened vault. We had been planning to divide it into five-gram fragments to use in the Killswitch, but right now it's still secure and in a single piece."

"Could they have made their own xenobium?"

"As far as we know, no one else is even close to obtaining the capability to manufacture it. The problem is that they might have found another source of the isomer."

"From where?"

Kessler took a breath and wiped his brow as he sat. "From outer space."

"Excuse me?" Grant said with a laugh and looked at Tyler while pointing at Kessler. "I thought he said outer space."

"That's what I heard," Tyler said.

"I did say outer space," Kessler replied, not getting Grant's sarcasm. "The sample at Pine Gap was found in Western Australia ten years ago. In 1993 a few truck drivers and gold prospectors reported a bright light and a series of thunderous booms. The explosion was so large that it registered 3.9 on the Richter scale. Because the area was so remote and because no one was injured, nobody went to investigate it for years. Some theorized it was a nuclear blast set off by the Aum Shinrikyo cult."

"Come on!" Grant said incredulously. "The group that gassed the Tokyo subway system?"

"I didn't say I agreed with such ludicrous speculation. No one ever detected radiation, so the likelihood of an atomic weapon was minimal. However, the impact of an iron meteorite like the one that created the Barringer Crater in Arizona was also ruled out because no crater was found at the site of the seismic event."

"Leaving what?" Tyler said.

"We now believe it was an airburst explosion of a meteor above twenty thousand feet. With no trees in that part of the desert to be blown down by a shock wave, it's possible that the evidence would be hard to find. When geologists went to investigate the mystery long after the event, they conducted a careful search of the area around the seismic event and came back with a single sample from the location's epicenter. After extensive testing, it was determined that the material was an unusual isomer of hafnium called xenobium."

"Is that the only sample in the world?" Vince asked.

"To our knowledge it's the only one that still exists. The first known sample was discovered a century ago by a Russian scientist named Ivan Dombrovski."

Grant snorted. "He sounds like an offensive lineman for the Green Bay Packers."

Kessler ignored him. "Dombrovski escaped from Russia during the Bolshevik revolution. He claimed to have recovered the material from the area of the Tunguska blast and used it to buy his American citizenship."

"The Tunguska blast?" Tyler said. "So we know it was caused by an exploding meterorite?"

"No one's ever been able to definitively prove what caused the blast. Explanations include a meteorite, comet, or even black hole. And some crackpots theorize it was an alien spacecraft that crashed and vaporized in the explosion."

Tyler and Grant exchanged looks at the mention of aliens. The subject did seem to keep coming up in the last few days. Tyler felt his ironclad skepticism cracking just a bit.

"You're saying that this xenobium could be an alien artifact?" Grant said.

"Don't be absurd," Kessler said. "It could have easily been part of the meteorite or comet that exploded.

Dombrovski just found the remnants that didn't detonate. And so did the Australians."

"What happened to the sample Dombrovski brought to America?" Tyler asked.

"For the next thirty years, he experimented with it. He established a project to take advantage of xenobium's unique properties and named it Caelus for the Roman god of the sky. Dombrovski was also trying to figure out how to produce more xenobium, but he never was able to."

"What was the goal of Project Caelus?"

"We don't know," Kessler said. "In 1947 his lab was destroyed in a fire set by Soviet spies, taking Dombrovski and the xenobium with it. Most of the records about Caelus were lost as well, but there were enough surviving files to confirm that his xenobium was the same material as the specimen found in Australia."

Collins entered and nodded at Morgan and Vince. "The Australian police need to talk to one of you."

"Why?" Morgan said.

"They found the bodies of the men who picked up the Killswitch from the airport."

"I'll take it," Vince said.

"Find out where the crime scene is," Morgan said. "Tell them we'll head there in five minutes."

Vince nodded and left.

Kessler stood. "While we're taking a break, I need to take my own." He left at a trot, as though he were barely going to make it to the bathroom.

Grant grinned at the quick exit. "When you gotta go, you gotta go."

"They've been looking for xenobium ever since," Tyler said under his breath.

"What was that?" Morgan asked.

Tyler suddenly stood when it clicked. "The Russians. They've been looking for more xenobium for almost a hundred years."

"But if that's what Colchev's men were looking for," Grant said, "why did they attack Fay?"

"Maybe they thought she had a sample of it. She said they were asking about a multi-hued metal object, colored like an opal. Hafnium becomes opalescent when it oxidizes, so I'm guessing xenobium does, too. But why did they think she had some?"

"Xenobium!" Grant said, slapping the table. "Remember? It was in the phrase Fay said in the video."

Grant was right. Tyler wanted to smack himself for not making the connection faster. He wheeled around to Morgan. "Can we get to the Internet from in here?"

"No. Every computer in here is cut off. Why do you need it?"

"We need to see Fay's video. Take me to a computer with Web access."

Morgan was dubious but led Tyler and Grant back to the office where her laptop was, passing Vince speaking on his phone in the hallway. She opened the computer and let Tyler find Fay's video on YouTube. He dragged the slider until he got to Fay's appearance and the phrase she was told by the creature she'd encountered.

"*Rah pahnoy pree vodat kahzay nobee um.*"

"My God," Morgan said.

"She must have gotten the pronunciation wrong. Whoever or whatever spoke to Fay was trying to tell her something about xenobium."

"Where is she now?"

"The last we heard, she was with Jess McBride at the warehouse where Colchev locked us in the truck."

Vince burst into the room, breathless, as if he'd been running.

"Morgan," Vince said, holding out his phone. "You have to look at this."

She took it. From his vantage point, Tyler could see it was a photo of five men, three white and two black, lying on the ground, each with a bullet in his forehead.

"What is this?" she said. "I recognize Josephson, but who are the other men?"

"A private pilot spotted them in the desert south of town. The police found them next to a Pine Gap truck. They're the men from the security detail who were sent to pick up the Killswitch."

Morgan looked back at the photo, first with a puzzled expression, then with dawning horror.

"Are you sure?"

"They all had their Pine Gap IDs on them."

"What's the matter?" Tyler said.

Vince looked up, his eyes clouded with dread. "The men we saw at the airport were all Caucasian. That means the hijackers had to have taken out the men before they reached the airport. The men we met were the impostors."

"So?" Grant said.

"So," Morgan said, her jaw clenched, "Kessler arrived at the airport with them."

TWENTY-SIX

M organ didn't waste time on self-recrimination for not detecting Kessler's treachery earlier. There would be plenty of time for that when her superiors found out. Her priority was to find him and make him tell her where she could find the stolen Killswitches.

"We've got a major security breach," she barked into her phone to Herman Washburn, Pine Gap's chief of security.

"What kind?"

"Charles Kessler. He left Pine Gap with your security team and arrived at the airport with the hijackers. He must have been there when your men were killed."

"But Kessler was at Pine Gap when the truck bomb was supposed to hit. He would have been killed."

"When we check the records," Morgan said, "I'll bet we find out that he was in the underground vault at the time. It would have been the only safe location during the blast."

"Dammit! All right. I'll post guards on every side of the facility to keep him from escaping."

"He can't be far. He left the lab just a few minutes ago. He may be trying to steal the xenobium sample."

"His badge isn't showing up on our internal monitoring system. We'll do a room-by-room search. He won't get away."

"Make sure he isn't harmed. We need him for questioning."

A voice came over the intercom. *This is a security alert. All non-security personnel are instructed to remain where they are. This is not a drill.* The message repeated.

"Wait a minute," Washburn said. There was an excruciating pause. "Agent Bell, I've got Kessler. He's in the vault with the xenobium. He's asking for you."

"All right, I'll head down there."

"No, he wants to talk to you over the intercom. You'll have to come to the security bunker."

Morgan grimaced. "I'll be right there." She hung up and turned to Vince. "Kessler's in the vault. Head down there and make sure any escape routes are cut off." She pointed at Tyler and Grant. "You're both with me. I don't want you out of my sight."

Grant put up his hands. "Whatever you say."

"Let us know if we can do anything to help," Tyler said.

"Come on." She sprinted for the security room with Tyler and Grant keeping up behind her.

When they arrived, the room was bustling with activity.

Washburn, a grizzled veteran, eyed Tyler and Grant. "Who are they, and what are they doing here?"

"Locke and Grant. They blew up the truck bomb."

Washburn appraised them, then grudgingly nodded.

"Where is he?" Morgan asked.

Washburn pointed at the center monitor. "I've got the vault sealed."

Kessler was looking up into the camera.

"Can he see me?" Morgan said.

"No."

She leaned into the mic. "Dr. Kessler, this is Special Agent Bell. I know you are involved with the hijacking."

"I want safe passage out of Pine Gap, and I'm taking the xenobium with me."

"You know I can't do that."

"You *will* do that or I blow it up." Kessler held up an object the size of a grapefruit.

Morgan put her hand over the mic. "Can he do that?" she asked Washburn.

"How the hell should I know?"

Morgan looked at Tyler.

He nodded slowly. "Given that I just learned about this stuff, it's hard to say. But if that thing he's holding is a detonator with the xenobium inside, I'd say it's possible."

"How much damage would it cause if it went off?"

"Kessler said they had a hundred grams of it and that it was twice as powerful as hafnium-3," Grant said.

She could see Tyler doing the math in his head. "That gives it the explosive power of over sixty tons of TNT. How thick are the vault walls?"

"Twelve feet of concrete on the sides," Washburn said. "The door is two feet of hardened steel."

"That's not enough to contain the blast. The vault is ten stories underground?"

Washburn nodded. "At the edge of the facility."

Tyler glanced at Morgan. "You'll get some serious foundation damage if it goes off in the vault. But if Kessler gets topside, it would take apart half the buildings in Pine Gap."

"What if that's his plan?" Grant said.

"We can't risk letting him get out," Morgan said. She removed her hand from the mic. "Kessler, disable the device and we'll talk."

"No." He tapped on the device in his hand. "I've just set this for sixty seconds. If the door doesn't open in one minute, it goes off. Starting now."

Morgan checked the clock on the wall. "Kessler, if you did this for money, we can work something out. We can get you help."

"Let me out! Now!"

"Maybe someone kidnapped a loved one. Tell us and we'll figure out how to solve the problem."

"I've got nobody. I dedicated my life to this project. And for what? Two divorces that milked every cent out of me, a pitiful pension, and an empty apartment. Why shouldn't I be able to retire in luxury?"

Forty-five seconds.

"Kessler, I'm not letting you out of there."

"Then I have nothing to live for."

"Yes, you do. We can work this out."

"So I can sit in a cell in Guantanamo for the rest of my days? I don't think so."

Thirty seconds. She could tell he wasn't bluffing, but there was no way she could let him leave with the xenobium.

She put her hand over the mic and turned to Washburn. "Get your men out of there right now." He scrambled to call his men. Vince would be with them. She tried not to think about it.

Speaking to Kessler, she said, "The Killswitch is useless without the xenobium. You said so yourself."

"I'm sure they have a backup plan."

Fifteen seconds.

"Kessler, I'm not bluffing. That door will not open."

"I know."

"Then don't do this," Morgan said, desperate to convince him to give up.

"There's no alternative."

Five seconds. Kessler began to mumble to himself.

"Where are Vince and your men?" she said to Washburn.

"Headed up the stairs. I don't know what lev—"

The screen went white and a massive tremor shook the ground. Morgan held onto the console as the floor rattled beneath her. Mugs, headsets, and books clattered to the ground.

After a minute, the trembling subsided.

"Is everyone all right?" Washburn said. A few people said yes. Others who were more shocked just grunted.

Morgan was already running toward the stairwell to see if Vince had made it out alive.

TWENTY-SEVEN

Even from outside the entrance of Pine Gap, Tyler could easily see the depression caused by Kessler's detonation of the xenobium. It had been an hour since the blast, and all non-essential personnel had been told to evacuate the premises. Only the emergency crews who had been pre-screened for security clearances were allowed into the facility to scour the rubble for survivors.

Grant was helping Morgan search for her partner while Tyler waited for Fay and Jess to arrive. He knew they wouldn't be permitted inside, so he paced along the outer fence.

He recognized the Jeep as it sped toward him. He waved it over and saw that Jess was driving.

She threw the door open, jumped out, and launched herself at Tyler in a tight hug. "I'm so relieved you're all right."

Tyler savored the embrace for a moment, then extricated himself and saw that Fay had joined them. "Are you two okay?"

"Other than being psychologically scarred by finding

five dead bodies in the warehouse, we're fantastic." Jess gestured at a passing emergency vehicle. "What the hell is going on here?"

"There was another explosion, this one inside Pine Gap. That's all I'm allowed to say about it."

"What happened at the warehouse?" Fay said. "We thought the worst when we found those bodies."

"That's a long story. I'll have to tell you later."

"We heard about the truck bomb," Jess said. "Actually, we *heard* the truck bomb."

"People in Adelaide would have heard the truck bomb."

"What's this all about anyway?"

"We think Fay may have stumbled onto a terror plot accidentally."

"Because of the artifacts from Roswell?"

Tyler nodded.

"Well, we finally found out what the phrase that alien told me means," Fay said. "'Rapa Nui leads to zaynobium.' We know that Rapa Nui is the Polynesian name for Easter Island, so we think the map on the wood engraving marks a particular spot on the island. But the other part of the phrase is still a mystery. Do you know what zaynobium is?"

Tyler ignored the question because even correcting her pronunciation would require breaking about twelve laws. He focused on Jess as he shook his head. She would understand that meant he *did* know but couldn't discuss it.

"Whatever it means," Fay said, "we're getting on the first flight we can find to Easter Island."

"Nana, you've seen what's happened here today. It's too dangerous."

"Dear, do you think I care about the danger? This is the greatest adventure I could have possibly imagined. I'm *this* close to finding the solution to a puzzle that's tormented me for sixty-five years. But I'm going without you. I don't want you hurt."

Jess objected. "The hell you are. I'm not letting you go anywhere without me. We go together or you don't go at all."

Fay paused for a moment, searching Jess's eyes, then smiled and patted her granddaughter's hand. "That settles it." She turned to Tyler. "Are you coming with us?"

Tyler looked from Fay to Jess. He wouldn't be able to persuade them to change their minds, and Morgan Bell had no legal authority to keep them from going.

"I'm in," he said. At least he knew what they were looking for.

Fay clapped her hands. "Excellent!"

"Where's Grant?"

"He's helping search the wreckage."

As he spoke, an ambulance hurtled out of the front gate, followed by a car with Morgan driving. She pulled to a stop next to them and got out. Grant hopped out of the passenger side.

"Did you find Vince?" Tyler said.

Grant nodded. "He was in the stairwell when the bomb went off. A concrete archway kept him from being completely crushed, but he broke both his legs and punctured a lung."

"Mr. Westfield heard him before anyone else did," Morgan said. That looked like the closest she'd get to saying thanks.

"It's not the first time I've seen this kind of damage, so I just knew where to look."

"The medics said he could be back in action in a few months."

"That's good to hear," Tyler said. He introduced Morgan to Fay and Jess.

"The government again," Fay said. "I knew they were behind this."

"It's all right, Fay," Tyler said. "The US had nothing to do with the attack in New Zealand. Rogue Russian agents are responsible for all this."

"Russians?" Fay said with awe. "That explains why the alien spoke to me in Russian."

Tyler told Morgan about the translation of Fay's phrase.

"Rapa Nui as in Easter Island?" Morgan said.

"Yes. And these two are going whether we want them to or not."

"When?"

"As soon as possible," Fay said. "Tyler's right. You can't stop us."

Morgan pursed her lips as she thought for a minute. Finally, she said to Tyler, "Do you think more xenobium could be there?"

"There's only one way to find out."

"Is that how it's pronounced?" Fay said. "What is xenobium?"

"That's classified, ma'am. All I'm allowed to tell you is that the Secretary of the Air Force has received clearance from the President to declare this situation a national security matter. The information you have may be critical to keeping a dangerous item from being used as an instrument of terror." Morgan took a breath. "I am authorized to use any and all means to bring this matter to a close, and since you are going anyway I'm requesting your help."

"We don't even know what all this is about," Jess said.

"Dr. Locke does, but he's bound by Executive Order 13292 from disclosing it, and I expect him to adhere to it. Therefore, I want him to accompany you."

"Yeah, we've already decided on that. You know, we're in Australia, so while we may choose to help you, we are under no obligation to."

"Ms. McBride and Ms. Turia, I checked your status. You're both dual citizens of New Zealand and the United States. I'd hope you'd have a sense of patriotism in the matter."

Tyler put up his hand to stop Morgan. This kind of heavy-handed approach wouldn't work, and she didn't need to use it. "We're all on board here, Agent Bell. Fay, Jess, I can tell you that whatever is on Rapa Nui may have global implications. If we don't find out what's there, millions of people may be at risk."

Jess set her jaw, still miffed at being bossed around, but Fay nodded with satisfaction.

"If the US government wants to help me solve the Roswell mystery, then I'll go along with it."

"Okay," Jess said to Tyler. "We're trusting you."

Tyler hoped he was doing the right thing including Fay and Jess and putting them in more danger, but he didn't really have much choice. They were too involved to exclude now, and Fay could have information crucial to solving the riddle on the artifact.

"By the way," Grant said, "I won't be coming with you."

"Why not?"

Grant tilted his head, a signal that he wanted to speak in private. He, Morgan, and Tyler took a few steps away from the Jeep.

"Morgan has a lead that the Killswitches may be in Sydney," Grant said.

"After we sent Vince to the hospital, I searched Kessler's office and found a burner cell phone," she said. "Kessler didn't know it, but all communication signals coming in and out of Pine Gap are intercepted and recorded. He called Colchev right after you blew up the truck bomb. Colchev instructed him to deliver the xenobium to a dead drop in Sydney tomorrow by midnight. It's possible he's unaware that Kessler was killed."

"Do you know where the drop is supposed to take place?" Tyler asked.

"I went back to two Internet discussion board messages

that we suspect were sent between Colchev and Kessler. One of the messages was posted under the false name George Hickson and mentioned a black box cheat code. It took only a simple Google search of 'George Hickson' and 'Sydney' to discover that there are two intersecting streets in Sydney named George and Hickson. There's a black flower box on the corner sidewalk. It's in a neighborhood called The Rocks near the opera house."

"Because I saw Colchev's men in the warehouse," Grant said, "Morgan wants me to go with her to see if I can spot someone checking the drop spot."

"If we can keep a lid on Kessler's death, they won't know he's not coming. We might be able to stop this whole thing there."

Tyler nodded. "That makes sense. But if they don't show, they're going to be looking for another source of xenobium."

"That's why you need to find it before they do," Morgan said.

"Agent Bell," Tyler said, "given all that's happened, don't you think some protection for us would be prudent?"

"It's already been arranged. Four NSA agents from Pine Gap are going with you. They'll be fully armed."

"I don't think Qantas will let them carry assault rifles on board."

Morgan shook her head. "You're taking our plane. The discussion forum message also hinted that July twenty-fifth was an important date, and Nadia Bedova seemed to confirm it. Whatever Colchev is planning will happen four days from now. That's why we've got the C-17 on the runway fueled and ready to go. After it drops me and Westfield off in Sydney, it's taking the three of you directly to Easter Island."

RAPA NUI

By eight a.m. Monday morning, Colchev's men were almost finished repacking the two Killswitch weapons into their new containers. One was already closed up and would be shipped on a cargo flight from Sydney to Mexico City labeled as "computer parts". The second would be coming with Colchev on a private jet supplied by a Russian oil tycoon. Compromising photos of the macho billionaire with some underage boys meant that Colchev could use the plane with no questions asked.

Before he let his men close up the second padded container they'd specially designed for the Killswitch, Colchev ran his fingers over the sleek copper casing. The weapon, four feet long and a foot in diameter, was tapered at both ends.

According to Kessler's report, the Killswitch was an advanced version of an explosively pumped coaxial flux compression generator. Science had never been a strength of Colchev's, so the description was gibberish to him. His understanding of its operation was that the plastic explosive inside the tube detonated the xenobium, causing the copper coils within to amplify the resulting gamma rays in a high-energy blast which would radiate out and interact with the Earth's magnetic field. The cascading effect of the magnetic flux would overload any electronic devices within its effective range.

At lower altitudes, the range was minimal, no more than a few dozen miles. But the effect was magnified at higher altitudes due to its closer proximity to the ionosphere. The higher Colchev could get it when it went off, the more damage it would cause.

Designed to account for the possibility that future sources might be discovered, the weapon allowed for any amount of xenobium up to five hundred grams to be inserted by unscrewing one end of the Killswitch. Sixteen metal teeth came together to clamp the material in place. The detonation was controlled with a digital display that had been fitted to the case. Once the security code was entered, the weapon was activated by setting the built-in timer.

Colchev shook his head in disgust. He had the weapon now, but Locke had destroyed his plans to get the xenobium. The purpose of the road-train bomb hadn't only been to cover the theft of the Killswitch. Although it would have taken investigators time to ascertain that the weapon wasn't in the wreckage, the theft would be revealed when the bodies of the security men and their truck were eventually found.

The true reason for the truck bomb had been to allow

Kessler to smuggle out the xenobium. In the confusion following the explosion, Kessler was to replace the xenobium sample with an identically sized hunk of regular hafnium, which wasn't radioactive or difficult to obtain. The two would be indistinguishable from each other except by testing for radiation emissions, and no one would think to do so for weeks. By that time Colchev's mission would have been over.

Now, with no distraction to cover his theft, he gave Kessler only a ten percent chance of successfully getting out of Pine Gap with the xenobium. Unless Colchev found more xenobium, the Killswitch would be worthless.

He stood and nodded for Zotkin to close the container. Nisselovich and Oborski carried it out to the car, leaving Colchev and Zotkin alone.

Zotkin frowned, reflecting Colchev's own concerns. "Do you think we should continue with the mission?"

Colchev couldn't give any indication that his confidence in the mission might be faltering. "Of course we continue. We'll never get another chance like this."

"But we cannot complete our plan without the xenobium. What if Kessler can't get it to us?"

"Then we find the other source."

"You think it really exists?"

"The evidence from Ivan Dombrovski's lab indicates there is more than enough for our purposes."

Zotkin scratched his head. "Why not just take the weapon back to Moscow?"

"Because we are all now enemies of the state. The deaths of Nadia and her team assured that. We are fully committed to this mission, Dmitri. If we don't succeed and show Moscow the true extent of our patriotism, there's no going back."

Zotkin hesitated, then nodded. "Of course you are right. How should we divide up?"

With four operatives lost in the last two days, Colchev was down to only eight men, including him and Zotkin. He thought for a moment about how to allocate his forces.

"Nisselovich and Oborski will take one weapon to Mexico as planned. Kiselow and Chopiak will accompany you and me to Rapa Nui. Buran and Vinski will stay in Sydney to see if Kessler made it. If he's not at the dead drop by noon, they should head to Mexico."

"Speaking of Mexico," Zotkin said, "Andrew Hull was the one who gave us that contact."

Colchev nodded. There was only one way Nadia Bedova could have tracked Colchev down as quickly as she did. He'd known Hull could be bought, but he hadn't counted on Bedova meeting the price.

"I can't have any more leaks," Colchev said. "The Americans will find Hull soon, so we'll have to pay a visit to our helpful arms dealer before we leave. You procured what I asked for?"

Zotkin nodded and went into the next room. He returned with a black case the size of a carry-on bag.

With reports of the truck-bomb explosion at Alice

Springs all over the news, surely Hull would realize he was now a marked man, but even someone with his vast security measures could be dealt with by using the correct approach.

And Colchev had the perfect method. He flicked open the clasps on the case and smiled as he inventoried the pieces of the disassembled sniper rifle. Even from a distance of five hundred yards, Buran would not miss.

TWENTY-NINE

B y the time the C-17 reached Easter Island, it was dusk. Despite Jess and Fay's eagerness to get started, Tyler convinced them that the trek to the location on the map would have to wait until morning.

He had spent most of his waking time on the flight planning the security arrangements with the NSA operatives and the pilots, who never questioned the diversion from their planned paratrooper training op in Japan. In between catnaps Fay and Jess researched Rapa Nui history using a dozen books and articles they'd downloaded during the stopover in Sydney.

On arrival they quickly determined that there was no way Colchev had beaten them to the island. The tarmac of diminutive Mataveri Airport, the most remote commercial airport in the world, was devoid of aircraft. There were only a few scheduled flights per day, most of them from Santiago and Lima. Colchev couldn't have made it all the way to South America and caught a flight to Easter Island in that time, and the airliner from Tahiti wasn't scheduled to arrive for two more days. The only other way to the island was by private jet, and according to ground control, none had landed in weeks.

Still, because they believed Colchev had heard Fay's Russian phrase, Tyler assumed he'd come to Easter Island eventually. Two of the NSA operatives would stay behind with the three C-17 crew members to keep an eye out for him while the other two would accompany Tyler, Jess, and Fay in their search of the island. Formed by an extinct volcano, Easter Island measured only fifteen miles across at its widest point, and the airport was not much more than a two-mile-long landing strip next to Hanga Roa, the town where virtually all of the five thousand inhabitants lived.

The Air Force and NSA men opted to stay with the plane for the night and take shifts sleeping on the crew bunks inside. When he was in his twenties, Tyler would have thought nothing of stretching out on the plane's spartan accommodations, but now that he was in his thirties, he'd gotten used to a bit more comfort. Besides, Fay and Jess wanted to stay at a hotel, so they found two rooms at the Tupa Hotel near the main street.

After settling in, Tyler suggested that the three of them get some dinner, but Fay, who had snacked on the plane, said she was too tired for dinner and retired early. That left Tyler and Jess to find a restaurant by themselves, alone together for the first time since New Zealand.

They chose a place called Au Bout du Monde that was popular with tourists who came to gawk at the island's incredible Moai statues. It was winter on the subtropical island, so half the tables were empty.

Tyler and Jess were seated on a second-story patio warmed by heat lamps to fend off the evening chill. The position gave them a dazzling view of the moonlit Pacific. The expansive sea suggested just how isolated they were on the tiny island. Beyond the distant horizon, the ocean was uninterrupted by land for another 1,200 miles.

As they waited for their green curry appetizers and pisco sours made with Rapa Nui's native grape hard alcohol and lemons, they quietly took in the scenery, avoiding eye contact as much as possible. Once the food and drinks arrived, Tyler filled the awkward silence by asking Jess about her research during the flight.

"Did you and Fay figure out exactly where the map is taking us tomorrow?"

"We think so," Jess said. "The map shows a jagged line going from the center of the island to the point on the coast where we're supposed to find whatever it is we're looking for. Comparing it to the satellite photo of Rapa Nui, we narrowed it down to a dry creek just south of the Ahu Maitake Te Moa."

"What are we looking for? One of Easter Island's famous statues?"

Tyler had seen photos of the stoic monoliths, some with the creepy white eyes still in place, but he didn't know much about them other than their general appearance and massive size, some of them weighing in at more than eighty tons.

"I doubt what we're looking for is one of the Moai," she said.

"Why not?"

"From what I read on the plane, it seems clear that all eight hundred and eighty-seven of them have been well studied and documented. They're either located on Ahu—those are the ceremonial stone platforms—or they are still lying in the quarries where they were carved."

"How do you think they're related to Roswell and Nazca?" he asked.

"I don't know the link to Roswell, but a connection to the Nazca is a possibility. Nana is a much better authority on Nazca than I ever will be, but my understanding is that there was an exodus from the Nazca plain of Peru sometime between AD 500 and 700. No one knows for sure why they left or where they went, but some anthropologists think South American migrants settled this region of Polynesia around that time. The Nazca people could have been among them. Thor Hyerdahl proved that it was possible by building a raft called *Kon-Tiki* using only materials that would have been available to people at that time. Now scientists mostly dismiss that notion, but nobody has proven it with certainty either way."

"Could the Moai have been created by the same people who drew the Nazca lines?"

"Supposedly the Moai came hundreds of years later, but who knows? Maybe the statues were created by their descendants. The height of their construction was in the

1600s until it came to an abrupt halt and the island's population crashed."

Tyler nodded. "I remember there was a book called *Collapse* a few years back. The theory was that the natives cut down all the trees on the island to transport the statues, and when that happened, they didn't have building materials for canoes or shelter anymore."

"Right. Jared Diamond popularized that theory."

"Theory? Looks like a slam dunk. I didn't see more than a couple of trees when we were coming in for a landing."

"They've replanted some trees in the center of the island, but it's still mostly barren grassland. They could have used trees to move the statues, but that's just one theory."

"Really? I thought it was pretty well established the islanders transported the Moai on rolling logs."

"There have been arguments about that for decades. Another theory is that they may have been moved by human sweat alone by dragging the statues with ropes made from the trees."

Tyler chuckled. "Come on. Dragging rocks weighing over a hundred thousand pounds?"

Jess smiled. "Which is why some of the more out-there ideas include alien intervention and tractor beams."

Tyler grinned at that. "There we go with the aliens again. Fay sure seems convinced that we're dealing with spacemen."

"She's got me doubting myself. What about you?"

"I'm a skeptic, but I'm also open-minded. However, I'd like some more evidence before I conclude that the Nazca lines and the Moai were created by beings from outer space."

"Right now, theories are all we have to go on. Another bizarre hypothesis for how the statues were moved comes from an old woman who told the first European explorers that the Moai walked to their current positions."

"Now you're just trying to make the aliens seem reasonable."

"No, really. A man named Pavel Pavel tied ropes to one of the smaller twelve-ton Moai and by rocking it back and forth, he and a crew of seventeen men were able to move it, covering ground at a rate of six hundred and fifty feet per day."

"Sounds possible if the base were shaped correctly and the statue had an optimal center of gravity—not so low that it would be hard to rock, but not so high that it would topple easily."

"The problem was that it chipped the base, and none of the Moai show that kind of damage."

Tyler scooped up the last of the curry. "The Moai were moved from quarries. Do you think the wood engraving is leading us to something like that?"

"It's possible, but Nana had an alternative theory. The map is steering us toward the northwestern edge of the island. Rapa Nui's ocean-side cliffs are riddled with caves that were painted by the natives. Her guess is that we'll find one at that location."

Tyler groaned. "More caves?"

"What's the matter?"

"I've just had a lot of experience with caves lately, none of it good."

"Suck it up. We'll get some ropes and flashlights in the morning in case Nana's right."

Their main course of Chilean sea bass arrived along with another round of drinks.

Tyler took a bite and then saw that Jess was only staring at her food.

"What's wrong?" he said.

"I was just thinking how odd it is to be here—on Easter Island of all places—having dinner with you like this after all these years." She picked up her fork and began eating. "It seems so normal."

"Especially after the last few days."

"Do you remember that time during that snowstorm right before Christmas when I dared you to run across the quad naked with me?"

Tyler laughed. He hadn't thought about that night in more than a decade. "I remember thinking that you were crazy."

"Why wouldn't you do it?"

He shrugged. "I was a ROTC cadet. I couldn't afford to get caught doing something like that."

"Are you still that uptight?"

"Uptight? Just because I wouldn't freeze my ass off running around campus in my skin?"

"Nobody would have seen us."

"I just didn't want to do it."

"That's what I mean. You were—are—charming, smart, competent, stable. You're also logical to a fault. You measure the pros and cons of everything you do. Every action is an equation with you. I just wanted you to be more impulsive sometimes. Like when you saved Fay in Queenstown."

"That wasn't impulsive. That was necessity. Two men were shooting at us."

"What about coming to Australia with us?"

Tyler focused on his food before looking at Jess again. "You and Fay needed help."

Jess smiled. "You always were a sucker for the damsel in distress." She picked at her food. "Nana told me the details about your wife's car accident. That must have been rough."

"Thanks. It's not something that's included in my Gordian Engineering website profile."

"Did you ever wade back into the dating pool?"

Just like the Jess he recalled. Never one to beat around the bush. Tyler downed the rest of his drink.

"Since Karen died I've met a couple women I got close to," he said, "but unfortunately we couldn't make it work. My job takes me all over the world. Makes it difficult to maintain a relationship."

"Is that on purpose?"

"A consequence."

"Huh."

"What does that mean?"

"You were so adamant about settling down right away,"

Jess said. "I just never figured you for the love-'em-and-leave-'em type."

"A lot's changed since college," Tyler said.

"I see that."

"But not with you."

"I tried marriage once. Not a good match."

"Was he too logical?"

"The opposite. He was a pretty surfer boy. Mooched off me for two years before I called it quits."

"And now?"

She shrugged. "I used one of those online matchmaking services, but after the fourth drooling weirdo showed up to meet me at some coffee house, I gave up trying to find a soul mate. Now I just use it for sex."

Tyler gaped at her, dumbfounded, until she let out a huge belly laugh.

"Kidding! Boy, maybe you really haven't changed."

Tyler shook his head and smiled. Then he ordered another drink.

They lost track of time and didn't stumble out of the restaurant until eleven p.m. Reminiscing about college days had resulted in lots of laughs and an extended period at the bar.

Tyler had realized too late that his five drinks were more pisco than sour. He downed a couple of waters before they left, but the walk back to the hotel only accelerated the absorption of alcohol into his system.

Not that Jess was any better. She'd had the same

number of cocktails that he did and weighed about half as much. They leaned on each other as they veered down the hall toward their rooms.

Jess stumbled and Tyler barely caught her, causing them both to stifle guffaws.

"This is what I should've done," she said.

"What? Gotten me drunk? I still wouldn't have run around naked in the quad."

"How about now?"

"No way."

"You're no fun."

They reached their doors, which were right across from each other—Fay and Jess's room on one side and Tyler's on the other.

Jess patted her pockets, then said, "Dammit."

"What?"

"I left my key in the room."

Tyler's head cleared for a moment. He didn't think Jess would try such a transparent ploy. "You did not."

"If you don't believe me, search my pockets."

"I believe you." He raised his fist, but Jess grabbed it before he could knock on the door.

"If Nana's sleeping, I don't want to wake her."

In some distant part of Tyler's brain, a little voice screamed that what he was about to say was a terrible idea, but his alcohol-lubricated id put the cautionary alarm on mute.

"Sleep on my bed," he said with more confidence than he felt. "I'll take the couch."

Jess went motionless. "I . . . I can't."

He took out his key and raised one hand like he was swearing on oath of office. "I promise I'll be a gentleman."

She grinned. "Impulsive."

"Practical."

"Right." Jess took a long look at him, but her eyes eventually flicked back the way they'd come. "I think I'll go get another key from the front desk."

Tyler nodded and tried to laugh his way out of the situation. "That would also work."

Jess gave him a hug. "I had a great time tonight."

"Me too."

She let him go and headed to the lobby. Tyler waited until she was out of sight. She never once looked back.

Tyler opened his door and went inside, where he planned to bang his head against the wall until his id was in a coma.

THIRTY

With Easter Island sixteen hours behind Sydney, Grant thought Tyler was probably asleep by now. Too bad he was missing the view.

The steel arch of Sydney Harbour Bridge, its spine dotted with tourists partaking in the BridgeClimb experience, provided the backdrop for the three-way intersection below. The sunny afternoon meant that the street was crowded with strolling pedestrians who'd wandered away from the nearby waterfront attractions in search of food or window shopping along the tree-lined streets. Well-maintained brick buildings, common to The Rocks, as the area was known, provided a quaint respite from the bustling business district only a few blocks away.

Grant didn't need binoculars to see the planter at the corner of Hickson and George where Kessler was supposed to drop off the xenobium, but he used them anyway. Morgan, lithe in a sports bra and Lycra leggings and pretending to be out for an afternoon jog, stretched her legs on the planter, surreptitiously depositing a fist-sized metal container into the box of geraniums.

When she peeled out of her stretch, she threw a pointed glance at the window before she trotted away. Morgan knew Grant was watching her through the blinds and wanted him to know it.

Eh. He didn't care that she knew he was staring. Grant had been sitting in the third-floor apartment for six hours now. He didn't mind Morgan's fine form spicing up the day, even if she had been nothing but a pain the entire time.

She'd picked a room at the Holiday Inn high enough to give them a good view of the area, but low enough that it wouldn't take them long to reach ground level if they spotted the target. Their luggage lay on the beds and Chinese takeout containers littered the small kitchen nook.

Two tactical squads of the Australian national police waited in vans around the corner, ready to move in if Grant recognized one of the targets.

But they'd decided they needed bait. The scientists at Pine Gap rigged up a small device that would emit just enough radiation to set off a detector. Now all they had to do was wait until midnight to see if their trap would snare any varmints.

Five minutes later, a key rattled in the door and Morgan walked in.

"Have a good run?" Grant said cheerfully.

"Did you get a good look while I was down there?" she said with a deadpan expression.

"Of you? Bird's-eye view."

"You're not around women much, are you?"

"Are you kidding? I grew up with four older sisters. There were nothing *but* women in my house. That's why I appreciate them so much." He waggled his eyebrows at Morgan, then smiled and turned back to the window.

As she rummaged in her bag for a change of clothes, Morgan said, "If you're trying to bother me, it won't work. After spending time in a squadron with fifteen guys, this is a breeze."

"You were a pilot?"

She sighed, as if she were sorry she'd brought it up. "F-16."

Fighter jockey. Grant was impressed. "Then what are you doing in the OSI? You get drummed out of the service?"

"I still hold a rank of captain in the reserves, Sergeant."

"I'm not in the reserves, so you can just call me Grant. Although I like the way you say 'sergeant'. Very authoritative."

She ignored him and took her clothes into the bathroom. When she came out, she was dressed in her suit again. Disappointing.

She picked up the second pair of binoculars and peered at the street.

After a few minutes of silence, Grant sat back in his chair, thinking to himself how boring stakeouts were. Well, that was easily rectified.

"So what happened?" he asked Morgan. "Did you sleep with a colonel and his wife found out and they bumped you down to investigator?"

"None of your business."

"Come on, Morgan. Lighten up. We're going to be here for a long time. And don't forget I saved your life yesterday. Might as well tell me your story."

Another sigh. "If I tell you, will you shut up?"

"Absolutely."

"Fine. It happened when I was stationed in South Carolina at Shaw. I had an old Corvette—"

"Sexy."

"Do you want to hear the story?"

"Sorry. Continue."

"It was late one night. I was on my way back from leave at my grandparents' house in Atlanta when a deer jumped onto the road. I missed it but lost control and spun off the road into a tree. They tell me I hit my head on the steering wheel and blacked out. Because it was down in a ravine, I was unconscious for an hour before someone spotted the skid marks and found me."

"You look fine to me. And I mean that in the health sense."

"I was in the hospital for a couple of days with two broken ribs and a concussion."

"Then what happened?"

"I was cleared to fly the next month, but when I was up in the air and performed some routine maneuvers, I got severely dizzy. I tried to shake it off, but on landing I nearly ran off the runway. When I got out of the plane, I tossed my cookies all over the tarmac."

"Because of your head trauma?"

Morgan nodded but didn't look at him. "A rare form of benign paroxysmal positional vertigo. In my case it only shows up under high-g maneuvers. The doctors tried everything, but they couldn't find the source. MRIs. Exploratory surgery. Even did tests inside a centrifuge at Brooks. Nothing worked. After a year of not flying, my career was stalled, so I asked for a discharge. Since I majored in criminology in college, I applied to the OSI. Been there five years now. Now you know the story."

"I'm sorry to hear about your flying status. I just dabble. Got my helo license a few years back. But Tyler's logged a couple thousand hours in jets. I know he'd be crushed if he could never fly again."

"There's nothing I can do about it, so there's no sense dwelling on it."

Morgan went to her bag and pulled out two pairs of night-vision goggles. She handed a set to Grant. He recognized them as thermal imagers, but they seemed to have been modified.

"You really think we'll need those with all the streetlights?"

From her coat she removed a vial of what looked like gray dust. She took off the cap and dipped the tip of her pinkie into it.

She nodded to his goggles. "Take a look."

Grant donned them and flipped the switch. Most of the room was a cold green, and Morgan glowed yellow. The end of her pinkie, though, was covered with bright red crosshairs.

"What's going on here? I thought I knew all the latest toys." He reached out to touch her finger. He just barely brushed against it, and when he withdrew his index finger, it too had red crosshairs on it.

"This technology is still classified top secret, so you can't discuss it with anyone else."

He removed the goggles and looked at his finger. The dust was now invisible.

"Is this ID dust?" He'd heard about it, but he thought it was still in the testing phase.

"Yes. Because we suspected a leak, we didn't tell the team that we coated the inside of the Killswitch containers with tracking dust. Pine Gap internal sensors are configured to identify the RF signature of the dust. We were planning to see if any unauthorized personnel were accessing the containers. Anyone handling the open container would have been tagged with the ID dust."

"So why didn't you track it?"

"The range is limited. No more than a few hundred yards. These goggles are tuned to sense it. If someone walking by down there has it on his hands, we'll see it."

"What if they wash their hands?"

"The nanoparticles are so small that they embed themselves in skin and clothes. It would be like trying to wash off the markings of a Sharpie. Because it transmits a radio-frequency ID, the signal is even visible through walls and thin metal casings."

Grant wiped his finger on his clothes, but all it did was transfer a few of the particles. "Is it safe?"

"It's not FDA approved, if that's what you're worried about."

"I'm not worried." But he couldn't shake the sensation that the motes were pricking his finger.

"Just keep an eye on the street. Our target may not have handled the Killswitch crate, so we need you to identify anyone who might be one of Colchev's operatives."

"Got it."

He took off the goggles and scanned the street with the binoculars.

After five minutes, he said, "You ever shoot anybody down?"

"I thought you were going to shut up."

"I did. You are going to find out that five minutes of shut-up is a long time for me."

Morgan ignored him, but he smiled when he heard the faintest sigh.

THIRTY-ONE

With a warm mug in her hand and the thick bathrobe wrapped around her, Jess sat on the balcony and watched the reflection of the dawning sun glitter on the Pacific. She sipped the coffee, and the caffeine jolt soothed her throbbing head.

The sliding glass door opened and Fay stepped to the railing, stretching her arms.

"What a beautiful sight. You were tossing and turning all night. Did you get any sleep?"

Jess stifled a yawn. "Some. How are you feeling?"

"Oh, nothing a few antacids couldn't fix." Fay sat in the other lounge chair. She stared at the sea for a minute before continuing tentatively. "Tyler's the one that got away, isn't he?"

Jess nodded. "I nearly didn't come back to the room last night."

"He's interested in you. The eyes don't lie."

"A lack of passion was never our problem."

"Then what was?" Fay swiveled in her chair. "Did he cheat on you in college?"

"Tyler? God, no. He'd be the last guy to do that."

"Then what?"

"I was young. New to college. He wanted a commitment. I wanted to have fun. Maybe it was just bad timing." Jess shook her head. "Tyler's a good man. He deserves the truth about my situation, about Andy."

"You'll know when the time is right to tell him, dear. Just follow your heart."

"My heart is saying I made a big mistake all those years ago. I know they say you shouldn't go through life with regrets, but sometimes it's hard not to."

"The people who say that are sociopaths," Fay said.

That surprised Jess. "You have regrets?"

"Too many to count."

"Like what?"

"Smoking, for one. But we didn't know any better." Fay held out her hand, and Jess took it in her own. "Regrets will always be a part of you, Jessica. The mistake you shouldn't make is letting those regrets keep you from enjoying the rest of your life."

"I won't."

Fay smiled. "Me neither."

Jess stood. "We've got a lot to do today. I'm going to take a shower."

Thirty minutes later came a knock on the door. Jess watched as Fay answered and let Tyler in. His eyes were bloodshot and he hadn't bothered to shave, but his windbreaker, T-shirt, and jeans didn't look too rumpled.

He nodded at Jess, but spoke to both of them. "The NSA guys found a Suzuki four-by-four that'll fit all of us. They'll be here in a few minutes. We'll stop for supplies at the hardware store. I'd wear a jacket. It'll be cool out there."

Fay excused herself to change in the suite's bedroom. The silence grew thick.

"Tyler, I'm sorry about last night."

"No need to be. I must have gotten the signals wrong."

"No. You didn't. You know you didn't."

"I know," he said. "I was just trying to make this a little less awkward."

"I shouldn't have broken up with you."

"Well, now you're making it more awkward. Besides, I broke up with you. Not to get into a pissing match about it."

"Yes, but you wouldn't have broken up with me if I could have committed to you back then. I was stupid."

"So we both agree on that," Tyler said with a twinkle in his eye.

Jess couldn't help but smile. "You're not making this any easier. I wanted to tell you—"

Tyler's phone rang and he put up a finger. He looked at the display, then answered. "Hello ... all right, we'll be down in a minute," he said and hung up.

As he pocketed the phone, Fay came back in. "Are they here?"

Jess sighed, realizing that she'd missed her opportunity. Turning to Fay, she asked, "Are you ready to do this?"

Fay beamed. "I've been ready since I was ten years old."

The store had the caving equipment they needed: four flashlights, a couple of shovels, and a hundred meters of nylon rope. Jess was an experienced spelunker, so the idea of delving into a dark, creepy hole didn't bother her in the slightest.

Tyler drove the Suzuki. Fay was in the passenger seat, and in the back Jess squeezed between two wiry security men, a blond kid in his twenties named Harris and a curly-haired guy called Polk who smelled like a locker room. Both were armed with silenced submachine guns. She thought the extra men were an unnecessary precaution, but Tyler had insisted.

It took only fifteen minutes to reach their destination four miles to the north. Once they left the paved road, the Suzuki bounced over the rough grassland toward the sea while Jess navigated. With the dry creek bed to their right, Tyler inched along to make sure they didn't bog down in any unseen gullies.

Fifty yards from the cliff leading down to the Pacific, Tyler came to a stop, and they all climbed out. Far from any of the tourist spots, the area was deserted. Jess checked her cell phone and saw that it wasn't getting a signal.

"Now what?" Tyler said.

"The map seems to indicate that whatever we're looking for should be on the very edge of the island," Fay said.

"There's probably a marker of some kind, possibly carved into a stone."

"Let's fan out. If you see anything unusual, give a shout."

"Unusual like what?" Polk said.

"The Rapa Nui people were known for cave paintings and rock art," Fay said. "Something like that might be what we're looking for."

Tyler devised a grid pattern for the search. They would space apart at five-yard intervals and walk parallel paths to make sure they didn't miss anything, starting a hundred yards south of where the creek mouth met the cliff.

Jess chose the spot closest to the cliff face with Fay next to her. They methodically walked the route. Every few minutes someone would stop to check out something more closely, but it always turned out to be nothing.

The group slowed as they reached the dry creek bed's mouth since that seemed to be the location of the dot on the map. They spent a half-hour meticulously combing the grass before Jess's foot scraped across an abrasive flat surface. If she hadn't been walking so deliberately, she would never have noticed the red stone almost completely buried in the soil. The eighteen-inch-wide slab looked nothing like the brown dirt surrounding it. She recognized it as scoria, the pumice-like rock that was used as a material for the gigantic hats adorning some of the Moai.

Jess called out, and everyone came running over to her find. Centuries of growth and accumulated earth had nearly covered the stone.

Tyler took one look at it and said, "That had to be placed there on purpose."

Jess knelt and pulled the grass away. "Help me dig it out."

Tyler went to the car to retrieve the shovels. After ten minutes of digging, they were able to see the carvings that adorned the sides of the circular slab.

A spider, a bird, a monkey, and a human figure. They were identical to the drawings on the engraving.

"Oh, my God," Fay said, her hands trembling. "This is it!"

"Is that what the map was leading us to?" Jess said. "It doesn't have any other drawings on it."

"It must be a marker for something nearby."

They fanned out to look again. Jess remembered her conversation with Tyler about the sea-side caves and walked to the part of the cliff closest to them, which was obscured by some low shrubbery. She pushed it aside and peered over the edge, where she saw a path carved into the cliff-side that was wide enough to accommodate an elephant. Without the marker, finding the path would have been pure chance in spite of its width.

"Hey!" she yelled. "Take a look at this."

Everyone joined her at the edge.

Jess turned to Tyler. "Shall we see where this goes?"

"All right," Tyler said. "Let's get the rope and flashlights." The three men returned to the vehicle.

"Nana, you should stay here."

Fay looked at her as if she were insane. "That would be a big no."

"We don't know how safe that path is."

"If you think I'm staying behind while you get to make the discovery of a lifetime, you don't know your grand-mother very well."

"Then just let us scout it out first."

"Absolutely not." When Jess began to object again, Fay said, "Unless you plan to tie me up and lock me in the car, I'm going."

Jess shook her head in defeat. "Okay. But I want you right behind me."

"That's my girl."

Tyler and Polk returned with the equipment.

"I asked Harris to stay with the car in case anyone comes nosing around," Tyler said, and led the way down the path, followed by Jess and Fay, with Polk bringing up the rear.

Once they were on the path, Jess could see that crude handholds had been notched in the cliff, making the descent relatively easy.

After two switchbacks, Tyler disappeared around an out-cropping. When Jess came around it, she saw Tyler standing on a ledge large enough to fit three SUVs.

"Looks like this is the end of the line," he said. "Other than the path back up, there's no way off."

While Jess guided Fay onto the ledge, Tyler inspected the cliff face, but there didn't appear to be any passages leading into a cave.

He knelt in front of a large boulder that was lodged against the cliff face, running his fingers along its base.

"Jess, look at this."

She bent over and focused a flashlight where he was pointing. The bottom of the boulder was scored with small divots chipped out of the stone.

Tyler looked at her. "Didn't you say last night that one theory for how the natives moved the Moai was that they rocked the stones back and forth using ropes?"

"Right, but they stopped because they were chipping—" It suddenly dawned on Jess what Tyler was getting at.

"If they wanted to hide this cave entrance from someone paddling along the coast," Tyler said, "they would block it with one of their stones. I think we're going to need more muscle here. We'll have to chance leaving the car alone for a little while."

Polk called on his walkie-talkie for Harris to join them.

"You really think this is the way in?" Fay said.

"Only one way to find out." Tyler began rigging two ropes around the top of the boulder, one to be pulled in each direction.

"How much do you think this weighs?" Jess said.

"Oh, probably a few tons. But if they were as good at this as you said they were, I'm guessing they made the boulder maneuverable."

When Harris arrived, Tyler gave him and Polk one rope while he and Jess took the other. Then he explained the procedure that he thought would work best. By alternating pulls, they started a rocking motion in the stone, and while it was tipped in one direction, the two people on the other side would move out and tug it in the opposite direction.

Tyler was right. The stone was perfectly weighted. Even with only him and Jess pulling, they were able to budge the rock so that it tilted a fraction in their direction. As they let it return to center, Harris and Polk pulled, causing it to tilt farther in the other direction.

After eight more pulls, they had enough momentum to start walking it out. It only moved an inch at a time, but that was all they needed. In ten minutes Jess could see a space big enough for a person to slip through and darkness beyond.

"All right," Tyler yelled. "I think we got it."

They let the boulder wobble to a standstill and caught their breath. Tyler sent Harris back to the car. Jess agreed that the last thing they needed was a passing tourist following their path down to the ledge.

Tyler pointed his light at the side of the boulder that had been hidden until now. "I'd say we've found who's been keeping an eye on the place."

They crowded around and saw what he meant. The side that had been against the cavern opening had the prominent brow and wide nose of the Moai they'd passed on the way here.

"Imagine," Fay said with reverence. "No one has seen this in over thirteen hundred years."

"I can't believe you were able to do this," Jess said. "We never would have figured out how to get in there."

Tyler shrugged at her. "I guess MIT wasn't a total loss. Let's take a look, shall we?"

Before Jess could respond, he was swallowed by the cave.

THIRTY-TWO

With midnight come and gone, Morgan still kept an eye on the intersection below, though she didn't think there was much point. She had reviewed the dossier the CIA had on Vladimir Colchev. Given his history and how well he'd planned the attack on Pine Gap, she thought it was very possible he had another mole in the Killswitch project besides Kessler. If that were the case, he would know the theft attempt had failed, and Colchev and his men would be long gone from Sydney.

"They're not coming," Grant said.

"They could be giving Kessler some extra time to make it."

"Not likely. I think it's safe for me to take a leak." He headed to the bathroom.

As the fan came on, Morgan's cell rang. She frowned when she saw it was Vince.

"You're supposed to be sleeping," she said.

"The doohickey they have me hooked up to is beeping every five seconds, so I can't sleep. The morphine's great, though."

"What did the doctor say?"

"She said I won't be playing rugby any time soon."

"How long until you're back?"

"They'll let me check out in a few days and fly back to the US. I'll be a desk jockey for the six weeks I'm on crutches. Have you made contact yet?"

"The targets haven't shown up. We'll give it another hour, but they probably won't take the bait."

"Sorry I can't be there."

"Yeah, thanks for sticking me with Westfield for the duration."

"Is he there?"

"In the john."

"I thought you two got along really well."

Morgan snorted in response. "It's been a joy."

"No sparkling conversation?"

"It's actually not that bad. I'm getting used to him."

"Wait a minute. Are you sweet on him?"

Morgan felt herself blush. "Don't be ridiculous. Army grunts aren't my type."

"He didn't seem dimwitted to me, especially for a former pro wrestler."

The toilet flushed and Grant came out of the bathroom. Morgan looked at him with a raised eyebrow.

"Oh, he's not stupid," she said. "Just annoying."

Grant nodded happily and took his seat.

"Whoa," Vince said with a moan.

"You okay?"

"Now all of a sudden I'm tired. Keep me posted. And stay safe."

"Will do. I'll see you back in the States."

She hung up.

"Who was that? Your boyfriend?"

"My partner."

"How is he?"

"Fine."

"That the official prognosis?"

Morgan smirked. Annoying.

"So what's the plan now?" he said.

"We wait here another hour."

"Then when they still don't show up?"

"Then we find out what the link to the Baja drug cartel is."

"It sounds like Andrew Hull won't be any help."

Morgan couldn't argue with that. The arms dealer had been shot by a sniper in front of his office building this morning. It wasn't until the afternoon when the police were searching his files and found the reference to a truckload of "gravel" going to Alice Springs that they made the connection to the Pine Gap explosion. Colchev must have offed Hull to cover his tracks.

The problem for her was that it worked. Unless their liaison at the Drug Enforcement Agency could find a lead, they were at a dead end.

"You really think Colchev wants to smuggle a Killswitch back into the US?" Grant said.

"That's the only reason I can come up with for why he would want to seek out a drug gang. They're the best smugglers out there. It'd be much easier to fly it into Mexico and drive it across the border than land in the US and try to get it through customs."

"Seems like a lot of effort when the weapon was already in America a couple of days ago."

"Until it got to Australia, the Killswitch was on an Air Force base the entire time. Trying to steal it there would have been suicidal. And they needed the xenobium from Pine Gap to make it operational."

"Well, we know they ain't suicidal," Grant said. "That's why they needed the robotic truck. None of his men were fanatical enough to blow themselves up."

Either that or they were saving themselves for a suicide attack on American soil. But where?

"You're an expert on explosives and electronics," Morgan said. "What would be the likeliest target?"

Grant considered that for a moment. She was impressed that he didn't just blurt out an answer.

"I've been wondering about that. Nadia Bedova mentioned Wisconsin Avenue. How many are there in the US?"

Morgan brought up the data on her cell phone. "Ten. Six in Wisconsin, two in Illinois, one in Iowa, and one in DC."

"I don't think this guy wants to take out corn farmers, so I'm betting DC is the target."

"It could also be Chicago. One of the Illinois locations is in a suburb."

"We know that if Colchev gets a large enough sample of xenobium, it could take out the entire city's grid. I'd still say Washington, unless Air Force One is visiting Chicago any time soon."

Morgan nodded. "We'll check on that. But if a terror attack is his plan, then taking out either Washington or Chicago would meet that goal."

Grant rubbed his head. "That's the part about Wisconsin Avenue that I don't get."

"Why?"

"Well, we know the Killswitch's effective range goes up the higher it is when it detonates. So why set it off at ground level? I spoke to Collins before we left Pine Gap just to get a sense for what this thing could do. If Colchev had the same amount of xenobium that was at Pine Gap, he could have flown the Killswitch to thirty-five thousand feet and taken out a huge swath of territory."

"How huge?"

"In the right location it could take out everything from Washington to New York."

Morgan went silent for a moment as she realized the enormity of the situation.

Grant put on his night-vision goggles and swept the street.

"Colchev could be selling it on the black market to a terrorist network. Maybe the buy is going to happen somewhere on Wisconsin Avenue in DC."

She shook her head. "If he were in this for the money, he could have found a hundred easier ways to make it."

"And why specifically on July twenty-fifth? Why is the date so important to Colchev? Is that when he's planning to set off a Killswitch or is that when he's going to acquire another component he needs for his scheme?"

"I don't know. There's something we're missing."

"Then we need to find out what it is. Let's hope I'm wrong about his men not showing up." After two more sweeps, Grant said, "I wonder if we have any kung pao chicken left."

Without taking the goggles off, he stood and turned, then abruptly halted. He cocked his head up, slowly moving it down as if he were watching something drip from the ceiling.

"What are you doing?" Morgan asked.

"You need to put your goggles on."

For a second she thought he was joking, but she realized his voice was deadly serious for the first time today.

She whipped the goggles off her lap and fitted them over her eyes. When she saw why Grant had told her to put them on, she whispered, "Damn it."

She could see red ID dust crosshairs descending, superimposed over the bedroom wall like ghostly apparitions.

Right where the hotel's elevator shaft was located.

She could have kicked herself for making such a bone-headed oversight.

Morgan's targets had been watching for Kessler from the hotel the entire time, several stories directly above her. And because the scientist hadn't shown up, her only links to the Killswitch were about to get away.

THIRTY-THREE

T he light piercing the narrow crack they'd opened in front of the cave entrance did little to penetrate the gloom. Except for the thin beam of his flashlight reflecting off the basalt walls of the lava tube, Tyler could see nothing.

Although the Moai protecting the cave had done an admirable job of concealing the entrance, apparently the seal had not been tight enough to prevent moisture from entering. The cave surface felt damp to Tyler's touch, and the air reeked of fungal decay. If mold had grown unchecked in here, whatever they were meant to find might have been destroyed centuries ago.

Jess guided Fay into the tight confines of the cave. Tyler instructed Polk to guard the entrance outside, but it was as much to keep him from seeing the results of their search as it was for protection. Not that he didn't trust the guy. After all, Polk was the one with the gun. But Tyler saw the wisdom in following Morgan's need-to-know rationale.

"Be careful," Tyler said, his voice reverberating into the distance. "The floor's slippery."

"You watch your head," Jess said. "Without hard hats, you could get a nasty bump."

"It sounds like you have some caving experience."

"Nana introduced me to it in New Zealand."

Fay took a deep breath. "Do you smell that? It's the aroma of history."

She removed a state-of-the-art video camera from her knapsack and turned on its powerful floodlight. It provided as much illumination as the two flashlights put together.

When she saw Tyler's appreciative look, she said, "I use this to record all my trips."

"*Paratus et validus*," Tyler said.

"What does that mean?"

"Ready and able. It was my Army unit's motto." He showed Fay the Gordian camera he'd had delivered to the C-17 during the Sydney stopover. The equipment was only slightly more advanced than hers. "You would have fit in well. Especially with the way you handled that shotgun."

Fay grinned. "Flatterer. Come on. I want to see what's in here."

She led the way into the darkness. No fear at all. Tyler was even more impressed.

Ten yards in, the path turned, and the echo effect increased. Tyler was shocked that he could now see light coming from the far end of the tunnel.

He exchanged glances with Jess. She was as surprised as he was. They continued on until they emerged into a massive chamber, its thirty-foot-high ceiling domed like a planetarium. Sunlight streamed through a one-foot-diameter hole in the ceiling, providing a weak supplement to the illumination cast by their flashlights. The tall grass must have hidden the hole from view when they were topside.

They all stopped, slack-jawed, as they laid eyes on what the Rapa Nui people had been hiding for more than a thousand years.

The ceiling was covered with images that were exact copies of the Nazca lines. Tyler took out his smart phone and brought up the map of the lines that he'd stored on it. Not only were the symbols identical to the geoglyphs on the Peruvian plain, but they were arranged in exactly the same locations and orientations. Each of the symbols was stippled with dots that didn't appear on the Nazca plain. Straight lines connecting the symbols matched straight lines in Peru, but there were far fewer of them on the ceiling.

"My God," Fay whispered as she focused the camera on the drawings.

"This is spectacular," Jess said.

Tyler made his own recording as he gawked.

Jess took his phone and looked back and forth between it and the ceiling. "Some of them are missing."

"What?"

"The ceiling isn't a complete representation of the drawings in Peru. See? The whale is missing. And these two that look like flower pots aren't here either."

Fay and Tyler crowded around the phone and saw that she was right.

"What do you make of that, Fay?" Tyler said. After all, she was the expert here.

"Based on how the drawings were made and arranged, archeologist theorize that some of them came much later. Perhaps hundreds of years."

"Which ones are here?"

Jess counted them off. "The monkey, condor, dog, hummingbird, pelican, spider, lizard, parrot, tree, flower, iguana, and human."

Tyler watched her as she tapped her fingers for each one. Twelve in all. Then he realized the significance of the dots.

"Twelve drawings," he said. "That can't be a coincidence."

Jess immediately got it. "One drawing for each lunar cycle in a year."

Fay gaped at the ceiling. "Then the dots are—"

Jess nodded. "Stars. These are constellations. How come no one has ever figured that out before?"

"With all of the extraneous drawings added to the Nazca plain over the years since the original twelve were drawn, it was impossible to know that they represented constellations."

"If those dots correspond to visible stars," Jess said, "we should be able to figure out which parts of the sky they appear in."

"What's that?" Tyler asked, pointing at an image located away from the others and connected to the monkey drawing by a single line. Instead of a crude animal symbol, this image was a complex geometric pattern. A circle encompassed two perpendicular overlapping rectangles with a bright white starburst in the center. Girding the circle were two squares offset like the triangles in a Star of David.

Fay got closer. "That's the Mandala. The drawing is on a high plateau north of the Nazca plain. No one knows what it means."

Tyler made sure to get a good shot of each symbol, then photographed the path of each line connecting them. When he was done, he looked around to see if there were any other exits from the chamber.

That's when he noticed the other drawings. He'd been so focused on craning his neck at the ceiling that he hadn't seen the wealth of stone carvings decorating the walls.

"Guys," he said, "take a look at these."

The intricate artwork encircled the entire chamber. Primitive paint filled the grooves so that the lines glowed white under the beams of their flashlights. Rather than drawings of animals, each etching seemed to illustrate a scene. Tyler started taking pictures beginning with the first one to his left.

The first image showed a streak coming down from the sky, trailing fire in its wake. In the next drawing was a starburst matching the one inside the Mandala figure. Above the starburst rose the unmistakable profile of a mushroom cloud.

Whoever drew this had either witnessed a gigantic explosion or had been told what one looked like. The same as at

Tunguska. And as with the event in Western Australia, there would have been no downed trees to record the blast in the arid Peruvian plateau.

"This tells a story," Jess said.

Fay nodded. "The migrants from Nazca must have recorded their history in this cave so it wouldn't be forgotten."

"It's funny that no one has ever found a drawing like this before," Tyler said.

"Not at all," Fay said. "Remember that for five thousand years no one could translate hieroglyphics. Then the Rosetta stone was discovered and revolutionized our understanding of the Egyptian language. A single artifact changed everything. This cave could be a pre-Columbian Rosetta stone for the Nazca culture."

"Why haven't they found drawings like this in Peru?"

"They might yet. An ancient city called Cahuachi lay hidden south of the Nazca plain until it was discovered in the 1950s. Only when further excavations started in the 1980s did archeologist realize it was a ceremonial pilgrimage site for the Nazca people."

"Would it be possible for something like this to be hidden there?"

"Of course. The site is huge. One and a half square kilometers. The largest pyramid is thirty meters high, a stepped structure built of adobe bricks. Somewhere in the complex, there might be an exact duplicate of this story, originally protected by the religious order that lived there and now buried in the city."

They continued on with the story, with Fay interpreting the scenes.

"Here we see someone discovering a circular object in the aftermath of the explosion. They carry it back to their people as a treasure. Oh, my goodness. Are those dead bodies?"

The next drawing showed a landscape scattered with what appeared to be corpses. The circle seemed to be sending out beams to each of them, striking them down.

"Whatever they found must have been deadly," Tyler said. If the culprit was a large chunk of xenobium, the intense gamma rays emitted from it would cause anyone in close contact to become sick within days from radiation poisoning.

Fay lowered her camera and squinted at the next drawing for several minutes. Kneeling human figures sat before what appeared to be an altar with the circular object resting upon it. "Here it looks as if they're offering the object as some kind of sacrifice. Perhaps they hoped the gods would come to retrieve it and relieve them of their burden."

"They could have just thrown it away," Jess said.

"They wouldn't if they considered it the property of the gods. They would want to safeguard it in case the gods ever returned to claim it. I think that's what the next etching describes."

The next image showed the object being encased inside a pyramid. A line led straight from the top of the pyramid up to the ceiling where it intersected with the human figure.

Fay looked up at the ceiling. "They're recording the event that led to the drawing of the Nazca lines."

Jess followed her gaze. "My God, it's a code."

"A code?" Tyler said.

"They wanted the gods to come and get their treasure back, but since the Nazca took it from its original location—the Mandala—they thought they needed to provide instructions to the gods about where it was hidden."

"And what better code for the gods to follow than the constellations," Fay said.

Now Tyler understood why the Nazca lines had to be so large. They were a message to the heavens, and the Nazca people made sure no person on Earth at the time would have been able to decipher the code.

THIRTY-FOUR

They should have had Colchev's men cornered, but an errant tire squeal blew an easy outcome.

As soon as Grant had shown Morgan the red crosshairs descending toward the first floor, he bolted out of the room with her close on her heels, shouting instructions to the Australian police into her phone.

They charged down the stairs expecting to intercept their targets in the lobby, but as they eased open the door to the lobby, a tire screeched outside just as the elevator opened. The pair of tactical team vans skidded to a halt in front of the main entrance and black-clad policemen poured out.

Then all hell broke loose.

Grant saw two men who he recognized from the Alice Springs warehouse dressed in light jackets and khakis. Both of them pulled semiautomatics and sprayed the lobby with rounds. Grant, armed with a SIG Sauer .40 caliber pistol on loan from the NSA, took aim at the men, but the screaming guests and hotel staff running for cover blocked his sightline. The tactical teams must have realized they could easily hit innocent bystanders and didn't return fire either.

The gunmen ran; Grant and Morgan gave chase. She yelled for someone to intercept them at the rear entrance of the hotel, but it was far too late. Colchev's men were already out the back exit.

Grant approached the glass door cautiously, sidling up next to it with his back to the concrete wall. He poked his head out to see through the door and was met with a hail of gunfire that shattered the glass.

He dropped to his knee and took five quick shots through the broken glass. The men ducked around the corner of a building, and Grant's rounds pinged off the brick.

"Watch where you're shooting!" Morgan shouted. "We need them alive."

"They started it!" Grant had been a soldier. Trained to kill, not to maim, not to read someone their rights.

He and Morgan burst through the gaping doorway and sprinted after the gunmen, who were fifty yards ahead. Morgan called into her phone. "They're heading down a diagonal street. Somebody cut them off before they head under the bridge."

The steel span of the Harbour Bridge began just a hundred yards ahead. If the gunmen got out of sight, they could easily disappear in the wharfs on the other side. They must have had a car parked around somewhere, but the hotel's offsite lot was in the opposite direction.

A police car came to a stop and blocked off the road ahead. The tac teams were busy setting up a perimeter in a ten-block radius around the hotel. Grant thought the

Russians were cut off until he saw them shoot at a locked door and duck through.

"Where'd they go?" Morgan said.

"I don't know." It looked like it was in the foundation of the bridge. But as they got closer, Grant saw the sign next to the door.

BridgeClimb. The tourist entrance for the guided walk up the spine of the bridge.

The gunmen would be taking the bridge over the roadblocks set up on the streets underneath it. If they got onto the bridge's vehicle deck, they could carjack someone and get away into the northern suburbs.

Grant and Morgan reached the door and stopped.

"You want to wait for the tac team?" Grant said.

"No," Morgan said. "I'm not letting these bastards get away. You stay here."

Grant shook his head. No way was she going by herself. "If you go, I go."

She didn't hesitate. "All right. You pull the door open. One. Two. Three."

Grant yanked it wide, and Morgan went in crouched, ready to take the shot if she had to.

"They're on the catwalk." She darted through the door and up the iron stairs. Although he was fast for his size, Grant had to dig deep to keep up with her.

Once they were up to the catwalk level that ran the length of the span underneath the bridge, Grant could make out the shadows of two men pounding across the steel grating. They were too distant to take clear shots, but that didn't stop them from blasting away. Rounds pinged off the girders.

Not very effective, Grant thought, *but they might get lucky just by sheer quantity*.

Morgan never hesitated. She charged headlong down the walkway, not even flinching when bullets whizzed past.

Grant made sure to keep his balance as he ran. The street was now a hundred and fifty feet below. If the bullets weren't fatal, the fall would be.

They reached a massive stone masonry pylon that served as the southern anchor for the bridge. The catwalk passed through an opening bored through the center of the pylon. Out the other side of the tunnel, Grant saw the two gunmen approach an intersecting catwalk and split up. One went straight ahead toward the northern terminus of the bridge while the other took a perpendicular path toward the opposite side of the bridge.

When Grant and Morgan reached the same point, she nodded at the man heading for the northern terminus. "You take that guy. Make sure he doesn't get to the other end of the bridge before the police set up their roadblocks."

"But don't kill him."

"Right." She didn't even sound out of breath.

"Easy enough," Grant said, wondering how he'd do such a thing.

Without another word, she took off.

*

Though Morgan didn't like leaving Grant on his own, she felt she'd had no choice other than to let him chase the second gunman. Given how well he'd handled himself so far, she thought it was an acceptable risk.

If she didn't catch up with her target soon, he might be able to escape in the maze of steelwork that made up the bulk of the bridge. Built as an arched span of girders between the masonry pylons, the Sydney Harbour Bridge was the main connection linking north Sydney and the business district. Eight lanes of street traffic and two rail lines made it one of the busiest stretches of road in the city. If he got to the vehicle deck, the gunman would have multiple options for his getaway.

Morgan's target headed for the set of stairs used by the BridgeClimb tourists as they descended from the main arch. Because the last tour group had come down hours ago, at least she didn't have to contend with bystanders getting in her way.

The Russian climbed the stairs leading up to the vehicle deck two at a time. The steps were so steep that it was nearly a ladder, with switchback platforms every five yards.

Morgan reached the stairs, holstered her pistol, and began climbing after him. She could see that her quarry had made the mistake of trying to climb without holstering his weapon, so he was hampered enough for her to be able to make up the distance.

She was just one platform below him when he turned to

fire. He got off two shots that caromed off metal before the slide locked back, indicating he was out of ammo.

She had him.

He hurled the pistol at her, catching her in the shoulder, but she ignored the blast of pain.

As he reached the vehicle deck, which still bustled with cars and trucks, she lunged for his feet. He kicked, barely missing her hand, and kept going.

On the next platform, she could take the shot that would disable him. Then it would be an easy task to haul him in.

At the vehicle deck, the stairs were wrapped with a ten-foot-high steel mesh cage to keep the BridgeClimb hikers from exiting onto the sidewalk. Instead of continuing up, the Russian grabbed the top of the cage, intending to vault over it and onto the sidewalk. If he did that, he might get into a car before Morgan could stop him.

She leaped up, but she didn't try to latch onto him. She pushed the exposed soles of his feet, toppling him over the side of the cage before he was ready.

He somersaulted over the edge, tumbling off the sidewalk and onto train tracks.

Morgan climbed up, drew her pistol, and aimed down at him, covering any possible escape.

With her free hand, she dialed her police contact to tell him that she had the subject ready for apprehension near the south pylon.

The Russian, seeing that he was caught, stood and put his hands over his head.

Her contact answered, but before she could make her report, the squeal of metal brakes interrupted her.

The Russian must have realized what was coming a split second before it happened. His mouth made a silent O just as a train roared through the pylon and smashed into him.

Grant wondered where in the hell this idiot thought he could go.

They were running up the arched spine of the bridge, and Grant wasn't afraid to admit he was starting to get winded. The guy he was chasing was wiry, with more of a runner's body, so Grant could do no better than keep pace behind him.

For some reason, the man had forsaken the chance to go over the metal cage they'd passed and onto the bridge deck. He just kept climbing until he was padding up the inclined walkway, only a thin steel railing on either side between him and a long and lethal drop to the road deck below.

Up ahead Grant saw what the guy was heading for. The bridge had four maintenance cranes that jutted from small sheds. The sheds housed the equipment to lower the maintenance platform that dangled over the side like a window washer's scaffold. The shed also encased the motor used to move the crane up and down the arch's span. Each housing was pierced by a small tunnel over the walkway to let the tourist climbers pass through.

If the Russian could get to the closest of the cranes, he'd use the platform to lower himself to a walkway below and climb down one of the ladders to the vehicle deck. Given that there was only one scaffold, Grant would have no way to follow.

He wasn't going to let that happen no matter what Morgan said.

He'd have one chance, when the man was getting onto the scaffold suspended from the crane's wires. After that the man could train his full attention on shooting Grant, who would have to lean awkwardly over the side to have any kind of shot.

When the man got to the crane, he turned and fired some covering shots, and Grant went prone. The man was at the very limit of Grant's range, and the odd geometry of the arch made the shot even tougher.

But this was Grant's best opportunity. The gunman began climbing onto the hanging platform.

Grant fired. It hit. Right leg.

Bull's-eye. Morgan would be proud.

The man reflexively grabbed his thigh, releasing his grip on the platform. His left foot, which was already planted on the platform, sent it swinging away from the bridge. He tried to regain his balance, but his feet were too far apart to recover. He scrabbled to grab hold of anything he could and came away clutching nothing but air.

With a terrified scream, the man plunged through the space between the bridge and the platform. The sound didn't stop until he smacked into the road below.

Grant got to his feet and leaned over the railing. Blood

pooled around the head of the corpse. No way this one was going to talk.

Grant frowned at the mess. "Huh," he said. "I really thought that would work."

THIRTY-FIVE

I t was when Tyler got to the astronaut drawing that Jess knew something was wrong.

As Fay explained to them, the astronaut figure depicted on the Nazca plain was one of the primary reasons that ancient alien theorists thought that spacemen had helped the Nazca people draw the lines. It was a simple humanoid with one arm raised and the other at its side. Although it had two legs, the head was round with the eyes being its only distinguishing features. Because the nose and mouth were missing, some thought it looked more like an alien creature than a human.

It seemed a stretch to Jess. To her it resembled a slightly more complicated stick figure. So what if the designers forgot to put the mouth on?

The astronaut drawing on the ceiling wasn't the issue. There was a second one at the end of the story drawn on the walls. It was identical to the ceiling figure, except this one was drawn with a large round object in its raised right hand.

Tyler had taken out a small electronic device and was

circling the cave, waving it over the walls until he reached the astronaut drawing. He stopped, and a strange look crossed his face. He took the Leatherman from his belt and unfolded the knife. Fay yelped when she saw him dig into the lower hand of the astronaut with the blade.

"You'll damage it!" Fay yelled.

"Sorry, Fay," Tyler said, and pried at the etching until a stone divot fell from the wall.

When Jess's flashlight passed across the resulting hole, a multi-hued glint reflected the light. It was about a tenth the diameter of the object in the raised hand, but this wasn't drawn on. It was embedded in the wall.

Tyler checked his device's display, and even in the dim light she could see his expression of alarm. He shouted toward the entrance.

"Polk, I'm going to need the case from the truck!" When he got an affirmative, he turned to Fay and Jess. "Let's step to the other side of the chamber."

"Why?" Jess said. "What is that device?"

"It's a radiation meter."

Instead of retreating, Fay moved closer to the dime-sized object. "That's radioactive?"

"Please, Fay, step back."

"How dangerous is it?"

"We'll be okay provided we don't stay here too long."

They moved to the opposite side.

"All right," Jess said, "I think we deserve to know what's going on."

Tyler paused for a moment, then sighed. "Fay, can you turn off your video camera, please?"

Fay looked puzzled, but complied.

"I'm not supposed to tell you because it's classified," Tyler said, "but you're right. You need to know the risks. What I'm about to say could send me to prison. You cannot under any circumstances talk about this with anyone else. Do you understand?"

Jess and Fay both nodded in bewilderment.

"The material embedded in the wall is called xenobium, a form of the element hafnium. We think the Nazca people found it after an explosion in their region. One of its properties is that it emits gamma radiation. I was hoping we wouldn't find any, which was why I didn't say anything until now."

"That's the reason Morgan Bell sent the Air Force jet to bring us here?" Jess asked. "This is related to the truck bomb in Australia, isn't it?"

"In a way. They stole a weapon called the Killswitch. This material is the trigger that powers it. If the people who have the Killswitch got their hands on this, it could result in a devastating terrorist attack."

They stayed to one side of the chamber until Polk called from the entrance that he had the case. Tyler ran out and came back carrying what looked like an aluminum suitcase, but by the way he was holding it, it seemed to be much heavier than Jess would have thought.

"Lead-lined case. Agent Bell gave it to us in the event that we found any xenobium."

Tyler pried at the hole until the xenobium popped out and rolled across the floor.

"Put a light on it, but don't touch it."

Tyler used the pliers on his Leatherman to pluck the xenobium off the floor. Jess had a hard time believing that something the size of a pea could be lethal.

He put it inside the foam interior of the case and closed the lid. After another wave of the radiation meter, he declared that the gamma emissions were back down to a normal level.

Jess returned to look at the story on the wall and saw that it made perfect sense now.

"So the Nazca people found the xenobium," she said, "but they didn't realize it was deadly until those with extended exposure started to get sick and die. Why bring it here?"

"We may never know," Fay said. "Perhaps they brought a small piece with them as an offering of thanks to the gods wherever they landed."

Tyler pointed to the astronaut figure. "Look at his hands. This bit of xenobium was in his left hand. The right hand is raised holding an object that is much bigger."

"The drawing would imply that they left a larger piece behind somewhere in Nazca," Jess said.

"Then we need to find it before anyone else does," Tyler said, aiming his flashlight at the ceiling. "But where is it?"

Fay pointed at the Mandala geometric figure on the ceiling. "See the starburst in the center? It looks like the explosion is taking place there. It could be that the Nazca people saw the fireball come down from space, and when they went to investigate, they found the xenobium."

Tyler walked over to the pyramid in the pictogram story. "Notice how the Mandala looks like the overhead view of a pyramid. Now look at the lines in the overhead chart. If you follow them, they go from the Mandala, through every one of the animals, and then straight to the Cahuachi pyramid."

"Of course!" Fay shouted in triumph. "The Nazca would have wanted to protect their find from thieves and separate it from the main population so that the people wouldn't get sick. The priests would have been the only ones allowed to have access to it. Not only would they hide how to get inside the pyramid, they would have constructed booby traps to keep invaders from taking the treasure. But they didn't want to hide it so well that the gods wouldn't find it."

"The gods weren't very powerful if they needed instructions," Tyler said.

"They weren't considered infallible like the God of Abraham."

"The pyramid would have been pretty noticeable at the time. Why not just put a big drawing on top of it to draw the gods there?"

"The Nazca might have thought the gods would return to the Mandala to retrieve their treasure. So they created the lines as a pathway to lead the gods from there to Cahuachi. It's only ten miles away from the Mandala."

"But the Tunguska blast was huge," Jess said. "Wouldn't a similar explosion have destroyed Cahuachi?"

"We don't know if Cahuachi was built before or after the explosion," Tyler said. "Maybe it was destroyed and then rebuilt. Fay said the city was only uncovered fifty years ago, and it's still being excavated."

"On the other hand, we could be wrong," Fay said. "The xenobium could be buried at the Mandala and the pyramid has nothing to do with it. But won't it be fun to find out?"

Fay's giddy excitement was contagious, and Jess couldn't help getting caught up in it.

"Have the archeologist discovered any way inside the pyramid?"

"A few chambers, but to my knowledge they've never found anything like that metal."

"If the Nazca line drawings form a code," Tyler said, "how does it tell the gods where to find it?"

"I've been thinking about this," Jess said. "If these are astrological symbols representing constellations, then they must go in order from the beginning to the end of the year. The straight lines connecting them could be the pathway that Nana mentioned."

"We can figure out the astrological link by matching the dots in the symbols to star charts. The question is, how does that tell us where to go in the pyramid?"

"Maybe the symbols have something to do with that as well."

"We'll try to figure that out on our way there," Fay said.

Then her voice took on an awed tone. "This could be the single greatest discovery of pre-Columbian archeology, even though it's found on Easter Island. Not only does it prove that the descendants of the Nazca people came here, but it also provides an answer to the mystery of the Nazca lines."

"Are you sure you're up for more travel?" Jess said.

"If you ask me that one more time, I'm going to put you over my knee."

Tyler laughed. "I'd like to see that. All right, you two. We're all going."

When they exited the cave, Tyler handed the case to Polk. "Take this to the car and bring Harris back with you to help us reset the boulder."

"I'll go with him," Fay said. "I want to load this video onto my laptop."

Jess smiled. Most of her friends' grandmothers were afraid to even touch a computer, let alone download video. Polk led Fay back up the trail.

"Why put the stone back in place?" Jess said. "Colchev doesn't have the map."

"We don't want anyone else to retrace our steps and find the cave until we're ready to reveal it to the world. Once the stone is covering the opening, I'll add some marks on the ground to disguise the ones we made."

Jess gave Tyler a quick hug. "Thanks for being honest with us."

"It's only fair. You're both sticking your necks out to help."

"Yes, but we dragged you into this. You could have blown us off in New Zealand."

Tyler leaned against the cliff face. "Remember in college when you asked me why I was in ROTC?"

"Something about your dad saying you shouldn't do it."

"Well, there was that. But it was really *because* of my father that I did it. His service in the military inspired me. It sounds corny, but there's a lot to be said for being part of something greater than yourself."

"Then why did you leave the Army?"

"The prospect of getting blown up all the time was one big reason."

"Did Karen have anything to do with your decision?"

Tyler nodded. "Not because she forced me to, but because being with her was being part of something greater than myself. She was good for my soul. Boy, that sounds like a sentiment on a greeting card."

Jess stroked his arm in a comforting gesture. "I think it's sweet. I'd kill to get a greeting card like that. But what does it have to do with this trip to Easter Island?"

"Do you know what Grant and I were doing in New Zealand? Testing the performance of a new car in winter conditions. Fun and important work, but not earth-shattering."

Jess nodded. "Our find here *is* earth-shattering."

"Exactly. The last few years I've been part of discoveries that have been revolutionary."

"And saved a lot of lives in the process. Yes, I did follow

your exploits in the news, even though you shunned the press and kept your private life out of the stories."

"Grant is the glory hound, not me."

"So you do it for another reason."

"After Karen's death, I thought the world had ended. And it had, for me. But since then I've realized that I don't want to go through the motions in life. I want to make a difference. Not to have my name in the history books, but because it's what makes me feel worthwhile."

Jess's lip curled into a grin. "So you're being selfish, is what you're saying."

"See? You get me. You always—"

Before Tyler could finish, he was interrupted by a honking horn, then the clatter of gunfire.

THIRTY-SIX

Before his private jet had landed on Easter Island an hour earlier, Colchev's men in Sydney reported that they were leaving the hotel because Kessler never arrived, which meant this path to the xenobium was his only option. He didn't hear from his men again, so he had to assume that they'd been caught or worse.

With the next flight to Easter Island from Peru not scheduled to arrive until later that evening, the only other jet on the island was a C-17, which must have been sent by the Americans to intercept Colchev. The Gulfstream's refueling stop in Tahiti had to be the reason the Air Force had beaten him here. The C-17's range was much farther, so it could fly nonstop, perhaps even refueling in mid-air on the way. Colchev's jet had to go far out of the way to make the vast distance across the Pacific.

He was sure that the Americans noted his Gulfstream's arrival, but the tail number would only lead them to the billionaire's front company based in the Bahamas. Still, seeing a bunch of men step off the plane would raise suspicions, so Colchev had hired two models in Sydney to come along on the trip. When the private jet landed and went through the cursory immigration and customs check, the observers on the C-17 would see two of his men, Kiselow and Chopiak, deplane with the girls and think they were nothing more than extravagant tourists.

Colchev's late arrival on the island meant that the Americans had a head start. Simply going out to the site mapped out on Dombrovski's photo of the wood engraving wouldn't work. And his first order of business was to cover his rear, which meant taking out anyone on the Air Force jet.

Instead of attempting a direct assault, Colchev, who stayed on the plane with Zotkin in case he'd be recognized, decided deception was the better choice. He instructed Kiselow and Chopiak to drop the models at a hotel in Hanga Roa, where they checked into a reserved room. Then his men took their rented vehicle to a remote location along the shore and called the police asking for help. When the lone police car arrived, his men shot the policeman and dumped him into the ocean.

The whole plan had gone smoothly. Kiselow and Chopiak drove the hijacked police car to the C-17 leisurely, as if they were just making a courtesy call. Before the man guarding the plane could tell that they weren't Easter Island cops, he was shot twice, the action shielded from the tower's view by the immense plane's fuselage. With the element of surprise complete, an ambush took out all four men aboard the jet without drawing any attention at the sleepy airport.

Colchev and Zotkin joined the two other men in the police car and set out for the location described on the map. From a distance they saw a Suzuki 4x4 parked near the ocean-side cliff.

Colchev had instructed Zotkin to drive toward the SUV slowly so that the vehicle's occupants wouldn't become suspicious. There were three people in view, a woman inside the Suzuki and two men holding assault rifles walking toward the cliff. They had to be security guards protecting Tyler.

The woman honked the SUV's horn, causing the two guards to whirl around. When they saw that it was a police car, the younger blond man waved and started walking toward them while the older curly-haired one stood near the cliff.

When they got within twenty-five meters, Colchev raised his own AK-47 and shot the blond man, who crumpled to the ground. Chopiak fired at the other man who fell over the edge of the cliff. Neither of Tyler's guards got a shot off.

Zotkin then sped toward the SUV as the woman, whom Colchev now recognized as Fay Turia, jumped out and ran toward the ocean. They intercepted her just as gunfire rang out from the cliff's edge. A bullet slammed through the rear driver's side window, killing Chopiak instantly. Chopiak must have missed or only injured the second man, who had to have landed on a ledge. Kiselow returned fire, and the guard ducked for cover.

"Keep your aim on him," Colchev said. "If he shows his head again, blow it off."

Colchev leaped out and grabbed Fay. She kicked and punched him but was no match for Colchev's bulk. He put her hand in a controlling grip, making sure not to snap it.

"Calm down, Mrs. Turia. There's nothing you can do now."

"Screw you!"

"You are a feisty grandmother, aren't you?"

"Let go!"

"No." He plucked a video camera from her hand. "What do we have here?"

"Family photos."

"I don't think so. I think you found something. Let's see what."

Kiselow fired again, but his shot missed. It did, however, keep the guard pinned.

Colchev peered at the LCD display and saw that it was video from inside a cave. He fast-forwarded through it, watching Tyler Locke and Jess McBride occasionally making appearances. Intriguing. It provided everything he had to know to find the xenobium. He slowed the playback when he got to the part showing Tyler waving around a radiation detector. After a look of alarm crossed Tyler's face, he turned to Fay and the video ended.

"Where is the xenobium fragment?" Colchev asked her.

She remained silent, but her eyes inadvertently flicked to the Suzuki.

"Zotkin," Colchev said, "search their vehicle."

Zotkin scuttled over to the 4x4, keeping the police car between him and the guard. In a minute he returned carrying a silver case. He put it down in the grass and opened it.

"No!" Colchev shouted when he saw the pea-sized bit of xenobium. It wasn't the large specimen in the photo from Dombrovski's lab. "*Blya!*" He slammed the case shut.

"That isn't ..." Zotkin said, stumbling over his words. "If that's all there is, our mission is over."

"I know that!" Colchev yelled before calming himself. "It's all right. All this does is prove that Dombrovski was right. The photograph we found wasn't a forgery. The xenobium we need was in fact hidden by the Nazca. Mrs. Turia has given us the information we need to get it."

"Colchev!" came a man's shout from the cliff's edge. "Colchev!"

Colchev peeked around the corner of the police car but couldn't see anyone. "Who is that?"

"My name's Tyler Locke."

"Dr. Locke, you keep popping up in the wrong place. I remember you from the hood of my road train."

"And I remember you killing Nadia Bedova. Now let Fay go!"

"Why should I?"

"Take me in her place."

"Again, why should I?"

"Because she'll slow you down."

"She seems spry enough to me."

"What do you want then?"

"Come out with your hands up."

"No. We know you stole the Killswitch weapons, Colchev."

Colchev grinned. "So?"

"So Kessler is dead. Your plan went up in smoke in Alice Springs."

The grin vanished. "You're the one who forced me into this action, Locke. If you hadn't interfered with my truck bomb, none of us would be here right now. Don't make me kill Mrs. Turia."

A woman's voice yelled out. "If you hurt her, I'll cut your nuts off and feed them to you!"

"That must be Ms. McBride. I won't hurt Mrs. Turia. She's going to be my guide."

"The hell I will," Fay said. "Don't listen to them, Jessica!"

Colchev took a handkerchief from his pocket and stuffed it in Fay's mouth.

"Colchev!" Tyler yelled. "Let her go, and I'll guarantee you safe passage off the island."

"It's too late for that, Locke."

"We can't stay here," Zotkin said. "Somebody might have heard their gunshots. We have to kill them now."

"Their position is too well defended," Colchev said. "We don't have the manpower to outflank them."

"Keep them distracted. I'll crawl through the grass and shoot from over there." He pointed to a rocky outcropping a hundred and fifty yards away.

"There's no time. We're not even sure you'll have a clean view of them. We'll take out Locke's car so he can't follow us back to the airport. By the time he gets there, we'll be long gone."

"But even with his car disabled, it's only four miles to the town. Locke will be able to call the mainland before we can get there. The police will intercept us as soon as we land in Chile."

Colchev's eyes fell on the case. There wasn't enough xenobium for his ultimate goal, but it would be sufficient to power the Killswitch he had with him. He buried his head in his hands, trying to think of another solution, but he wracked his brain and nothing came. It was either use the Killswitch or risk total mission failure. At least it would give him a chance to test the weapon and verify that it worked.

Colchev glowered at Zotkin. "We'll make sure he can't call the mainland when he gets back to town. Put the Suzuki in neutral and then get in the police car." He turned to Kiselow and pointed at Fay. "Keep her head toward the cliff so they won't fire. I'll drive."

Shielded by the police car, Zotkin ran to the Suzuki and back. He and Kiselow climbed in the car with Colchev taking the wheel. He drove forward until the police car's front bumper touched the back of the Suzuki's. Colchev gunned the engine, pushing the vehicle toward the cliff.

When he got within four car-lengths of the drop-off, he wrenched the wheel to the right. The Suzuki's momentum caused it to go sailing over the edge just as the guard popped up to see what was going on. The SUV smashed into him, taking him down to the rocks below.

Fay screamed through her gag, but the momentary appearance of two heads above the cliff edge meant that Tyler Locke and the granddaughter were still alive. Not that it mattered. Once Colchev's car was gone, he was sure the Americans would head back to Hanga Roa on foot. At a fast trot the two of them could reach the outskirts of town in a little over thirty minutes.

They would arrive just in time to die.

THIRTY-SEVEN

When Grant climbed down to the bridge's vehicle deck, only Morgan's intervention kept twenty police officers from training their weapons on him. He jogged over to her as he eyed the train stopped halfway up the bridge. Officers swarmed over part of the track behind the last car. The suited man she was speaking to got a phone call and retreated to take it.

"Who was that?" Grant asked.

"Roger Abel. Australian federal agent."

"Are we all playing nicely?"

"Grudgingly on their part. They know this is related to Pine Gap. They're leading the investigation here, but they're instructed to share any info they find."

"Given that you're not interrogating your runner, I'll bet he didn't come quietly."

Morgan nodded at the rails. "Pulped by the commuter train."

"Anything useful left over?"

She shook her head. "He's spread across a hundred feet of track. The Aussies will collect the pieces. They'll tell us if they come across anything pertinent, but I'm not holding my breath."

"We might have more luck with my guy."

"I saw him hit the ground. What happened? I told you not to kill him."

"Look who's talking."

"My guy was an accident."

"So was mine."

"I heard that you shot him."

"Yeah, but only in the leg. It was a good shot, too."

"Let's go look."

"By the way, anyone hurt at the hotel?" Grant asked as they walked toward the center of the bridge.

"No. We got lucky. These guys were just trying to sow confusion so they could escape."

"It almost worked."

The agent caught up with them. "That was my director. I don't know what's going on here, but I don't like it."

"You don't have to," Morgan said.

"Nicely handled," Grant said.

"We've got two dead gunmen," Abel said, "one of whom your partner shot before he fell to his death. I need to know whether we have more of them out there."

"You don't. Did your director tell you to cooperate with us?"

They reached the corpse sprawled in the middle of the right lane. Abel crossed his arms. "According to him, I retain custody of anything we find, but you can see it before it goes into evidence. I'm allowed to get your statements, but then you're free to go."

"Good. We need to examine anything found on this man."

Abel scowled and then nodded at a uniformed officer carrying a plastic baggy. He handed the package to Morgan.

The baggy contained a wallet, a US passport, phone, car keys, and a scrap of paper with an address. She opened the wallet to find two hundred Australian dollars and nothing else.

"This is it?" Morgan said.

Abel nodded. "We're running down the ID on the passport."

"It'll be fake, just like the ones on the bodies we found in the warehouse in Alice Springs."

"Were these men responsible for the explosion there yesterday?"

"That's what we're trying to find out."

The phone was still operational. Since the guy landed on his back, Grant assumed it had been in his front pocket.

Morgan scanned through the recent calls and text messages. They'd been wiped clean. Same for the contact list.

"This guy didn't make or receive any calls?" Morgan said.

"It must have been erased remotely," Grant said. "My company worked on similar technology. It's a common feature on secure phones used by foreign intelligence services in case they're caught or lose the phone. That's why this one's not password protected. The remote erasure took that out, too."

Abel stared at the body. "He's with the CIA?"

"We think he may be a Russian," Morgan said.

She glanced at the piece of paper and then showed it to Grant. It said 22 Lic. Jose Lopez Portillo Ore.

"Does that mean anything to you?" she asked Grant.

He shrugged. "A town in Oregon? Maybe someone he's planning to meet with?"

"Or a street address where they're going to meet." Morgan jotted down the phrase in her notebook and handed the items back to the officer.

After making their reports of the chase to Abel, they walked back toward their car.

Grant searched for the phrase on his phone while Morgan was lost in thought. The entire phrase failed to yield anything useful, so he started plugging subsections of it into a search engine.

"When Kessler didn't show to make the drop," Morgan said, "their next move would probably have been to leave Australia. We think that they had some connection with the Baja drug gang. This could be related to their contact in the cartel."

Grant continued trying different combinations. "Like we said earlier, a drug gang would be a good way to smuggle the Killswitches back into the US. They've got the systems already in place, and they'll do anything if the price is right."

"We can't send out a blanket alert to the Border Patrol describing the Killswitch because of its secret status. And unless we send a detailed description, they won't know what to look for. We'll have to see if we can narrow it down to a particular city."

"Got it!" Grant said triumphantly. "That guy had the abbreviation wrong or we couldn't read his handwriting. It should have been 22 Lic. Jose Lopez Portillo Ote. It stands for 22 Licenciado José López Portillo Oriente. It's an address in Tijuana. There's a border crossing a quarter-mile from there."

"That could be where they're planning to meet to repack the shipment for the smuggling operation."

"If we can intercept them there, we might be able to retrieve the Killswitches before they even cross the border."

"We'll have to coordinate with the Mexican Federales to put a stakeout on the location. When the weapons arrive, we'll raid the place and get them back."

"How will you know when the Killswitches are there?"

"Because you're coming with me. You know what the Russians look like."

"Do I get to have a gun?"

Morgan squinted at him. "I guess so. You've come in handy so far."

Grant smiled. "Then I'm in."

She got on her phone. "This is Special Agent Bell. How fast can Grant Westfield and I get to San Diego?"

THIRTY-EIGHT

Jess had been shocked when Polk was dashed on the rocks by the falling Suzuki, but she'd been outraged by the kidnapping of her grandmother. Her instinct had been to charge up over the cliff edge to get Fay back, but Tyler had restrained her when he saw how well Colchev's gunmen had them pinned. Harris's lifeless form in the grass only confirmed that they would have had no chance.

When Colchev's car was out of firing range, Tyler and Jess gave chase. Her feet crunched on the hard-packed dirt as she ran next to Tyler. They'd settled into a fast jog after sprinting for five minutes behind Colchev's rapidly receding SUV, which was now long gone.

"How far ... to the airport?" she asked between breaths. She wasn't struggling for air, but Tyler's long legs made it a challenge to keep up. He didn't seem to be huffing and puffing.

"At least four miles," he said. "At this pace it'll take us another half hour."

"They could take off by then."

"I know. We have to stop them before they get airborne."

She wanted to get reassurance from Tyler that Fay would be all right, but wasting her breath on extracting meaningless platitudes wasn't going to help her get to the airport any faster. She concentrated on sucking in air through her nose and exhaling through her mouth as she did on her twice-weekly jogs.

Tyler jerked his head around at the sound of an engine behind them.

She turned to see two motor scooters puttering toward them. Two skinny guys, both in their twenties, waved as they approached.

"We need those scooters," Tyler said. "Follow my lead."

The kids seemed like college students on summer break, backpacks slung over their shoulders.

Tyler smiled and flagged them down. The look was non-threatening, just a dirty, sweaty man and woman who were out in the middle of nowhere.

The riders came to a stop. Both of them paid more attention to Jess than Tyler.

"*Hola*," one of them said to Jess. "*¿Qué pasa?*"

"*No hablo Español*," Tyler said. "*¿Habla Inglés?*"

The men shook their heads.

"Do you speak Spanish?" Tyler said to Jess.

"No," Jess said. "And we don't have time for this."

With a quick nod at the bikes, she took a running lunge and pushed the closest guy off his scooter, grabbing the handle before it could fall.

Tyler didn't hesitate to follow her cue. He ripped the second man off his bike as if he were a doll. The man hit the ground with an "oof".

"Sorry," Tyler said, and hopped onto the seat.

They gunned the engines and zipped away before the men could get to their feet. In her rearview mirror she could see them give chase, but their cursing and arm-waving didn't help them catch up.

The scooters could hit forty miles an hour, but the frequent potholes meant that thirty was pushing the safest top speed. Tyler pulled even with her.

"That's one way to do it," he said over the wind.

"Those guys will be fine. We can't let Colchev get away with Nana."

"We'll park a truck across the runway if that's what it takes to keep them from leaving."

"I hope you're right. She doesn't have her medication."

"What medication?"

"Insulin. She'll tire quickly without it. If she doesn't get another dose within a few days, she could pass out and go into a coma."

"Is she diabetic?"

Jess hesitated, but she had to tell him. "Nana has pancreatic cancer. She wanted me to keep it quiet."

"She seemed fine to me."

"She had some rough days earlier in the month, but she's been okay the past week."

"How far along?"

"Stage four. Terminal. I'm not giving up hope, but most people in the same situation last only a few months. She's supposed to start chemotherapy next week."

"I'm sorry. You're right. I would never have let her come along if I'd known."

"I tried to talk her out of it, but you've seen how stubborn she can be."

"She's a tough bird. Maybe the doctors are wrong."

They were only a few miles from town, but a thunderous roar coming from that direction made Tyler stop. Jess pulled to a halt next to him.

It sounded like a jet engine.

"Damn it," he said. "We're too late."

The roar receded into the distance until she saw a white twin-engine private plane take to the air above the far end of the runway.

"No!" she cried out. "No!"

"It's all right. The C-17 should be able to match the speed of Colchev's jet. We'll get into the air as soon as we reach the airport, and we'll make sure to have a SWAT team waiting wherever they land."

He revved his engine and took off.

"Why are they doing this?" Jess said when she caught up. "What's so damned important about this weapon?"

"The Killswitch is an electromagnetic pulse device. Xenobium, the material we found in the cave, is detonated by explosives in the Killswitch, and it sends out a cascade of gamma rays that disrupts any magnetic field within range."

"Which would do what?"

"It would cause a surge of electricity that damages electronic devices. Anything with a transistor would immediately shut down. Computers, communications, electrical grids, vehicles, airplanes would all be affected."

"Do you think he's planning to use this thing?"

"Possibly, but we don't know what Colchev's target is. Now that he has the components to make it work, he could take out a major city with it."

"Good God! Imagine if he set it off next to an airport."

"Every plane within range would crash. Hospitals would have no power. With no working fire trucks or water pumping stations, fires would rage out of control. Nuclear plants would melt down. We're essentially talking about a worst-case terrorist event."

Jess's stomach twisted at the nightmare scenario.

"This is some kind of classified US weapon?" she said.

"Yeah, and I committed twelve felonies telling you all that. But I need your help to get it back. And we'll get Fay back with it. I promise."

He still knew her well. The platitudes helped.

They made better time once they hit the paved road going into Hanga Roa. In another two minutes they were on the airport tarmac.

Tyler came to a stop next to the huge cargo jet and jumped off the scooter without bothering to pop the kickstand. Jess did the same and followed him up the stairs into the C-17.

She stopped suddenly when she saw dead bodies scattered on the cargo floor. The plane's three crew and the two other security men. All of them had been shot.

Tyler ignored the corpses and knelt on the opposite side of a copper-colored device four feet long. The sleek piece of machinery had an inherently menacing quality.

"Is that the Killswitch?" she asked.

He met her eyes. "Yes. And it's armed."

"What?" She went around to Tyler's side and saw a LCD display counting down. It read 15:23. 15:22. 15:21.

"Colchev must have set it before he left." He waved the radiation meter over the weapon and grimaced when he saw the results. "The xenobium we found must be in here."

"Oh, my God! Can you disarm it?"

Tyler examined the device and shook his head. "It looks like it requires a security code. Do you think you could decipher it?"

"Not without knowing anything about its internal safeguards to prevent tampering. What about cutting the wires?"

"I'm not even sure how it works. I could set it off just by tinkering with it."

"Then let's get it out of the plane. We'll put it far away and then take cover."

"That's not going to work."

"Sure it'll take out the electronics, but at least it won't blow up the plane."

Tyler stood. She could see the gears in his head turning, weighing a set of bad options.

"What's the matter?" she said.

"When it goes off, the xenobium in the weapon will emit high-intensity gamma rays. That's how it causes the magnetic flux."

Jess felt her gut twist. "Radiation?"

Tyler grimly nodded. "It doesn't matter where we take it. If this bomb goes off, everyone on the island will die."

THIRTY-NINE

Tyler briefly considered dumping the Killswitch in the ocean, but he had no idea whether that would short circuit it, causing a detonation before it got deep enough to remove the radiation threat.

"What are we going to do?" Jess said. "How far away do we have to get it?"

"I don't know the effective range, so as far away as we can ..."

Tyler paused and fixated on the dead pilot. The C-17. If he still had enough time, he *could* get the Killswitch far away. He checked his watch, comparing it to the countdown timer. To have a chance of succeeding, he'd have to start right now.

He ran for the staircase leading up from the cargo deck to the cockpit.

"Where are you going?" Jess yelled as she came after him.

He sat in the pilot's seat and fired up the auxiliary power unit that he would need to start the engines. Tyler thumbed through the checklist while the APU whined as it spooled up. It would take eight minutes to get all four engines warmed up.

"If I can get the plane over the open ocean," he said, "it might be far enough to keep everyone safe."

"Will it keep the island from getting hit by the electromagnetic pulse?"

"I don't know."

"But this is suicidal!"

Tyler thought back to what the pilot had told him about their previous mission before it had been scrubbed to ferry them to Easter Island. The C-17 was supposed to be going from Alice Springs to a paratrooper training op in Japan. That meant the crew had brought their own parachutes, standard procedure for an airborne drop.

"There are chutes on board somewhere. I'll jump once I get into the air and set the autopilot."

"Have you ever jumped from one of these?"

"A couple of times," he lied. He'd done a few jumps at Grant's urging, but those had been out of a propeller-driven skydiving plane, not a full-sized jet.

She looked around the cockpit. "Where are the chutes?"

"I don't know. But they've got to be here somewhere." He handed her his camera. "This has a wireless connection. Send every photo and video in there to your email address." In case the Killswitch knocked out the island's electronics, he wanted to make sure they had a record of the cave drawings.

Jess tapped on the camera's display while Tyler worked on getting the engines started, the checklist on his lap. What he didn't tell her was that it would take only one missed detail to screw up his entire plan. While he'd flown jets for years now, he'd only flown sleek twin-engine private planes, not four-engine monsters like the C-17. The principles were the same, but the handling was altogether different. And now he would have to skip all but the most important steps in the checklist to get into the air in time.

Tyler knew he was making a big assumption about the chutes. Aircrews always packed their own parachutes, to be used only in an emergency during the drop, but he didn't actually have confirmation that they were on the plane already. He was willing to take the risk, but there was no reason to tell Jess.

"Done," she said, looking up from the camera. "It'll take a few minutes to upload them all, but they're on the way."

"Thanks," Tyler said. "Now get off the plane."

"What about you?"

"I'll be fine."

"This is crazy!"

"Go!"

She stopped typing and dashed into the cabin behind the cockpit, but instead of leaving, she threw open locker doors.

Tyler didn't have time to ask what she was doing. With the APU at full power, he started the number one engine. The engines had to be started in sequence from port to starboard, approximately ninety seconds for each one as the rotors reached the minimum RPM needed.

Jess returned carrying two parachutes. "Found them,"

she said, dumping them onto the floor. "Even if you jump out safely, you'll be miles from shore. You can't swim that far."

"There are life rafts embedded in the fuselage. I'll deploy them before I jump."

"Where are they?"

Tyler felt the color drain from his face when he realized that wasn't going to work. He'd been part of the team investigating the crash of a C-17 in Alaska a couple of years before, so he was familiar with the aircraft. The plane's Floating Equipment Deployment System, or FEDS, consisted of three rafts ejected from the top of the aircraft.

Idiot, he thought. *You should have remembered that the rafts are attached to the plane so that they won't float away after a water landing.*

Jess must have noticed his ashen pallor. "What's the matter?"

"The life rafts are tethered to the aircraft. If I eject them in mid-air, they'll just flutter behind the plane like kites."

"Are there any inside the plane?"

"No."

"Then we need to bring one of the other ones on board."

She was right. He had to deploy them now. He ran to the loadmaster's station, armed the deployment mechanism, and pulled the T-handle.

Three bangs jolted the aircraft. Two rafts sailed into the air on either side of the cockpit, trailing nylon ropes behind them. The protective clamshell coverings clattered apart on the ground, and the rafts began to inflate automatically. A third raft would be behind the starboard engines. The blown hatches would have a negligible effect on the plane's aerodynamics.

He took the Leatherman from his pocket and pressed it into Jess's hand. "Take this. There's a knife on it. Cut the ropes loose on all of them, starting with the port raft, but be careful of the engines. Drag the forward rafts behind the engines. Then drag the other raft in through the rear cargo door and get out. I'll close it when you're clear."

"No way. I need you alive if we're going to save Nana. That's why I'm coming with you."

"Oh, no, you're not."

"Tyler, I've done more than forty jumps. Discussion over."

Tyler could see she was going to be just as stubborn as Fay was. And she was right. He didn't have time. Only ten minutes left to detonation.

"All right," he said. "You win. Pull the raft in and close the crew door. There should be a button next to it. It'll show green when the door is secure."

She left and Tyler opened the massive rear cargo door. He saw Jess dash out and cut the cord on the port raft, using the line to drag it backward as she strained at the weight of the enormous raft. When she was clear, he started number two engine.

Jess repeated the process with the starboard raft. Tyler wanted to go help her, but doing so would have wasted time they didn't have.

As soon as she was out of sight, Tyler started engine three.

He put the pilot's headset on. It was already on the tower frequency.

"Tower, this is Air Force flight ... uh, this is the Air Force C-17. Permission to taxi for takeoff."

An accented voice answered after a pause. "I don't have your flight plan, C-17."

"This is an emergency takeoff. We'll file the plan en route."

"Negative, C-17," came the shocked response. "Not without your paperwork. There could be traffic in your proposed flight path."

"Tower, traffic won't be an issue unless they're on final approach. This was just a courtesy call to tell you to keep the runway clear. I don't see anyone out there, so I'm taking off. Out."

Engine three was still warming up, but he could use the first two engines to taxi.

A minute later, Jess returned and climbed into the right-hand seat, sweat pouring from her brow. "Those bastards are heavy," she said between breaths, "but I got one aboard. The side door's closed."

Tyler closed the cargo door, pushed the throttles forward, and released the brakes. The C-17 rolled across the tarmac at a stately pace.

"Wait a minute," Jess said. "You've only started three engines."

"The plane is designed to take off with an engine out. We can't wait to start the fourth. Put your seat belt on."

He swung the big beast around and headed for the two-mile-long runway, lowering the flaps and making sure he didn't miss anything critical on the checklist. Taking off wouldn't do much good if he crashed at the end of the runway.

As soon as he had the nose lined up on the centerline, Tyler pushed the throttles until the fan speed reached ninety percent.

The engines howled in response. The plane surged forward, pressing Tyler against his seat.

He couldn't help thinking, *This is about the dumbest thing you've ever done.*

"If we're going to die," Jess said, "I need to tell you something."

"We're not going to die." *Yes, we are.*

"The reason I didn't come into your room with you last night is because I'm seeing someone."

"You really think this is the best time for this?"

"I wanted you to know that it was a tough decision. Even after all these years, I still love you."

Tyler was so shocked by her profession that if his hands hadn't been glued to the yoke, he would have keeled over. He could have chosen from a thousand possible responses, but he had to keep his attention focused on the task at hand. Now he had a real reason not to die just yet.

His eyes met Jess's for just a moment. "We'll have plenty of time to talk in the raft."

The C-17 hit takeoff velocity with a half-mile of runway to spare. Tyler pulled back on the yoke, and the massive plane rose smartly into the air. Easter Island receded behind them.

"I'll get us up to three thousand feet," he said. "I'll keep us at a hundred and sixty knots for the jump and hope that's slow enough, but I'm going to set the autopilot to speed up just before I leave the flight deck. That way we'll get the maximum distance between us and the plane by the time it blows."

"What should I do?"

"Go down to the cargo deck and keep hold of the life raft. I'll open the cargo door, but don't launch the raft until we're ready to drop. At this speed we're going a mile every twenty seconds. I'll give you a minute to get down there and open the door, then I'll join you and we'll jump."

Jess nodded and got out of her seat, taking one of the parachutes with her. "I'm not jumping without you."

"I know. Go!"

She sprinted away. Tyler eased the jet to a heading of 180 and kept it steady at an altitude of three thousand feet at a hundred and sixty knots. He changed the transponder code to squawk 7700 and adjusted the radio to 243 megahertz, the guard emergency frequency.

"Mayday! Mayday! Mayday! This is Air Force C-17 from Easter Island. We are ditching six miles due south of the island. Request rescue boat. Repeat we are ditching on heading one eight zero from Easter Island VOR. Request rescue boat."

He glanced at his watch. Six minutes to detonation.

A nervous reply bleated from his headset. "Air Force C-17, this is Easter Island control. We read that you are ditching six miles due south—"

That was enough for Tyler, who just wanted to make sure he'd been heard. He tore off the headset, opened the cargo door, and dialed up the autopilot for maximum cruising altitude and speed. Then he stood and put on the parachute. When the harness was buckled, he initiated the autopilot command.

The engines powered up and Tyler could feel the altitude increasing. He shot down the stairs and ran to the back of the cargo deck where Jess was waiting at the open door. She had a death grip on the life raft to keep from being sucked out by the airstream.

"You ready?" he shouted over the wind.

She nodded, no trace of fear. If anything, she looked pumped for the experience.

Tyler put both hands against the raft, and Jess did the same. He called out, "One! Two! Three! Push!"

They surged toward the cargo door, until the raft tipped over the edge and flipped out.

"Go!" he yelled, and Jess sprinted forward with a whoop, as if she were on one of her extreme tourism adventures. She leaped off the lowered cargo door, and the slipstream ripped her away.

Tyler, who was right behind her, wished that he were as exhilarated by the jump. The only thing that was making his feet move was the knowledge that this was no longer a perfectly good airplane.

Then he was freefalling into space. The air was sucked from his lungs as he was bombarded by a wind shear unlike anything he'd experienced in previous jumps.

Tyler watched the C-17 rise into the sky above him, so mesmerized that he almost forgot he wasn't on a static line. He pulled his ripcord and strained at the harness as the chute yanked him to a sudden stop.

He scanned the ocean for the other chute and saw Jess floating lazily below him. The bright banana-colored raft splashed into the water only a few hundred yards away. The fully inflated boat's wind resistance had kept it from getting too far behind them.

The calm ocean rose to meet Tyler quickly, and he readied himself to release the chute. Drowned by his own parachute was not how he wanted to go.

He plunged into the water and held his breath as he wriggled out of the harness. After an agonizingly long thirty seconds, he was free and swam for the surface.

He burst into the air and took a deep breath. He whirled around looking for Jess and the raft.

He saw the raft first, its color easily spotted against the blue horizon. Then he saw Jess paddling toward it with a smooth stroke.

It took him several minutes to meet her there. They

climbed in and caught their breath. The flashing light of the homing beacon was activated automatically by the water, but the survival kit was gone, probably lost while the life raft was tumbling through the air. They could do nothing now but wait for rescue.

Jess sat up and leaned against the outer tube.

"You all right?" Tyler said.

"That was amazing! You?"

"As good as can be expected."

She drew the folded Leatherman from her pocket and handed it to Tyler. "I thought we might need it if we're out here for long."

"I can't seem to lose this," he said, and put it in his own pocket. "Unfortunately, I don't think the Air Force will consider it a fair trade for a two-hundred-million-dollar jet."

"I can't see it," she said. "How far away do you think it is?"

Tyler checked his watch. Fifteen seconds to detonation.

"I'm hoping it's at least thirty miles away by now. It should still be accelerating."

"Will we be able to see the blast from here?"

As if in response to her question, Tyler squinted as a fiery orange glow pierced the sky. He counted while he awaited the sound of the explosion.

Two minutes later a tremendous crack split the air.

"Twenty-five miles away," Tyler said.

"Is that far enough?"

"At this distance the gamma radiation is going to be

minimal." He pointed at the extinguished homing beacon light. "But the electromagnetic pulse reached us. That's why the electronic beacon shut off. We'll have to hope someone with a sailboat is headed our way."

"I hope it's soon," Jess said, her teeth chattering.

Tyler's adrenaline subsided and he realized he was shivering as well.

"Come here," he said.

She nestled against him, and he wrapped his arms around her for the shared warmth.

That was about all they had going for them. No food. No fresh water. And because of the EMP, the only populated area within two thousand miles was now a technological wasteland.

FORTY

Halfway to Santiago, Colchev finished watching the video from Fay's camera for a third time. He concluded that there were two possibilities for where they would find the xenobium at the Nazca plateau. Either it was at the Mandala geometric figure or it was somewhere in the pyramid of Cahuachi.

The photo from Ivan Dombrovski's lab in 1947 proved that the Russian scientist had found a ball of xenobium three inches in diameter as a result of his search all those years ago. The unnamed cave had pointed the way, he'd recorded, but Dombrovski never explained why he didn't bring the xenobium back with him. The only puzzle piece Colchev had been missing was the location of the cave. Thanks to Fay Turia and Tyler Locke, he'd found it.

The problem now was deciding where to begin the next part of the search. Fay was going to help him decide.

He walked to the rear of the Gulfstream, where Fay stared through the window at the ocean below.

He took a seat opposite her. "Mrs. Turia."

She turned her gaze on him, her eyes blank. "What?"

"You seem to be an expert on the Nazca lines, and I need your assistance."

She barked a raspy laugh. "You must be dumber than the sheep on my station."

Colchev wasn't accustomed to women talking to him like that. He clenched his armrest tightly. "If you don't help me, I don't have a reason to keep you alive. You're saying I should just shoot you right now?" He drew his pistol and aimed it at her head.

Fay didn't flinch. "Go ahead. I'll be dead in a few months anyway."

That was not the reaction Colchev was expecting. He lowered the pistol. "What do you mean?"

"I mean I have malignant pancreatic cancer. Apparently it's not a pleasant way to go, so you'll actually be doing me a favor by pulling that trigger."

He'd never seen someone so unafraid of death. Men he'd threatened like that were more likely to wet their pants than talk back. He put the gun away and tried a different tactic.

"I'm giving you a chance to save your granddaughter."

Fay's eyes softened. "You will *not* hurt Jessica. I won't allow it."

"You *will* allow it if you don't help me."

He didn't tell her that the armed Killswitch would have irradiated the entire island with gamma rays. It was quite likely that both Jess and Tyler were now dead or soon would be, along with the two models Colchev had left behind in the hotel.

He leaned forward to make his point. "If, for some reason, my mission fails because you didn't help me, I will have no choice but to hunt your granddaughter down and kill her."

"How do I know you won't do that anyway?"

"Because I won't have any reason to."

"I'm not naïve. I've seen your faces. I know that you have something called the Killswitch. And I know you're after more xenobium. Why would you let me live?"

"I won't go into the details, but I will tell you that Washington, DC, will cease to be the center of global power once this is over. Once America is on its knees, China will fall with it, as dependent as it is on the US economy. Moscow will take its rightful place on the world stage as the dominant force, and so I will have nothing to fear."

"The US will go to war with Russia."

"That's a risk I'm willing to take, but I don't think so. After all, if they are attacked by their own secret weapon, how can they blame Russia for the attack? No, the US will have too many problems at home to want to start another war. Besides, why do you care? You live in New Zealand now."

"I'm still an American."

"Mrs. Turia, I admire your patriotism, but I'm going to succeed whether you help me or not. However, it will go faster if you point me in the right direction. If you don't, I guarantee that I will carry through on my threat. Your granddaughter will live in fear for the rest of her days, never knowing when or where I'll strike. You don't want her to go through life like that, do you? I may let you go just to deliver that message to her."

Fay glanced out the window again before she looked back at Colchev. "What do you want me to do?"

Colchev smiled. "I need your expertise. I've narrowed down our search to two spots based on the video you filmed in the Rapa Nui cave. The first is the center of the Mandala and the second is the Grand Pyramid of Cahuachi. You seemed to indicate that the Nazca animal symbols were important to the search. What do they mean?"

"I don't know. We were hoping to learn more when we got there."

"Got where?"

She sighed heavily. "The Mandala. The alien told me it's in the center of the figure, buried under the starburst pattern."

"The alien?"

"The one I met at Roswell. He drew it in the dirt before he died."

"You met an alien?"

"Of course! What do you think started all this?"

"You're talking about the Roswell incident."

"Yes. A spaceship crashed. An alien climbed out and saved me. He gave me the wooden engraving and then drew a rectangle in the dirt before he died."

Colchev stifled a chuckle.

"You don't believe me?"

"Actually," he said, "I do. For reasons that you can't

comprehend. Is your theory that the same aliens visited the Nazca people?"

"How else do you explain the xenobium? A material like none other found on Earth falls from the sky at Tunguska, remote Western Australia, and the ancient Nazca plain of Peru. Obviously an alien spacecraft crash landed just like at Roswell, but the spacecraft power source survived. Given how many times they've visited our planet over the last few thousand years, it's only reasonable to assume they've had some accidents."

Colchev smiled. "That's a fascinating theory."

"There's no other possible explanation."

"So you think the xenobium is buried in the dirt at the Mandala?"

Fay nodded. "We think that's where it landed over fifteen hundred years ago. The Nazca people buried it there so the gods would be able to retrieve it."

"And you're sure it's not in the Grand Pyramid?"

"I can't be sure of anything, but the chambers inside the pyramid have been searched thoroughly. If the xenobium was there, it would be gone by now."

"That would be very bad for you and Jessica."

Fay looked scared. "That's why I'm sure it's at the Mandala. When you find it there, I expect you to keep your promise."

"Of course."

Colchev returned to the front of the plane and told Zotkin her wild story.

"Do you believe her?" Zotkin said.

Colchev shot him an amused look.

"I mean about the burial place for the xenobium," Zotkin said quickly. "The rest of her theory is obviously ridiculous."

Colchev looked back at Fay, who had resumed staring out the window. "She's a tough old woman. I really believe she's more afraid of losing her granddaughter than dying herself. I think she took my threat seriously."

"And if the xenobium isn't at the Mandala?"

"Then we'll take her to the Grand Pyramid of Cahuachi. We may still need her to interpret the symbols."

"Tonight?"

"No, it'll be dark soon. We'll start the search at sunup."

"She better be right," Zotkin said. "We only have two days left."

"Yes," Colchev said. "Only two more days for the United States to enjoy its position as the world's lone superpower. And then it is our turn."

FORTY-ONE

A high-pitched screech jolted Jess awake. Until she sat upright and experienced a mild head rush, it didn't register that she'd actually been asleep.

"What was that?" she said, searching for the source of the noise.

"Just a seagull," Tyler said, leaning against the side of the raft. "He's been circling us for ten minutes."

"Like a buzzard."

"No, but I do think he's hoping we'll give him some food."

"No chance. If I had any food, I'd wolf it down." Salt crystals clung to her still-damp jeans, and her mouth felt like the inside of a cotton ball. At least she was no longer shaking like a seizure victim. "How long have I been out?"

"My watch isn't working because of the EMP, but I'd say an hour and a half. Almost getting blown up can be tiring. Believe me, I know."

"Probably. Plus I didn't sleep much last night."

"Me neither."

She scanned the horizon for sign of a rescue boat or

plane. Nothing. Easter Island beckoned in the distance, tantalizingly close, but if they tried to swim for it, they'd be exhausted before they got halfway there.

"Do we have any supplies?"

"A flare gun. One shell. But we shouldn't use it until we're sure someone is looking this way."

"You seem pretty confident that's going to happen."

"It will," Tyler said. "I just don't know when."

"How can you be so sure?"

"Because I sent out a distress call before we jumped. As long as we don't get a storm, we should be fine."

"Great. You just jinxed us."

"I don't believe in jinxes."

"Why am I not surprised?"

"If it happens, it'll happen whether we talk about it or not."

"Very logical of you."

"And your boyfriend isn't?"

Jess brushed away some of the salt from her pants. "I shouldn't have told you that. Well, not at that moment."

"Who is he?"

"His name's Andy. He's a doctor."

"In New Zealand? How come I didn't meet him?"

"He's volunteering for Doctors Without Borders. He's in the middle of the Congo right now."

"Does he know anything about what's going on?"

"I left him a message, but phone service out there is unreliable."

"Is it serious?"

"He asked me to marry him before he left. I told him I'd give him an answer when he got back."

"You? Settle down? I thought you found out it wasn't your thing after the surfer dude. It sure wasn't what you wanted at MIT."

"Tyler, we were young, all right? In college I wasn't ready for that kind of commitment. You caught me at a bad time."

Tyler looked distinctly uncomfortable. "Looks like I did it again."

She chuckled. "You know the ironic thing?"

"What?"

"He's a lot like you. Dashing, smart, funny, kind, reliable."

Tyler cleared his throat. "So what's the answer?"

"To what?"

"To the question he asked."

"I haven't made up my mind yet."

"What's stopping you from saying yes?"

She smiled. "He's a lot like you. Stubborn, arrogant, workaholic, impatient, logical."

He returned the grin. "So what you're saying is, he's flawless."

She shook her head. "He's a pain in the ass."

"Sounds like my kind of guy."

"You're not going to make this easy, are you?"

Tyler paused, then said, "Jess, I was blissful with Karen, but I never stopped loving you, either."

Jess started shivering again, but she couldn't tell if it was from the cold or something else. She put her head against Tyler's shoulder.

"Why couldn't all this have happened a year ago?" she said.

Tyler didn't answer, but he put his arm around her. She looked up at him and felt his eyes pulling her toward him.

They kissed. Lightly at first, then ravenously. She forgot all about the cold, the dampness, the hunger, the discomfort.

It would have become more but for the drone of an engine in the distance. They drew apart, checking with each other to see if they'd heard the same thing.

The sound disappeared in the wind and then came back stronger. They both shot up and looked toward the island.

A small boat cut through the ocean, distant but approaching quickly. They got up on their knees and waved frantically. The boat's two occupants waved back.

"Looks like someone on the island had an old diesel," Tyler said.

"We're being rescued. You were right again."

He looked at her with a serious expression. "You need to make up your mind."

"I know."

"But for now we need to get Fay back and stop Colchev."

"I know," Jess said again, but she felt like she didn't know anything.

NAZCA

The drone of the six-seater plane's engine was so monotonous that the coffee in Tyler's hand had been the only thing keeping him awake on the early morning flight. There wasn't much to see as they flew over the mountainous terrain from Lima toward southern Peru, but now that the aircraft was in its final descent, he perked up, and Jess's tension was palpable. In a few minutes they would be flying directly over the Nazca lines.

Yesterday when the scuba company owner who rescued Tyler and Jess took them straight to the island, Tyler found that all communications were out except for an old battery-powered short-wave radio. While Jess gathered their belongings from the hotel, including Fay's medication and cash, he helped get the antique radio working by the time the LAN flight from Lima arrived just ahead of sunset. Unable to make contact with the airport, the airliner pilot had nearly turned around before they were able to reach him and convince him to land.

If there was one small piece of luck, it was that the jet

didn't need to gas up to return to the mainland. Rapa Nui had no refueling equipment to be rendered inoperable by the EMP blast. All airliners to the island had to load enough fuel to make the round trip on one tank.

Though it was the low season of winter, the tourists who were there swarmed to the airport when they realized that the power outage wasn't going to be a short-term inconvenience. The plane had been only half full, but none of the arriving passengers was getting off, so seats were at a premium. It was only through Jess's fast talking and Fay's bankroll that she and Tyler secured two of the spots on the return flight to Lima. The local police were too busy with the sudden chaos to question them about the downed cargo jet, and Tyler wasn't going to volunteer any information that would get them confined to the island for an extended period.

By the time they arrived in Peru, they were too tired to do anything but crash in a hotel for the remainder of the night. Tyler had tried reaching Grant and Morgan, but he'd been told by Morgan's supervisor that they were en route from Sydney to Los Angeles. He also informed her supervisor about the men killed by Colchev, the detonation of one of the two Killswitches, and the crashed C-17, though he left out the part about him being the one who destroyed it. Tyler didn't have time for the complications that admission would bring. He'd come clean when the entire situation was resolved.

Without Morgan's help, he and Jess were on their own in

contacting the Peruvian authorities. Tyler spoke with a policeman in Nazca who could understand English and told them about Fay's abduction and the connection to the incident at Easter Island, but he said nothing of the Killswitch or xenobium. The policeman agreed to accompany them to Cahuachi in the hopes that they could intercept Colchev there and liberate Fay. Once Morgan was available, Tyler would consult with her on how to work with the Peruvian government to secure the xenobium.

After only a few hours' sleep, they woke up to get to the stores by the time they opened. Jess acquired more cash and new cell phones while Tyler made a couple of quick stops of his own to cobble together the hardware he needed. With their purchases in hand, they hurried to the airport and bought tickets on the next flight to Nazca.

The plane's only occupant other than Tyler and Jess was the pilot. As they neared their destination, he pointed down, and Tyler peered out the window at the desolate plain below. The empty desert beneath him made the landscape around Alice Springs look like the Garden of Eden.

Other than the distant fields that hugged the banks of narrow rivers, there was no sign of vegetation. Rocky peaks engulfed the flat expanse of the Nazca plateau, which seemed to be a uniform rust color until he focused his eyes and saw his first glimpse of the famed white lines.

The construction of the drawings—from the miles-long straight lines to the most intricate animal symbols—was a simple process, aided by the unique geography of the region.

A thin layer of red pebbles overlaid the white substrata of chalky clay underneath. All that was needed to make the lines was a pair of hands and time to painstakingly remove the red pebbles. Because the desert experienced almost no rain or wind, erosion was minimal, allowing the drawings to persist for over a thousand years.

Although the construction technique was simple, how the huge drawings were created so precisely and for what purpose had been the subject of heated debate for almost a century. Hundreds of feet long and unrecognizable for what they are at ground level, they remained undiscovered until planes began flying over the desert in the 1920s. It was only then that the lines were revealed to the world as one of the great mysteries of a forgotten people.

Now that he could see them with his own eyes, Tyler could understand why the lines captured the public imagination. The first image he could identify was a giant hummingbird winging its way across the northwestern corner of the plateau. Like the other drawings, it resembled a child's doodle, but its wings, tail, and beak were outlined in recognizable detail.

Next was a great monkey, its prehensile tail curled into a spiral. Straight lines intersected the drawings and each other in all directions. A casual observer might come to the conclusion that these majestic symbols were alien spaceship landing instructions. It defied belief that a primitive culture could not only make them, but envision a reason for doing so in the first place.

Jess waved for him to check out her side of the plane. He leaned over and saw the shape of a massive condor, and beyond that the eight legs of a tarantula.

"Nana has seen this view a dozen times," Jess said. "She'd come here just to fly over the lines and see if she could figure out why she'd been chosen by the alien to be entrusted with its secret."

Tyler admired Fay's tenacity. He had never believed in aliens—at least not in ones that had visited Earth—but he understood her need to find the truth. Her experience at Roswell had obviously set all of this in motion, and until he had the answers he was ruling nothing out. He was a skeptic, but he was also a scientist. The scientific method meant doing away with preconceived notions. He would go wherever the evidence took him, no matter where it led.

Jess gazed at the desolate landscape with a haunted expression. "Do you think she's down there somewhere?"

"Yes, and I believe we're going to find her."

"Why?"

"Because I don't have any reason to think we won't."

"Sometimes I like your arrogance."

"It comes in handy."

Jess pointed at the astronaut drawing waving to them from the side of a hill. Tyler had to admit it did look like an otherworldly figure, two round eyes gazing from its otherwise featureless bulbous head.

"You think he's going to lead us to Nana?" Jess asked.

Tyler nodded. "And to the xenobium."

"Why are you so sure?"

"Because Colchev is sure."

"What do you mean?"

Tyler lowered his voice. "We know that Colchev got away with two Killswitches, each one worth hundreds of millions of dollars."

"And we know that they're useless without the xenobium trigger."

"Right. So what does he do when he finds the only xenobium that we know about?"

Jess frowned. "You mean, why did he set off one of his two Killswitches?"

"Exactly. Colchev had to be absolutely sure that there was more xenobium. And it's possible that the specimen from the cave wasn't big enough for whatever he has planned. The sample that Kessler destroyed in Australia was twenty times bigger than the speck we found."

"The drawing at Easter Island did imply that the Nazca had a much bigger specimen hidden in the pyramid."

"Kessler told us about a scientist from Russia named Dombrovski. What if Dombrovski was a Russian spy who found the xenobium but couldn't get it out of its hiding place for some reason? That would explain why Colchev is so positive it exists."

"He just didn't know where to look until Nana made that appearance in the video."

"It also means that Dombrovski found a way inside the

Grand Pyramid more than sixty years ago, before anyone even started doing a thorough excavation of the site."

"So we shouldn't be looking for the entrance anywhere that's been uncovered since then."

Jess's eyes lit up as if she remembered something and she plunged her hands into her bag. She opened a notebook and leafed through it.

"This is Nana's. It contains her notes for the book she's planning to write. She left it in our room because she had scanned everything into her computer and didn't want to risk losing it at the site of the cave. It has a detailed map of Cahuachi in it, including dates."

Jess flipped the pages until she got to the map. Jess pointed to a spot on the northwest corner of the Grand Pyramid.

"Look! This is one of the first discoveries of the adobe bricks that led to them uncovering the pyramid."

"Did floods bury it?" Tyler asked. "The river looks close by."

"No, that's the odd thing. The pyramid is more than thirty meters tall. It would have taken centuries of natural floods to cover the entire four-hundred-acre site. For some reason, the Nazca buried the whole city in mud themselves before they abandoned it."

"Why would they do that?"

"Maybe they didn't want anyone to ever find the xenobium."

"So it was literally a massive cover-up, but they left one

point of access into the pyramid, something only they and the gods would have known about."

"They drew the Mandala to show how to get into the pyramid," Jess said. "Then they drew the Nazca lines as a map to the pyramid. A map that would be decipherable only to those with the ability to see it from the sky."

"Speaking of that, I took some time last night to compare our photos to southern hemisphere star charts. The animal constellations match up perfectly. If you follow the lines according to the sequence of constellations ordered by their position in the zodiac, they lead directly from the Mandala to the Grand Pyramid."

As their plane touched down at the Nazca airport, Tyler could see a police car waiting for them on the tarmac.

"If Colchev figures all this out," Jess said, "he might know how to get into the pyramid."

Tyler didn't have to respond. They both knew the ominous outcome if Colchev had beaten them to Cahuachi. Fay would be no further use to the Russian spy once he had all the components of a weapon that could kill millions.

FORTY-THREE

Morgan noted that getting out of the US was much easier than getting in. Even at the break of dawn, the line of cars at the Highway 905 US–Mexico border crossing stretched half a mile—on the Mexican side. On the US side it was a clear road to the immigration checkpoint. Morgan flashed her credentials at the officer, and he directed her to the customs building.

She elbowed Grant, who dozed in the passenger seat, still sleeping off the effects of the Ambien he took for the flight back to LA. He had awakened just long enough to make the transfer to the helicopter that took them to the San Diego airport, and then again when they got in the car.

His eyes flew open. "What?"

"Wake up. We're here."

"I'm awake."

"Next time, just take one pill."

"For someone *my* size?"

"You took enough to down a bull elephant."

"Well, I'm up now," Grant said, yawning. "Remind me. Who are we meeting?"

"Captain Filipe Benitez of the Mexican Federales."

"*Excellente*."

"You speak Spanish?"

"*Tenemos los exitos más calientes*."

"You have the hottest hits?"

"It's from a radio station I listened to when I was at Fort Hood."

"If the Killswitch played music, you'd be a big help."

"It's the only Spanish I remember."

"Let me do the talking."

"*Si, si, señorita*."

She pulled into a parking spot next to the customs building. When she opened the car door, a blast of hot air hit her, reminding her that it was summer now that she was back in the northern hemisphere.

"Good God," Grant said as he got out. "I must have really been out of it at the San Diego airport not to notice this heat."

"We're ten miles inland here."

"Aren't you hot?" He nodded at her suit. He was wearing a T-shirt and jeans.

"I'm fine."

"Suit yourself. Ha! Get it?"

"I'm amused." She wouldn't admit it to him, but she actually almost cracked a smile. His bad jokes were starting to grow on her.

They went inside, where they were met by air conditioning and Policìa Federal Captain Benitez, who was dressed in full tactical gear.

"Special Agent Bell?" he asked in precise English.

She nodded and showed him her ID. He responded in kind, then eyed Grant.

"This is Sergeant Grant Westfield," Morgan said. "He's on temporary assignment with me from the Army Rangers."

They shook hands.

"I was instructed to give you every cooperation I can, Agent Bell."

"I appreciate your help. This is a dangerous situation, and I understand that you are this state's top anti-cartel officer."

"Until they kill me," Benitez said without a trace of humor. Mexican anti-drug officials had a depressingly short lifespan.

"We think the Baja cartel is going to attempt to smuggle some explosives into the US sometime today," Morgan said.

"You think they will meet at this address that I was given?"

"It's possible. Do you have it under surveillance?"

"Yes, for eight hours now."

"Any unusual activity?"

Benitez shrugged. "A few men came and went. Nothing strange."

"Were any of the men Caucasian?"

"No. All Hispanic." He showed her and Grant the surveillance photos.

Grant shook his head. "None of them look like our guys."

"Captain," Morgan said, "it is vital that we get those explosives before they enter the US." She wasn't going to share that they were looking for a top-secret weapon, only one of which now remained in existence according to the message she'd received about the EMP blast that disabled Easter Island.

"We are prepared for a full tactical breach once you confirm that the explosives have arrived on the premises," Benitez said.

"We'd also like to capture these men alive, but the explosives are the top priority."

Benitez shook his head. "The Baja cartel is responsible for over a hundred murders in the last month, including a night club where twenty-five were killed. If this house is theirs, they won't come quietly."

"Sounds like our boys have connected with some real winners," Grant said.

"If your suspects need smuggling assistance, they chose the right gang. The Bajas have moved three tons of cocaine out of Tijuana this year, and we've intercepted none of it going into the US."

"Could this house be their staging area?" Morgan asked.

"Possibly. It's very close to both the truck and car crossings. It's also possible that they could be planning to smuggle your item under the border. Some of the cartels' drug tunnels have been found to be more than a quarter-mile long."

"I'll let my team in the US know to be ready for anything. Let's get over to the house. Oh, and one other thing. Westfield and I need to go in with the tactical team. Sergeant Westfield is a bomb-disposal expert, and we may need him in there."

Benitez nodded. "Of course. Come with me. We will supply you with uniforms and weapons." He walked toward the rear of the building. Morgan and Grant fell into step behind him.

"He didn't bat an eye," Grant said under his breath. "That was easy."

"That's what happens when the Secretary of the Air Force calls up the Commandant of the Federales," Morgan said.

Ten minutes later they were fully geared up with black fatigues, ballistic vests, M4 rifles, comm units, and helmets.

"You'll have to leave your car here," Benitez said. "They'd spot the US plates immediately."

"Lead the way," Morgan said.

They went outside to a beat-up Chrysler minivan with blacked-out windows.

Benitez saw Grant's bemused appraisal. "Our black Suburbans would be noticed even faster than your car."

They climbed in the back. The driver was one of Benitez's men dressed inconspicuously in a dingy white tank top.

When the sliding door closed, he steered onto the road leading south from the border.

"We'll only be able to drive by the house once. Any more would be suspicious."

"How are you watching the house?" Morgan asked.

"Someone abandoned construction of a four-story building across the street. Only the girders have been put up. I had one of my men climb up late last night and install three wireless cameras facing the house."

"And your man wasn't seen?"

"It was a moonless night, and I made sure the streetlights went out for a short time."

In two minutes they were cruising down a boulevard paralleling the border only two hundred yards away. On the left were enormous warehouses supplying the truckers shipping goods back and forth to the Mexican factories. On the right were tiny stores, freight yards filled with semis, street food vendors just setting up shop in their trucks, apartment complexes, and homes. It wasn't Beverly Hills, but it wasn't a slum, either.

"There's the construction," Benitez said, pointing out the windshield.

A chain-link fence protected the skeleton of bare girders rusting in the sunlight.

The driver turned right at the next street.

"This is Licenciado José López Portillo Oriente. Number 22 is the pink house on the left."

The second house down from the boulevard was a

rundown home set back from the road just enough to make room for a paved front yard. The paint was peeling, tiles on the roof were missing, and old lawn furniture was piled against the garage door.

The only thing that looked out of place was the new iron fence and gate that protected the parking area.

The driver didn't slow down for Morgan and Grant to get a better look.

"The garage looks big enough for a full-sized van," Grant said.

"Trucks are very common in this area," Benitez said. "If they're planning to move the package across the border that way, it would take only a few seconds to put it on a passing semi."

"Grant and I are going to need line-of-sight to the house," Morgan said. "It's the only way we can identify our subjects." The night-vision goggles for the ID dust had a limited range, and the cameras on the abandoned building wouldn't pick up the signal.

"I told you that's impossible," Benitez said. "They would see you."

"Well, we have to figure out something. Otherwise, they could drive straight into that garage, and we wouldn't know if the explosives had arrived."

Grant raised his hand. "I have an idea. Is anyone else hungry?"

"You're hungry?" Morgan said. "The only thing you did on the plane besides sleep was eat."

"I'm always hungry, but that's not the point."

"What *is* your point?"

Grant smiled. "My obsession with food will get us that surveillance spot."

FORTY-FOUR

Zotkin swept the ground with his radiation meter.

"Anything?" Colchev said.

Zotkin shook his head. "Just a tiny amount of elevated background radiation."

The Mandala was positioned at the summit of a flat-topped mountain twenty miles northwest of Nazca. After arriving in Santiago without incident, Colchev had the jet refueled and immediately flew on to the town of Ica, Peru, which was the closest airport to the Mandala. It had been a short drive to the turnoff from the Pan-American Highway, then another mile to the path that led them up to the plateau.

The trek up the mountain hadn't been an especially hard one on anyone except for Fay, who stood off to the side panting from exertion as she watched their search. There was no need to closely guard her. If she ran, Kiselow, the only man Colchev and Zotkin had left, would chase her down.

From this ground-level vantage point, the massive drawing just looked like a random collection of lines strung together. Holes in the dirt punctuated the intersections of lines in several places, but they served no discernible purpose and hid nothing.

They had concentrated their initial search on the center white space that radiated lines in multiple directions. Unless the xenobium was buried deep beneath the surface, the radiation meter would detect a pronounced signal, but nothing significant registered on the device.

Zotkin shook his head. "I've been over every inch of this drawing. The xenobium might have been here at one time, but it's gone now."

"We never had a chance to find it here," Colchev said. "Did we, Mrs. Turia?"

Zotkin and Kiselow turned to Fay, who smirked.

"You really are stupid if you thought I would tell you anything."

Colchev nodded appreciatively. "Very good act. Convincing, although I gave it a fifty-fifty chance that you were lying."

Fay laughed. "I'm sure."

"It doesn't matter. I would have chosen this location to visit first anyway. More isolated and easier to get the xenobium if it really was here."

Zotkin took Colchev aside. "Do you want me to kill her?"

Colchev sighed. "Eventually."

"Now."

"Not yet. The news from Rapa Nui this morning said that all power was out, but there were no mass casualties."

"What if Kessler was wrong about the gamma rays?"

"No. The experiments they did with the Australian sample proved that gamma ray emissions from the weapon would be deadly at that range. Somehow they got it off the island."

"Do you think Locke survived?"

"If he did, we may need Fay as a bargaining chip. But when we do find the xenobium, we will kill her. Satisfactory?"

Zotkin looked as if he were about to protest again, but held his tongue.

Colchev turned around. "All right. Back to the car." He checked his watch. "We should be at Cahuachi in forty-five minutes."

Girdled by adobe brick walls, the terraced Grand Pyramid loomed over the sprawling Cahuachi complex. In the days when the city served as the religious center of the Nazca culture, its citizens would ritualistically climb the myriad stairs in a procession that snaked around the forty structures built to house the civilization's heritage and treasures.

Today the city was uninhabited, awaiting the arrival of the first tourist buses.

Jess was surprised that Tyler had been able to convince the police to provide six officers for the search at Cahuachi, but the show of force had been for naught. Jess shouted Fay's name repeatedly. Silence was the only response. There was no sign of her or Colchev.

"Do you think they've come and gone?" she said to Tyler.

"I doubt it. They wouldn't have made it before nightfall yesterday, and searching in the dark would have been difficult."

After a thorough inspection of the grounds, the lead officer called his men back to the main plaza, where he approached Jess and Tyler with a combination of regret and annoyance.

"Señor Locke," he said. "She is not here."

"Are you sure they couldn't be hiding somewhere?" Jess said.

The policeman shrugged. "Señor, this place very big, but we look everywhere. Nobody here."

"Officer," Tyler said, "I think the best option is to leave some of your men here and take us to the Mandala. They could be there instead."

The policeman frowned. Jess had never gotten the feeling that he believed their story. "I'm sorry, señor," the officer said. "We go now."

"We're staying for a while to look around."

"We are?" Jess asked. "What about the Mandala?"

Tyler nodded slightly to show her that he had a plan.

The policeman shrugged. "Okay. If you see these people, call us and we come back."

The officers returned to their cars and drove off, leaving the rental as the only car in the lot.

"What are we supposed to do now?" Jess said.

Tyler started walking toward the Grand Pyramid.

"Without some muscle, we'll never be able to take Colchev. We don't even have any guns. If Colchev *is* at the Mandala, he's in the wrong place."

"Which means he'll come here."

"Right. And if the xenobium really is here, we need to find it before he does."

Jess suddenly understood. "Then we'll have something to bargain with!"

"If we find it, that is. We'll do better to search on our own. Since this is probably a Peruvian national monument, the police wouldn't look too kindly on us breaking in and stealing an artifact from it."

"That kind of thing didn't seem to bother Indiana Jones."

"Yeah, but they never show you the actual sequel to his tomb raiding: Indiana Jones and the Museum's Repatriation Lawsuit."

"You're not going to trade the xenobium for Nana," Jess said. "Are you?"

Tyler's jaw clenched. "We can't. I'm sorry. It would be too dangerous for Colchev to get his hands on it."

"I'm getting her back!" Jess cried out. "I don't care about the damn xenobium!"

He put his hands on her shoulders. "We will get Fay back. We can use the xenobium as a lure."

"Then what?"

"We'll think about how that will work later. Let's get the xenobium first."

Jess grunted and shrugged his hands away, but she didn't argue further.

Tyler and Jess checked the interior chambers that had been excavated, including the large tunnel that seemed to be the main entrance inside, but it ended at a brick wall and there was no indication of a way further into the pyramid. They climbed to the top of the exterior so they could get a better lay of the land. A maze of walls, trenches, and stairs had been unearthed around it, revealing the smaller mounds that seemed like pale imitations. Beyond that were sere hills and pocked terrain that could have served as a backdrop for a film set on the moon. The blue of the clear sky was the only reminder that she wasn't looking at a sepia-toned photo.

"Where do we start?" she said.

Tyler consulted his camera, then pointed to the northwest corner of the pyramid. "According to Easter Island, that's where we're supposed to look."

They clambered down the steps until they reached the spot that corresponded to the photo of the drawing on the cave ceiling.

"I bet if we did a survey of the actual Nazca lines, they would eventually intersect right here," Jess said.

Tyler nodded. "Dombrovski had a lot more time to analyze them than we've had. But now that the pyramid is completely uncovered, the entrance should be much easier to find."

"One question: if we do find the xenobium, it'll be radioactive. How are we going to carry it?"

Tyler tapped the backpack he'd taken from their rental

trunk. "This morning I stopped at a medical supply store and bought one of those protective vests used for patients getting x-rayed. I also picked up a couple of lanterns and a short crowbar."

Jess was agog. "You knew this might happen."

"I didn't want to worry you."

"Next time, give it to me straight. I can take it."

"Will do."

The wall at this corner, like the others, was built out of adobe brick, fabricated by mixing mud and straw. The pieces fitted together in a zigzag pattern, mimicking the stair-step construction of the pyramid itself.

Tyler knelt next to the bricks, running his hands over the rough surface.

"It wouldn't be an obvious opening," Tyler said, "or someone would have found it long ago merely by accident."

"Do you see any symbols?" Jess asked.

"Nothing."

"If this is a secret entrance, why would the Nazca make it so you had to tear the bricks apart to get in?"

"They wouldn't. Dombrovski entered through here somehow. If he'd hammered the bricks away to get in, there'd be evidence, and these bricks are intact. We just have to figure out how to open it."

"Maybe it has something to do with the Mandala image," Jess said. "That would fit the pattern of the drawings, that the Nazca were providing a set of instructions to the gods."

Tyler nodded. "Makes sense. It has a square overlaid with another square that's turned at a forty-five-degree angle. Which implies that something needs to be turned to set it to the proper alignment." He studied the picture from the cave, then an aerial photo of the Mandala itself. "But what has to turn?"

Then Jess saw the difference between the drawing and the photo. She snatched the camera from his hand. "Look at this line in the drawing. It's faint, but you can see that it bisects only the northwest corner of the larger square."

Tyler's eyes widened. "It's as if that corner is supposed to divide in two."

He didn't have to utter the same conclusion that they had both reached. The bricks would have to swing away in either direction to reveal the secret opening.

Tyler's finger followed the path of the stair-step seam created by the bricks. Then he stuck the tip of the crowbar between the bricks. The dirt fell away.

"The mortar's crumbling," Jess said.

"It's not mortar. It's dirt that's worked its way into the crack. That explains why no one has noticed the gap."

He jammed the crowbar farther in and pried at the bricks. At first they didn't move, but Tyler pulled again, and Jess heard the bricks scrape against each other.

"It's working!"

Tyler put his back into it, and the bricks separated far enough for Jess to get her fingers in. While Tyler pulled, Jess pushed from her side. The more room they got, the easier it became to swing it aside until the adobe segment was flush against the pyramid wall.

They repeated the process for the other side. With the other half of the corner out of the way, this one was no problem to move. Only three feet across, this hole was even less inviting than the one on Easter Island.

It didn't matter. If this was the way to get Fay back, Jess wanted to get started as quickly as possible.

She held out her hand. "Give me a damn lantern."

FORTY-FIVE

The passageway into the pyramid was not much wider than Tyler's shoulders, so he had to adjust the backpack to keep it from scraping the walls. Jess led the way, holding her electric lantern high enough to illuminate the tunnel sixty feet ahead.

Tyler could make out soot on the ceiling from the torches that must have been carried through here over fifteen hundred years ago. The sunlight quickly receded behind him, and at the first turn in the passage, it was completely gone.

They crept forward another forty feet where they reached an opening on the left. The tunnel continued straight ahead.

"Which way?" Jess said.

"Let's see what's in this room."

She turned and stopped so suddenly upon entering that Tyler almost ran into her.

He didn't have to ask why. The room was filled with debris, a haphazard pile of bricks that stretched halfway to the ceiling thirty feet above.

"What the hell happened here?" Jess said. "Sure is a weird way to store bricks."

Tyler raised his lantern to get a better look at the ceiling. Around the edges he could see a few bricks still teetering atop the inner wall that made up part of the room.

"It looks like they built an outer room around the inner room and the inner ceiling and walls collapsed."

"Or they built the outer room over it after the old one caved in. But why would they do either one?"

"You've got me," Tyler said. Even if there was another outlet on the other side of the room, it would be a dangerous trek to get to it. "Let's keep going down the tunnel."

They exited and this time Tyler took the lead.

After another forty feet, the tunnel opened into a vast space, this one so large that their lanterns barely illuminated the opposite side. Tyler estimated the ceiling was sixty feet high, and the circular space was big enough to hold a couple hundred people.

They had to be in the pyramid's primary chamber.

Jess walked to the other side of the room and shone her lantern into a large opening.

"This must be the main entrance," she said.

"Is it walled off?"

"Not that I can see from here."

In the center of the room was an enormous pillar holding up the domed ceiling. Stepped risers surrounded the brick tower and led up to its mid-point. Something about the layout seemed familiar . . .

He whipped out the camera and checked the aerial image of the Mandala.

The layout of this room was exactly the same as the shape of the inner part of the Mandala—a circle inside a square with rectangular steps surrounding a starburst image in the middle. The starburst had to represent the xenobium locked inside the pillar.

The Nazca designers had drawn an overhead plan of the pyramid for their gods.

"This is it!" Tyler said.

Jess ran over to him. "The xenobium?"

"It has to be in the center pillar." He took out the radiation meter and pointed it at the brick structure.

The reading was in the middle of the scale. He climbed to the second level of steps, and the reading increased.

"It's up here on the pillar." He removed the lead apron from his pack and draped it over his front so it dangled from his neck. Even with it on, he didn't want to remain there any longer than he had to.

He climbed the next step. The reading reached the top of the scale.

He looked at the pillar to see if he could spot the xenobium. Halfway up the pillar, the bricks were supplanted by a stack of twelve thin circular stone disks that partially supported the thick vertical wooden beams. The top disk was pierced at irregular intervals by slots that were the same diameter as the beams. The dry desert air had preserved the yard-long segments of lumber.

There was a finger-width gap between each of the beams. He held the lantern up to one of the gaps, and the iridescent sheen of the multi-hued xenobium reflected the light. From the limited view he had, it looked to be an oblong specimen the size of a plum.

The gaps were too small to fit his hand through, and even if he could have, the xenobium specimen was too large to extract.

The Nazca must have created a way to retrieve it. But how?

Then he noticed that wooden handles extended from the disks. He looked closer and saw that drawings of the Nazca zodiac symbols were etched around the rim of each of the disks.

That had to be it. If the disks were rotated to a particular alignment, the wooden beams would slip off their main supports and fall into the disk's slots like the tumblers in a lock. Tyler supposed he shouldn't have been surprised about such a sophisticated design from a people who had created the wealth of lines on the Nazca plateau, but it was an amazing revelation all the same.

"Can you get it?" Jess said.

"Let me give it a try."

Tyler grabbed hold of the handle attached to the topmost disk and pulled to his right until the spider figure was aligned with the hummingbird figure in the disk below.

Just as he suspected, a wooden beam slid down a few inches into the topmost disk.

What he wasn't expecting was the cascade of bricks that

fell from the roof. He hugged the pillar and they barely missed him as they crashed to the floor.

When the dust cleared, Jess said, "What the hell happened?"

"I got a little overconfident."

"Surprise, surprise."

"At least we know what happened in that other room. They had a similar pillar setup in there and some tomb raiders found out the hard way that the Nazca didn't want anyone but the gods messing with their stuff. It'd take a week to dig through there and see what they were after."

Jess gazed at the pillar. "You mean, if those disks are turned in the correct pattern, the wooden beams fall far enough to let you get at the xenobium, but if you don't align them perfectly—"

"We get buried under a few hundred tons of bricks. Some of the wooden beams seem to act as keystones. Drop a couple of the wrong ones down into the slots, and it would start a chain reaction."

"You say the symbols from the Nazca lines are on the disks?"

"Some of them, but I don't have any idea how they should line up to get the xenobium out. I could try to pry the beams apart, but I'm afraid I'd bring down the entire roof."

Jess looked thoughtful then broke out her smart phone, to which she'd transferred the cave photos they'd emailed from Easter Island. After scanning it for a few minutes, she said, "Are all twelve symbols on every disk?"

Tyler walked around the pillar, counting each of the drawings etched into the stone.

"All of them are here," he said. "Why?"

"Because I think I know why the Nazca symbols were connected by lines. The map shows each of the drawings connected from the Mandala through each other all the way to Cahuachi. What if the lines were drawn to show the gods how to unlock the xenobium?"

"It's a combination lock." Tyler gaped in awe of the Nazca people's ingenuity. "The stone disks are the dials. But what's the zero position?"

"The Nazca apparently liked lines. See if you can find one above the top disk."

Tyler did another circumnavigation on the top riser and sure enough, there it was. He'd missed it before because it was just a single notch. It lined up with a notch below the bottom disk.

"Found it. Okay. Tell me the order."

"One problem. I don't know whether the Nazca would order them from top to bottom or bottom up."

"What's your best guess?" Tyler asked. "We've got a fifty-fifty shot."

"As long as my theory about the combination is correct," Jess said. "All right. They drew the lines leading from the Mandala to here through the constellation symbols. They were leading the gods to the xenobium. That means the disk symbols should go in the same order."

"So you think the top disk would be the last symbol the line on the Nazca plain goes through?"

"Or it could be top down because the gods would start in the heavens."

"But then the xenobium would be underneath the disks. I think your first instinct was right. We'll start with the bottom and work our way to the top."

"Are you sure you want to do this?" Jess asked. "After that preview of the collapse, we may not get a second chance."

"If Colchev gets here and figures out what we did, he could walk away with the xenobium before we get back with any kind of force. And if I fail, at least he won't get his hands on it."

"Don't even say that."

"Believe me, if this starts to buckle, I'm going to run like hell. Stand over by the exit in case this doesn't work."

Jess hesitated, then reluctantly moved to the passageway opening.

"Now what's the first symbol?" Tyler asked.

"The spider."

Tyler found the tarantula and rotated the bottom disk until the etching was matched up with the line.

"Next?"

"The condor," Jess said. "Don't mix it up with the hummingbird."

"Bigger wingspan on the condor, I assume." He rotated the second stone disk until the condor was above the spider.

They continued on in the same way for the next nine symbols. None of the wooden beams had moved, but Tyler wasn't expecting them to until he reached the last disk.

"What's the last symbol?" Tyler asked. His back ached from pulling on the heavy disks.

"The astronaut."

"Okay," Tyler said. "Get ready to run if this doesn't work."

"If you start to feel it buckling, get out of there."

"I will." Tyler put his hands on the disk's handle and paused to look at Jess. "I've often thought about running into you again. I'm glad I did." He smiled. "It's been fun."

Before she could reply, he pulled the handle. The disk ground against the other stones as it rotated. Tyler put every bit of remaining strength he had into the final heave.

The astronaut etching lined up with the notch and something snapped inside the column. Two of the wooden beams fell all the way into their slots on the pillar. Tyler prepared to jump, but all the other beams remained in place.

The xenobium gleamed from its honored resting place nestled on a cradle of obsidian glass, within reach of human hands for the first time in over a thousand years.

"It worked!" Jess yelled.

Tyler exhaled sharply. "And I'm not dead!"

"That too."

He used the crowbar to nudge the xenobium out of its holder, and the ovoid relic fell out, thumping onto the top riser before rolling off and coming to rest on the floor of the chamber. Tyler clambered down, took the lead-lined apron out of his pack, and carefully wrapped it around the specimen.

"Is it safe to hold?" Jess asked.

Tyler ran the radiation meter over it. "Not for long. I'll be getting an x-ray-equivalent dose every two minutes while I'm carrying it."

"Then let's go." She scooped it up.

"Let me hold it," Tyler said.

"You've been next to it for ten minutes already." She walked quickly toward the exit while Tyler followed carrying both lanterns. "That officer is going to be pretty surprised at what he missed."

"We can't tell him," Tyler said. "If the Peruvian government finds out what we've done, they'll lock us up and who knows what will happen to the xenobium."

"What about Nana?"

"We'll leave the pyramid open when we exit. Once Colchev finds out we have the xenobium, *he'll* find *us*."

They retraced their path out of the pyramid. When they reached the opening, Jess climbed out first. But before Tyler could do the same, she barreled back down the steps.

"What happened?"

"It's them!"

"Colchev? Where?"

"At the parking area. I saw his gray hair. He's got two men with him."

"And Fay?"

Jess nodded. "They've got her, Tyler. And they're coming this way."

FORTY-SIX

Grant munched on a second breakfast burrito, the salsa running down his hand. From his position he had a good view of the house where they were expecting the Killswitch to arrive. The food vendor had been only too happy to rent out his truck for the day at a reasonable mark-up. Although the vehicle was closed for business, with the awning rolled up and side window closed, its familiar presence wouldn't arouse suspicion to any occupants of the drug gang's hideaway.

In the hour they'd been observing the home, no one had come or gone. Grant thought they might be in for a long wait, so he helped himself to the vendor's supplies. He figured it should be included in the price.

"How can you eat that?" Morgan said with a measure of disgust on her face.

"Easy," he said, and stuffed the rest of it in his mouth. "Best burrito I've had in months. Seattle isn't known for its Tex-Mex."

"I don't want to think about what kind of meat that is."

"Doesn't matter. My stomach's like an iron cauldron."

He wiped his hands on a paper towel. "This was a great idea, if I do say so myself."

"I won't be able to get the smell of taco sauce out of my hair for weeks."

Grant rubbed his bald head. "You could always try my hairstyle."

"It wouldn't look as good on me."

"Why, Agent Bell, is that a compliment?"

She snorted in feigned exasperation, but she also turned red. Grant smiled. It seemed like he was starting to make an impression.

A van approaching from the opposite direction slowed to turn onto the side street where the house sat.

Grant and Morgan donned their goggles. Bright red crosshairs bloomed on the back of the van.

"We have a winner," Grant said.

The gate to the house slid aside, and the garage door opened. The van pulled inside, and the door closed behind it.

Morgan took off the goggles and radioed Benitez. "That's our van. The explosives are in the house."

"We're ready to move in."

"Remember, no one touches the explosives except us. When the house is secure, Westfield and I will take possession of the explosives and bring the couriers into custody."

"Understood. We move in two minutes."

"Copy that."

They weren't going for subtlety in this operation. Two tactical teams would approach the house, one from the front and one from the back to make sure no one escaped. Everyone on the team had gas masks. Benitez had wanted to use concussion grenades for the breach, but Morgan was afraid of damaging the Killswitch, so she insisted on tear-gas grenades instead, telling him that the explosives might be detonated by the concussive blast.

Three men would cover the garage door in case the targets attempted to escape in the van. The rest of them would go through the front door, prepared to shoot anyone who resisted.

Once they found the Killswitch, Benitez would provide escort back to the American border, where they would secure the weapon until the Air Force could arrange for protective transport back to Wright-Patterson.

Grant squeezed into his ballistic vest and put his helmet on over his mask. Morgan did the same.

"You don't have to go in with us," she said, her voice muffled.

"You think I'm going to wait in the truck?" Grant said.

"I dragged you along on this. It's not your job."

"Morgan, I've done this kind of raid dozens of times in Iraq and Afghanistan. If there's a better way to get the adrenaline pumping, I don't know what it is."

"You enjoy this?"

"You don't?"

"Flying does it for me."

"Taking down bad guys does it for me."

"If that's true, why aren't you still in the Army?"

"Because I hate sleeping in barracks and eating MREs." There was a lot more to it than that, but Grant wasn't going to go into the details now.

Benitez's voice came through the radio. "We're set to move in, Agent Bell."

"Ready here," she said.

"Do not get out of the truck until my unit is deployed."

"Understood."

Grant positioned himself at the food truck's rear door, his M4 assault rifle at the ready. Morgan checked her own weapon twice. Her breathing quickened to the point that she sounded like Darth Vader hyperventilating.

"Have you ever done this before?" Grant asked.

She hesitated for a moment, then shook her head. "Only in simulations."

Grant fell back on his days as a sergeant leading soldiers fresh out of boot camp into battle.

"Remember to verify your targets before firing. This probably won't take more than thirty seconds, but if it does, things will get confusing fast. Stay with me and you'll be okay."

She gave him a thumbs-up with a rock-steady hand, and her breathing slowed.

The tactical team's truck sped past them, its tires squealing as it came to a stop in front of the house. Men in full assault gear spilled from the rear.

"That's our cue," Grant said, and threw open the back door.

He ran at top speed around the corner until he was in the

shelter of the massive black truck, Morgan on his heels the whole way. He took up a position next to Captain Benitez, who gave a command in Spanish.

A policeman took aim with the grenade launcher. With a thud, the tear-gas grenade shot across the fence and through the front window with a perfect bull's-eye.

That's when all hell broke loose.

As smoke billowed from the target house, a hail of gunfire rained down from the homes to the left and right of it, taking out two of the policemen in the first few seconds.

The police opened up, and the neighborhood was instantly transformed into a war zone.

Grant saw a face appear in the window to his left. He took aim and fired. For a soldier trained to hit targets at over two hundred yards without a scope, the distance to the neighboring house across the street was practically point-blank range. The man's head disappeared in a red mist.

Morgan fired her own weapon, but Grant didn't take the time to see if she hit anything.

Bullets from high-powered rifles continued to slam into the tactical vehicle. The armor would protect them, but Grant knew that some of these drug cartels carried heavy weaponry like rocket-propelled grenades. If they used one of those, the situation would deteriorate quickly.

More gunfire erupted from the back of the three houses. Benitez yelled at his men in Spanish. Grant hoped he was telling them to fire gas at the other houses because if they stayed out here much longer, they'd be cut to ribbons.

Grant had expected coughing gang members to spew from the main house after the tear gas took effect, but he realized that no one had left the house. It was highly unlikely that a drug cartel would have gas masks, and in a confined space like that, covering your face with a rag wouldn't do much good.

So what were they doing? Maybe they were holed up in the garage.

He saw that Morgan still had her goggles hanging from her neck. He tapped her on the shoulder, and she twisted around, a wild look in her eye betraying how amped up she was by the gun battle. He gestured at the goggles and took them from her. He leaned out so he could see through the truck's windshield and held them up to his mask.

No red crosshairs in the garage. He panned over the rest of the house. Nothing.

Until he looked down.

The crosshairs were descending below street level. Then they disappeared, no longer able to penetrate the dirt that shielded the ID dust from the sensors.

Grant dropped the goggles from his face.

"We've got to move in now!" he shouted to Morgan. "We're losing the Killswitch!"

"What? How?"

"Captain Benitez was right. They've got a drug-smuggling tunnel."

FORTY-SEVEN

"**D**id Colchev see you?" Tyler asked Jess. She was sure he hadn't turned her way when she popped out. "No, but they're headed straight for us. They'll see the opening any minute."

With Colchev and his men only a few hundred yards away, Tyler and Jess couldn't come out of the secret passage without being spotted. Unarmed, Jess knew they'd be easy prey.

"At least we won't be ambushed like on Easter Island," Tyler said. "That gives us a small advantage."

"What are we going to do?"

"I've got to collapse the chamber. It's the only way to be sure. We can't let Colchev get his hands on the xenobium."

"You'll be killed!"

"This isn't a discussion." He took the lead apron from her and stuffed it in the backpack. He gave her the crowbar and said, "Come on."

Carrying the backpack, Tyler ran toward the central chamber. Jess followed, expecting him to climb back up to the pillar, but instead he crossed the chamber and went out through the larger main entrance on the opposite side.

The wide passageway turned right and ended at a brick wall after another thirty feet.

With a look of concentration, Tyler examined the wall, then turned 360 degrees.

"What are you doing?" Jess asked.

He laid a hand on the wall. "This is facing south, right where we found the entrance to the pyramid when we were searching for Colchev. I'll bet the priests walled it up before they buried the whole place with mud."

"What's your point?"

He dropped the crowbar by the wall. "You're going to use that to hack your way out of here. You'll need to hammer the crowbar with another brick to chisel out the mortar."

"Are you serious?"

"We can't go back the way we came in, so this is the only other choice."

"But it could take hours. They'll be here any second."

"Which is why we will have to make them think you're dead."

"What do you mean, 'dead'?"

"Just trust me." She began to protest, but he shoved the backpack into her hands. "Follow my lead."

"But Nana—"

"You and Fay will be all right."

"Will *you*?"

"That's not important." He rushed back to the central chamber. Several approaching lights reflected off the walls of the secret passage on the other side. They didn't have much time until Colchev and his men entered the room.

When Jess moved to join Tyler on the pillar's riser, he stopped her before she got out of the chamber's main entrance.

"Stay there with your back against the wall," he said. "Don't make yourself a target."

She turned off her lantern and stepped to the side so that the pillar stood between her and the secret passage, leaving just enough space so that she had a slim view of the opening.

Tyler set his lantern down and pulled on the top disk. A few more bricks rained down. Another strong pull, and the whole ceiling would fall.

He waited, keeping tension on the handle.

The lights stopped just outside the chamber.

"Come in, Colchev!" Tyler called out. "But don't shoot. We're unarmed."

Colchev's lights were extinguished. After a moment, Jess could see a man crawl out of the gloom, survey the chamber, and pull back quickly.

"Let us see your hands!" came a booming basso voice.

"I can't do that," Tyler said, the body of the pillar between him and the secret passage. "Did you see the collapsed bricks in that chamber you passed?"

A pause. "Yes."

"The same thing will happen in here if you try to fire at us."

The lights went back on. A young man dressed in jeans

and a denim jacket emerged carrying a submachine gun. He took a look around the chamber, including the ceiling. Then he nodded.

Colchev and a bearded companion, both armed with pistols, followed the first man into the chamber with Fay propped in front of them. Colchev put down the metal case Tyler had used to secure the Easter Island xenobium.

"Nana!" Jess shouted. "Are you all right?"

"I'm fine. Don't give them anything for me."

Still as gutsy as ever. Jess breathed a sigh of relief.

Colchev's eyes went from Jess to Tyler. "This isn't going to end well for you, Dr. Locke."

"Maybe not. But then you won't get the xenobium."

"You have it?"

Tyler nodded in Jess's direction. "She does."

"How do I know that?"

"I'm sure you have a radiation detector. You should be able to tell from there."

"Zotkin," Colchev said. The man next to him took out a meter like Tyler's and waved it around.

"There's a strong radiation source in the room, but I can't tell where it is from this far away. She may have it."

"What are we going to do about this standoff?" Colchev said.

Jess held her breath. She had no idea what Tyler was planning.

"A trade," he said. "Fay for the xenobium. Then you leave."

"Really?"

"It's that simple."

"I accept. Have the girl bring over the xenobium and we'll let her grandmother go."

"No. One man goes with Fay and the radiation detector over to Jess at the main entrance. Your man checks out the backpack she's carrying. When he verifies that the xenobium is inside, Fay stays there and he goes back. Then you head out one at a time with the flashlights so we can see that you've all left. When you go, you'll take your weapons but leave the ammo on the floor so that you can't ambush us on our way out."

Colchev thought about it for a moment, then nodded. "Agreed. Give the detector to Kiselow."

Zotkin handed it over to the man in the denim jacket. Before Kiselow started walking, Tyler said, "One more thing. Kiselow drops his gun. I want to see that he's unarmed before he makes the trip. Turn out your pockets and show me your waistband and ankles."

Kiselow looked at Colchev, who nodded again. The man handed over his submachine gun and a pistol from his belt holster to Zotkin, then showed Tyler that he was now unarmed.

"Okay. Go ahead. Slowly." Tyler kept watch on Colchev and Zotkin, who had the submachine gun trained on Fay. "If you fire or if you or Zotkin take one step farther in, the whole place comes down."

"I only want what's mine," Colchev said.

"It's not yours!" Fay shouted.

"It will be in a minute unless you all want to die."

"I'm dying already."

"But Locke and your granddaughter aren't."

"It's okay, Fay," Tyler said. "Please."

Fay huffed but started moving. Kiselow kept her in front of him while they crossed. His eyes moved from Tyler to the ceiling and back to Fay.

When they reached the other side, Jess ran into Fay's arms and grasped her in a tight hug.

Jess pulled away and studied her grandmother's eyes.

Fay didn't look frightened. She looked angry.

"You shouldn't be doing this for me," she said.

"We weren't going to let these assholes kill you," Jess said.

"The bag!" Colchev commanded.

Jess unslung the backpack and gave it to Kiselow, who unzipped it and ran the detector over the opening.

"This is it," he said to Colchev triumphantly.

"Bring it back," Colchev said.

Kiselow zipped it up and started to walk back across the chamber.

Jess glanced at Tyler, who gave her a slight nod.

This had been Tyler's plan all along. *We can't let Colchev get his hands on the xenobium.*

She shook her head, pleading for him not to do it, but when she saw the corner of his mouth go up in a lopsided, heartbreaking smile, she knew there was no convincing him otherwise. He was going to stop Colchev even if it meant sacrificing his own life.

When Kiselow was beside the pillar, Tyler wrenched the disk's handle.

Three wooden beams fell into the column, and bricks began to plummet from the ceiling.

Kiselow, startled by the crackling of the adobe bricks, froze just long enough for Tyler to leap from the platform, his fist aimed at the Russian's head. Kiselow saw him in time to avoid the brutal punch, but couldn't keep Tyler from slamming into him. As bricks rained down, they wrestled for the backpack.

A burst of rounds from the submachine gun peppered the wall beside Jess. The weapon was in Zotkin's hands, but Colchev had shoved the barrel toward the ceiling, sending bullets ricocheting around the chamber.

"Don't shoot, you idiot!" Colchev yelled at Zotkin. He turned back to the melee. "Kiselow, throw the bag!"

Kiselow wound up to toss the backpack, but Tyler grabbed the top of it. The bag zipped open, dumping the contents on the ground. The xenobium rolled out of the protective apron, flashing its brilliance in the light.

The hail of ceiling chunks was so thick now that neither Colchev nor Zotkin could make a move for it.

Tyler tried to kick the ball of xenobium away, but Kiselow grabbed his foot. While they struggled, a falling brick caught Tyler in the side of the head. He reeled from the blow, and Kiselow kicked him in the chest.

Tyler stumbled backward. He tripped and landed on his back only twenty feet from Jess's location. If he stayed there, he'd be crushed in another few seconds.

"Get up!" Jess yelled, but he didn't move.

She had to help him. She shrugged out of Fay's grip and ran into the storm of bricks.

Kiselow grabbed the xenobium and hurled it away before he was buried by a shower of bricks.

Jess reached Tyler and yanked him to his feet. Debris narrowly missed her head as they staggered back toward Fay, who turned on the lantern to guide her.

Jess pushed Tyler ahead and she launched herself at the opening just as the rest of the ceiling finally gave way, sealing off the main entrance from the chamber and trapping the three of them inside the tunnel.

They fell to the floor. Tyler rolled over and groaned, his eyes fluttering.

"Stay still," Jess said, stroking his hair. She felt a huge bump on the side of his skull.

"Are you all right?" Fay asked.

"I'm fine, but I think Tyler has a concussion. Did you see what happened to the xenobium?"

Fay nodded solemnly. "It bounced and rolled into the secret passage. Colchev has it now."

FORTY-EIGHT

As soon as the tear-gas grenades hit the windows on the two homes to either side, Grant sprinted for the target house, Morgan at his side. The tactical team covered them with a barrage of gunfire.

Grant saw a muzzle flash in the window to his right and let loose with a volley of his own, stitching the wall underneath the window with a row of bullet holes. The thin drywall was no match for the high-velocity rounds, and the gunman disappeared.

The headlong rush to the house wasn't the best tactic, but they had no time to wait. Morgan had already called into the OSI team waiting for the Killswitch that the tunnel exited somewhere on the American side, but without knowing how far the tunnel went or in what direction, there was no way for them to narrow the location down to less than a square mile of stores and warehouses.

Grant vaulted the fence, landing in the tiny front yard. He charged straight for the front door.

Hit with the battering ram of his 250-pound bulk, the flimsy door was demolished. It flew off its hinges, smashing into a gunman hiding behind it. Grant went down onto the door, pinning the pummeled man beneath him.

As Grant rolled over, trying to bring his M4 to bear, he saw a gang member with a bandanna wrapped around his face. The man turned and raised an AK-47 just as Morgan ran through the open doorway and fired a three-round burst into his chest, killing him instantly.

She kept moving forward, sweeping with her rifle for other targets. Grant took the living room, staying low in an attempt to avoid the random shots piercing the thin walls.

"In here!" Morgan yelled.

Grant found her in a small kitchen with a gaping hole cut in the floor, an extension ladder poking out of it.

They both edged over to the hole on opposite sides and crouched. Grant did a silent countdown with his fingers. When he reached one, they jumped up and unloaded their magazines into the pit. Two screams were followed by the thump of falling bodies and the sound of ejected shell casings clinking on the metal steps of the ladder.

The tear gas had dissipated enough that they didn't need the masks anymore. Grant took his off, and Morgan did the same. Both of them reloaded.

They peered into the hole and saw two corpses. Neither looked Russian.

The hole had been dug through the concrete slab into the dirt below to create a pit large enough for six men to stand comfortably. A four-foot-high tunnel opened to the north.

Grant climbed down the ladder while Morgan covered

him. Keeping his rifle aimed at the tunnel, Grant hopped off the ladder next to it in case someone was lying in wait inside. He gave the tunnel the same treatment as the pit. Rounds bounced around the shaft. No one returned fire.

He ducked down and saw that the tunnel was empty. But this was no bare-bones prison escape tunnel. A track was laid down its center and electric lights had been strung along the entire length of its ceiling, powered by wires leading back up to the kitchen. The tunnel curved a few hundred yards away so that the other end was out of sight. Walking that far in a crouch would take time they didn't have.

Grant was happy to see a five-foot-long flatbed cart lay at their end of the track. One of the dead men had fallen against it, and Grant nudged him aside with his foot. A simple lever control protruded from the front of the cart.

Morgan jumped off the ladder and saw the railcar.

"They don't mess around," she said.

"This is high-quality construction," Grant said. "The cart's electric-powered, controlled either from the cart or from this lever on the wall. They could move a lot of drugs this way."

"Looks like our two corpses were getting ready for their turns."

"There's only one cart. And it's too far to scuttle."

Morgan stared at the cart for a moment, as if she were fishing for another option. "There's not much room for two of us."

She was right. The small dimensions of the cart meant they'd have to snuggle up. "You ride behind me and keep your rifle pointed straight ahead while I drive."

"All right. Get on."

Grant knelt on the cart and slung his rifle over his shoulder. He positioned himself so that he could operate the controls. "Climb aboard."

Morgan squeezed on, pressing herself against Grant's back. Her breath was hot on his neck.

"Ready?" he said.

"Just go."

Grant put the cart in gear, and the small electric motor hummed. They rolled forward at a decent clip. Other than the threat of imminent death, the ride was quite relaxing.

"Vince hears nothing about this," Morgan said.

"Are you telling me that you're going to file an incomplete report?"

A beat, then, "Shit."

"I hope you include that I was a perfect gentleman."

"You're enjoying this."

"What's not to enjoy? I'm about to go into battle with a beautiful woman behind me and a gun at my side. Could I be any studlier?"

Grant wasn't sure, but he thought he heard a faint chuckle.

They rounded the bend, and Grant saw movement a hundred yards ahead at the end of the tunnel.

"Maybe we're not too late," he said.

"Just a little closer and I can take a shot. All I can see are legs."

"They're going to be expecting one of the other guys. Wait as long as you can before you shoot. We might surprise them."

As they got closer, Grant could hear the men speaking in Spanish. They were standing in a pit similar to the one under the Mexican house. Two pairs of knees were visible.

Neither man was paying attention to the tunnel.

The cart rolled forward, and only when they were within thirty feet did one of the men crouch down to see who was coming.

"*Vamanos*, Carlos," he said, sounding annoyed at his friend's tardiness.

Morgan answered with the crack of her M4, cleanly dispatching him. She shot the other man in both legs. He collapsed in pain but defiantly drew a pistol, and she finished him off.

Shouts came from above as Morgan scrambled out of the tunnel, her rifle aimed skyward. Grant crawled after her. They stood with their backs to opposite sides of the pit, each covering one half of the rim.

This would be the tricky part. The enemy had the high ground.

"Were you ever a cheerleader?" Grant said.

She looked at him like he was nuts. "What?"

He gestured that going up the ladder was a bad idea. The men up there would have a bead on it and take her out as soon as her head rose above floor level. To surprise them, Grant would have to give her a boost.

Morgan frowned and then nodded reluctantly.

While she kept her rifle to her shoulder, Grant grabbed her around the hips and hoisted her up. Even in her full battle gear, he lifted her easily. *And who said all those hours in the weight room were wasted?*

He raised her until she could see over the rim.

Bullets zinged by and she returned fire.

"One down!" she cried out. "They're in the next room. Let's go!"

Grant dropped her and went up the ladder two rungs at a time. At the top he knelt beside the ladder and aimed his weapon at the door while Morgan climbed up. It looked like they were in a storage room of some kind of office-park rental.

As Morgan came up out of the pit, a man suddenly appeared in the door to Grant's right, aiming a pistol at her head. Grant didn't have time to bring his gun around.

He did the only thing he could. He jumped in front of Morgan. Two slugs hit Grant in the chest. The flak jacket took the brunt of the rounds, but it still hurt like hell, as if he'd been pounded by a sledgehammer.

Despite struggling for breath, Grant rushed the man and grabbed his arm, breaking it against the door jamb. The gunman screamed. Grant swung him around and tossed him past Morgan into the pit.

The man landed on his neck with a sickening crunch.

Morgan hopped off the ladder and put the rifle to her shoulder. "Thanks."

"*De nada*," he wheezed, holding a hand to his battered chest.

"Where's the Killswitch?"

Tires screeched outside in reply.

Two men in the next room shouted toward the fleeing vehicle.

"*¡Salen!*"

"*¡Esos pendejos rusos!*"

Grant barreled through the doorway while they were distracted and took each of them down with one shot.

Morgan dashed to the front door, and Grant went after her. They emerged into bright sunlight beating down on a long row of warehouses and offices.

He got out in time to see a white van tear around the corner and out of sight. They didn't even get a shot off.

"Did you get the plate?" Grant asked.

Morgan shook her head. "Too far away. Dammit!"

She took out her phone to report their location using her GPS, but there was no way the roadblocks would be in place yet. A plain white van like that was on every other street. Finding it would be virtually impossible.

They'd lost their best chance to get the remaining Killswitch back. Now it was loose in the United States.

All Grant could hope was that Tyler had better luck.

FORTY-NINE

Still groggy from the blow to his head, Tyler took turns with Jess chipping at the wall with the crowbar. Two hours after being trapped in the tunnel between the collapsed central chamber and the bricked-up barricade, his head continued to throb, mostly from the injury but also because he was angry at himself that his plan hadn't worked. He'd fully expected to die from the cave-in, but he thought the xenobium would have been buried with him. His wooziness made it hard to tell if he'd come up with a poor scheme or if Colchev had just gotten lucky.

His only consolation was that Grant and Morgan probably had done a better job of retrieving the Killswitch.

Even so, he needed to get out of the pyramid and warn them that Colchev had the xenobium.

They'd removed twenty bricks so far. There was no way to know how thick the wall was, so they were racing to break through before the battery on their single lantern died.

Fay sat against the wall with Jess's arm around her. A day without her insulin had made her weak, but the situation was not yet life-threatening. As Tyler hacked at the mortar, she told them about her conversations with Colchev.

"Did he say what his target was?" Tyler asked.

"He mentioned Washington, DC, and that America would be on its knees. The attack would take China down with it."

"Nadia Bedova, his former colleague, asked me about Wisconsin Ave. There's a Wisconsin Avenue in downtown DC. The nation's capital is a tempting target."

Tyler turned toward them and frowned at the scenario.

"What's wrong?" Jess asked.

"Something doesn't make sense about it."

"Why?"

"Fay said she heard them say that they only had one day left, which would be July twenty-fifth, the same day that Bedova asked me about. If Colchev plans to take out DC, why does it have to be tomorrow?"

"Is something special happening in Washington?"

"Could be, but we're past the Fourth of July. And the President's plane is protected against EMP bursts better than any other plane on Earth. Colchev would know that."

"The gamma rays. He could be trying to kill the President."

"But again, why tomorrow? Bedova also mentioned the Baja drug cartel and the word 'Icarus'. Did he say anything about them?"

Fay shook her head. "Sorry."

"You have nothing to be sorry about. I was the one who

let them ..." Tyler trailed off. No sense rehashing his mistakes.

"You did your best," Jess said. "You saved me and Nana."

Tyler didn't answer. Failure didn't sit well with him. He slammed the crowbar into the mortar.

The brick moved, but this one jutted away from him.

He pounded again, and the brick fell outward, letting a sliver of muted daylight through. He could make out the dimly lit interior of one of the pyramid's previously excavated chambers.

"We're through!"

Jess and Fay got to their feet and cheered.

Now that he could wedge the crowbar between the bricks and force them out from inside, the hole got bigger quickly. In five minutes the gap was wide enough.

Jess went first and helped Fay traverse the breach. Tyler wriggled out and flopped onto the ground, only to find himself face to face with a family of four gaping in astonishment at the trio covered in dust and squirming out of a wall that had been there for centuries.

The father, who was wearing a Pittsburgh Steelers jersey, asked, "What in the world is going on?"

Tyler ushered Jess and Fay out. As he passed the astonished tourist, Tyler handed him the crowbar and said, "You will not believe how long we've been in there."

After a quick refueling stop in Lima, Colchev's private jet lifted off for North America. The xenobium was safely ensconced in the leaded case. Bomb-sniffing dogs might have detected the explosives in the Killswitch, but he was confident he could get the small specimen of xenobium past customs.

He called Oborski to find out the status of the Killswitch. They should have smuggled it through the Mexican drug gang's cross-border tunnel by now.

"Where are you?" Colchev said when Oborski answered.

"On our way to Phoenix. Our charter is ready to take off when we get there."

"And the package?"

"Safe. We had some problems at the border. The black man and some woman were there and tried to take it back, but we got away before they could see our vehicle. Our friends on the peninsula won't be happy about us revealing their smuggling route."

"I don't care about them. Is everything on schedule for tomorrow?"

"Yes. The latest reports show no problems with the launch. It's still set to go off at noon."

"Good. We're on schedule to meet in Shelby. Have the plane there tonight."

"Understood."

He hung up and told Zotkin the news.

"I have to admit, Vladimir," Zotkin said with a smile, "after everything we had to overcome, I did not think this would happen."

Colchev slapped him on the back and laughed. "Never

lose faith, my friend. I will chill the vodka tonight, for tomorrow we will be toasting the downfall of America and the establishment of Russia as the most dominant nation on the planet."

While federal operatives on both sides of the border combed the Mexican drug houses and the nondescript office on the American side for evidence, Grant and Morgan gave their reports to the FBI. Separately. Grant had been through enough debriefings to know that wasn't a good sign.

His interview finished long before Morgan's, so he tried calling Tyler again from the lobby of the San Diego field office while he waited.

No answer, but he did have a voicemail waiting.

Grant, it's Tyler. We found the xenobium in a Peruvian pyramid, but Colchev got away with it. It's about the size of a tennis ball, so it could take out an entire state if it gets reunited with the Killswitch.

Other than a bump on my head, I'm okay, and so are Jess and Fay. Fay said Colchev mentioned something about Washington, but I don't think that's the target for a few reasons that I'll tell you about when we get in to LAX tonight at eleven o'clock.

Tell Morgan to track any incoming private plane flights from South America. That's the only way he could get a radioactive element through customs.

Whatever he's planning will happen tomorrow. You've

got to get the Killswitch back. I hope you have better luck than we did.

The message ended, and Grant clicked the phone off. *Great*, he thought. *The news just keeps getting better and better.*

Morgan slammed the door open and stalked past him out of the lobby. He caught up with her outside as she plunked herself in the driver's seat of the pool car. She opened the passenger window and said, "You coming?"

He got in, and she sped off, merging onto the freeway.

After a minute of nothing from her, Grant said, "That bad?"

"Now that the Killswitch is in the US and a threat to national security, the FBI is taking over the case. I'm put on suspension pending an investigation into my actions of the last four days."

"That's idiotic! Why?"

"They had a lot of good reasons." She held up a fist and flicked it open one finger at a time. "I allowed the Killswitch to be stolen, the Australian xenobium was destroyed, our suspects in Sydney were killed before they could be interrogated, and I failed to stop the weapon from being smuggled back into the US. Oh, and the Air Force lost its two-hundred-million-dollar cargo jet and crew that I convinced them to send to Easter Island."

Grant grimaced. "When you put it that way, it doesn't sound good. What do we do now?"

"We don't do anything. They took my OSI ID and gun. I'm supposed to fly back to Andrews tomorrow morning."

"Tyler left me a message. He said Colchev has the xenobium. He thinks the attack is going to happen tomorrow."

"I know. He called our office and left me the same message."

"What is the FBI doing about it?"

"They disagree with Tyler's assessment that Washington isn't the target. The President is being moved to a safe location away from the city, and they're shutting down Wisconsin Avenue and doing a building-to-building canvass along the street."

"Colchev's too smart for that. He'd just move to a different location."

"The FBI thinks this is the best option," Morgan said with disgust. She took the exit for Mission Hills. Grant didn't know San Diego well, but he assumed she was heading for the airport.

"You're not giving up are you?"

"What else can we do?"

"Tyler gets into LAX in eight hours. I say we meet him there and trade information. Maybe we'll come up with something."

"All right," Morgan said, "but I need to shower and change first."

"So do I. Motel?"

She pulled to a stop in front of a tidy two-story home and put the car in park.

"My parents' house. They're at work right now."

Grant took the guest bathroom while Morgan used her parents' master suite.

By the time he was finished with his shower, Grant felt like a new man. After he toweled off, he wrapped it around himself and walked out of the hallway bathroom to find Morgan standing in the guest bedroom doorway wearing only a robe. Her skin radiated a fresh glow, and her damp hair dipped across her shoulder in an alluring flourish.

"Hi," she said.

"Hello," Grant said, not sure if the vibe he was getting was correct. But he was damned interested to see where this was going. His adrenaline surged more than it had during any of the explosions or firefights of the last few days.

The seconds ticked by as they eyed each other. Grant got the distinct impression that he was being ogled, which didn't bother him one bit.

Without saying a word, he walked over to Morgan and stopped inches in front of her. Her breath was hot on his chest.

He didn't care if he was wrong. He swept her into his arms and kissed her.

When she returned the kiss so forcefully that she twisted him around and pushed him backward into the guest bedroom, he knew he was right.

FIFTY

The nine-hour flight from Lima left Tyler, Jess, and Fay exhausted, but at least they made it out of Peru before anyone discovered that they'd had a hand in destroying part of a major Nazca monument. Tyler dozed fitfully during the flight, preoccupied with speculation about where Colchev was headed.

Now that Fay had access to her insulin, she was feeling better, but the experiences of the last few days had drained her. Jess decided to get her a hotel room in LA, so when the plane landed, Tyler texted Grant to meet them at the airport Radisson.

The shuttle dropped them at the hotel lobby, where Tyler saw Grant and Morgan standing awkwardly next to each other.

Tyler clapped his friend on the back and said, "How are you doing?"

"We're fine," Grant said. "Well, Morgan's not ... she's had a rough day. I'm trying to keep her spirits up."

Tyler raised an eyebrow at Grant, who knew exactly

what he was silently asking. Grant's lightning-fast grin answered the question.

"We should find somewhere to talk," Morgan said.

"I reserved a suite," Jess said. "The living room should be big enough for all of us."

After the quick check-in, they settled into seats around the coffee table. Even Fay stayed, despite Jess's pleas for her to get some rest. It took them an hour to swap stories about Sydney, Rapa Nui, Peru, and Tijuana. Although they had whittled away at Colchev's crew, he had bested them at every turn, and they were nowhere close to catching him.

Tyler ran his hands through his hair in frustration at trying to figure out Colchev's ultimate goal. The Russian's original plan had been to steal both the Killswitch and the xenobium in Australia. He not only was going to bring them back to the US, a risky proposition in any case, but he had a timetable to get them into the country in time for an attack to occur on July twenty-fifth.

"Could this be related to money?" he asked Morgan.

"Anything's possible," she said. "If he's playing the market, he could profit when an attack devastates stock prices."

"But why tomorrow?"

"Maybe he has to short sell by then," Jess said.

"That means he created the short timeline for himself. That seems ambitious, even for him."

"But what would be on Wisconsin Avenue?" Grant said.

"It does seem like an odd place to attack," Morgan said.

"I've looked over the satellite and street maps in detail. It's far away from any of the critical government functions."

"That doesn't matter. Colchev has a huge amount of xenobium. Not only will the gamma rays kill everyone within miles, the EMP burst could take out every computer all the way to Baltimore, whatever street he detonates it on."

"It sounds like we're missing a vital piece of the puzzle," Fay said. "Like when I didn't know that the phrase the alien told me was Russian. If he *was* an alien, that is."

Tyler grinned. That was the first time she conceded that perhaps what she experienced wasn't a close encounter with a spaceman. He was impressed with her ability to change her mind, even after sixty-five years.

"Fay's right," Tyler said. "Bedova asked me if we'd heard the word 'Icarus' from Colchev's men when they were in New Zealand. I bet that's an important piece."

"I have one possibility, though it doesn't make sense," Morgan said. "I couldn't tell you before because our knowledge of it is classified. Sorry, but I was bound by law."

"And now?" Grant said.

The corner of her mouth turned up. "I can't screw up much more than I already have in the eyes of the OSI. Icarus is a Russian code name for a parachute."

Jess looked at her dubiously. "A parachute that's classified?"

"It was developed for their military space program. It allows them to bail out of a sub-orbital spacecraft and parachute back to Earth from up to eighty miles high."

Grant laughed. "You're kidding. I'm pretty much a badass, but that sounds like an impossible stunt."

"Maybe not," Tyler said. "There was a US program called Excelsior in the late fifties. The Air Force was worried about pilots ejecting from the high altitudes that the U-2 flew at, so they designed a multi-stage parachute to prevent fatal spins. Icarus could be a Russian version of the same thing."

"And you know about Excelsior how?" Jess said.

"My father was in the Air Force. He knows the guy who tested the chute, Joseph Kittinger—probably the gutsiest man in history."

"Why?" Fay asked. "How did they test it?"

"They put Captain Kittinger, who was wearing a pressure suit, into a gondola attached to an enormous helium balloon, then let it float up to a hundred thousand feet."

Grant whistled. "Almost twenty miles."

"For all intents and purposes, he was in space. When he stepped off that ledge, it was like jumping into a satellite photo. He fell for four and a half minutes, still the record for the longest parachute freefall."

"And he lived?" Fay said.

Tyler nodded. "He not only survived, he earned a slew of medals for the mission and eventually became a colonel."

"Fascinating, but what does this have to do with the Killswitch?" Jess said. "Does Colchev have one of these Icarus parachutes?"

"We don't know," Morgan said. "We can't exactly check

with the Russians to see if they've lost track of one. Besides, Icarus is a common reference. The boy with wax wings who flew too close to the sun and fell to Earth. You could do a Google search and get a thousand hits."

"I doubt he's going up in a balloon."

"From Wisconsin Ave?" Grant said. "Not likely. Those things are gigantic."

"If he did get it that high," Tyler said, "the Killswitch would do a lot more damage."

"Why?" Jess said.

"Because the EMP effect would be amplified by the magnetic flux in the ionosphere. Military planners have worried for years about a nuclear weapon detonated over the central United States. It could wipe out the entire country's infrastructure. In an instant every machine in the US would go quiet."

Jess gasped. "With all the computers and communications systems down, nobody would even know that Armageddon had arrived."

With a faraway look, Morgan said, "'And we should die of that roar which is the other side of silence.'"

"Who said that?" Grant asked.

"George Eliot."

"Who's he?"

Morgan rolled her eyes. "*She* wrote *Middlemarch*, you illiterate dolt."

"Hey, if you had said Curious George—"

"The question is," Tyler said, trying to get them back on

track, "how could Colchev deliver the Killswitch to that altitude?"

"Maybe he found the Roswell spaceship," Fay said. When she saw the looks the rest of them gave her, she continued, "I'm just saying the Russians designed Icarus to be used with a spaceship, and I saw a spaceship at Roswell. That's awfully coincidental if you ask me."

Tyler chuckled. Maybe she wasn't giving up on her fantasy.

Grant snorted. "Right, instead of a balloon, Colchev has a spaceship taking off from Wisconsin Ave."

Tyler started to laugh, then stopped himself and sat bolt upright. *A spaceship taking off from Wisconsin Ave.* Something about that jogged Tyler's memory.

He asked for Grant's laptop and opened the browser.

Grant edged closer. "What did I say?"

"Bedova said Wisconsin Ave, not Wisconsin Avenue, right?"

Grant shrugged. "That's the way I remember it."

"What's the difference?" Morgan asked.

"Either Colchev had been using a code or Bedova interpreted the abbreviation the wrong way. It's not Wisconsin Ave. It's pronounced Wisconsin A Vee."

"What do the letters A and V stand for?" Jess said.

"AirVenture."

"Wisconsin AirVenture?" Fay said. "What's that?"

Grant slapped himself in the forehead. "Of course! The EAA."

"The Experimental Aircraft Association has a huge air show every year," Tyler said. "It's in Oshkosh, Wisconsin, smack dab in the middle of the country. Thousands of private aircraft pilots fly their planes to the show. It's so big that for one week, Oshkosh becomes the busiest airport in the world, with over ten thousand takeoffs and landings. I flew to it a few years ago, but I didn't make the connection until just now because I always called it the Oshkosh Fly-in."

Morgan looked at the tablet. "This is tomorrow's schedule."

Tyler pointed to the middle of the schedule. "Check out what happens at noon."

Morgan peered at it, then her eyes went wide. "I'll call the FBI." She jumped up and furiously dialed her phone.

"What is it?" Jess said. "What happens tomorrow?"

Tyler put a hand on Fay's shoulder. "I'm sorry I laughed at you."

"Why?"

"Because you were right. Tomorrow a company called ExAtmo is making a demonstration flight at noon of their brand new product, the Skyward."

Grant recognized the name instantly. "Damn! You think Colchev is planning to hijack it?"

Tyler nodded grimly. "He must be planning to fly the Killswitch up to an altitude of seventy miles."

"I don't understand," Jess said. "What's ExAtmo?"

"They're a commercial sub-orbital tourism venture. Skyward is their experimental spaceplane."

SPACE

From the co-pilot's seat of the Cessna 340A, Colchev could see vast rows of planes lined wingtip to wingtip on the grassy field bordering the northern runway of the Oshkosh Whitman Regional Airport. The previous night, he and Zotkin had landed in Calgary, Canada to refuel the Gulfstream, where they were able to sneak off the plane disguised as pilots. Two other men dressed as pilots took their places and the jet continued on its way toward Moscow. Then Colchev and Zotkin drove across the border into Montana using a new set of false passports and boarded the smaller twin-prop six-seater at a tiny airport in Shelby.

To cover his tracks, Colchev planted a small explosive device on the Gulfstream, timed to blow up over the remote Canadian tundra. It would take days to confirm that he and the xenobium were not on board.

Zotkin, who was flying the Cessna, got clearance to land on runway 27, which was closer to their parking spot in the north field than the main 36L runway used for the demonstration flights and daily air shows. They made their final turn, Lake Winnebago glistening just a few miles to the east under the azure sky. Excellent conditions for the launch.

As they came around, Colchev got his first glimpse of the Skyward spaceplane. It was situated in a place of honor at the primary taxiway leading to the main runway. Even from this distance, the vehicle was a technological wonder to behold.

The Skyward was slung underneath its carrier plane, the Lodestar. Like a mother hen, the wing-shaped Lodestar sat atop the spaceplane, which nestled into the curvature of the larger aircraft's concave underside and was already in place for the launch in two hours.

The most distinctive feature of both the Lodestar and the Skyward was the unusual design of their fuselages. The carbon-fiber bodywork was constructed with criss-crossing struts that seemed to be oriented in a haphazard fashion. The delicate-looking framework was optimized to provide the maximum strength to the spaceplane for its weight, much like the hollow bones of a bird. The spaces in between the struts were filled with state-of-the-art polymer windows that gave intrepid passengers a 180-degree view of the Earth when the spaceplane reached its maximum altitude of seventy miles.

Colchev had been following the news about the Skyward ever since its existence had been made public. By acquiring the rights to use Burt Rutan's SpaceShipTwo, Richard Branson's company Virgin Galactic had a huge head start on ExAtmo's effort to bring spaceflight to the commercial market, so the newer company had to come up with an attention-getting ploy to wrest some of the spotlight away from the pioneer and showcase its own advanced technology. The exhibition flight at the premier experimental aircraft show in the world was the answer. As soon as Colchev had heard about the planned demonstration six months ago, he knew it would be his best chance to cripple the entire United States in one blow.

Getting information about the Skyward out of the notoriously secretive ExAtmo files had been difficult, but not impossible. One of the gems they'd acquired had been film of a test flight, showing the cockpit operation of both the carrier and spaceplane. With that, they knew their plan was possible.

The flight profile of the spaceplane was straightforward, helpfully sketched out in a CGI video on the ExAtmo website. The Lodestar could take off from any commercial runway. When it reached an altitude of fifty-thousand feet, the Skyward dropped from the belly. Once it was clear, the Skyward ignited its liquid rocket engine, propelling it to three thousand miles per hour, or mach four, twice the speed of Concorde. Shooting straight up toward space, the engine disengaged after seventy seconds, giving the six passengers five minutes of weightlessness as the spaceplane was pulled back toward Earth, its fuel spent. Twenty-five minutes later, it glided in for an unpowered landing at the airport just like a space shuttle.

Of course, there was a pilot in case anything went awry

during the flight, but on a typical trip he was superfluous during the launch. The Skyward was completely automated, the computer controlling the entire powered portion of the flight. As soon as the Skyward dropped from the carrier, the pilot didn't need to do anything but monitor the gauges until it was time to land.

That automation was going to make it possible for Colchev to fly into space.

Building anticipation for the flight, ExAtmo had garnered extensive publicity by withholding the names of the pilots of the spaceplane and carrier aircraft as well as the two passengers. Fully suited and helmeted to maintain the mystery of their identities, they would be taken by shuttle bus to the flight line, where they would get on board the craft in full view of the crowds. The entire flight was to be recorded by telescopes on the ground. When the Skyward returned, the successful crew and passengers would be revealed in a massive press conference right on the tarmac.

Only it wouldn't happen quite as planned.

Colchev and his men would take the place of the pilots and passengers. Zotkin, an experienced pilot rated on many different types of aircraft, would fly the carrier plane. Colchev and the other men, Nisselovich and Oborski, would climb aboard the Skyward. Once they were in the air, Nisselovich and Oborski would crawl through the mating hatch into the Lodestar, leaving Colchev alone to pilot the Skyward.

Colchev's sole task during the Skyward's launch would be

to cut off the rocket early. After arming the Killswitch, he would depressurize the Skyward and eject the weapon, where it would continue on its ballistic arc. Then Colchev would fire the engine and use up the remaining fuel to get as much distance as he could between him and the Killswitch.

When the Killswitch went off, the electronics in the Skyward would be useless. It would be destined to crash, which was the reason Colchev needed the Icarus parachute. He'd bail out just as the Killswitch timer counted down to zero. Zotkin and the others would use traditional chutes from a much lower altitude. Ten minutes later, Colchev would land in an utterly changed world. He'd rendezvous with his comrades at a garage where they had stored an ancient diesel truck equipped with extra fuel. Together they'd make the difficult trek back to Russia through the North American wasteland, departing on a ship that they'd already contracted to meet them at the port of Seattle.

The Cessna's wheels touching down brought Colchev out of his revelry. Guided by the flag-waving attendants, they taxied through the maze of aircraft and tents to their parking space.

Zotkin shut down the engines. He nodded at a hangar to their right along the edge of the airport.

"That's the Weeks hangar. The flight crew is getting ready in there."

The hangar door was closed for privacy. The shuttle bus that would take the crew to the plane was parked outside.

No security was visible. The guards were all stationed around the spaceplane. The prep location had been withheld from the media, but Colchev had acquired the information from the ExAtmo files.

"Is everyone clear on the plan?" Colchev said.

Three nods.

Nisselovich and Oborski left to inspect the area around the spaceplane and verify that everything was as they anticipated.

Colchev opened the container carrying the Killswitch. He carefully removed the xenobium from its protective case and inserted it into the weapon. The tines latched onto the metal and drew it into the compartment, closing over it and shielding the radiation. Now all he had to do was enter the arming code and set the timer.

He and Zotkin unloaded the container from the plane and put it on a handcart they'd brought along. With all of the camping equipment and barbecues set up around them, no one glanced twice at them moving their luggage toward the unguarded hangar.

FIFTY-TWO

The banner on the control tower proudly declared that Oshkosh was the world's busiest airport. The constant drone of propellers and engines reminded Tyler that the proclamation wasn't hyperbole. Every minute there were aircraft taking off or landing, sometimes simultaneously on the two runways. More airplanes buzzed around in flight, including a squadron of P-51 Mustang fighter planes flying in formation.

There was also constant motion on the ground. As Tyler, Jess, Fay, Grant, and Morgan made their way toward the Skyward spaceplane, a Navy AWACS plane crossed in front of them and was ushered to a spot next to a white Air Force T-38 supersonic trainer and an Army Chinook helicopter, two of the many military aircraft on display. Lines of visitors formed at each of them, and the pilots were on hand to answer questions from the gawking fans. Some of them even allowed the curious to sit inside the cockpit.

On the other side of the tarmac were vintage aircraft of every stripe, from World War I biplanes to Vietnam-era choppers. Further down the runway Boeing and Airbus were giving tours of their latest airliners.

Enormous tents housing manufacturer showcases, vendor displays, and restaurants stretched five hundred yards in every direction. Outside most of the tents were innovative private plane models and experimental prototypes that the builders wanted to spotlight, hoping to make sales to the enthusiasts who came from all over the world.

The wide thoroughfares were crammed with pedestrians taking in the sights, tractors towing shuttle trams, and gas-powered carts ferrying workers and supplies in every direction. For the entire week, the airport was transformed into a small city, with a population approaching 100,000 visitors on sunny days.

"I've never seen so many planes," Fay said. "This is enormous."

"Are you doing all right, Nana?" Jess asked her. "We should have made you stay in Los Angeles."

"I'm fine."

Tyler thought she looked anything but. They were all exhausted from the constant travel and fitful sleep on planes, but Fay had gotten the worst of it. Dark circles under her eyes and a haggard droop in her shoulders gave away that she was on the ragged edge. Though she was the fittest seventy-five-year-old he'd ever known, age and illness were catching up with her.

When they had made the connection between the Killswitch and the Oshkosh AirVenture, Morgan had tried to convince the FBI and her superiors to send agents to stop the launch of the spaceplane or at least guard it until it took off. But her suspension had seriously undermined her credibility, and they wouldn't listen because of a new development.

The private plane carrying Colchev had blown up over an unpopulated region of Canada. Homeland Security suspected that he got cold feet about bringing the xenobium into the US and continued on to Russia. All indications were that the explosive material was mishandled and detonated in flight. Canadian authorities were rushing an investigation team to the area, assisted by forensic units from the FBI and US Air Force. With the trigger gone, Homeland Security felt that the threat from the Killswitch had evaporated, though there was still a massive effort to locate the expensive prototype.

But Tyler didn't believe Colchev would be so careless or would give up so easily. Which meant his group had to get to Oshkosh and either obtain proof that Colchev was coming there or stop him themselves. Jess had suggested calling in a bomb threat, which would cause the event to be evacuated and the flight to be aborted, but Morgan nixed that idea. She was worried that if Colchev suspected interference in his plans, he might panic and set off the Killswitch in the middle of the air show.

Overnight flights to Chicago were fully booked, so Tyler called for one of Gordian's executive jets in Seattle to come down to Los Angeles and pick them up. It had the range to take them directly to the air show. He also requested that pistols be packed on the jet since Morgan's weapon had been confiscated. If they were going to meet up with Colchev's men again, doing so unarmed would place them at a disadvantage to the Russians.

A maintenance delay taking off from LA made the trip longer than it should have been, so they didn't land in Wisconsin until only an hour before the launch was supposed to occur. It didn't leave much time, and despite Fay's valiant effort, she would only slow them down.

"Fay," Tyler said, "how are you feeling?"

She smiled wanly. "Just a little tired."

"Nana, why don't you take a seat under those umbrellas by the food court?" Jess said, picking up on Tyler's intention. "That way you can keep an eye on the Skyward and let us know if you see anything unusual."

Fay looked like she was about to protest, but Jess's hand on her shoulder changed her mind.

"Maybe you're right. I can stay out of sight there. If I see Colchev, I'll call you."

"Perfect. And remember to drink some water. You could get dehydrated quickly in this heat."

Fay squeezed Jess's hand. "Be careful."

"We will."

"Oh, and if *you* see Colchev, I wouldn't mind very much if you shot him." With those parting words, she left.

Tyler, Jess, Morgan, and Grant picked up the pace as they headed toward the spaceplane.

"She's a good role model for you," Tyler said.

"I want to be just like her when I grow up," Jess said.

"When will that be?"

"In about forty years."

At the cordon separating the crowds from the area around the spaceplane, they got a good look at the unusual aircraft. Ground crews swarmed the exterior making the final checks before the flight, and yellow-shirted security personnel surrounded the airplane.

"We need to convince them to abort the flight," Morgan said.

"Without your credentials, that'll be difficult. Why should they believe us?"

"I'll disable the plane myself if I have to."

"We won't get within twenty yards of it," Tyler said.

A man from the ground crew passed them. Morgan grabbed his arm. The surprised technician must have thought she was an overzealous onlooker, until she lifted her shirt to show him the gun tucked in her waistband and gave him one of her cards.

"I'm Special Agent Morgan Bell," she said. "We've gotten a report that someone may try to interfere with today's flight. Has anything unusual happened this morning?"

The nonplussed crewman looked at the card and then at Morgan with wide eyes. The confidence in her tone convinced the man she was who she claimed to be.

"No, ma'am," he said. "We've got everything under control, and all systems are go for the launch."

"What about the crew?"

"They're still in the Weeks hangar getting prepped. Should be here in thirty minutes."

"Who's in charge here?"

"That would be Robert Gillman. He's the flight director. You'll find him in the mobile control center over there."

He pointed at a trailer with a satellite dish mounted on its roof.

"Tell him I'm coming to talk to him," Morgan said, releasing the man. He nodded and trotted toward the trailer.

"What do you think?" Grant said.

"You and I will meet with the flight director, try to get him to scrub the demonstration. But I don't want to put all our eggs in that basket. Tyler, you and Jess go find the flight crew and see if you can delay them until we get some real security out here. And if you spot Colchev or his men, do not engage. Call me first."

"Sounds like a plan," Tyler said.

As Morgan and Grant trotted to the command center, Tyler and Jess headed back the way they came. Tyler checked the official guide and found the Weeks hangar on the map.

"That's all the way over on the opposite end of the airport," Jess said. "Even if we jog, it'll take a while to get there."

Tyler spotted a utility cart parked behind the EAA Welcome Center. He took Jess's hand and ran to it. The key was still in it.

"We'll borrow this. Hop on."

Tyler started it up and aimed it toward the northern hangars, dodging pedestrians until they got into the open and he could floor it.

"Is this what your life is like now, Tyler?"

He suddenly realized that this was the first time he and Jess had been alone together since leaving Peru.

"You mean, gallivanting around the world on caffeine and no sleep, barely living through each day?"

"Not to mention stealing vehicles and blowing up Air Force jets."

"I don't do this kind of stuff all the time," Tyler said. "But it does seem to be happening more frequently the last couple of years. Do you like the craziness of it?"

"Yes. No. Both."

"It sounds like your doctor friend does something similar."

"This Doctors Without Borders job is short-term. Andy's not going to be doing it forever."

At the north field Tyler cut through the entrance to the aircraft parking area. The gunmetal gray hangar was up ahead.

"Then what's next for you?" Tyler said. "The house in Queenstown? A private practice where he's stitching up snowboarders and bungee jumpers? Kids?"

"Do *you* want kids?"

"I did when I was with Karen."

"And now?"

"Does it matter?"

"It does to me."

"Only with someone I love."

"Would you be willing to give up the globe-trotting?"

"Someday. If the right person came along."

"But you didn't with Karen."

"That was a few years ago. A lot's happened since then."

Jess gave his leg a squeeze and remained unusually silent. He didn't know what that meant, and this wasn't the time to delve into it further. They had reached the hangar.

Tyler and Jess got out of the cart and walked to the door. He tried the handle, but it was locked. He knocked and after a few moments heard the rhythmic squeak of rubber soles on a polished concrete floor. The footsteps stopped on the other side of the door.

"Yes?"

"I need to speak to someone in charge," Tyler said.

"What is this about? We're very busy."

Tyler was about to respond, then stopped himself. The voice. He'd heard it just yesterday.

Zotkin.

He and Colchev were inside. With less than thirty minutes before the launch, Tyler and Jess could go back with this definitive proof and get the entire police force to surround the hangar.

"Oh. I guess we can come back later."

But with that response, Zotkin must have recognized Tyler's voice, too. The door flew open.

Zotkin took aim with a pistol, but Tyler barreled forward before he could fire, knocking Zotkin backward. He kneed the Russian in the groin, then elbowed him in the side of the head. Zotkin went down before he knew what had happened.

Tyler took his weapon and gave it to Jess. He yanked Zotkin to his feet and drew his own Glock, pressing it against the man's temple.

"Move," Tyler said, pushing him forward, one hand clenching his collar.

They turned the corner and saw six men lying against the hangar door, all of them bound and gagged.

"Put your gun down," came a voice from behind him.

Tyler whirled around. Colchev was hunched over an open container holding the Killswitch.

His finger lay on the red arming button.

"I've set this timer to zero, Dr. Locke," Colchev said. "Put your gun down or I push this button and a hundred thousand people die."

FIFTY-THREE

Despite Morgan's arguments, the flight director wouldn't call off the launch. He said that the company had everything riding on this demonstration to secure more investment funding, and without a direct court order, the flight was going forward. With no official identification, her speculation about a stolen weapon being snuck onto the spaceplane sounded like the ravings of a lunatic, even with Grant there to corroborate her story. She would have threatened him at gunpoint if she thought it would change the man's mind, but she knew that would just divert attention to the control center, leaving the spaceplane unguarded.

They exited the trailer and resorted to their only option. Sitting on a bench near the spaceplane, they used the infrared goggles to scan the crowd. Bystanders would think they were using high-tech binoculars to watch the airplanes.

"Do you think these guys will still be tagged?" Grant said.

"The ID dust is persistent," Morgan said. "The ones

who escaped in San Diego will still have some of it on them."

Grant sighed dramatically. "Ah, San Diego."

"Oh, my God. You're not going to get all mushy about what happened, are you? You were just there at the right time."

"Mushy? Hell no. Can't a guy reminisce about a fun afternoon?"

"Good. Because that's all it was."

"Fine with me."

They scanned for a few more minutes before Grant said, "But just for the record, I wouldn't mind having another afternoon like it."

Morgan smiled. "Maybe we'll find the right time again."

"I know a great hotel in Chicago. When this is over ... " Suddenly Grant went quiet and tensed up. "There's one of them. Twenty yards away." He was pointing at a man with a rounded face and dark hair wearing a gray T-shirt and jeans. He must have just come from behind the trailer housing the control center. She put the goggles up and saw the man covered with red crosshairs.

"How do you want to take him?" Grant said.

"I'll approach from the front and distract him while you sneak up behind him."

"You mean like this?" a voice behind them said. Morgan felt the barrel of a gun jammed into her back. "Move and you die."

The man they'd been observing strode toward them, a

pistol tucked underneath the event program in his hand. He cautiously pulled the pistol from her waistband, then took Grant's.

The guy behind them leaned closer to her. "You should have picked a partner who's less conspicuous than Mr. Westfield. I spotted him the moment you walked into that mobile control trailer."

He removed her goggles and used them to look at his cohort.

"The intelligence was correct. They did develop ID dust. I told you that's how they knew we were in the house in Tijuana." He lowered the goggles and put them in the pocket of his cargo pants.

"Where's Colchev?" Morgan said.

"Nearby. We'll take you to see him. Get up slowly."

She and Grant both stood. She could now see that the men had silencers on their SIG Sauers. A jacket over the arm concealed the other man's weapon.

"Now move." They started walking, a pistol in each of their backs.

"We know what your plan is," Grant said.

"So?"

"So I'm just letting you know it won't work."

"Why's that?"

"We convinced the flight director to abort the launch."

The Russian smiled. "If that were true, there would have been an announcement. Now keep walking or I'll kill you right here."

"That would ruin your plans, wouldn't it?" Grant said. "A couple of gunshots would bring a lot of attention out here. Might even stop the flight."

"That's a risk we're willing to take. Are you?"

Grant glanced at Morgan, and she shook her head. With the constant noise, two silenced gunshots might be mistaken for a backfiring aircraft engine.

As they walked, the Russians had to stay right behind them to keep their weapons concealed. The close range was a double-edged sword. The Russians couldn't miss if they got shots off, but it also meant that Morgan had a chance to disarm one of them. All she needed was the proper distraction.

"Where are we going?" she asked.

"Does that matter?" Grant said, glaring at her. At first she thought he was genuinely angry with her, but then she saw the slightest widening of his eyes.

He was trying to give her a distraction. She played along.

"Well, I wouldn't ask," she said, "except that we got caught so easily because of you."

"Oh, this is my fault now?"

"I knew I shouldn't have brought you with me. You've been nothing but a pain in the ass since I met you."

"And since I met you, you've been nothing but a raging bitch!"

Both Russians laughed at the comment. That was her cue.

She whirled to her right and raised her hand as if she were going to smack Grant in the face with her left hand. Grant made a show of twisting to avoid the slap. Their momentum carried them around so that they both rotated 180 degrees.

Grant struck the man behind him with a crushing blow to his shoulder. Trusting that Grant would live up to his billing as an expert in hand-to-hand combat, Morgan focused on her own guy. She grabbed the man's pistol wrist, clasped his trigger finger, and bent it backward. The ligament snapped, causing the man to scream and drop the SIG.

The man elbowed her with the other arm, the point striking her in the ribs. She went to her knees but got back up and whipped around, grabbing the man's hair as she slammed her shin into his thigh.

He cried out and went down. Morgan helped him, bashing his head into the pavement with a crack. The man went limp.

She looked up in time to see Grant's opponent topple to the ground unconscious.

He stood, brushed his hands off, and walked over to Morgan. "You all right?"

She stretched her back. "I'll be fine. Looks like you handled your guy almost as well as I handled mine."

"His head had an unfortunate encounter with my knee." He put his hands on her shoulders. "Sorry about the 'raging bitch' comment."

She pulled him to her and kissed him hard. Damn adrenaline.

When she let him go, she said, "I have to say, you are sexy as hell when you hit people."

"You should see some video of my wrestling days."

"I have," she said with a smile. "Never missed one of your bouts."

He grinned. "Why you little ... And you let me think all this time that you hated me."

"I could tell your ego was already big enough. No sense gushing over you."

He chuckled and picked up one of the SIGs. "We have to show these guys to your bosses. Should be the proof we need to get the flight shut down. I'll text Tyler to let him know that Colchev is down two more men."

While Grant sent the message, Morgan scooped up the other gun and searched the man for any additional weapons or information about their plans. She came up empty and was about to tell Grant to wait here while she got security, but she didn't need to.

Two policemen ran up to them, guns drawn. They saw the two men laid out, and pointed their pistols at Morgan and Grant.

"Drop your weapons now!" both of them yelled.

They let go of their guns and put up their hands.

"I'm a federal officer," Morgan said.

"Show me your ID."

"Don't have it on me."

The men exchanged looks, then one said, "On the ground! Do it!"

Morgan and Grant lay face down next to each other. As they were frisked, Grant said, "Maybe this isn't going to go as smoothly as we thought."

FIFTY-FOUR

Seething with anger, Colchev read the text message on Tyler's phone and knew he'd have to alter his plan. According to Grant Westfield, Nisselovich and Oborski were in custody. Colchev knew they were too well trained to talk, but without them the crew would be two passengers short when they got to the spaceplane. The flight director would certainly know something was wrong. They'd never get off the ground.

Only eight minutes remained until they were supposed to drive to the Skyward.

Colchev considered using the original passengers, who were now locked inside the hangar's storage room, but he needed them alive, so he couldn't take them on the space-plane with him. He turned and eyed Tyler and Jess. Their sizes were slightly off: Tyler was taller than Nisselovich and Jess was shorter than Oborski, but they'd do.

Colchev picked up the pressure suits and thrust them at Tyler and Jess.

"Put these on."

"Why?" Jess said.

"You two are going to be astronauts." Seeing that they were about to protest, Colchev said, "If we don't make it onto the Skyward, I will have no choice but to detonate the Killswitch on the ground. The gamma radiation will kill everyone at the air show. Now do it."

Zotkin was already in his pilot's uniform and helmet. Because he was going to fly the carrier jet, he didn't need a pressure suit. The crash helmet and sunglasses would be enough of a disguise for him.

The three blue and gold pressure suits, however, were fully enclosed. The Skyward was pressurized, but the suits were required in the event of a hull breach. The lightweight material wasn't exactly form-fitting, but it wasn't nearly as bulky as the old suits the Apollo astronauts had worn. While they were on the ground, a small slit in the base of the helmet allowed them to breathe. On the spaceplane the slit would be closed and an oxygen hose from the on-board environmental system could be plugged into the suit.

Colchev was wearing his, and the absence of air-conditioning in the hangar was beginning to make the suit stifling. Tyler and Jess struggled into the suits, which consisted of both an inner insulating layer—to protect against the freezing cold of the vacuum at seventy miles— and an airtight outer skin.

"What are you going to do with those men?" Tyler said, pointing at the storage room.

"They're going to ensure my legacy," Colchev said with a smile. "Did you recognize any of them?"

"Call me crazy," Jess said, "but I'm pretty sure one of them is Trent Walden."

"The action movie director?" Tyler said.

Colchev nodded. "Correct. He was supposed to be one of the passengers on the flight. The other passenger is a Russian producer named Mikhail Arshan. They were planning to film shots of the Earth from space for an upcoming movie they're making together. They and ExAtmo thought it would be good cross-publicity for both ventures. Who better to reveal what I've accomplished here today?"

"You're letting them live?"

"Of course. Not only will the Russian government have no doubt about my patriotism, but the Russian people will hear of my glorious triumph."

"And the American government won't rest until they bring you back here or kill you."

Colchev smiled. "*If* they thought I was still alive. But why would they think I could survive such a cataclysmic event? Then it will just be a matter of getting a new face once I'm back in Russia. Your country isn't the only one with a program to give its citizens new identities."

Static from the pilot's walkie-talkie told Colchev a call was coming in from the flight director. He left Zotkin to watch them while he answered.

"Yes?"

"We're ready out here. Are you suited up?"

"Acknowledged."

"Good. The driver is on the way to get you. Out."

438 / BOYD MORRISON

Colchev returned and gave Tyler and Jess their helmets. The mirrored visors would make them unidentifiable.

"I will be by the Killswitch at all times. The helmets stay on. If you take them off or you make any gestures for help, I will press the button. You understand?"

"We understand," Tyler said. "If you do that, you'll kill tens of thousands of people for nothing. And if you set it off in space, it'll be just as meaningless."

"Wrong! It will finally tip the scales in Russia's favor. With this single action, I will change the equation that has dominated world culture since the Cold War ended. Now America will know what it's like to be a second-class world citizen."

"You don't know my country very well. We'll bounce back like we always do."

"You don't understand the power of chaos. I've seen it myself when the Soviet Union fell. All it takes is a push to unbalance the situation. And thanks to your own military-industrial complex, we have the weapon to give that push. I'll never tire of the irony."

"If your men were captured, the police will know you're here," Jess said. "They'll stop us before we even get to the spaceplane."

"Then why did I get a call from the flight director a few minutes ago saying that they're ready?"

"Maybe it's a trick to lure you out."

Colchev knew she was right, but he had no choice now but to march on assuming victory. "For the sake of everyone here, I hope you're wrong."

A knock on the door, followed by a shout. "Your bus is here!"

Colchev put on his helmet and told Tyler and Jess to do the same. Zotkin hefted the bag containing the Icarus parachute system and his own normal parachute as well as several bungee cords. Colchev took the handcart, the Killswitch now in a black padded duffel. His hand was inside the zippered opening, his finger near the arming button.

"They'll notice you're carrying that," Tyler said.

"Oh, you mean Walden and Arshan's film equipment?" He gestured at a pile of cameras and lenses heaped on the floor.

That shut them up. They couldn't see it underneath his helmet, but Colchev was grinning.

Zotkin opened the door and ushered Tyler and Jess outside. Colchev followed with the handcart. When they all got on the bus, he made sure to keep the Killswitch between him and Tyler.

The driver eyed the luggage but said nothing. He closed the door and drove off.

As they approached the Skyward, Colchev spotted the massive crowd that had gathered to watch the crew board the ship. They would have plenty to tell their grandchildren someday, provided they weren't in an airplane or a car when the Killswitch went off.

Colchev leaned over to Tyler and Jess. "Remember: wave, but no other gestures. And say nothing to the ground crew. I will be listening."

When they got out of the bus, the crowd cheered. Colchev gave them the thumbs-up, and the mob went wild. They had no idea that he was sending them an insult. As opposed to signifying that everything was great, in Russia the *thumbs-up* meant "up yours".

Tyler waved, and Jess put up both her hands in the V-sign to the crowd's delight.

After a few more waves, the ground crew escorted them to the open hatch of the Skyward. With Zotkin making sure that Tyler stayed too far away to attempt anything, Colchev went first and brought the Killswitch up with the ground crew's help. Then Tyler and Jess climbed aboard. Zotkin was last and pulled the hatch closed behind him. The Lodestar's four engines were already spooled up and humming.

The interior of the Skyward was flooded with light from the myriad triangular windows covering the fuselage, so they were still in full view of the spectators. Three rows of seats, one on each side, straddled the center aisle. The pilot's chair sat in the front center of the ship. With weight at a premium and flights costing more than $200,000 per person, there was no room for a co-pilot.

"Rear seats," Colchev said.

While Tyler and Jess were standing at the rear of the space-plane, Zotkin ordered them to turn their backs to the windows. Pretending he was adjusting their suits, he wrapped bungee cords around their wrists and guided them into seats across the aisle from each other. Zotkin belted them in with the four-point safety harnesses so that their arms were under the nylon straps. Once they were secure, Colchev and Zotkin lashed the Killswitch and Icarus between the seats.

Zotkin climbed into the carrier jet, and Colchev closed the hatch behind him before taking his seat in the pilot's chair. He plugged his helmet into the on-board communications system. By switching the unit between channels, he could either talk to the flight control or to Zotkin on the Lodestar.

"All right, Skyward," the flight director said, "now that you're on board, let's begin the checklist."

"Roger, control," Colchev said. Before the director could get any further, Colchev switched to Zotkin's channel. "Are you ready?"

"The flight controls are exactly what I anticipated. I'm ready to taxi."

"Then do it while they still think you're the real pilot."

Colchev switched back to the flight director's channel just in time to hear, "—Skyward, do you read me?"

"I read you loud and clear, control."

"Why aren't you following the established takeoff procedure? What's the problem?"

"No problem here. Skyward signing off."

He should have closed the channel, but he rather enjoyed listening to the flight director's confused shouts as the engines powered up and the spaceplane rolled across the tarmac to the runway.

FIFTY-FIVE

G rant strained at his handcuffs as he watched the Lodestar reach the end of the runway. The aircraft began its takeoff roll a second before he heard the engines go to full power. After ten minutes of telling their tale to the arresting officers, he and Morgan were not getting a sympathetic ear. The policemen's major concern was clearing them out of the busy pathway so that the incident wouldn't disrupt the event.

"You have to listen to us," Grant said to the officer guiding him to the oversized utility cart. "You have to call the flight director of the Skyward and tell them there is someone here who may have planted a bomb on their plane."

"Right. And those unconscious guys are Russian spies." They'd already carted the Russians off in medical units. "Look. We've relayed your concerns to the appropriate people. We'll take you to the security office. If your 'story' checks out, then we'll see if we can find the other Russians."

Grant and Morgan were shoved into the cart, and they motored away.

As the cart passed the main food court, a shout called out

to them. When the cart didn't slow, the shout became a scream of bloody murder. That finally got the officer to stop.

"What the hell is going on now?" he said.

Fay ran over to them waving her arms, dashing around to the driver.

"I need their help," she said, breathing hard.

"Do you know these people, ma'am?"

"They're friends of my granddaughter. What's going on?"

"We caught them after they beat two men to the point of unconsciousness. We're taking them to the security office. You can meet us there."

The officer's radio squawked. "Moline, where are you?"

"Moline here. We're at the food court near the Heli Center."

"We've got a major problem with the spaceplane demo. They lost contact with the pilot, and then he just took off."

Grant felt his stomach sink. Colchev was already on his way up.

"That's what I'm telling you!" Grant said. "The spaceplane is being hijacked."

"And for all we know, you're in on it. Now shut up!"

"Moline," the voice on the radio said, "get over to the flight ops and see if you can give them a hand."

"We've got suspects in custody."

"Damn it! All right, bring them back here. I'll get someone else."

Moline put the radio away. "Ma'am, we have to go—"

Fay jabbed the muzzle of a Glock pistol against Moline's rib cage, taking care to keep it out of sight of passing patrons. "No. You let them go. Now."

Moline snickered at the seventy-five-year-old. "Is this a joke?"

"Do I look like a comedian?" Fay said with a deadly serious stare. Moline's smirk faltered.

"Fay," Morgan said, "where did you get that?"

"Tyler gave it to me. You didn't think I would be the only one to come here unarmed, did you?"

Grant supposed he shouldn't have been surprised that she'd want her own weapon after the way she handled that shotgun in New Zealand.

When Moline hesitated, Fay poked him with the Glock. "Don't make me shoot you."

Moline nodded at the other officer, who unlocked Morgan's cuffs and then Grant's.

"What do we do with them?" Morgan said, retrieving their weapons and the officers' guns as well.

Grant looked around and saw a row of Port-a-Potties on the other side of the food court. "Over there."

As inconspicuously as possible, they put the two officers into the potties and locked the doors with the handcuffs. The men might scream for help, but it would take time for anyone to get them out.

"Good job, Fay," Grant said.

"I had to do something. Tyler and Jess are on that plane."

Grant and Morgan looked at each other in confusion, then back at Fay.

"Are you sure?"

Fay nodded. "They were wearing spacesuits, so when I was watching them get out of the shuttle bus, I thought they were the crew. But then I saw the shorter one put up her hands in the 'V for victory' sign."

"I don't get it."

Fay's words came out in a gusher. "In New Zealand if you do the sign palm-out, it means 'victory'. But if you do the sign palm-in, it means 'screw you'. You know, like giving the finger. Well, the shorter one gave the palm-out version to the crowd, but then she definitely gave the palm-in version to the two men on either end. Then when I saw the taller man put his hand on her hip to escort her to the plane, I recognized their walks. It was Tyler and Jess. Now they're on board the plane with that madman. You have to help them!"

"They must have the Killswitch on board," Morgan said. "How long until they launch the spaceplane from the carrier?"

Grant had read up on the Skyward on the flight there. "If the pilot climbs hard, they can be in launch position in fifteen minutes."

He could see Morgan doing mental calculations. She shook her head. "Not enough time. The closest air base is in Madison. Unless they scrambled right now, they won't be able to get here in time to ... " She glanced at Fay. " ... to force them down."

446 / BOYD MORRISON

Grant shook his head. "You're right. Who knows how long it'll take to convince them that there's enough of a threat to send up the fighters."

"What about the fighters here?" Fay said, pointing at the T-38, whose portable start cart was already attached. "They could go up and find the spaceplane."

"No good," Morgan said. "The T-38 is a trainer. It's unarmed. All the planes here are. Besides, without orders from their chain of command, they wouldn't do it."

"You could," Grant said.

"Me?"

"You were a fighter pilot. Can't you fly that?"

Morgan looked at the T-38 again and then back to Grant. "You're serious?"

"What other choice do we have?"

Morgan pursed her lips in thought before she finally nodded. "You're right. Come on!"

She sprinted toward the T-38, leaving Grant to pull Fay along behind her.

The trainer's pilots were standing next to the jet talking to a patron. Morgan pushed the man out of the way.

"Captain, I'm a federal agent. I'm commandeering your airplane."

The baby-faced pilot smiled at her and then started laughing hysterically. He turned to his subordinate, a lieutenant. "Hudson, did you put this pretty lady up to this?"

The puzzled lieutenant joined in the laughter and shrugged.

"I don't have time for this," Morgan said, pulling out her pistol.

The pilots got quiet fast.

"I'd listen to her," Grant said.

"What the hell is this?" the captain said.

"I don't have time to explain, and you wouldn't believe me anyway. Give me your helmet."

"The hell I will."

She looked up the stairs leading to the cockpit. "That's okay. It must be in the cockpit. Is your plane prepped and ready to fly?"

"You're taking my plane over my dead body."

Fay pulled her pistol and pointed it at him. "That might happen, son. Because my granddaughter is a hostage on the spaceplane that took off. Now give this woman the keys or whatever she needs, or I'll shoot you myself."

"This is truly a matter of national security," Morgan said. "There is an EMP weapon on board the spaceplane. If it reaches launch altitude, the entire US infrastructure could be destroyed. I'm a former F-16 pilot, and I'm going to bring them back down before that happens. Understand?"

"What's your call sign?"

Without hesitation, she said, "Buster."

Despite the situation, Grant couldn't help a slight smile. He was quite sure that Buster stood for "Ball Buster".

The captain frowned at her. "I'll fly up myself if I get confirmation about this."

"No time. Fay, keep an eye on them."

Morgan ran up the stairs. Grant dogged her footsteps. At the top she turned to see him right behind her.

"What are you doing?"

"I'm coming with you."

"No, you're not."

"What if you get vertigo up there? I've got a helicopter license. I can't take off in one of these things, but I could keep the stick steady if you black out."

"I'll handle it."

"Are you willing to bet the future of the country on that?"

She pursed her lips.

"I know what you have to do up there," Grant said. "If they won't land, there's only one other way to bring them down."

"That's why I don't want you there."

"That's my best friend we're talking about. If you have to ram them, I want to be there to make sure Tyler doesn't die in vain."

She paused, wrestling with the decision, but he could tell she knew he was right.

"Okay," she said grudgingly. "Get in the front seat. I'll fire up the start cart."

As Grant climbed in and squeezed into the pilot's helmet and parachute, she ran back down the stairs and gestured frantically at Fay, who waved her gun at the two pilots when they didn't respond quickly enough. Morgan ran back up the stairs and got in the rear cockpit seat.

"I told Fay to get the pilots to release the start cart once the engines are powered up. She'll also get them to retract the stairway."

They closed the canopies and strapped in. Grant kept his hands off the controls. The instrument panel was ten times more complicated than the light helicopter he flew.

The engines rumbled to life. He cranked his head around. The APU was pulled away, as were the stairs and wheel chocks. He gave the V-sign to Fay, palm out. She returned the gesture.

Grant thought they didn't build them that tough any more and had to correct himself. The woman sitting behind him was the real deal, too.

Morgan released the brakes.

"Time to intercept?" Grant said.

"Can't say. Even using afterburners, it'll be close."

Morgan informed the tower to clear all air traffic because she was taking off no matter what the controller said. A minute later the T-38 screamed down the runway, and Grant wondered if he'd ever touch the ground again.

FIFTY-SIX

Although the Lodestar carrier plane shaded the sun, Tyler had an expansive view of the horizon for 180 degrees around him thanks to the unorthodox window design. If he were prone to acrophobia, he'd be catatonic by now.

Tyler explored the limits of his restraints, but it was no use. The bungees were too tight to get any leverage against the belts. Zotkin had been very thorough, taking everything Tyler had on him, including his Leatherman.

He breathed in the smell of the Skyward's interior through the slit in his helmet, a scent that smelled oddly like a car fresh off the factory floor, no doubt due to the newly installed upholstery. The tiny hole kept him from suffocating, but it did nothing to cool him down. He was already drenched with sweat.

Judging by their climb angle, he guessed they would hit the fifty-thousand-foot launch altitude in another five minutes.

"You okay?" Tyler whispered to Jess so that he wouldn't be heard over the muted engine noise. He could see her struggling to no avail.

She gave him a plaintive look. "We're going to die, aren't we?"

"Not if I can help it."

"What can we do? I'm trussed up like a turkey. Can you get out?"

"I'm trying." He pulled again. This time he was able to move his arms up just a little. He tried twice more, but he'd reached his maximum range of motion. Unless he could figure out a way to loosen the belts, he was stuck.

Colchev had stripped out of his original flight suit and was now getting into the Icarus suit. It was somewhat bulkier because of the attached parachute and small oxygen tank. If Tyler could somehow break free, he'd at least have the advantage in mobility.

In situations like this, Tyler had one rule: doing something was better than doing nothing. He'd start by talking. He found it helped to get inside the mind of his enemy.

"I know what you're planning to do, Colchev. You're going to leave the Killswitch on here and jump out. Won't work. We'll both be in freefall. You'll just float next to us outside the spaceplane until the bomb explodes."

"Wrong." He didn't elaborate, but Tyler didn't really think he was that stupid. Colchev was probably going to do it the other way around, dumping the Killswitch overboard once the timer was set, then using the rocket to put some distance between him and the explosion before bailing out.

At least that's how Tyler would do it.

"Are you sure Icarus even works?" he asked.

"It was designed by top Russian engineers."

"That's what I mean."

Colchev smirked at him. "Don't forget that we were the first country into space. First satellite. First cosmonaut. First space walk. And now America rides on Russian rockets to the space station. I trust this parachute more than I trust this spaceplane."

Tyler tried a different angle. "You can't shoot us in here, you know. The bullets might rip through us and penetrate the hull."

"True. If you're worried about how you're going to die, I'm planning to make it easy for you. Instead of letting you scream in terror as the disabled Skyward plummets back to Earth, I'll just leave your suits unplugged from the environmental system. When I decompress the ship, you'll fall unconscious and simply fade away. Much more pleasant."

"That's very kind of you."

"I'm not a monster."

"Even though you've killed a dozen people already and you're planning to kill thousands more?" Jess said.

"Soldiers are given medals for killing men while trying to take some godforsaken hill somewhere. I killed men on the way to resetting the global order. Which is more justified?"

"Yeah, you're a regular hero."

"One country's villain is another's hero. George Washington may be a hero in America, but to the British he was a vile traitor. If the colonies had lost the war, the city of

Washington would be named Kingsville. It will be the same with me in Russia."

"Colchevgrad?" Tyler said. "Not very catchy. There's one other thing I've been wondering. How did you know about the cave on Easter Island? You didn't have Fay's relic to guide you there, but somehow you ambushed us."

Colchev looked at them in amazement. "You really don't know?"

"Know what?"

"About Dombrovski."

"I know Dombrovski was the one who made the connection to the Nazca lines."

Colchev shook his head and chuckled. "You Americans *can* keep secrets. Dombrovski was the one who originally brought the xenobium from Tunguska to the United States in exchange for asylum. He's the one who created Project Caelus for the US Air Force. That's why he was trying to find another source of xenobium."

"Project Caelus?" So Colchev had additional information about Dombrovski's secret project that Kessler hadn't shared with them. Colchev must have had access to the records that the Soviets stole.

"It's funny how we know more about it than you do," Colchev said. "Dombrovski was obsessed with two things: Project Caelus and his second wife, Catherine. I suppose she became his fixation after the death of his first wife and daughter in Russia, but then Catherine died as well. Every morning he would visit her grave and then go straight to his lab."

"Was Dombrovski a Russian spy?"

"No, he hated the communists. But we had someone in his lab who was sympathetic to our cause. That's how we got possession of his notes. We're the ones who torched his laboratory. We sabotaged his plane. We thought we had everything, including a photo of the xenobium in its Nazca hiding place. Dombrovski documented its existence but didn't attempt to remove it because he hadn't figured out how to do it without the chamber collapsing."

"He planned to return to retrieve it," Tyler said, "but the Soviets killed him before that happened."

"We were going to complete his task," Colchev said. "The old Soviet files had photos of the wood engraving, but Dombrovski died before we could find out the location the map was referring to. All we knew was that the xenobium was at Nazca. Then when I saw the video of Fay and heard her say, 'Rapa Nui leads to xenobium', I thought she possessed the Nazca specimen. When I realized that wasn't the case, I went to Easter Island to claim whatever clues were there for myself. You just happened to beat me to it. I set off the other Killswitch to keep you from following me."

Tyler pulled at his restraints. "And yet here we are."

Colchev strapped up the final piece of the Icarus suit. "At least you'll die for your country. Maybe they'll even name a monument after you. I know they will name one after me in my country."

Colchev put his hand to his ear and nodded.

"We're nearing our departure point, lady and gentleman. You'll be dead in a few minutes, so I'll bid you farewell. As for me, destiny awaits."

He walked back to the pilot's seat and buckled in.

As Tyler continued trying to stretch his seat belts, he made one promise to himself.

He wasn't going to die sitting on his ass.

FIFTY-SEVEN

Morgan had stopped talking, and that's what worried Grant the most as he kept his hand on the T-38's control stick. Being a trainer, the jet was easy to fly, but all he could do was follow a straight line or make minor adjustments in their heading. He needed Morgan for anything more complex, and the two-minute vertical ride to thirty thousand feet had brought on a fierce bout of her vertigo.

He thought she was okay until they nosed over and leveled off. It was bad enough for him, the blood pooling in his head from the negative g's, but for her it must have been overwhelming. She told him to keep hold of the stick and then went silent.

Thanks to chatter on the radio, they had enough info to vector in on the Lodestar. It was fifteen miles away, climbing at two thousand feet per minute. At their closing speed of mach 1.2, the T-38 would rendezvous with it before the Skyward was in position for launch.

Ground control continued to try to raise the Lodestar on the radio without success, so they had requested the Air

Force to scramble two F-16s to intercept it. Their ETA was another fifteen minutes, far too late to do any good. The T-38 was the only plane in range to intervene. Although ground control was also trying to reach Morgan and Grant, they maintained radio silence.

The situation reconfirmed for Grant that the Killswitch was on the Skyward. If there had simply been a communications malfunction, the pilot would have returned to Oshkosh. The only explanation was that Colchev was making his attempt to detonate the weapon in the ionosphere, causing a doomsday scenario for the American infrastructure.

Grant was sick at the thought of being responsible for Tyler and Jess's deaths. He wracked his brain for any other option, but he kept coming up empty. If they simply made a warning pass or attempted radio contact with the Lodestar pilot to threaten him, Colchev might launch before the T-38 could intercept even if the Skyward weren't at the optimal altitude. They'd only get one pass at bringing the carrier down. This had to be a sneak attack.

Grant tried to console himself with the thought that Tyler would agree he had no choice. The good of the country came first. Tyler had been an officer in the Army, with responsibility for ordering men into harm's way. But Jess was an innocent victim. She'd never made the pact that you would give your life for the greater good.

Both military veterans, Grant and Morgan *had* made that bargain. It didn't need to be said between them that they were willing to die to keep the spaceplane from launching.

"Morgan, talk to me."

After a few seconds, he heard, "I'm here."

"How are you doing?"

"I was able to hold down my lunch. My vision's a little blurry, but it's clearing up."

"And the vertigo?"

"Better. I can handle the stick now."

Grant let go and she put the plane into a steady climb on the intercept heading. She seemed to be doing okay.

"We're going to come up from below and behind them. Even if they're aware of us from listening to ground control, they won't be able to see us until we're almost upon them. When we're close, I'll slow to a one-hundred-knot closing speed so that I make sure not to miss. At that velocity we'll still do enough damage to destroy the plane."

"And ours."

"That's why we're going to eject just before impact. Under each of your armrests is a trigger. Feel for them but don't pull them."

Grant touched them. "Got 'em."

"When the time comes, you'll pull both armrests straight up and squeeze the triggers. The canopy will blow off and a rocket will eject the seat. Sit up straight to minimize the possibility of fracturing your spine. The wind will slam into you. Your mask should stay on, but if it doesn't you'll pass out before you reach twenty thousand feet. The parachute will open automatically."

"How will that affect the flight path of the plane?"

"At the speed we'll be going, the plane will be like a missile. The inertia will keep it steady for a few seconds."

"We pull at the same time?"

"No, pulling the handle will eject both of us, one after the other."

Morgan was the expert, so Grant had to take her word that all this would work.

"I still expect that afternoon together," he said.

"I promise. I'll be there."

A distant white speck caught Grant's attention.

"Target dead ahead," he announced to Morgan.

In seconds he could see the bone-white Lodestar, its enormous wingspan cleaving the blue sky. They were coming up directly behind the carrier, which grew in size rapidly.

"I've got it," Morgan said. "Are you ready?"

"Just tell me when."

"I'll count down. Throttling back."

Grant's chest strained against the safety straps as the afterburners cut off. They were now doing a stately six hundred knots. Ejecting at this speed and altitude was dicey at best, especially because he wasn't wearing a flight suit. If he didn't die of hypoxia, he might freeze to death before he got to a lower altitude.

The Lodestar was now close enough that Grant could make out the Skyward below it.

Tyler and Jess had no clue what was coming. Grant rationalized that they would die anyway if the Killswitch were detonated, but the taste of guilt was too strong to ignore. If he could trade places with them, Grant would do it in an instant.

"I'm sorry, guys," he said under his breath. "So sorry." He silently prayed for them.

"It's time, Grant," Morgan said. "I'll see you on the other side."

"Can't wait."

The Lodestar loomed in the windshield. Morgan was aiming dead center. The T-38 would tear through the middle of the fuselage. Grant hoped that Tyler and Jess would never know what happened.

Morgan began her countdown.

"Pull on one. Five."

Grant wrapped his fingers around the armrests and triggers.

"Four."

Morgan's voice sounded strangely at peace.

"Three."

Like she knew this was a moment to be savored.

"Two."

Like she was finally back where she belonged.

"One. Bail out, bail out, bail out!"

Grant jerked the armrests up, and his world became a rush of sensation. The sound of the explosive bolts blowing the canopy off. The intense cold of the air lashing his arms. The crushing force of the seat catapulting him out of the plane. The coppery taste of blood as he bit his lip. The tunneling of vision from sudden deceleration as the air dragged him to a stop.

As he tumbled through the air, a drogue chute deployed to halt the spin, and that's when he saw that she had over-estimated their closing speed. He'd ejected when they were still hundreds of yards from the Lodestar.

But Grant couldn't see Morgan's chute anywhere. She hadn't bailed out.

For an instant Grant thought something had gone wrong with the ejection mechanism. But then he realized she'd tricked him into ejecting. Morgan was staying with her plane until the end.

The Lodestar pilot must have seen the plane behind him because at the very last moment he banked to the left. If Morgan had ejected, the T-38 would have flown right by it.

Instead, Grant saw why she'd been selected as a fighter pilot. Morgan reacted to the evasive maneuver by snapping the T-38 sideways and flying through the starboard wing of the Lodestar.

The T-38 was transformed into a fireball so large that Grant could feel the heat of the burning fuel. Morgan didn't have a chance to eject.

The starboard engines of the Lodestar cartwheeled away. Flames shot from the stub of remaining wing, and the Lodestar did a barrel roll, turning upside down.

Grant struggled to breathe in the thin air, fighting to maintain consciousness. He owed it to Tyler to be a witness to the end.

Grant expected the carrier to break up from the extreme aerodynamic forces, but the Lodestar fuselage remained intact, demonstrating the strength of the bird-bone frame holding it together. The aircraft continued its lazy spin until it was right-side up again.

Then to Grant's horror, the Skyward was released from the Lodestar. It dropped away and the Lodestar fell behind, the fire eating away at the carbon wing.

The Skyward's rocket fired just before the Lodestar exploded, taking it safely out of range of the burning wreckage.

True to its name, the Skyward stood on its tail and shot into the blue atop a tongue of fire propelling it to four times the speed of sound.

Grant had never felt so helpless as he watched the plane disappear into the heavens.

"So sorry," he whispered as the blackness took him.

The deep indigo mesmerized Colchev. As they accelerated toward the stars, the color of the sky faded through a rainbow of blues. He turned his head against the punishing g-forces and saw the Earth receding at a pace he couldn't have imagined. Distinct ground features became imperceptible, only the shoreline recognizable as they soared over Lake Michigan.

The myriad windows of the Skyward had saved the mission. With nothing to do until the Skyward launched, Colchev had been taking in the panoramic view when he happened to look over his shoulder and saw the jet bearing down on them.

He had screamed a warning at Zotkin, but only in time to avert a catastrophic collision. In one last heroic effort before the Lodestar disintegrated, Colchev's old friend jettisoned the Skyward, initiating the automated flight sequence.

He admired Zotkin's sacrifice and vowed that his name would have a place of honor along with those of the other men who gave their lives in support of this mission.

Colchev suddenly felt the weight of responsibility crash

down upon him. Now he was the only one left to carry out their plan. The future of the world was up to him.

Although they had launched prematurely, Colchev was confident that they would reach a sufficient altitude to make the operation a success. All he had to do was shut down the engines when the fuel gauge neared the five percent mark, leaving him enough to get clear of the gamma radiation emitted when the Killswitch detonated.

Colchev tore his eyes away from the hypnotic sky and focused on the task at hand. The engine was gulping liquid hydrazine at a prodigious rate, embodied in the five g's that plastered him to the back of his seat. It was a tremendous effort to raise his arm, but the engine shutoff switch was within reach.

Just two more minutes.

Tyler was too busy trying to wrestle his way out of the bungee cord to admire the view.

He didn't know who had made the kamikaze attack, but he thanked them for giving him a sliver of hope. During the violent roll he had hung upside down in his belt, providing just enough slack to pull his hands from underneath the restraints.

The Skyward's engine howled behind them, but he knew the sub-orbital trip would last only a few minutes more. He contorted his arms in an attempt to undo the belt release, but the angle made it impossible to reach with his fingers. His best shot was to use his elbow to unlatch it.

He had to remember to keep silent as he worked. Colchev

was still attending to the instruments. Tyler had been thinking about how Colchev would bail out of the Skyward, and it occurred to him that the spaceplane wouldn't have a control to manually depressurize the fuselage as Colchev had said he would do.

Once Tyler realized Colchev's likely depressurization method, he knew Colchev wouldn't hesitate to shoot both of them. Tyler had to get to Colchev before the Russian discovered that he was free.

Tyler got his elbow under the latch and pushed it out, his muscles overtaxed by their quintupled weight. But the effort was enough.

The straps fell back into the seat. Although he was loose, the bungee was still wrapped around his wrists, and he had no way to untie it. He would have to get Jess to do it, but the brutal acceleration glued him to the chair.

Then the rocket cut off. One moment he weighed a thousand pounds and the next he was floating above his seat like a balloon.

Using his tethered hands, Tyler propelled himself over to Jess, who was shaking off the effects of the g-forces. He raised both hands for her to be quiet. He hoped Colchev's helmet would prevent him from hearing their movement.

Tyler unbuckled her as silently as possible. He attached her seat's oxygen hose to her suit, then closed her visor and locked it shut, making the suit airtight. He quickly unraveled her bungee cord and then held his hands out for her to reciprocate.

His cord was cinched up even tighter than hers, so she had trouble getting at the knot. She looked up, frustrated, and then her helmet twisted as if she spied something over Tyler's shoulder.

He turned and saw Colchev getting out of his seat, the SIG Sauer pistol in his gloved hand.

The engine had cut off on schedule, and Colchev experienced freefall for the first time. For a moment it felt like his innards would come pouring out of his mouth, but the sensation passed quickly. In the movies astronauts in zero gravity are often portrayed as if they're swimming through molasses, but Colchev had the opposite feeling, as if he had no more corporeal form than a ghost. The slightest nudge could send him flying.

After checking that his internal oxygen supply was functional and his helmet was closed, his next task was to decompress the cabin so that he could open the hatch. The differential between the cabin and the vacuum outside resulted in twenty thousand pounds of pressure on the door. He had to equalize them, which was what the pistol was for.

Shooting a hole in the skin of the Skyward was necessary for Colchev's plans. It was a common myth that puncturing a plane's window would cause the fuselage to explosively decompress and that anyone near the hole would be sucked out. Experiments on various aircraft had shown that the only effect would be the slow leak of air until it was depleted. At this altitude the blood of anyone not protected by a pressure suit would boil.

No sane aircraft designer would provide a way to intentionally depressurize a cabin, so Colchev had to resort to a cruder method. He couldn't shoot through the windows because they were stronger than ballistic glass, but the carbon-fiber body was not bullet resistant. His plan was risky, but the whole venture had been risky. Besides, he would arm the Killswitch beforehand so that if something went wrong and he died as a result of the decompression, the weapon would still detonate.

He rose out of his seat and grabbed the headrest to turn around. Even in the bulky pressure suit, he felt as graceful as a butterfly.

His gleeful mood was suddenly chilled by the unbelievable sight of Tyler Locke, his bound hands outstretched, sailing toward him.

Tyler was only halfway through the cabin when Colchev saw him, but he was committed to his course. There was no way he could duck if Colchev fired at him, and he hadn't had time to let Jess untie him, so his wrists were still stuck together.

The pistol came around, and Tyler thought he was dead.

But Colchev didn't account for the effects of microgravity. As he swung his arm around, the change in angular momentum was enough to throw his aim off. He fired, but the bullet whizzed past Tyler's helmet and punched through the fuselage behind him.

Colchev rapid-fired two more shots, but he'd apparently forgotten about Newton's Third Law of Motion: every action has an equal and opposite reaction. He hadn't anchored himself before firing, so the recoil of the gun sent him flying backward. His second and third shots embedded themselves in the windows.

Though the first shot hadn't hit Tyler, the .40 caliber hollow-point had done its original job. Wind whistled as air rushed through the ragged bullet hole. It would be a matter of seconds before the cabin atmospheric pressure was zero.

Tyler shut his visor as he soared toward Colchev, but it was only a delaying action. The air inside his suit was extremely limited. Without the connection to the spaceplane's internal oxygen, he'd be hypoxic in about a minute.

He reached out and kicked the pilot's seat, altering his trajectory so that he hit Colchev squarely in the stomach with both fists. The pain he could see on Colchev's face through the Icarus suit's clear visor told him the impact made an impression.

Tyler swung his elbow out and knocked the pistol away. Colchev slapped at Tyler's helmet, causing him to somersault backward. He was already getting light-headed from the lack of oxygen, but holding his breath wouldn't help. He had to make this a short fight. The whistling of the air was gone, meaning the pressure inside was now equal to the vacuum outside.

Colchev launched himself toward the Killswitch, but Tyler grabbed his ankles before he could reach it. Tyler halted his own forward momentum by looping his toes around the edge of the pilot's seat.

The sudden stop whirled Colchev toward the hatch. Too late, Tyler saw Colchev grasp the emergency release handle and yank it.

The hatch door swung open. Colchev pushed away from it back toward the Killswitch. As Colchev struggled mightily against his grip, Tyler held on, but Colchev now had the advantage.

Because Tyler wasn't hooked to the internal oxygen, the carbon dioxide level in his suit would soon reach a lethal concentration. He could already feel himself getting dizzy. It was only a matter of time before he passed out.

Jess had to do something. Tyler was in a war of attrition with Colchev, and the Russian had the upper hand. And if Tyler was unable to beat him, she wouldn't stand a chance in a fight with him.

The Killswitch was what Colchev was stretching for. She realized that with the hatch open, she could put the unarmed weapon permanently out of reach no matter what happened to her and Tyler.

Her heart pounding, she detached herself from the oxygen hose and pulled herself along the seats until she was floating above the Killswitch. Though the LCD timer read three minutes, it wasn't counting down; Colchev hadn't activated it yet. It didn't matter that Jess had no idea how to disable the bomb. She had another solution.

Colchev waved his arms violently from four feet away, straining to get to her, but Tyler wouldn't let go even as he was on the verge of unconsciousness.

Jess unhooked the quick-release bindings that were holding the Killswitch in place. She grabbed the end of it, and as she expected, the heavy bomb was now easy to maneuver.

With a firm grip, she aimed it at the open hatch. She braced her feet against the fuselage wall and then sprang forward.

Jess flew across the cabin, and when she was sure the Killswitch would clear the opening, she let go and flailed for purchase to prevent herself from following it out into the abyss.

Her hand latched onto the armrest of the nearest seat, and she swung around, her legs dangling through the open hatch.

Jess screamed at the thought of falling into space and used all of her strength to pull herself back inside. She glided to the back of the cabin where she saw the air hose floating next to her seat. She attached it and inhaled the cool oxygen blowing through.

Her terror abated, and she came to her senses long enough to see Tyler go limp. Colchev wriggled free from his grasp and pushed himself forward.

Jess steeled herself to fight him as best she could, but instead of coming for her, he went toward the base of the first row of seats. He rummaged around for a moment and then came up holding a fire extinguisher.

He placed his feet against a window and bent his knees. Then he did something that made Jess gasp in astonishment.

Colchev pushed off from the window and shot out the Skyward's hatch into open space.

FIFTY-NINE

Tyler's limbs were numb. A coldness seeped through his veins. His ears buzzed as though he were listening to a conch shell. Fog covered the inside of his visor. Or maybe the fog was in his mind.

Through the haze, Tyler made out a figure swimming toward him.

Colchev. Colchev was trying to get to the Killswitch. Tyler had to stop him. He reached forward but his fingers wouldn't flex. The cold was unbearable.

He was vaguely aware of being pulled by the leg. His back hit something soft and yielding.

Knocking ... Knocking ...

His eyes snapped open.

His body was being shaken, and he heard a rapping on his helmet. Then he was suddenly aware of the air coursing through his suit. Jess floated in front of him, mouthing words he couldn't hear.

He looked around and saw that he was in the first row of seats, and the oxygen hose was connected.

The hatch was closed. Wasn't it open before? Yes, because Colchev had opened it.

And that's when he realized two things were missing: the Killswitch and Colchev.

He pulled Jess's helmet to his until they touched.

"Can you hear me?" he said.

"Yes." Her voice sounded tinny, but it was understandable.

"What happened?"

"I threw the Killswitch out the hatch, but Colchev went after it. He's propelling himself with a fire extinguisher. I don't know how long we have."

Tyler unhooked himself from the hose and launched himself over to the pilot's seat. He could see Colchev about four hundred yards away. The coppery exterior of the Killswitch flashed in the distance beyond him.

They had a few minutes at most. Once Colchev reached the Killswitch, he wouldn't bother with a delay. It was a suicide mission now. The detonation would be nearly instantaneous.

Jumping out of the spaceplane himself wouldn't do any good. He'd never catch up to Colchev.

But the fuel gauge said the rocket still had some life in it.

Tyler had no time to tell Jess what he was planning. He motioned for her to buckle up and strapped himself into the pilot's seat before attaching the air hose.

Suddenly he heard Jess's voice. "Tyler," she muttered, "I hope you know what you're doing."

"Me too."

"Tyler! How can you hear me?"

The air hose must also have had an audio umbilical so that the pilot could communicate with the passengers, but he didn't take time to explain it.

"I'm going to ram Colchev. It's our only hope."

According to the online literature, the Skyward had tiny gas thrusters for altitude control in zero gravity so that the pilot could orient the spaceplane for optimal passenger viewing, important when they were spending the price of a condo on the trip.

With no airflow over the wings, the control stick wouldn't be able to affect the orientation of the spaceplane. Tyler searched the panel and saw a dual-joystick control. That had to be it.

He toggled the left joystick and the nose slewed around. Tyler had put too much into it, so he compensated in the other direction. The sticks had been modeled on a videogame controller. It took Tyler only a few seconds to understand how they functioned. They couldn't move the vehicle sideways, so he would need to line himself up precisely to hit his target.

A quarter-mile ahead, Colchev made his own course corrections using the fire extinguisher as a crude thruster. He was closing on the Killswitch.

It was now or never.

"Hang on!"

With one hand on the thrusters, Tyler hit the button for the rocket.

The Skyward blasted forward. Tyler kept his fingers on the sticks, making tiny adjustments as the spaceplane shot at Colchev.

The one advantage he had was that the roar of the engine wouldn't be heard by Colchev in the vacuum of space.

But something tipped him off that he was being pursued. Perhaps the light of the flame reflected on the inside of his helmet. Whatever it was, he twisted around and raised the fire extinguisher to blast out of the way just as the spaceplane reached him.

Time seemed to slow. As he passed, Tyler saw Colchev's horrified expression glaring at him. He knew his own face was obscured by his darkened ExAtmo helmet, so Colchev couldn't see the look of satisfaction as the leading edge of the Skyward's wing clipped the fire extinguisher, sending it tumbling away. He hadn't killed Colchev, but the spy wouldn't reach the Killswitch either.

Tyler switched off the rocket. At this point, even if he thought a second pass would be needed, the engine didn't have enough fuel for it.

"Did you get him?" Jess said. "Please tell me you got him."

"I think so. We'll know in a few minutes."

Tyler stretched his torso to look behind him, but he couldn't see anything. The freefalling weapon and the thief who'd brought it to this desolate location had already faded into the indigo blue.

SIXTY

The Killswitch taunted Colchev. Only a few meters away, it might as well have been a thousand. Without the fire extinguisher to fine-tune his path, he couldn't get close enough to push the arming button.

Even if he could reach it, he might not have been able to press the button anyway. When the extinguisher had been ripped from his hands, the wrist seals on his gloves had been damaged to the point that they were bleeding air. The leak wasn't fast enough for him to lose consciousness, but the cold seeping in chilled his hands to the point of numbness. At least he'd been able to deploy his drogue chute before they were completely frozen.

As they fell together, Colchev could only glower at the impotent Killswitch. He'd come so far to be denied his success by a few arm's-lengths. When he landed, he could guarantee one thing. He'd follow through on his promise to Fay. If Tyler and Jess somehow survived their landing, he would find them and erase them from this earth.

The air resistance gradually began to increase, and the Killswitch, which lacked the stabilization of the drogue, started to spin as it plummeted toward Lake Michigan at over six hundred miles an hour. The thickening air would diminish its velocity, and the eventual impact wouldn't be strong enough to detonate the unarmed weapon before it sank. The sturdy casing would likely even keep the xenobium from irradiating the water. Colchev, who was slowed by the small parachute, could only watch as the Killswitch disappeared from view.

The agony from his frozen hands was excruciating, forcing tears of pain to dribble down his face. But he would not cry out. That was for the weak. The defeated. He held his rock-hard hands to his body.

For seven minutes the ground rushed toward him, and he used the increasing air resistance to angle away from Lake Michigan toward the Wisconsin shoreline. During that time he realized that he would still be hailed as a hero of the Motherland. He would survive the longest freefall in history. He would bring back crucial evidence of a top-secret American weapon. And he would boast of the success of destroying a threat to his country's national security.

Despite the torture of his immobile hands, Colchev greeted the howling air rushing past his helmet as a sign that he was nearly through the worst of it. Tyler Locke had won the battle, but Colchev would come out of the situation unbowed.

He checked the wrist altimeter, which read eight thousand meters. At five thousand meters the parachute would automatically deploy. He was now over green pastureland, and upon landing he would have to formulate a plan for exiting the country.

But five thousand meters came and went without the sudden jerk of the chute opening. Colchev realized in horror that in the mayhem of his fight with Tyler, he hadn't switched on the automated chute deployment mechanism.

He scrabbled at the manual ripcord, but his rigid hands would not grasp the metal ring. In a panic he pummeled his chest. No matter what he did, the ring stubbornly stayed in place.

As Colchev stared at the verdant countryside, he could make out the shape of cows grazing. Though it looked lush and soft, the approaching meadow would be as lethal as concrete. His destiny was no longer to be a hero. Instead of devastating America, he would be nothing more than a stain on it.

The thought of such a humiliating fate was too much for Colchev. Terror finally seized him. His last ninety seconds were an eternity of fear, and the sound of screams echoed through his helmet until he slammed into the grassy field.

While the Skyward plummeted during its freefall descent, Tyler was able to make contact with flight control and get a crash course on guiding the unpowered spaceplane in for a landing. He just hoped the term wasn't literal in this case.

They had been far over Lake Michigan, so once the Skyward reached enough air resistance for the wings to have some lift, Tyler had to steer the craft back toward Wisconsin, aiming for Oshkosh thirty miles to the west.

It wasn't until the Skyward was halfway from the shore to the airfield that the controller informed Tyler he didn't have enough altitude to make it. Ditching in Lake Winnebago seemed like a bad idea, so he asked them for the closest runway and was told that, if he turned, he might make it to the Sheboygan County Memorial Airport. They had cleared a runway for his landing.

He made the turn and realized he'd bled too much altitude.

"Damn it!"

"How are you doing up there?" Jess said nervously.

"Why don't you help me look for a nice straight piece of highway to land on."

"Are you serious?"

"Time's a-wasting."

"Can't you use the rocket motor?"

"Only if you want to crash more quickly." Tyler thumbed the switch for the fuel-dump valve.

"This is the last time I go up in a spaceship with you."

They looked for a landing spot. Tyler could try setting the spaceplane down in a field, but that was a tricky proposition. The Skyward could snag on a rock or depression and roll, potentially igniting the remaining rocket fuel vapors.

"There!" Jess cried out. He looked where she was pointing and saw a road curving away from a small town before it straightened for a two-mile stretch. He immediately recognized the ribbon of asphalt next to it. As a racing fan, he knew Elkhart Lake Raceway well. Even from this distance he could see the stands packed with spectators. Cars buzzed around the track.

"We have a winner," he said and banked toward the highway. The spaceplane wasn't much larger than a private plane, and roadway landings weren't unprecedented and were often successful. He just had to hope that anyone driving on that stretch of highway would see him in time to get out of the way.

It wasn't until he was committed to his approach from the north that he saw an unfortunate obstacle.

The highway was under construction. Orange cones dotted the pavement, and yellow pavers and backhoes littered the road.

He had one other choice. The straightaway at Elkhart was just barely long enough.

Tyler nudged the stick sideways until he was lined up with the track.

Jess realized what he was attempting. "Are you insane? We can't land there!"

Tyler grimaced as he concentrated on the narrow strip of straightaway. "If you have a better idea, tell me three minutes ago."

"You haven't even lowered the landing gear!"

"Our speed's too hot. This will only work as a belly landing. As long as the racecars stay out of my way."

"Oh, my God!"

"Hold on."

The track's final turn flashed below him, and he could see that the racers were vintage sports cars. Then he saw the pedestrian bridge that marked the beginning of the flat straightaway. Miraculously, the segment of the track in front of him was devoid of cars.

As the spaceplane flew over the bridge, he could make out the faces of amazed race fans craning their necks to watch him come in.

Tyler pulled the nose up and the Skyward settled toward the tarmac as gently as if it were falling onto a bed of hay. Then the peaceful landing was interrupted by a grinding din as the pavement tore at the spaceplane's belly with a vibration that rattled Tyler's seat.

As the craft slid down the straightaway, Tyler's control was gone. He was as much a spectator as the dumbfounded people sitting in the stands on either side. The first turn came up fast, but the end of Elkhart's front straightaway was bordered by a spacious run-off area instead of a catch fence. The Skyward plowed into it, sending a tsunami of sand to either side, and came to a halt.

The sudden silence was deafening. Tyler got out of his chair and went over to Jess.

"Are you all right?"

Jess nodded and unhooked her belt. She stood, shaking. But when she removed her helmet, Tyler could see it wasn't because she was terrified.

"After that, bungee jumping just won't have the same

rush," she said with a huge smile. "You think my company can offer this as a ride?"

The rest of the day was a blur for Tyler. The police took him and Jess to the Milwaukee FBI office for interrogation before the phalanx of journalists that had descended upon Wisconsin could start hounding them for information. It had been quickly verified that the Killswitch had been on board the spaceplane because of the container found in the Weeks hangar with the spaceplane's gagged original crew, all of whom attested that Tyler and Jess had also been hostages of Colchev and Zotkin.

Tyler told the FBI that the spaceplane had been over the lake when the weapon was tossed out, so they'd have to plumb its depths if they ever wanted to retrieve the Killswitch. A search for it began immediately.

Colchev's bloody mess of a corpse was found by a rancher on a property near Lake Michigan. His two accomplices, the ones that Morgan and Grant subdued at the air show, had regained consciousness and were spirited away to an undisclosed location.

It wasn't until that evening that Fay and Grant, who had endured their own questioning, were allowed to see them. While Jess and Fay talked, Tyler went into one of the conference rooms where he found Grant staring at the table. Tyler put his hand on his friend's shoulder and sat next to him.

The agents had told Tyler about Morgan's sacrifice with

the T-38. He saw that Grant was mourning more than just the loss of a colleague, but now wasn't the time to go into it. Tyler recalled when people tried to console him after his wife's death. Words of sympathy rang hollow, but they were appreciated all the same.

"I'm so sorry about Morgan," Tyler said.

Grant swallowed hard. "She tricked me into ejecting before she rammed the Lodestar. Stupid. She promised."

"She's a hero," Tyler said. "Without her, Jess and I would be at the bottom of Lake Michigan, and Colchev would be celebrating the ruination of the United States."

Grant flashed a joyless smile, then changed the subject. "Do you think they'll ever find the Killswitch?"

Tyler sighed. "Possibly. The search area is going to be huge, and the weapon was probably destroyed on impact, but the xenobium will be intact. If they can find the radiation signature in all the muck at the bottom, they'll get it. Maybe they'll even restart the program, although that may be difficult without Kessler's expertise."

"One thing's for sure," Grant said. "If they do find it, we'll never know about it."

Tyler nodded, and he silently pondered what other secrets the government had kept quiet for the last sixty-five years.

EPILOGUE

One month later

The lush grass of Roswell's South Park Cemetery defied the blazing August sun. Tyler wiped his brow in the sweltering heat and admired the landscapers' efforts to keep the lawn watered. It was a pleasant setting, shaded by the occasional oak tree, and he could see why Ivan Dombrovski had chosen it for his wife's grave. Tyler and Jess continued their search for Catherine's headstone.

Though Jess and Fay weren't allowed to leave the country until the inquiries into the events in Wisconsin had come to a conclusion, a personal trip to New Mexico was allowed. At least that's what the FBI thought it was.

Tyler had been intrigued by what Colchev had told them: that Dombrovski had visited his wife's grave every day during his final year and that the Soviets never knew to which island the wood engraving's map had been referring.

It was only when Tyler put it together with Fay's Roswell encounter that he made the connection.

The dying alien Fay said she met had drawn a K, a

backward E, and a T inside an upright rectangle.
Latin alphabet, they were puzzling, but not if the word
was writing had been Russian. In the Cyrillic alphabet, the
first three letters translated to C, A, and T. It was the start
of the word "Кэтрин".

The alien had been trying to spell Catherine in his native
tongue.

"Here!" Jess called out.

Tyler found her standing in front of a modest granite
headstone. It read, "Catherine Dombrovski. Beloved wife.
1890–1946."

"I wish Nana were here to see this," Jess said with a tear
in her eye.

Tyler put an arm around her shoulder and gave it a
squeeze. "Me too. But she insisted we come without her."

He knelt in front of the headstone and inspected the
granite without seeing any obvious seams on either side. He
ran his fingers over its surface, feeling for a hidden latch or
button.

When his index finger ran over the dot of the raised "i"
in "Catherine", he felt it give slightly. That had to be it. He
pressed it, and the entire outline around her name popped
open like a door hinged on the bottom, confirming his suspicion for the reason that Dombrovski had been such a
devoted visitor.

Even in his most distraught days after Karen's death,
Tyler didn't visit her grave daily so he was sure there had to
be another explanation for why Dombrovski had come so

en. Tyler thought it was because the scientist knew his lab had been compromised, so he'd needed somewhere to stash his most crucial files. The headstone was the perfect hiding place.

Tyler carefully tilted the compartment open and peered inside. The watertight gasket was still intact, preserving the contents perfectly.

The first item he removed was an ancient unmarked film reel. He gave it to Jess.

"We'll see if we can find a projector for that in town," he said.

The other item was a thick file folder containing a raft of yellowed documents.

He smiled when he saw the file's title and showed it to Jess.

It was labeled *Project Caelus*.

It took some effort, but they finally found a teacher at a local high school willing to loan them a compatible film projector from their store room. After they put the antiquated device in the trunk, Jess drove down a street lined with buildings like the International UFO Museum and the Roswell Space Center while Tyler flipped through Dombrovski's files. It took only a few minutes to appreciate the significance of their find.

By the time Jess turned into the driveway of the Roswell Regional Hospital, he had enough information about Caelus to understand what Fay had experienced all those years ago.

They parked and carried the projection equipment to the hospital's third floor. In room 308 they found Fay dozing.

Although she'd received chemotherapy treatment, the cancer had ravaged her over the past month. Despite her weakened condition, she had elected to make the trip to Roswell with Tyler and Jess, her intense need for closure before death evident. But upon arrival at the airport, she'd collapsed and they'd rushed her to the hospital. Jess had wanted to stay with her, but Fay prodded her to go to the cemetery with Tyler to find out if his theory was true.

Tyler set up the projector, and while they waited for Fay to wake up, he walked Jess through the files. An hour later Fay blinked her eyes to see the two of them at her bedside.

"Well?" she said, her voice wavering. "I don't have much time for suspense."

"We found it," Jess said. "Catherine Dombrovski's headstone. There was a compartment hidden inside."

"It wasn't an alien, was it? I know that now. I just want answers, whatever they are."

Tyler sighed. He didn't want to disappoint her, but she deserved the truth. "I think you should see this."

He turned down the lights and flicked on the projector. While the silent film played on the wall opposite Fay's bed, he narrated what they were watching.

The first shot was of a smiling bald man in a white lab coat. He had his arm around a beautiful white-haired woman.

"Dombrovski and his second wife. They were the scientists who conceived of Project Caelus. Dombrovski was a physicist and Catherine was an aeronautical engineer originally from the Ukraine. Both of them defected from Communist Russia. She died of influenza in 1946."

In the background was an unsmiling man with round spectacles and crew-cut hair.

"That's Fyodor Dinovich, their colleague, also from Russia. Dombrovski suspected him of being a Russian spy but could never prove it. Based on Colchev's statement, I think it's now confirmed. Dinovich was the reason Dombrovski designed the hiding place for his most critical notes."

The next shot was a wide view inside a closed hangar. Spotlights focused on a massive silver wing that dwarfed the workers buzzing around it. The sleek aircraft was built from the plans of captured German designs.

"That's the XB-32, an experimental bomber that was powered by the xenobium. Project Caelus was designed to create an aircraft that could stay aloft—unrefueled—for days, and the flying wing shape was the most efficient platform for it. Dombrovski had high hopes that xenobium could be a safer power source than nuclear energy because it couldn't be repurposed to create atomic bombs."

"That's what I saw," Fay said weakly. "That's what crashed on the Foster ranch."

"Notice from the front it looks very much like a disk shape. The design was far ahead of its time. I can see why you would have thought it was a spaceship. The records show that the test flight was to take place on July second, 1947. I think Dinovich intentionally brought the plane down where it happened to crash near you. He must have been killed in the explosion."

Before Fay could ask her next question, the film cut to Dombrovski in a silver flight suit.

"He wore that for protection while they were airborne. Because of the lead lining, it's suffused with a liquid coolant to keep him from overheating while on board. If the suit were damaged and leaked, it would look like bright blue blood."

When he put the suit's helmet on and locked it in place, Fay gasped. Two softball-sized black lenses covered the eyes, and a narrow slit was slashed across the mouth.

Tyler turned to Fay. "The alien you met—the creature who saved you—was Ivan Dombrovski."

Tears streamed down Fay's face.

"Are you disappointed?" he said.

She shook her head. "He knew the xenobium would explode, so he used his last breath to save me. And although I lost my daughter, I now have a beautiful granddaughter because of his actions. I just wish I could thank him."

"You completed his search. I think he would have been pleased."

"But a few things still bother me. Why did he speak Russian to me instead of English?"

"The trauma of the crash might have caused him to revert to his native language."

"He did seem very weak at the end when he gave me the wood engraving. How did he find the engraving in the first place?"

"According to his notes, during his worldwide search for more xenobium, he came upon an antiquities dealer with the wood engraving that he claimed was from Easter Island. The engraving had a tiny speck of xenobium embedded in it, just large enough to suggest that more of it might exist."

"If Dombrovski went to Easter Island," Fay said, "why didn't he take the xenobium from the cave?"

Tyler shrugged. "My radiation meter was eighty years more sophisticated than whatever he had. He probably never realized it was there."

"And why the big US government conspiracy to cover up the Roswell crash?"

"After the plane exploded and Dombrovski's office files were destroyed, I'm sure the government didn't want the word to get out about its prototype in case there was more xenobium to be discovered. The remaining pieces of the plane are probably hidden deep in a cavern under Area 51."

The film ended, the strip flapping in the reel. Tyler switched it off and turned on the lights.

Fay smiled at Tyler. "What a great adventure you've given me. Thank you."

Tyler took her hand. He was going to tell her more, but she dozed off again.

He collected the film and files and went into the hall with Jess.

"What are you going to do with those?" she asked.

"I haven't decided yet. I may just hang onto them for a while. No sense in spoiling everyone's fun. Let them keep thinking it was a UFO."

"How illogical of you."

Tyler gave her a light but tender kiss. This was where they parted ways. She'd made her decision.

"If it doesn't work out with what's-his-name," Tyler said, "you know where I am."

"I love you, Tyler. I always will."

"You know I will, too. Give my best to Fay."

"Sure. I just wish we didn't have to dash her beliefs like that. She put on a brave face, but I know it must have been heartbreaking for her, especially because she's not going to write her book about Roswell. Even if she had time to finish it, she wouldn't want to get you in trouble for revealing classified information."

Tyler nodded his thanks. "She fell asleep before I could tell her something."

"About the Roswell incident?"

"In a way. About the xenobium. Tunguska. Australia. Nazca. They all suggest the metal has an extraterrestrial origin."

"Right. It's from space."

"But how was the xenobium made?"

Jess frowned in confusion at what he was suggesting. "Made? It's just a rock, isn't it?"

"Is it? I don't know. We humans couldn't produce it artificially, and Kessler didn't have a theory for how the xenobium could be created naturally. So tell Fay it's possible that she had an encounter with proof of extraterrestrial life."

"You don't believe that, do you?"

"Until proved otherwise, who can say?"

Jess smiled. "Thank you for that. She'll love it."

They embraced, just happy to be holding each other one final time before Jess drew away. After a last look, she brushed his arm and turned to go back into Fay's room.

Tyler lingered for a moment, then ambled down the hall with a melancholy grin. Although he was sorry to leave Jess, at least he'd given her grandmother some peace in the end. It felt good not only to fulfill Fay's last wish to find closure but also to leave her with something to dream about.

After all, Tyler thought, *what's the point of life if there isn't any mystery?*

In a thriller like this one that explores the boundaries of technological possibilities and posits alternative explanations for ancient mysteries, it's often difficult to know where the real world ends and the fiction begins. It might surprise you to find out how little I had to make up in this story.

The strange 1908 blast in Tunguska, Siberia, continues to be an enduring enigma. According to *The Mystery of the Tunguska Fireball* by Surendra Verma, a goldsmith named Suzdalev was the first Western explorer to visit the disaster area, but there were only vague rumors about what he found there. The fallen trees can still be seen in an area the size of London, and the flies are still nasty. A similar mysterious explosion occurred in Western Australia in 1993, and no one has yet determined the cause.

I've had the thrill of taking a ride on the Shotover River jet boats in Queenstown. The river isn't far from the Southern Proving Grounds, which does winter testing of cars during the northern hemisphere's summer.

The ultra-secret Joint Defence Facility Pine Gap is located

just outside Alice Springs, Australia. I wouldn't suggest driving down their private road, but you can get a good view of the facility on Google Maps.

Though Project Caelus is a fantasy, the Air Force did study the feasibility of building nuclear-powered aircraft, even going so far as to install a nuclear reactor on a B-36 bomber. To my knowledge, it was never attempted on the wing-shaped B-49, a jet-powered Air Force prototype built in 1947.

Four-trailer road trains are the longest street-legal trucks in the world and range across the vast Australian outback.

The Sydney Harbour BridgeClimb is another adventure I've been privileged to experience. The bridge is designed as I've described, including the maintenance cranes and catwalks.

The US military has poured millions of dollars into developing tracking dust, also called smart dust or ID dust, to be used for identifying and following enemies coated with the material.

Drug-smuggling tunnels burrowed under the border between Tijuana and San Diego continue to be discovered on a regular basis. The tunnel I feature in this book is cruder than some of the more sophisticated operations that have been constructed with concrete linings and elevators.

Privately built spaceplanes are already a reality with the launch of Virgin Galactic's SpaceShipTwo and will soon carry paying passengers into space seventy miles above the Earth. Airbus is exploring the feasibility of developing a plane with a bird-bone frame like I used in the Skyward. The multitude of windows would provide a great view, but you better have a strong stomach if you tend toward motion sickness.

Joseph Kittinger's real exploits on the Project Excelsior high-altitude skydiving program are even more incredible when you consider that he undertook his mission over fifty years ago and no one has duplicated the feat since.

I had a great time at the AirVenture show in Oshkosh last year, and the vast rows of airplanes lined up as far as the eye can see are truly overwhelming. If you love aircraft, for one week in July Oshkosh is your mecca.

The theories for how to move Easter Island Moai are even more varied than the few I list in the novel. However, rocking the statues back and forth to walk them forward does work. Lava tube caves and the colorful paintings on their walls abound on the island.

Although xenobium is fictional, hafnium-3 is an actual isomer of the element hafnium. Its explosive potential is vast, as is its cost to manufacture. Isomer bombs and induced gamma emission weapons are theoretically possible and could produce effects scarily similar to the ones produced by the Killswitch.

Electromagnetic pulse from a nuclear explosion is a very real threat. In fact war-game planners always assumed a Soviet first strike would consist of a massive hydrogen bomb detonated over the central US to disable its electronic infrastructure and hinder the military's ability to retaliate.

Now the same threat comes from terrorists and rogue nations. The target in this book was the United States, but the weapon would work equally well at setting the technological clock of any industrialized nation back by a hundred years.

The Nazca lines and symbols, the Mandala geometric pattern, and the ancient city of Cahuachi in Peru have all become popular tourist destinations, yet no one has deciphered their true meaning as of this writing.

The Roswell incident continues to fascinate me as it does the rest of the world. What really crashed there? Why did the Air Force's explanation of the event change? What happened to the wreckage that was found? An explanation as prosaic as a stray weather balloon would be a disappointing answer to say the least. But do I think it was an alien spacecraft? I'm a skeptic, though it sure would be cool to think so. However, I'd like to think an alien race that had traveled light-years to get here using technology we can barely imagine could make a better landing. If you'd like to give me a tour of Area 51 and prove me wrong, I will take you up on it.

ACKNOWLEDGMENTS

Writing a novel like this without the help of others would be impossible, so I'd like to take this opportunity to thank those who contributed so generously to making this book a reality.

My agent Irene Goodman has been a rock-steady presence throughout this process, and I couldn't think of anyone better to guide me on this roller-coaster ride. Her wisdom and support are invaluable.

It's a privilege to work with my foreign rights agents, Danny Baror and Heather Baror-Shapiro, who are not only the best at what they do, but are also really nice people.

Thanks to my editors Jade Chandler and David Shelley for believing in my storytelling and for helping me create the best book I can. Their enthusiasm got me to the finish line.

I often rely on experts in the field when my research requires, so I'm fortunate to have a talented pool of friends and family to draw on. Nevertheless, any mistakes or intentional alterations in technology, history, or locations are my responsibility alone.

I appreciate Jeff Davis, Noreen Moen, and John Hopkins for answering my questions at the EAA AirVenture show.

My friend, oncologist Dr. Craig Lockhart, provided crucial insights into pancreatic cancer.

My conference pal, Susan Tunis, once again bestowed her keen editorial eye on the manuscript.

Many thanks to my brother, retired Air Force pilot Lieutenant Colonel Martin Westerfield, for his expertise on the military and aviation.

Beth Morrison, in addition to being my sister and curator of illuminated manuscripts at the Getty, is also a whiz at pointing out my boneheaded plot holes.

I sincerely appreciate the time my father-in-law, Frank Moretti, spent in giving me feedback on several different revisions of the novel.

Finally, my wife, Randi, has been more than a mere supporter of my work. She has been instrumental at every phase of the story creation process, from late-night bull sessions on plot direction to character development decisions to multiple editorial passes. It's no exaggeration to say that I couldn't have done this without her. And she's just downright wonderful. I'm a lucky guy.

COMING SOON

**The breath-taking new standalone thriller
from Boyd Morrison . . .**

THE TSUNAMI COUNTDOWN

Over the remote central Pacific, a plane is suddenly
rocked by a massive explosion. Despite the pilot's valiant
efforts, the blast sends it plummeting into the ocean,
leaving no witnesses to the fireball.

Kai Tanaka, the new and untested director of the
Hawaii Pacific Tsunami Warning Centre in Honolulu,
notes a minor seismic disturbance in that region but
doesn't make the connection with the lost airplane. There's
no reason to be worried about his wife, manager of a
luxury hotel on the island, or his daughter, who is enjoying
the sunny holiday morning at Waikiki beach with friends.

But when all contact with Christmas Island is suddenly
lost, Kai is the first to realize that Hawaii faces a
catastrophe of epic proportions: in one hour, a series
of massive waves will wipe out Honolulu. He has just
sixty minutes to save the lives of a million people,
including his wife and daughter . . .

Visit www.boydmorrison.com to find out more.

After university, Boyd Morrison earned a PhD in industrial engineering, worked for NASA and tested Xbox games for Microsoft. A professional actor and outdoor-sports enthusiast, he is currently at work on his next thriller in the Tyler Locke series.

Join Boyd on Facebook – visit www.boydmorrison.com to find out more.